MR CHEN'S EMPORIUM

'A top read' *Reader's Digest*

'In a word: enchanting' *Gold Coast Bulletin*

'A real charmer and a fine debut' Deborah Rodriguez, author of *The Little Coffee Shop of Kabul*

'The narrative blends seamlessly between the two time periods, which are strong, stand-alone stories. I loved every page of this beautiful book' *Newcastle Herald*

'Perfect for book clubs, *Mr Chen's Emporium* is an enchanting historical love story, an East meets West in a sleepy NSW gold rush town' *Avid Reader*

'A fabulous new debut novel. Set in country Australia, I read it on my iPhone and it was such a great read, I went out and bought the print book so I could have it on my bookshelf!' Margareta Osborn, author of *Bella's Run*

'This is a great debut from Australian author Deborah O'Brien. I look forward to more from her' *The Big Book Club*

'O'Brien's captivating novel skilfully mixes solid research and fiction, telling a poignant, page-turning and heart-warming story within the framework of both historical and contemporary romance' *Flinders Indaily*

'While the two main protagonists are separated by time, they are both strong women and carry O'Brien's story well' *Western Advocate*

'*Mr Chen's Emporium* is a light, engaging novel which I think would particularly appeal to readers of historical and romantic fiction' *Book'd Out*

'Rich in romance and history ... An enjoyable and well-researched read' *Write Note Reviews*

'You'll end the book desperately trying to imagine the person who lived your life before you did ...'
Shop Til You Drop Magazine

DEBORAH O'BRIEN

MR CHEN'S EMPORIUM

BANTAM

SYDNEY AUCKLAND TORONTO NEW YORK LONDON

A Bantam book
Published by Random House Australia Pty Ltd
Level 3, 100 Pacific Highway, North Sydney NSW 2060
www.randomhouse.com.au

First published by Bantam in 2012
This edition published by Bantam in 2013

Copyright © Deborah O'Brien 2012

The moral right of the author has been asserted.

All rights reserved. No part of this book may be reproduced or transmitted by
any person or entity, including internet search engines or retailers, in any form
or by any means, electronic or mechanical, including photocopying (except
under the statutory exceptions provisions of the Australian *Copyright Act 1968*),
recording, scanning or by any information storage and retrieval system without
the prior written permission of Random House Australia.

This is a work of fiction. Names, characters, places and incidents either are the
product of the author's imagination or are used fictitiously. Any resemblance to
actual persons, living or dead, events, or locales is entirely coincidental.

Addresses for companies within the Random House Group can be found at
www.randomhouse.com.au/offices

National Library of Australia
Cataloguing-in-Publication Entry

  O'Brien, Deborah.
  Mr Chen's Emporium/Deborah O'Brien.

  ISBN 978 1 74275 555 7 (pbk.)

  A823.4

Cover illustration by Christopher Nielsen
Cover design by Christabella Designs
Internal illustrations by Deborah O'Brien
Internal design and typesetting by Midland Typesetters, Australia
Printed in Australia by Griffin Press, an accredited ISO AS/NZS 14001:2004
Environmental Management System printer

Random House Australia uses papers that are natural, renewable and recyclable
products and made from wood grown in sustainable forests. The logging
and manufacturing processes are expected to conform to the environmental
regulations of the country of origin.

MR CHEN'S EMPORIUM

AUTUMN

*'You shall have an emporium
selling fine silks and wondrous wares . . .
And you will be garbed in a suit,
befitting one of the great merchants of the town.'*

'Histoire d'Aladdin, ou la lampe merveilleuse'
Nuit CCCXVIII [Antoine Galland c.1710]

1
ARRIVALS

Then – 1872

Amy Duncan was only halfway through her journey and already she was longing for Sydney and its cool harbour breezes. As she waited at the coach stop outside Granthurst railway station, her new straw bonnet, tilted forward in the latest fashion, could do nothing to protect her face from the midday sun. If only she could board the next train back to Redfern terminal, she would be in her aunt's house by suppertime. But that was the wishful thinking of a selfish girl who cared only to lead her own life. And that life she must forget for the foreseeable future. Her father had written saying her mother was ill – not dangerously so, but serious enough to need help with the chores. It was Amy's duty to join her family.

While the Cobb and Co coach to Millbrooke stood waiting, the driver loaded her luggage on top. Two gentlemen were already seated among the bags, cabbage-tree hats on their heads and pipes in their mouths. Prospectors off to the goldfields? She pitied them having to spend five hours perched on the roof in this March heat. Thank goodness she would be sitting inside with the ladies and children, though, of course, being inside would provide no protection from a band of highwaymen. Surveying the flimsy structure with its quartet of weary-looking horses, she wondered whether it could even complete the journey, let alone outrun a gang of bushrangers. Not that she was carrying any valuables, bar a cameo belonging to her grandmother and a single sovereign hidden at the bottom of her trunk.

'Ye can board now, miss,' said the coachman.

'Thank you, sir,' she replied. 'Do you suppose there may be an encounter with a highwayman?'

'I 'ope not. For they ain't the swashbucklers ye might imagine 'em to be.'

Amy blushed. How could he possibly have guessed that she pictured bushrangers as Antipodean Robin Hoods, no matter what *The Sydney Morning Herald* said about them being thuggish brigands?

'Did you ever have a brush with the O'Reilly Gang?' she asked as the driver checked the harnesses.

'It was me great fortune ne'er to meet 'em in me travels. They was hanged last year, thank the Lord. Good-for-nothings, the three of 'em. Ne'er worked a day in their lives. Stole sheep and 'orses when they was boys and then graduated to the gold escorts. Shot one of their own in a public 'ouse in Millbrooke and buried 'im under the floor.'

'Millbrooke? You mean . . .'

'That was their home town. Used to visit their lady friends in a bawdy house in the main street, though the bleedin' coppers was jus' down the road. Pardon me French, miss.'

Amy smiled to indicate she wasn't offended and nodded enthusiastically for him to continue.

'Not a soul ever put those lads in. The folks there was too scared of bein' shot. Though I shouldna speak of such things to a young lady like yeself. It will only give ye nightmares.'

But it didn't. On the contrary, as the coach jolted its way through scrubby bushland, she daydreamed about the Gold Rush town which was to be her home, seeing a magical city like Mr Coleridge's Xanadu, its pavements inlaid with precious metals, its streets strewn with nuggets and its streams flowing yellow with gold dust. If this Millbrooke was indeed a glittering and sophisticated place, she might even be able to tolerate living in her father's house again.

Just as she was conjuring up the exterior of that very residence, complete with a shining fountain and jewelled peacocks, the coach arrived at a low building skirted by a broad verandah, and the driver announced the changing station. Here the mail was delivered and the passengers took refreshments. Amy had been sharing the carriage with a worn-out mother, her three restless offspring and a gentleman, who had introduced himself as a commercial traveller and was now entertaining the children by showing them haberdashery items from his sample case. The two men in cabbage-tree hats sat on the verandah, smoking their pipes and drinking from a flagon that Amy supposed must contain some sort of alcohol. The devil's drink, she could hear her father say.

When they set off again, Amy closed her eyes and tried to return to the golden city. But the heat was so oppressive, it was hard to concentrate. Suddenly there was a terrified bellow from the horses and the carriage came to a shuddering stop. A masked bandit on a white charger appeared at the window, brandishing a pistol. 'Stand and deliver,' he demanded, as he dismounted and ordered them out of the coach.

The children were cowering behind their terrified mother and even the prospectors looked nervous, but Amy was bewitched by the velvety voice and confident bearing. One by one, the passengers handed over their valuables. When Amy offered up her grandmother's cameo, the masked stranger pushed her hand gently away and told her to keep it. She smiled at his gallantry and ventured a glance at the mysterious brown eyes shining behind the mask. Then he lifted her into his arms and swung her onto his steed.

'Spare the young lady,' cried the commercial traveller, as the bandit mounted his horse with Amy behind him.

'Do not listen to him,' Amy whispered in the outlaw's ear.

He hesitated for less than a moment, then leaned forward and loosed the reins, crying, 'Gee ho, Fleetfoot,' and they galloped away. Not towards the golden city and the setting sun, but in the opposite direction, towards the harbour lights in the far distance. With her arms wrapped tightly around his chest, Amy clung to her rescuer as they cantered across fields and flew over hedgerows. When they came to a deep ravine, the charger baulked. Could they make it? She held her breath. Then they leaped into the air, landing with a jolt on the other side. And all at once she was awake, her mouth dry and her head aching from the heat. Opposite her, the children were napping and their mother was listlessly wiping her brow.

The eucalypt forests which had filled the landscape for most of the journey had given way to open fields and rolling hills. A row of hawthorn trees beside the road could have come straight from her native Scotland. They crossed a little creek, the horses straining as they pulled the coach and its load up a hill on the other side. Buildings were starting to appear and Amy tried to look out the window, but the children were in the way, jostling with each other for a better view. Then the road levelled out and the coach came to an abrupt stop.

Amy's head throbbed and her navy-blue dress stuck to her body as she waited on the boardwalk, her travelling bag and trunk beside her. Meanwhile her father was nowhere to be seen. Nor was there any sign of gilded streets or golden pavilions. In their place, she saw only a road made of earth and an odd mix of ramshackle huts with low, tin roofs interspersed with grander two-storey edifices, their parapets crowned with Grecian urns. It was hard to determine which buildings might be the public-houses her father had so railed against in his letters as the source of all licentiousness and debauchery, but Amy did wonder whether the ugly orange building near the coach stop could be one of them.

What a peculiar place this Millbrooke was. If towns were like people, this was a charlady donning her mistress's pearls and pretending to be a grand dame. Amy longed to be back in Sydney with its tearooms and emporia, its theatres and pleasure gardens, and dear Aunt Molly. But she would bear this place for her mother's sake. The Millbrooke chapter of her life couldn't last forever. She straightened her back and filled her lungs with the hot, dusty air. Now where was her father?

Five months ago, when the Reverend Matthew Duncan was transferred from his Sydney parish to St Aidan's in Millbrooke, seventeen-year-old Amy had stayed behind to finish her schooling, moving into the Newtown house of her Aunt Molly, a wealthy widow. With no children of her own, Molly had made a special place in her heart for her niece, allowing her all the gentle pleasures Matthew Duncan condemned as venial sins – singing, dancing, concerts and plays, not to mention adornments such as lacy dresses and sparkling necklaces. At Aunt Molly's Amy could laugh out loud whenever she wanted, and read her favourite books quite openly. In fact, her aunt liked nothing better than to sit in the drawing room, listening to Amy read aloud from the latest work of fiction, just arrived from London.

Matthew Duncan only approved of reading if it was from the Bible. 'The Good Book contains the best writing of all time, whether it be poetry or prose,' he would say. 'That is because it is inspired by the Lord Himself.'

Amy found the Bible beautiful, but she also enjoyed Mr Dickens and Mrs Gaskell, the Brontë sisters and Miss Austen. And above all, Sir Walter Scott, whose rousing stories made her proud to be Caledonian.

As a parting gift, her aunt had produced a pile of Amy's best-loved books. Her favourite was a volume of fairytales in French, collected by Antoine Galland at the start of the eighteenth century. Amy had topped her class in French at Miss Howe's School for Ladies and had no trouble reading the foreign text. Inside its pages, she discovered an intrepid Chinaman by the name of Aladdin, who had quickly become the hero of her dreams.

'I know you love this book,' Aunt Molly had said as Amy packed it into her trunk. 'All the same, I do not advise you to read it to your little brothers. Some of the tales are not entirely suitable for small children.'

'But I would be translating the stories for them, so I could easily omit the grisly incidents, and anyway it is only the villains who meet a nasty end.'

'Indeed. However, there is also a degree of immodesty some might find distasteful. I recall, for example, that Aladdin slept in the same bed as the princess *before* they were man and wife. It is your father I am thinking of, my dear. I don't want him to accuse me of being a bad influence. So do keep it out of his sight.'

'Don't worry, Aunt Molly. I shall hide it in my petticoat drawer.'

All around her, Amy could hear languages she didn't recognise, and unfamiliar accents speaking her native tongue. She herself had once possessed a distinctive accent, inherited from her father, but elocution lessons had softened the elongated vowels and rolled *rr* until she sounded exactly like her mother and her aunt, who both spoke in the genteel manner of the English Home Counties, despite being Glaswegian by birth.

She had never seen such a diverse group of people before – prospectors in their shabby clothes, men in high-necked suits, children with bare feet, and ladies in crisp cotton gowns and floral bonnets. Walking briskly along the boardwalk was a young woman with a parasol held aloft. She wore a shiny blue dress, not a sensible navy like Amy's, but the colour of a summer sky. What a fetching gown and such a sweet face with those cherry-red lips, rosy cheeks and milky complexion. The bodice of the girl's dress, however, was astonishingly low, revealing far more than was fashionable in Sydney. As she approached, Amy smiled and said, 'Good afternoon.'

A puzzled look crossed the girl's face and then slowly she returned the smile. 'Good afternoon to you, ma'am,' she responded with a bob of her head, though they were surely much the same age.

Then, with a deepening blush, Amy realised the girl was probably someone her aunt would refer to as a 'lady of ill-repute'. Close up, Amy could see the rouge applied generously to her mouth and cheeks. Aunt Molly had said such ladies were free with their favours. Amy wasn't sure exactly what her aunt meant by that. From the tone of her voice, she hadn't been referring to acts of charity.

The girl moved on and Amy turned her gaze back up the dusty road to see a column of Chinamen approaching. They almost seemed to be dancing, though it was more of a shuffle than a waltz. Across their shoulders they carried bamboo poles with calico bags hanging from the ends. As they came closer Amy could see that each wore his hair in a pigtail under his peaked straw hat. But what struck her most was their bronze-coloured skin, the exact colour of her father's communion chalice.

Shadows were lengthening across the main street as she finally caught sight of the Reverend Duncan, hurrying towards her in his dark suit and dog-collar, his face bearing the grim expression he wore like a penitent's hair shirt. When he stooped and gave her a peck on the cheek, Amy was suddenly aware of the frivolous bunch of velvet violets tucked into the brim of her hat, but he seemed not to have noticed them. He was too preoccupied with the procession of Chinamen shuffling down the street.

'Wretched Celestials,' he complained. 'They don't belong in this country.'

While Amy was wondering how anyone would partner a curse-word like 'wretched' with something as heavenly as 'celestial', he took her chin and turned her face to his.

'Ye didna speak to anyone, did ye, Amy Duncan?'

She didn't dare mention the young woman with the parasol. But before she could decide how to reply, he had hoisted her trunk onto his shoulder and picked up the travelling bag.

'Get a move along, lass. Yer ma has the tea ready.'

Now

Tears streaming down her face, Angie Wallace sat on the hardwood floor of the sitting room, hemmed in by a circle of cardboard packing boxes, most of them still unopened. She should have known better. It was the photos that had set her off – they always did. Just when she had passed a full day without a single tear. Just when she'd started to imagine little scenes from a possible future, instead of playing the past like a movie channel in her head, month after month.

Stupid of her to open the carton containing the albums and shoeboxes of photos and memorabilia. She should have followed Vicky's advice: 'Mark each carton with its contents and which room it should go in. Then open them in order of practical priority.' Which is of course what Vicky had done when she and Paul moved from their big house in Mosman to an apartment in Darling Harbour.

'You need to plan a move carefully,' Vicky had said. 'Moving house can be just as stressful as getting a divorce or losing a spouse.' Then Vicky had flushed pink as she realised what she had just said to a woman who had not long become a widow. Practical Vicky, but not always tactful. She was a veritable font of household hints and domestic do-it-yourself. She should have had her own column in a newspaper or perhaps an online blog: 'Vicky Lamb – domestic detective, solving your darkest and dirtiest problems'.

Angie hadn't deliberately ignored Vicky's advice, but somehow, in the chaos of wrapping things and putting them in boxes, she'd forgotten about it. Her sons had helped with the packing. It hadn't been easy for them to see the bits and pieces of their family life crammed into cartons. Ever since Phil's death, formerly meaningless objects had become the precious relics of lost relationships, between a husband and wife, a father and his sons.

Nor were the boys happy about their mother's decision to move to a town so far away from Sydney.

'This is a time when you need your support network,' said Blake. 'Moving away is the worst thing you could do. It's known as the geographical avoidance ploy. GAP for short.'

It sounded ridiculous, but he was doing his Master's in Psychology and he should know.

'It's like losing both parents,' said Tim.

That really hurt. Still, the boys were adults now with their own lives and Angie had to loosen her dependence on them and shake herself out of the lethargy that hung over her like a shroud.

Millbrooke had happened by chance. At the four-month mark, Vicky and Chrissie had bundled her up and taken her on a girls' weekend to the country. Lacking the energy to protest, she had allowed them to make a booking at a B&B and throw her clothes into an overnight bag. All the wrong things, as it turned out, but Angie couldn't complain, having shown no interest in the first place.

They had taken Vicky's Audi, plush and powerful. She set the cruise control to 110 and they purred down the highway, singing along to sixties and seventies music. Well, Vicky and Chrissie had sung a series of duets, while Angie sat in the back seat, feeling as though she was fighting off a cold. Finally they spotted a sign saying 'Tourist Drive. Millbrooke 68km'. It was an asphalt road, but so narrow two vehicles would barely fit side by side. At first there were open fields, dry and brown after the recent summer, with dusty sheep grazing around empty dams, then long stretches of straggly bush. Finally they came to a river, cascading over shelves of rock with sandy swathes of beach along its banks.

'Nearly there,' Vicky declared.

After the river the countryside opened up. There were more fields of grazing sheep, but this time the grass was a vibrant green, as if it were a secret place untouched by the prevailing drought. Chrissie drew their attention to a dead wombat beside the road, lying on its back with its stubby legs pointing into the air. The animal had been marked with a red painted cross.

'Thousands of wombats are killed on New South Wales roads every year,' she said. 'I read that somewhere.'

Nobody else spoke for a while. Then a procession of advertising boards heralded the entrance to the town.

'Welcome to Millbrooke - the Heart of Platypus Country'

'Don's Bakery. Open every day from 6am. Except Christmas Day'

'Millbrooke Antiques. Pre-loved Furniture and Collectables'

'The Old Schoolhouse B&B. Second on right'

'That's where we're staying,' said Vicky.

Deborah O'Brien

A road sign indicated a seventy-kilometre zone. Then an avenue of birch trees in yellow leaf led the way to a bridge with a large plaque set into its stonework, proclaiming: 'Millbrooke. Established 1836.'

After the bridge they passed a large park fringed by willow trees.

'Look, Angie, there's a platypus,' said Vicky, slowing down and pointing animatedly towards the park.

Angie turned wearily, only to see a walrus-sized bronze statue atop a block of stone.

'It's huge,' said Chrissie. 'How big is a real platypus anyway?'

None of them knew for sure, having never seen one.

Soon they found themselves in the heart of town. Iron lace verandahs and heavy corrugated awnings lining the main street reflected a boom time now long past. There were hitching posts for phantom horses at intervals along the kerb. They turned off the main street into a lane and pulled up outside the Old Schoolhouse, a stone building with dormer windows. When they knocked at the door, they were greeted by a generously proportioned woman who introduced herself as Nola. The interior of her B&B was chintzy and cluttered – doilies and dried flower arrangements on every table and cushions festooned with ruffles, beads and ribbons. Their hostess, who was an uncomfortable match for the décor, was effusive about the delights of Millbrooke. Having lived there six years now, she had passed the acceptance test, she told her guests. If you stayed more than five years, you were no longer considered a 'blow-in'.

The three of them browsed in the shops and galleries of the main street and had tea and Portuguese custard tarts in a café at the end of town, its old timber walls lined with shelves of local pottery, all for sale. Then, as tourists are wont to do, they examined the listings in the window of the estate agent. There was a hand-written sign on the door: 'Closed Sundays for Church.' It made Angie smile. A step back to a gentler time.

'I like this one,' said Chrissie, who was a dab hand at gardening. It was a large farmhouse with a wisteria-garlanded verandah, cottage borders and a hundred acres of land.

'Pricey,' said Vicky. 'I can't imagine doling out that much for a property twenty k down the road.'

Not just a domestic doyenne, Vicky was also a real estate expert.

Angie hadn't been paying too much attention. She was simply going through the motions, trying to smile when required and nodding at appropriate moments. Then she saw it. A faded photo of a fairytale house with a high gable and a fretted bargeboard. It reminded her of the gingerbread houses she and Phil had fallen in love with in northern California, only not as ornate. A description was pasted below the photo on yellowing paper with curled edges, as if it had been attached to the window for a long time.

THE OLD MANSE BUILT CIRCA 1870
CHURCH LANE
BUILT IN THE VICTORIAN ROMANTIC STYLE, THIS
HISTORIC WOODEN HOUSE FEATURES
FORMAL SITTING ROOM, SEPARATE DINING ROOM,
THREE BEDROOMS, TWO BATHROOMS
AND A KITCHEN WITH ORIGINAL EARLY KOOKA STOVE.
TWO OPEN FIREPLACES. NEW CORRUGATED STEEL ROOF.
OUTDOOR LAUNDRY.
A LARGE BARN ADJOINING THE HOUSE COULD BE
CONVERTED TO BECOME A STUDIO OR GALLERY.

Deborah O'Brien

ON THREE ACRES OVERLOOKING THE PLATYPUS HOLES OF
MILLBROOKE CREEK.
TRULY A RENOVATOR'S DELIGHT.

She must have been staring at it for a long time because Vicky remarked, 'Renovator's delight. You know that's real-estate-speak for decrepit dump.'

'Let's go and have a look at it anyway,' Angie said with such determination the other two just stared at her.

Vicky produced the town map their host had given them. 'Here's Church Lane,' she said, pointing with a long acrylic nail. 'We can walk. It's no distance. Nothing *is* in this town.'

In five minutes they were there, standing outside a picket fence, overgrown with burgundy briar roses that only partly concealed the peeling paint. A 'For Sale' sign stood next to a wooden lychgate opening to a path which led to the front door. The walls appeared to be cream, but it might have been layers of dirt disguising the original white. There was a new roof in heritage green that looked promising. An arched window sat in the gable end facing the front, with a sheet of plywood in place of glass.

The land around the house was thick with long grass stretching down to a creek that meandered its way across the bottom of the garden. Several grey boulders seemed to have been randomly scattered there.

'Oh, look at the rocks,' Angie said. 'They remind me of the dolmens and menhirs in Brittany – primeval monoliths.'

'It's a pile of ugly old stones, Angie,' said Vicky. 'Don't kid yourself.'

But nothing Vicky could say could put Angie off.

'I wonder if we'd be able to take a look inside,' she said, stooping to open the lych-gate and avoid the thorny roses.

Before Vicky could stop her, she was walking through the gate and up the path to the front door. She knocked, but nobody answered, so she tried to peer inside the front windows, which were draped with sheets. Stepping back to the edge of the verandah, she surveyed the downstairs façade. There was no doubt the house was shabby, yet it retained a sense of pride, as if it had once been beautiful and longed to recapture the past.

'Let's go and see whether the agent will take us through,' she suggested, watching Vicky and Chrissie exchange wary looks.

'It's lunchtime. They've probably closed for the day,' said Chrissie.

'It can't hurt to check,' replied Angie.

Morrison Real Estate was still open.

'The Manse has been on the market for two years,' said Doug Morrison, the agent.

'That seems like a long time.' Vicky spoke with an air of authority.

'It's a fact of life in a small country town,' he said. 'Things were busier before the government closed the branch line to Granthurst. Now the redundant railway station is an antiques centre and there's a daily bus to Sydney. But most of my vendors aren't in a hurry to sell.'

'What other choice do they have?' whispered Vicky in Angie's ear.

After lunch he took them on a tour. The walls and ceilings were water-damaged and in need of a fresh coat of paint. The kitchen was primitive. No hot water, a single power point and an Early Kooka stove that might have come from the 1930s. The upstairs bathroom contained an instant hot water heater and an old stained bath. Its downstairs counterpart had been refurbished with a new shower and modern toilet – the only room to have been updated.

But Angie didn't see the flaws. She was taken with the high ceilings and decorative plaster cornices, the elegant fireplaces and long central hallway with its dado rails and embossed metal panels. She ran her hand over the carved baluster of the cedar staircase and pronounced it smooth as silk. In the smallest upstairs bedroom she was drawn to a window seat from which she could see distant mountains and a dark line of trees defining the creek as it snaked towards the main river some kilometres away.

By the time she had looked inside the barn – a repository of old building materials and cardboard boxes filled with browning copies of *Post* and *People* magazines – Angie was in love.

'A perfect space for a studio,' she said, almost to herself.

After breakfast on Sunday morning, Angie returned to her room to pack. Then she phoned the agent, who was on his way to church.

'I love the house,' she told him. 'But I'm not in a position to buy it – for many reasons.'

'Well, there are other options,' he began, but Angie had seen Vicky loitering in the hallway. 'Just a moment,' she said, and pushed the door closed with her foot.

When she emerged from her room a few minutes later, it was with a gusto she hadn't felt for a long time.

'Well, thank goodness you've seen sense,' said Vicky. 'The Manse was a terrible idea.'

'Actually, I'm going to meet Doug later this morning at that cute café with all the pottery for sale. The owner's coming too. He might be prepared to lease the house.'

'What?'

'Perhaps you missed the end of the conversation,' said Angie, feeling smug.

'You mean you want to move down here and pay rent for a place that's barely liveable?'

'I could rent out the Sydney house. That would bring in a healthy income. And it would give me time to decide whether living in the country suits me or not.'

'That's insane, Angie.'

'It's not insane. It's keeping my options open.'

'Well, if you're going to do something like that, why not choose a nice little renovated cottage?'

Angie smiled benignly. 'Where's the challenge in that?'

She arrived a few minutes early and looked around for the real estate agent, but he hadn't turned up yet, so she ordered a cup of tea at the counter and chose a table near the window. The café was empty, apart from an elderly man sitting at the back, wearing a woollen cap pulled low over his forehead and a checked flannelette shirt which should have been thrown out years ago. She began leafing through a magazine from among a selection on the shelf beside her. A few minutes later she heard: 'Excuse me, are you Mrs Wallace?'

'Yes,' she replied tentatively, looking up to see the man in the beanie. His chin was covered in stubble which spread like grey moss onto his cheeks.

'I'm Richard Scott. Owner of the Manse.'

Angie tried to conceal her surprise. 'Nice to meet you, Mr Scott.'

When he extended his hand, she shook it, feeling calloused skin. Then she waited for him to say, 'Call me Richard', but he didn't. Obviously one of those old fogeys who were sticklers for formality.

'Doug Morrison sends his apologies,' he said, taking a seat opposite her. 'He forgot that his wife had invited the in-laws for lunch. Doug's in charge of the barbecue.'

'No problem. I'm sure we can handle things on our own.'

'He tells me you're interested in the Manse.'

'Yes, I'm afraid I've fallen in love with it. I suppose I shouldn't be saying that to the owner. You'll want to charge me a massive rent.' She laughed nervously.

'I gather you've ruled out purchasing the property. At least for the time being.' He lowered his voice. 'Doug mentioned your circumstances.'

Thank goodness for that. She hated having to tell people, even strangers.

'I'm very sorry,' he continued.

'Thanks.' Even though he had only offered clichéd condolences, tears were welling. Hastily she blinked them away, but one had already escaped, rolling down her cheek and onto her neck. At that moment the waiter arrived with a tray which he unloaded onto the table, and Angie was able to take advantage of the diversion to dab at her eyes and swipe a tissue across her dripping nose.

'I hear you'd like to use the barn as a studio,' Mr Scott said, adding three teaspoons of sugar to his tea.

Resisting the inclination to wince, she responded, 'Yes, I'm an artist. Well, I used to be. I haven't painted for a while. Not since . . .'

Another tear had dropped. If she wasn't careful, it would become a gushing tap.

'This town attracts artists,' he said. 'I suppose it's the old buildings and green countryside.'

'It seems so idyllic.'

'Nowhere is idyllic, Mrs Wallace. Not even Millbrooke. There are always issues.'

'Are you trying to talk me out of living here?' she asked lightly.

'No, just being honest.'

'So what kind of *issues* might I encounter in Millbrooke?'

'Well, for starters, there's a *foreign* mining company nosing around the area.'

'Foreign?'

'American.'

'Oh,' she replied, unsure how she was supposed to react to that.

'They're drilling holes and taking samples out by the river.' He sighed loudly. 'When I was a kid, Australia rode on the sheep's back; now it's all about mineral resources and commodity prices.'

'Times change, Mr Scott. And I'd rather have a mining boom than a recession.' It was a throwaway line, something she must have heard on the TV or the radio.

'You make it sound so cut and dried,' he retorted, giving her a withering look. 'But there are long-term repercussions to consider. It's a wildlife haven out there.'

For a while they drank their tea in uncomfortable silence. Then Angie asked, 'Is this mine close to town?'

'*Potential* mine,' he corrected like a schoolmaster. 'It's a few kilometres east of here, near the place where the Chinese had their camp in the Gold Rush days. Being across the other side of a wide river, it made them feel safer. Less chance of drunken white miners going on a rampage and attacking them in their sleep. The Chinese used to commute by punt to the diggings. That's why it was called Chinaman's Cove. Nowadays, only oldies like me use the original name. Millbrooke Shire Council changed it a while back in a burst of political correctness. They thought it might offend someone. So they came up with "River Cove" instead. Then they had new road signs made at ratepayers' expense.' He snorted in disgust. 'Bloody council.'

What a prickly character he was, one of those grizzled old curmudgeons Walter Brennan used to play back in Hollywood's golden age. But at least her tears were gone.

Finally she said, 'Well, I don't think this mi ... *potential* mining project is relevant to me or my decision to rent the Manse.'

After a long pause he replied, 'In that case, I suppose we should discuss money. Would four hundred dollars be reasonable?'

Four hundred a week. She wouldn't think twice about it in the city, but that was a bit steep for a rundown rural house, albeit a charming one. Perhaps Mr Scott was expecting her to bargain with him.

'It's more than I expected,' she said firmly.

'Well, how about three-sixty? That would work out at ninety a week.'

Angie felt her face flush. He'd been talking about *monthly* rent, not weekly.

'I need to pass this by my sons before I make any decisions.'

'Of course. No obligation. The house is just sitting there. I'd be glad to have someone living in it. It needs a human presence to make it feel wanted. Not that I'd expect you to renovate the place.'

'Actually, I wouldn't mind doing a bit of refurbishing. Nothing structural, of course.'

They spent another half hour discussing the technicalities and agreed that Angie would phone Doug during the week to let him know her decision. Then they shook hands at the door and he sauntered down the street in his funny hat, while Angie headed in the direction of the antiques shop where she had arranged to meet Vicky and Chrissie.

'What was the owner like?' asked Vicky as she picked up an old porcelain plate, turned it over and read the brand name.

'A bit odd. Looks like an old tramp, but Doug told me on the phone that he owns a big Georgian house just out of town and several shops in the main street.'

'Millbrooke's unlikely property mogul,' said Chrissie. 'What did he say?'

'He likes the idea of the Manse being occupied rather than sitting there bleak and empty. And he's prepared to offer it at a nominal rent.'

'So he should,' said Vicky.

'There would be a year's lease, and he won't sell it during that period.'

'As if anyone would want to buy it.'

'*I* might. At the end of the twelve months, if I found that I liked living in Millbrooke.'

'What the hell are you talking about?' asked Vicky.

'I would rent it for a year. And during that time I might give it a coat of paint and do some work in the garden.'

Vicky shook her head. 'He expects you to fix the place while you're renting?'

'It wouldn't be a renovation as such. Just a tart-up. He'd pay for the paint.'

'But you mightn't buy the bloody place. Then all your work would be for nothing. And if you did decide to buy it, what's to stop him charging you another hundred thousand for the privilege of owning a house that *you'd* fixed up?'

'He's agreed to lop twenty thousand off the current price if I buy it at the end of the lease.'

'Are they going to put any of this in writing?' asked Chrissie.

'We don't need to. I trust them both.'

'A real estate agent and a property owner?' Vicky was rolling her eyes.

'Things are different in the country, Vicky. People stand by a handshake.'

'Maybe in the nineteenth century they did,' she muttered. 'They saw you coming, Angie. The crazy woman from the city. Let's put one over her. She's so besotted with the old house she won't even notice.'

But Angie wasn't listening. It was something at which she had become adept over the past few months. Mostly she didn't even hear what people said. She just offered up responses in a manner she hoped was acceptable.

'Are you going to discuss this with the boys?' asked Vicky.

'Of course.'

'Oh, Angie, you don't even know a soul in Millbrooke,' said Chrissie.

'I do. There's Nola at the Old Schoolhouse and Doug Morrison. And Richard Scott, the owner.'

'I might be able to understand it if you were born here and you were deciding to move back,' said Vicky. 'But you're a city person. You have no connection to the country whatsoever. Honestly, I don't think you know what you're doing. You'll go mad in a town like this.'

'Phil and I used to talk about retiring to a little country town and buying a B&B.'

'Everybody does that – even Paul and I do, after a weekend away. It's the tree change fantasy. But nobody actually *means* it.'

'Phil did.' Angie felt her throat contract in the way it always did when she said his name. It really had been their dream, the two of them. They had discussed it for as long as she could remember. He would retire from the ER, run a consultancy two days a week and spend the rest of the time playing the jovial host. And she would have her own painting studio where she could work to her heart's content, while their guests were out sightseeing.

'Is this an attempt to keep Phil alive, by turning his dream into a reality?' asked Vicky.

'It was *my* dream too.'

'Angie, everything's happening too fast. They say you shouldn't make any major changes in the first year – no rash decisions that you'll regret later.'

'I haven't made a decision. I just said I'd phone next week to let them know.'

'You've latched onto this as a way of avoiding the grieving process. That's what people do when they can't confront the loss. They go on an overseas trip. Move to the coast. Move to the country. They fool themselves into believing a change of location will make things better.'

'Isn't there a possibility that it could?' Angie asked fiercely. Vicky was making her angrier than she'd felt in a long time.

Maybe that was a good thing. Was it possible the numbness was finally abating?

'It's running away,' Vicky continued, oblivious to the edge in Angie's voice. 'Like those movies where the woman loses her husband and goes off to Tuscany or Provence or somewhere equally foreign and exotic.'

'And does up an old house,' added Chrissie. 'And meets a local Adonis. He's usually the builder, isn't he? He doesn't speak much English, but he makes up for it in other ways.' She gave Angie a wink.

'Chrissie, don't encourage her. This is bloody Millbrooke, not the movies,' said Vicky. 'And you'll probably end up with lead poisoning from scraping off the old paint, and broken nails from pulling up those monster weeds out the back.'

Little bubbles of hysteria were building in Angie's throat, threatening to erupt as a cackle, yet if she burst into maniacal laughter, Vicky would be convinced she really was insane. Instead, she tried to sound rational and composed.

'It's not as if I would be cutting my ties to Sydney. I wouldn't be selling the house, only putting it up for rent. And you'd come and visit me, wouldn't you?'

'Of course we would,' said Chrissie.

Vicky gave her a dirty look.

'And the boys would love weekends in the country. They could stay during the uni holidays. I'd probably see more of them than I do now.'

Vicky was shaking her head again.

'You're such a wet blanket, Vicky,' Angie said more sharply than she intended. 'Something positive has happened to me this weekend. For the first time in months, I don't feel numb and helpless. And I think I'm ready to paint again. Millbrooke has inspired me. I could even offer painting classes to the locals. And if it doesn't work out, I'll just move back to Sydney.'

'Blake and Tim will blame *me* for this,' said Vicky. 'If there hadn't been a girls' weekend, the Old Manse would have continued to languish on its acreage, waiting for some other crazy romantic to take it on.'

When Angie didn't answer, Vicky added, 'It ought to be demolished and replaced with a spanking new subdivision. Except that it's probably heritage-listed like most of this bloody town.'

Little was said on the long trip back to Sydney. Angie sat in the back with a sketchbook she'd bought at the newsagent, drawing room plans and slotting in her furniture. By the time they reached the freeway interchange on Sydney's outskirts, she had added a conservatory at the back, a pergola at the side, a knot garden and a lavender hedge. There was a new streamlined kitchen adjoining the dining room and ensuite bathrooms for every bedroom.

As they pulled up outside Angie's house, Vicky told her for the umpteenth time to drop the idea.

'It's cloud-cuckoo-land,' she warned. 'Nothing good can come of it.'

Angie thanked them for a lovely weekend and waved goodbye. Then she let herself into the house and turned off the alarm. No need for one of those in Millbrooke, she thought to herself. A smile creased her face. It was then she realised that she'd already made up her mind.

2
ALADDIN AND HIS TREASURES

Then

What Amy's father hadn't told her in his letter was the cause of her mother's illness. That mystery was solved when Margaret Duncan confided to her daughter about a bairn arriving at the end of winter. Amy looked upon her mother's wan face and felt guilty at her own reluctance to leave Sydney. She couldn't remember such awful sickness with Robbie or Billy, not that Amy had known much about it, having been no more than a child herself when they were born.

In the mornings her mother sent Amy to buy bread from the bakery in the main street. 'Don't tell your papa,' she whispered, 'but I'm just not well enough to make my own bread.' The Reverend Duncan didn't believe in buying things you could make yourself.

One morning, towards the end of April, Amy slipped past her father's study where he was already up and working on his Sunday sermon. It was a brisk Millbrooke morning with a light frost on the grass, a portent of the winter to come. She wrapped her paisley shawl tightly round her shoulders.

Just after sunrise, the main street was unnaturally quiet. A man sleeping off the previous night's drinking binge was curled up in the doorway of the Telegraph Hotel. Amy shivered as she imagined an autumn night spent in the open. She skirted around him and headed up to the bakery, passing the millinery shop on the way. Sitting in the window on a wooden stand was an adorable straw creation with a mass of downy black feathers and a bold red grosgrain ribbon. Amy sighed out loud – she had a passion for hats. And although it might never be hers, she could always dream.

Even before she reached the bakery door, she could smell the bread, so fresh and enticing. The baker had just removed a tray of currant buns. His arms were bulging with muscles from kneading the dough; his face was flushed with the heat of the oven. Overcoming the urge to buy a warm bun to eat on the way home, Amy purchased the loaf she had been sent for. The sun was glistening low in the eastern sky. There was no need to hurry. So she pondered taking a stroll to the top of the street and down the other side, past a haberdashery she had spotted on her first day, its windows laden with rolls of ribbon and cards of lace.

Merchants were setting up their shops, placing crates of fruit and vegetables on the boardwalk. The smell of the bread nestled in her basket was becoming so irresistible she was tempted to break off a small piece of the crust. She didn't though, because she wanted to take her mother the loaf in all its perfection. She crossed the road and proceeded down the other side, stopping to gaze at the ribbons and lace. Aunt Molly's sovereign was still wrapped in a handkerchief inside her trunk, waiting to be spent.

'Just between us,' Aunt Molly had said. 'No need to tell your mama and papa.'

A new hair ribbon would be nice. Her father would never notice. She would think about it and come back when the shop was open.

Amy passed the boot mart, the pharmacy and Thompsons' general store. She was about to cross back to the other side of the road when her nose detected something even more mouth-watering than the bread. It was a mix of aromatic spices coming from the next shop. She looked for a sign. Most of the buildings were covered in painted lettering, but here she had to search for the name, written in elegant frosted letters on each of the windows.

MR CHEN'S EMPORIUM
IMPORTER OF FINE GOODS AND DEALER IN ORNAMENTAL WARES

At the top of each verandah post was a pair of decorative brackets made from cast iron. Nothing unusual there, except that the design within each bracket was a fire-breathing dragon, its wings outstretched. A pair of blood-red doors marked the entrance. One was shut, the other flung open.

She stood at the doorway, unsure whether to enter. She might have walked on, had it not been for the scent of the fragrant spices luring her closer – cinnamon, cloves, ginger and something earthy she couldn't quite identify. Tentatively she stepped over the threshold but didn't proceed any further, as if an invisible barrier was holding her back. From somewhere close she heard a tinkling sound. It took her a few seconds to discover the source. Hanging above her were strings of brass bells swinging in the breeze. The interior of the store was so dark her eyes took a while to make out the details, and then she could barely contain her excitement. The walls were lined with wooden shelves reaching to the cornices. Every shelf was crowded with beautiful things vying for her attention: teapots, bowls, cups and plates in tantalising colours and intricate patterns, and elegant vases with lids resembling Prussian helmets. Paper parasols painted with bright flowers and birds were suspended from the ceiling. Bolts of fabric were stacked in an open cabinet, arranged by colour. A brass lantern glowed on the counter and large porcelain urns patterned with intricate blue and white designs stood on the floor.

It was an Aladdin's cave, tucked away in the main street of Millbrooke.

A man was standing at the counter with his back to her, unloading something from a tea chest. She was about to leave when he turned and saw her. He squinted, trying to make out the figure backlit by the morning sun. Then she realised it couldn't be more than half past seven. The store was not yet open.

'I'm sorry to have disturbed you, sir,' she said before he could speak. 'Your shop smells like Christmas and I couldn't resist looking inside.'

He was dressed in a suit – a brown jacket, white shirt and black tie knotted loosely in a bow, with matching brown trousers. But it was the waistcoat which caught her eye: orange silk – the colour of a Millbrooke sunset. And then she saw his face. Bronzed skin, liquid brown cat's eyes, sleek black hair immaculately combed back from a high forehead, full lips topped by a black moustache, not the thick and bristly kind favoured by her father, but a thin line perfectly groomed. His cheekbones might have been sculpted out of clay. It was hard to judge his age.

As she looked at the face, it dawned on her that the merchant was a Chinaman, like the band of dancing people she had seen in the street. Like her beloved Aladdin of Monsieur Galland's *A Thousand and One Nights*, only without the pigtail.

Meanwhile, the Chinaman in the orange waistcoat was staring back at her, as though he hadn't understood her words. She was about to repeat them slowly when she heard: 'Good morning, madam. Please do not apologise. May I be of help to you?'

He was smiling, showing perfect white teeth. Perfect English too. If she closed her eyes, it would be easy to imagine he was Mr Dickens himself. Amy was disconcerted. She had expected him to speak in the odd, high-pitched sounds she had heard from his fellow countrymen when she passed them in the street. Not the cultivated accent of someone who might have recently come down from university.

'No, thank you, sir. I really should go. My mother is waiting for me to return with the bread for our breakfast. I am truly sorry to have bothered you.' At the same time she found herself advancing further into the shop.

'You spoke of the smell of Christmas,' he said.

The look he gave her was so odd that she wondered if she should explain the meaning of 'Christmas', but he continued. 'I wonder if it could be the spices in the tea? This one in particular smells like plum pudding.' He was pointing to a small wooden canister, part of a row of identical containers sitting on the counter.

'I've never known tea to smell like that,' she replied.

He removed the lid and filled a wooden scoop with tea leaves. As he held it towards her, Amy leaned forward and breathed in the fragrance. Her face was almost touching his hand.

'Yes, I think you are right,' she said.

'Dried chamomile blossoms, apple and cinnamon. It is a tisane. Would you care to try it? I have some water boiling on the stove.' He indicated a room at the back. Before she could decline, he was gone, returning soon after with a cast-iron kettle which he placed on a porcelain trivet. Next he took a white teapot, decorated all over with climbing blue flowers, added three teaspoons of the tisane, and poured the hot water.

'It must infuse for a few minutes. Pray take the opportunity to look around while you are waiting.'

'Thank you, sir.'

Although there was much to peruse in the Chinaman's store, it was the bolts of fabric which drew her to them. Jewel-coloured silks and brocades adorned with tiny flowers and birds. Next to the silks there stood a cheval mirror. How could she possibly resist the temptation to drape herself in one of those sumptuous silks and view the effect? Placing her basket on the floor, she took a bolt of turquoise and unrolled enough of it to wrap around her body like a toga. In her mind's eye she saw a wondrous ball gown. It would have no need of lace or any other trim. Then she posed in front of the looking glass, supporting the roll of fabric with one hand and placing the other on her hip.

What she saw made her smile. The greenish-blue tones were a perfect foil for her pale complexion, which was flawless, save for a dusting of freckles on her nose, the product of eight summers lived under the Australian sun. Her dark blue eyes had taken on the colours of the sea, and her golden curls seemed to shine as brightly as the silk.

Although she had been among the tallest in her class, the improvised turquoise ensemble flowing from shoulder to floor made her look even taller. However, thanks to Miss Howe's deportment lessons, she knew better than to hunch her shoulders in an attempt to camouflage her height. 'Stature may be God-given,' Miss Howe had preached, 'but posture is one's own doing.'

A noise at the counter indicated the Chinaman was back. As she turned towards him, she noticed a frown on his face. What must he be thinking? That she was a flibbertigibbet mesmerised by her own reflection? Flushed with embarrassment, she hastily undraped the silk, rolled it up and replaced it on the shelf among the blues and greens. As she smoothed her navy dress, she heard: 'I have always admired the silk makers of Hangchow. They are not afraid to use colour. Do you like the turquoise, madam?'

Still flustered, she simply nodded in reply.

'I think I have a small remnant of it. Not big enough for an item of clothing.' He riffled through a basket of fabric scraps on the counter. 'Here it is. Would you like to have it? You might be able to make a pincushion or a needle-holder.'

He handed her the square of silk.

'I couldn't.'

'It will only be used to patch someone's breeches if you don't take it.'

The silk was like a tiny piece of his exotic homeland. She placed it carefully in her basket.

'Thank you, sir.'

'People call me Mr Chen,' he said, offering his hand.

'I am Amy Duncan from St Aidan's Manse,' she replied, conscious that she had forgotten to wear her gloves. Although it was generally considered unladylike to shake hands with a gentleman, gloves or not, she couldn't very well ignore his proffered hand. As she shook it, she noted the long, bronze fingers and the skin cold and smooth like silk.

'It is a pleasure to make your acquaintance, Miss Duncan.'

'Likewise, Mr Chen,' she smiled, but at the same time took a step back. In the space of a few seconds, yet another rule had been broken. Miss Howe had taught her she should never give her name to a stranger. Furthermore, her headmistress maintained that a lady and a gentleman should be formally introduced by a third party who was a mutual acquaintance. But perhaps the rules of etiquette might not apply to an exchange between a merchant and his customer.

When in doubt, Amy always sought solutions from her reading. What would her namesake, Little Dorrit, have done in the circumstances? She remembered Mr Dorrit's insistence on keeping up appearances. He had even employed Mrs General to give etiquette lessons to his offspring. And then the image of her own father loomed. What would the Reverend Duncan make of his daughter indulging in a conversation with a Celestial shopkeeper, albeit one who spoke and dressed like a gentleman?

'Your tea is ready, Miss Duncan,' Mr Chen announced, pouring the fragrant liquid into a tiny cup with no handle.

'Aren't you going to have some yourself?' she asked.

He seemed surprised. 'Do you mind?'

Why would she mind? He poured a cup for himself and watched as she took a sip.

'It actually tastes like Christmas,' she said.

'It does indeed,' he replied, smiling at her.

They sipped their tea in silence.

'I think I would like to buy some of this tea, Mr Chen.'

'There is no obligation on your part, Miss Duncan.'

'I know that. Nonetheless, I am charmed by the notion of conjuring up Christmas, simply by smelling your tea.'

'You must remember to drink it as well.'

He produced a little square tin with a domed lid. On the sides were illustrations of Chinamen in colourful robes, standing among willow trees and flowering shrubs.

'Two scoops?' he asked.

'Yes, please.'

'When the tin is empty, I shall refill it for you.'

Amy had been so engrossed in tasting the tea and looking at the silks that she had forgotten there was only a shilling's worth of coins in her pocket. What if she couldn't pay him? How embarrassing. She would never be able to face him again.

'That will be threepence,' he said.

She sighed so loudly with relief that he added: 'We can put it on account, if you wish.'

'No, no, I have it with me.' She placed the tiny silver coin in his silken hand.

'Thank you, Miss Duncan,' he said, putting it in the tray of a brass cash register at the end of the counter.

Next minute she was standing on Miller Street, shading her eyes from the sunlight. Lying in her basket were the souvenirs of her visit to Aladdin's magic cave. If the tin and the fragment of silk hadn't existed as evidence of her encounter with Mr Chen, she might have thought it all an exotic dream.

On her return, Amy found her mother dressed and making a pot of tea. She was about to offer Mr Chen's tisane but decided to keep it for a time when she could be sure it was just the two of them. She had missed her gentle, quiet mother. Whereas Molly Mackenzie was all hustle and bustle, Margaret Duncan was the image of thoughtful repose. Two sisters, both easy to love, yet each so different.

'The doctor says the sickness should have passed weeks ago,' her mother said, slumping at the table. 'I'm so glad to have you back, Amy. I can barely cope with the chores, let alone manage the boys.' She lowered her voice. 'I wanted to send them to one of the schools in town.'

'Why didn't you do that, Mama?'

'Your father maintains public schools are unsuitable for a clergyman's sons.'

'Are there not private schools like Miss Howe's?'

'They are beyond our means.'

Amy blushed as she realised her gaffe. Aunt Molly had been paying for Amy's education for years. 'In that case, it is fortunate that I am back to help educate them,' she said, patting her mother's hand.

Over the next few days, Amy saw the boys' antics for herself. Robbie was nine and Billy seven, and both had energy to burn. They had become accustomed to running wild, chasing the chooks, lighting bonfires in the far paddock and disappearing down to the creek. They used sticks to prod the reed-fringed banks, claiming an odd creature called a duck-mole lived there. They were always trying to dislodge it from its burrow. For her part, Amy had dismissed the duck-mole as a figment of their imagination, like a fire-breathing dragon or a mythical unicorn, until the day Robbie appeared at the door, nursing his hand and holding back tears.

'What have you done?' asked Amy.

'It was the duck-mole. I tried to grab him and he stung me with his claw.'

Already Robbie's hand had swollen to twice its size. Amy thanked God that her mother was napping in the parlour. Then she went to tell her father.

'Don't worry yer ma about this, lass,' he said, dispatching Billy to find Doctor Allen.

As the doctor examined Robbie's hand, he said, 'I remember when Old Tommy Roberts was shooting duck-moles for their fur. He hit one and sent his dog into the creek to fetch it. But the creature was still alive and barbed the dog with its spur.'

'What happened to the dog?' asked Amy.

'It died the same day.'

She gasped, and the doctor continued, 'I haven't encountered a case in humans before. And I don't recall anything in the journals. I think he'll be all right. Best to keep the boy still. No moving that arm for the next few hours.'

How could anyone keep Robbie still, Amy wondered in frustration.

'Send for me if he becomes feverish. Otherwise, bring him to the surgery tomorrow and I'll check the wound.'

'What shall we tell Mama?' asked Amy after the doctor left.

Matthew Duncan stroked his beard in contemplation and replied, 'the truth, of course, but don't any of ye mention the dead dog or I'll gi'e ye the strap.'

Robbie couldn't use his arm for a couple of weeks, but in all other respects he was fine. And the duck-mole incident put an end to the boys' worst escapades. In the meantime Amy returned some structure to their lives. Three hours of lessons every morning – spelling, grammar, arithmetic and geography. There was no misbehaving because their father was directly across the hallway in his study, where a leather strap lay waiting to be used on a recalcitrant child. Of an afternoon Matthew Duncan would tutor them in Latin and Greek. Although Amy secretly wondered about the relevance of ancient languages to a life in the colonies, she held her tongue. Her father believed a gentleman's education was not complete without a thorough grounding in the classics.

Among the tedium of establishing routines for the boys and helping her mother with the housework, there was a saving grace. Amy had acquired yet another pupil – seventeen-year-old Eliza Miller, who lived in the grandest house in the district and had been schooled at home by a governess. With the formal part of her education over, her parents had planned to send her to a finishing school in Europe before launching her into Sydney society, but Eliza had other ideas. She had been born in Millbrooke and intended to stay there. When her parents heard about the arrival of the Presbyterian minister's daughter, fresh from Miss Howe's School for Ladies in Sydney, they approached the Reverend Duncan about the possibility of his daughter tutoring Eliza in English and French and perhaps some other niceties like calligraphy.

At first Amy had been apprehensive about the prospect. She was only six months older than Eliza. What could she teach a wealthy girl who had been educated for years by a governess? Fortunately Eliza turned out to be friendly and open-minded, neither stuck-up nor a know-it-all. For the first week, Amy insisted on being called Miss Duncan, but soon they were simply Amy and Eliza.

Friday afternoon was Eliza's grammar lesson. After they parsed an entire page of Mr Dickens, noting nouns in apposition and verbs in a variety of tenses and moods, Amy rewarded her pupil with an early finish. While a delighted Eliza rode home, Amy took a walk along the creek in the direction of the main street. She dithered in the haberdashery with no particular purchase in mind, which was fortunate indeed, seeing that she had left her purse at home. Afterwards she found herself standing on the boardwalk opposite the emporium.

In the fierce light of a Millbrooke afternoon, the store looked much like the others in Miller Street – low, verandahed buildings with tin roofs glinting in the sun. She began to wonder if she had been investing a special significance in the proprietor and his wares which was merely a product of her overactive imagination. Yet, as she gazed across the street at the blood-red doors and iron lace dragons, it seemed to her that this really could be an oasis of beauty in a dusty provincial town, a storehouse of possibilities in a world dominated by ironclad discipline and unbending rules. She was even tempted to pay a quick visit to Mr Chen to verify her theory, but the emporium was bristling with customers – ladies, immaculately coiffed and daintily attired. Amy's own hair had not been brushed since the morning, and she was wearing a dowdy calico apron over one of her mother's old dresses. Even if the emporium had been empty, there was simply no question of going there today.

Now

In her first month at the Old Manse Angie had learned that nobody was who they seemed. The amiable waiter in the pottery café had turned out to be a ceramicist, the creator of the shiny bowls and plates that lined the walls. Then there was Lisa, a friendly woman of around Angie's age, who owned the Millbrooke Arms. In a previous life, she had been a chef of some renown in a hatted Sydney restaurant. The elderly woman who sold plants every Saturday from the back of her ute was an award-winning screenwriter. The woodworker whose shop was only open on Fridays and Saturdays was also the editor of the local paper. And Nola from the B&B had been an actress in a series of seventies soap operas. This winter she was to be director of the annual *Millbrooke Follies*. Lisa said the town attracted refugees from the city seeking to reinvent themselves. She had christened their migration 'the Millbrooke phenomenon'.

Meanwhile Angie had run an ad in the *Millbrooke Gazette* offering painting classes – watercolour and acrylic. She supposed that she herself might be the latest example of the Millbrooke phenomenon – a nondescript fifty-something widow, who was actually an artist. She couldn't pinpoint exactly when she'd become nondescript, yet over the past decade the woman who used to turn heads when she entered a room had morphed into someone the world barely noticed. Phil had reassured her she was still attractive, but perhaps that was because he continued to see her as the teenage girl he'd first met in a Newtown pub. He had never noticed the strands of grey in her shoulder-length hair, the fine lines on her face, nor the stretch marks on her stomach. As for her art, it hadn't been the great career she'd envisaged. A couple of solo exhibitions before the boys came along and then it had fizzled out. With the long hours Phil had spent at the hospital, someone needed to be the mainstay in the children's lives and Angie had embraced the role. She enjoyed being secretary of the P&C, helper at the canteen, coordinator of the school fete, mother of the dux (Blake) and school captain (Tim). But one day the boys left home and she and Phil were empty-nesters, missing their offspring yet enthused by the possibilities ahead of them – the B&B they'd dreamed about for years, the painting career Angie had left behind. Then the man who had been a constant in her life for more than three decades woke with a crushing pain in his chest and died in the ICU two days later.

The ad in the *Gazette* produced five students – all women. When one of them confided on the phone that she had never painted before and was apprehensive about her skills, Angie reassured her: 'Everyone has an artistic side; we just need to tap into it.'

In the centre of the dining room she set up a big folding table with a groundsheet to protect the wooden floor. Then she primed five stretched canvas squares with Naples yellow hue. It was the colour Cézanne had used as the base for his paintings. Cézanne was Angie's favourite artist. She loved his use of autumn colours and the way he deconstructed objects into planes and angles. On the table she arranged a collection of blue and white Chinese vases and a matching ginger jar – luscious curving shapes with glossy surfaces that caught the light. The vases used to live in the yellow bedroom of the house that she and Phil had shared for thirty years and which was now leased to a young couple, no children, no pets. When she pictured the room and its bed, tears welled. But it wasn't the uncontrollable flood that would have once left her empty and exhausted. After a few minutes she resumed her preparation, picking a bunch of yellow tea roses from the garden, full-blown, ready to drop their petals, and placing them in one of the vases. Today the class would paint a still-life – Chinese porcelain with roses.

When the students arrived, it was obvious that they knew one another – they had completed a term of lace-making classes together and a year of quilting before that. One of them had brought a tray of chocolate mint slice, another a tin of ANZAC biscuits. They sat at the table, sipping tea and chatting. Although Angie wondered whether she should encourage them to start sketching, nobody seemed to be in a hurry.

'It's a lovely old house,' said Jennie, a young blonde woman in her early thirties with a cheerful face. 'I've always wanted to see inside.'

'Heaps of work to be done, though. It would give me nightmares,' said Ros who was in her fifties with curly brown hair and long acrylic nails like Vicky's.

'Don't listen to Ros, love. Just take your time.' Moira was a softly spoken woman of about seventy, wearing an immaculate white linen shirt which Angie feared might not be so clean at the end of a day's painting. Moira used to be the town's librarian, until the council forced her to retire at sixty-five. Now she was working there as a volunteer. 'Ever since George died, it's helped to fill the time,' she'd told Angie over the phone, her voice faltering as she said her husband's name. Another grieving widow. Angie had felt an instant bond.

'The house has been waiting for years for someone to do something with it,' Moira continued. 'The family who used to live here let it go to the pack.'

'They were only tenants,' said Tanya, who worked part-time as a receptionist at Morrison Real Estate. Then she flushed with embarrassment. 'Of course you're a tenant too, aren't you, Angie? But you're different to the others. You'll bring an artist's flair to the decoration.'

'Thanks, Tanya, but right now I'm overwhelmed by it. I've started little jobs all over the house, and nothing is finished.'

Finally they began to do a preparatory sketch. Angie suggested they work on a sheet of tracing paper and then transfer it to the canvas. As she looked at the emerging drawings with their wonky vases and unrecognisable roses, she knew it had been a wise idea to work on paper first. Eventually she dashed off a drawing herself, copied it onto tracing paper and gave each of them a pattern.

'Don't feel disheartened,' she said. 'Drawing is the most difficult skill of all. You'll find the painting process much easier. Really it's just about the application of colour and the play of light and shade.' She tried to sound persuasive.

By lunchtime everyone had transferred the design and they paused for Angie's vegetable soup and spelt bread from Don the baker.

'Just the ticket on a cold day,' said Ros.

'How was your date, Jennie?' asked Narelle, who had straight brown hair to her shoulders and a practical nylon tracksuit.

'Don't ask. It said on the website that he's self-employed, but it turns out he's actually *un*employed. Hasn't had a job in years.'

Narelle was laughing. 'When are you going to learn the code, Jen?'

'Code?' asked Angie.

'Yeah, you can't take a profile at face value,' said Tanya. 'For instance, "loves to dine out" means "loves to dine at your place".'

'And "looking for companionship" translates as "seeking sex",' said Narelle.

They were all giggling. Yet for a bemused Angie, it was a foreign world. 'So, Jennie, are you really looking for a partner on the internet?' she asked tentatively. Jennie was an attractive woman. Surely she wouldn't have a problem finding men.

'We all are,' said Tanya. 'It's not like living in the city where you can meet men in nightclubs or bars.'

'We've had our disasters though, haven't we, girls?' said Jennie. 'Remember Jamie.'

There were cries of 'Sleazebag!' and 'What a loser.'

Jennie explained: 'I used to drive over to Granthurst to see him. He couldn't get enough of me. Then one Sunday, after we'd been going together for six months, he announced: "I'm bored with this." When I asked him what had changed to make him say that, he said: "Nothing. That's the problem." And it was over, just like that. It turned out he'd met someone else – on the internet!'

Angie must have gasped because Jennie said: 'It's fine, Angie. I'm okay about it now.'

'Are you all doing this internet dating thing?'

'Yeah, except Ros,' replied Narelle. 'She's happily married.'

'Aren't there any nice men in Millbrooke?'

Angie's question provoked hysterical laughter.

'It's a man drought,' said Tanya. 'A rain shadow when it comes to finding a partner.'

'The eligible ones are taken,' said Narelle. 'As for the rest, they're either partial to the drink or a bit crazy.'

'Or they're gay,' said Tanya.

'What about Richard Scott?' asked Angie. 'Is he married?'

'Are you interested?' asked Tanya.

'In my landlord? Hardly. I just thought he might be a candidate for one of you.'

'Never even considered it,' said Jennie. 'He must be pension age if he's a day.'

'And he needs a complete makeover,' added Narelle.

When there was a brief pause in the conversation, Moira said, 'I know for a fact that Richard Scott isn't married and he's definitely not gay.'

Angie gave Moira a curious glance. How could she know Richard wasn't gay, unless . . . ? No, a relationship between the well-groomed widow and Angie's shabby landlord was too bizarre to contemplate.

'Then according to Narelle's theory,' Ros chipped in, 'he must be crazy.'

'Just a bit unconventional,' said Moira.

'For an unconventional bloke, he's done pretty well for himself,' said Ros. 'Millerbrooke House must be worth a motza.'

'But he's an alcoholic, Ros,' said Narelle. 'He almost lives at the pub.'

'If he's a drunk, how did he accumulate all that property?' asked Angie.

'Probably inherited it,' said Tanya.

'Moira, you've lived here all your life,' said Narelle. 'Give us the goss.'

'It's nobody's business but Richard's,' she replied firmly.

Which put everyone in their place.

The afternoon broke up at three when Narelle and Tanya, both single mums, went to collect their children from school.

'I'll have to go too,' said Jennie who was divorced with no children. 'I have a client coming at three-thirty.'

Angie must have given her an odd look because she added: 'I'm an accountant.'

Embarrassed, Angie said: 'In that case, you might be interested in doing my tax return when the time comes.'

'No problem. Do you keep your statements and receipts in a shoebox?'

'No. Why do you ask?'

'That's the standard filing system in Millbrooke.'

After Jennie and Ros left, Moira stayed behind. Angie made her another cup of tea.

'You know, this internet dating thing isn't as bad as you think,' said Moira. Then the genteel widowed septuagenarian with the neatly permed hair went on to explain that she had also ventured into the world of cyber matchmaking. No meetings in person though. Not yet.

'You should try it, Angie,' she said.

When Moira saw the shocked look on Angie's face, she added:

'Maybe it's too soon. But down the track when you're stronger ... You won't meet a man any other way. Not if you live in Millbrooke.'

3

THE GIRL IN THE MAGENTA DRESS

Then

Amy finished Mr Chen's tea sooner than expected, and not in the most pleasant of circumstances. Barely a week after her visit to the emporium she and her mother were sitting in the kitchen, sipping their cinnamon infusion, when the Reverend Duncan returned early from a visit to an elderly parishioner. As he entered the room, he demanded: 'What in heaven's name is that dreadful smell?'

'It is a Chinese tisane, Papa,' replied Amy, instantly regretting the use of 'Chinese'.

'Did ye buy it from one of the Celestials, Amy Duncan?'

Amy was tempted to dissemble. Although lying was a sin, evasion was acceptable, particularly when you lived in Matthew Duncan's house.

'What is a Celestial, Papa?'

'Do not obfuscate with me, lass.'

She had no choice but to tell the truth. 'If you mean a Chinaman, then yes.'

'From now on ye must buy provisions at Thompsons' and keep away from those heathens with their herbs and potions. Ye don't want to make yer ma ill, do ye? Not in her delicate condition.'

'I find it to be a most refreshing tonic,' protested Margaret Duncan.

'Poison disguised as a refreshment,' said her husband. 'Which store was it, lass? Was it that Chen with his fancy way of speaking?'

Amy looked down at the table and said nothing.

'He's the worst of them, pretending to be like us.'

'But Matthew, he attends church at St John's.'

'It is a ruse to ingratiate himself with Millbrooke society. I've heard that when he's at home, he wears pagan robes and plays cards with his brother.' Playing cards was among the Reverend Duncan's most despised social vices, along with dancing and, of course, drinking alcoholic beverages. 'I wouldna be in the least surprised if he smokes opium,' he added.

Amy could stand it no longer.

'Papa, what evidence do you have for saying that?'

'Are ye contradicting me, lass?'

'No, Papa,' she answered, biting her lip. Although her father's attack on Mr Chen seemed mean and unwarranted, it wouldn't do to defend him.

'Once he's made his fortune, he'll slink back to his homeland. Like the others.'

'He has a prosperous emporium. That hardly denotes the behaviour of a fly-by-night.'

Her father glared at her. 'Yer time in Sydney with yer aunt has made ye far too insolent, Amy Duncan. Now tip the rest of that vile concoction onto the garden, and dinnae let me see ye with it e'er again.'

The next morning, the sun was lingering on the eastern horizon, not quite ready to greet the day, when Amy donned her magenta dress, ready for her morning visit to the bakery. If she just happened to detour via the emporium on her homeward trip, it would be a secret she would share with no-one, not even Eliza.

This morning her mother was still abed, too ill to raise her head from the pillow, her father was already at work in his study, while the boys, Robbie and Billy, were respectively milking Lorna Doone, the cow, and collecting eggs from the chicken coop. At the last moment, she grabbed her straw hat with its bunch of velvet violets and trail of ribbons and placed it at a jaunty angle on her head. Then she slipped out the back door.

It wasn't until she reached Miller Street that she could admire her outfit full-length in a shop window. With its draped overskirt, the magenta dress was daintier than the navy, but still plain enough to be acceptable to her father, who had pronounced it modest and sombre when she had worn it to her first church service in Millbrooke. Being a man ignorant of fashion, he had only noticed the dark colour. Amy, however, was well aware that the overskirt accentuated the slenderness of her waist, while the purple tones flattered the milkiness of her complexion. As for the hat, it showed off her curls to perfection.

When Amy reached the emporium, she was relieved to see one of the doors was open. That meant Mr Chen was already inside, unpacking his boxes and preparing for the day. The smell of exotic spices enveloped her in a fragrant cloud. Taking a deep breath, she stepped into the shop. Above her, the brass bells tinkled like fairies' laughter. Mr Chen was standing at his counter, writing in a ledger. He looked up, as if he had been expecting her.

'Good morning, Miss Duncan. I hope you have been keeping well.'

'I have, Mr Chen. And you?'

'I am fine, thank you.'

As she walked towards him and her eyes adjusted to the darkness of the shop, she could see a shadow across the left side of his face, almost as purple as her magenta dress.

'Mr Chen, what has happened?'

'An incident, Miss Duncan. Nothing for you to be concerned about.'

'Did you have an accident?'

'Not as such.'

Amy wondered if he might have slipped from a ladder while arranging goods on the uppermost shelves. Then her instincts told her it was a human hand which had wrought the damage, and she was indignant.

'Did someone strike you, Mr Chen?'

'Please, Miss Duncan, do not be upset. It was a drunkard in the street.'

'Oh dear. Did you call the constabulary?'

'No, it was unnecessary. And I didn't want to make a fuss. Episodes of this nature are not uncommon. There are people who do not take kindly to foreigners.'

'Foreigners? Aren't we all foreigners in this land, sir?'

'Save for the native people, Miss Duncan.'

Amy had never seen a native person, let alone thought about them.

'But, you are right,' he continued. 'And some of us appear more foreign than others. Human beings are fearful of anyone who is different.' Then he smiled. 'But I wonder if you are the exception, Miss Duncan.'

Amy could feel a blush rising from her collarbones and up her neck. Soon her face would be as deep a colour as the Chinaman's bruise. She lowered her eyes, trying to think of a reply. Finally she said: 'It's all very well to label commodities such as tea.' She pointed to the wooden canisters lined up on the counter with their little signs written in Chinese and English. 'But we can't put people into boxes. Each of us is unique.'

He was smiling at her. 'I see you have brought your tin, Miss Duncan. Would you like to sample a different tea this time?'

'Yes, I would, Mr Chen.' What was the harm in trying a little tea? After all, she had already flouted her father's edict by entering the emporium.

'I recommend the Lapsang Souchong. A black tea from Foukien Province.'

'Is that your homeland?'

'I come from Kwangtung which is south of Foukien. They are both coastal provinces, but Foukien has fewer people and many mountains and forests. Would you care to smell the tea leaves?'

When he opened the lid of the canister, the smell was unmistakable.

'It reminds me of my father's pipe,' said Amy.

Mr Chen laughed. 'That is because the leaves are dried by smoking them over pine fires.'

'It's a comforting aroma. My father might even like it.'

'Did he enjoy the tisane?'

'Not exactly.' She wasn't going to tell Mr Chen about having to dispose of the remaining tea leaves on the marigold plants. 'I shall buy some of your smoked tea. And would you kindly write down the name for me? I will never remember it otherwise.'

'Certainly.' He took a piece of paper from below the counter, a jar of ink and a pen. She watched as he wrote the two words in perfect copperplate – the loop of the 'S' as sinuous as a morning glory vine. Then he placed one scoop of tea inside the tin.

'Only one scoop?'

'Yes, Miss Duncan. Then you will return sooner.'

His eyes met hers so briefly she might have imagined it. She took threepence out of her purse and placed it on the counter.

He put two pennies on the counter, in the same way she had done. When she retrieved her change, he said: 'I must apologise, Miss Duncan, for misjudging you. I have done the very thing you've just condemned. Placing people in tea boxes.'

Bewildered by his words, she tipped her head sideways.

'The first time you visited my shop, I only saw a pretty girl with yellow hair.' His voice was so low she had to strain to hear him.

'I'm ashamed to confess I assumed you to be flighty and frivolous, when, in fact, you are wise beyond your years.'

Amy didn't know how to reply to his remark so she gave him an embarrassed smile and wished him good morning. Outside, she took a deep breath. Things which had seemed so simple barely a fortnight ago had now become as complicated as a piece of bobbin lace.

On her return to the Manse, Amy found the boys playing with their tin soldiers on the front verandah.

'Have you finished your chores?' she asked.

Absorbed in their game, they simply nodded. As she entered the house and stole past her father's study, the pungent odour of his pipe filled the air, indicating his presence. She was halfway down the hall when she heard: 'Is that ye, Amy Duncan? Come in here, lass. I've been looking fer ye.'

Oh dear. Did her father know where she had been? She would have to make a confession, or at least a partial one.

'Coming, Papa,' she replied meekly, depositing her hat and basket in the hallway. Gingerly she put her head around the door. 'I'm sorry, Papa. I was at the bakery.'

There was a pause in which she prepared herself for the inevitable recriminations, but he only said, 'Guid. Ye must go there every morning – it will save yer ma having to make the bread. Be sure ye come straight home though.'

He didn't sound gruff at all.

She took a seat on the stiff-backed chair opposite him.

'Normally I would have asked yer ma to listen to my sermon, but I didna want to disturb her, seeing as she is having a wee lie-in. So I thought ye might hear me read it through before we take our breakfast.'

It was hard to love her father in the way a daughter should, but today Amy could see glimpses of the man her mother had found engaging enough to marry. As he read aloud in his rumbling Glaswegian accent, Amy closed her eyes and listened to his sermon for Pentecost Sunday. She had always been enthralled by the rushing wind and the speaking in tongues.

'What do ye think?' he asked when it was over.

Amy couldn't remember him asking her opinion about anything before.

'It's beautiful, Papa,' she said and meant it.

'Guid,' he replied.

There was a hint of a smile on his lips.

Two days later Amy was awake before dawn, lighting the kerosene lamp on her bed-stand and deliberating about what to wear. Not that she had much choice – either her magenta dress or the navy one. The occasion was her birthday and she intended to buy herself a present. Covertly, of course, because birthdays were neither acknowledged nor observed in the Duncan family, apart from Christmas and the Queen's Birthday.

Like a wraith, she tiptoed downstairs and out the door. Aunt Molly's shiny sovereign sat deep inside her pocket, clinking against the small coins she had brought for her morning visit to the baker. Once that task was over and the bread lay warm and inviting in her basket, she strolled down the main street, every step bringing her closer to the intriguing Mr Chen and his emporium. As she approached the store, the clock tower atop the School of Arts began to toll seven o'clock. Was she too early? Perhaps she should do another circuit of Miller Street and come back in ten minutes. Then she noticed one of the red doors was ajar. She pushed it open just enough to step inside.

Although Mr Chen was nowhere to be seen, he had been busy since her last visit. A new shelf had appeared on the side wall, holding ornaments made of a shiny green substance that looked almost translucent – animals, birds, plants and people, a whole world in miniature, carved with masterful dexterity. As she raised her hand to touch a figurine – a lady dressed in a flowing robe, with her hair pulled into a tight bun – Amy heard: 'Do you like the jade, Miss Duncan?'

Her heart began to race. Most likely it was from being caught by surprise. 'I do indeed, Mr Chen,' she replied, turning to see him in a red waistcoat dotted with dragonflies. The bruise on his face had faded to a light purple, barely visible on his golden skin.

'And how may I assist you this morning?'

'I am seeking a present.'

'What is the occasion, may I ask?'

'A birthday.'

'I'm afraid I have very few items suitable for children.'

'She is not a child. Not any more,' she said with determination.

'So it's for a lady.' He began to pace around the room, surveying the goods. 'I wonder what she might like? A necklace perhaps?' He held up a string of purple beads.

'A most attractive choice, Mr Chen, but unfortunately this lady does not wear jewellery.'

Then his gaze rested on a collection of hair ornaments, intricately carved out of bone. 'Do you think an ivory clasp might be appropriate?'

'Sadly she is not permitted to wear adornments of that ilk.'

'You seem to be well acquainted with the lady's tastes and requirements, Miss Duncan.'

'Yes, indeed,' Amy replied with a blush. She would have to tell Mr Chen the truth. He was not a person with whom she could equivocate. 'I have a confession to make. It is I who is having the birthday.'

'Really? I would never have guessed.' Although he maintained a straight face, she knew he was smiling inside. 'Many happy returns of the day.'

'Thank you,' she said demurely.

'A lady never reveals her age, does she?'

'I have no such aversion.'

'Then may I be permitted to ask which birthday you are celebrating?'

'It is my eighteenth.' She longed to pose the same question of him, but couldn't summon the courage.

'We should have a tea party, Miss Duncan. In honour of your special day.'

Before she could remonstrate with him, he had disappeared into the back room. In his absence she browsed the shelves, looking for something she could buy which would escape her father's detection. She was about to give up when she discovered boxes of stationery decorated with plum blossoms and peony roses. Now this was the perfect choice. She could use the beautiful paper for her correspondence with Aunt Molly and conceal it at the bottom of her bureau.

In a few minutes Mr Chen was back with a lacquered tray which he placed on a low table, its legs writhing with dragons. 'Let us imagine we are partaking of a sumptuous feast, even though it is only jasmine tea and currant buns.'

'I'm very fond of currant buns,' she replied.

'Likewise,' he said with a smile.

Perhaps one day she might encounter him at the bakery, away from his emporium. What would he be like without his delicate porcelain and fragrant teas? Would he remain dazzling, or would he just be a dapper gentleman in a silk waistcoat?

'Please take a seat, Miss Duncan,' he said, moving two wicker stools towards the table.

As they sat opposite each other, sipping from tiny cups and conversing as friends, she longed to remain locked in the moment like a jade figurine on Mr Chen's shelf. But that fanciful notion was quickly replaced by a worrying thought. What if a St Aidan's parishioner came into the emporium and caught her socialising with its proprietor? If her father found out, there would be no more visits to Mr Chen. She might even be locked up like Rapunzel and never let out again.

Mr Chen must have sensed her disquiet because he said: 'Your family will be waiting for their bread. You had best be leaving. But you must choose your present before you go.'

'I think I shall buy a box of your stationery. I'm quite taken with the floral motifs, though I fear the paper is so exquisite I shall be reluctant to write upon it.'

'Just as tea is there to be drunk, the paper is meant to be used,' he said as he placed the box in her basket.

'Is it from China?'

'Of course. The Chinese were the first to make paper.'

'Really?' She was sadly ignorant of Chinese history.

'A thousand years before the Europeans.'

'My goodness!'

'Can you guess what material they used?'

Amy shook her head.

'Mulberry bark. Are you familiar with mulberries, Miss Duncan?'

'I am indeed. We had a tree in our garden in Sydney. And I used to keep silkworms in a box and feed them the leaves.'

'We might think it is a vast world, but there are many connections,' he said softly.

The way he looked at her made her blush. 'How much is the stationery, Mr Chen?' she asked, by way of changing the subject.

'It is a gift, Miss Duncan. For your birthday.'

'No, I couldn't.'

'Please do not deny me such a small gesture.'

Amy didn't know how to respond. She knew she should insist on paying, yet part of her wanted to accept his offering. Finally she said: 'Thank you, Mr Chen. You must allow me to reciprocate on *your* birthday.'

'In China we all become a year older at the lunar new year. However, my *real* birthday is in April.'

'That's almost a year away,' she replied, 'but I shall not forget. Good morning, sir.'

Suddenly she was outside the emporium. The clock on the School of Arts showed it was five past eight. How could it be so late? An hour had passed in an instant. The street was filling with people. She panicked as she imagined her family sitting around the kitchen table, wondering what had happened to their bread. Although she knew it wasn't ladylike, she ran all the way home. Breathless she burst into the kitchen to find everyone silently eating their porridge, even her mother who looked better than she had in weeks.

'The baker was busy and I had to wait,' said Amy, surprised at how easily a falsehood could glide from her tongue.

But nobody questioned her, nor did they mention her birthday. After breakfast she finished her chores, removed the stationery from its hiding place in the basket and went upstairs to her room. There she took a single leaf from the box and stared at it for a long time, pondering what to write to Aunt Molly. *She* was the kind of person who might understand Amy's fascination with the emporium and its owner. Then again, sharing your secrets, even with a kindly aunt, would be like wishing on a shooting star and telling someone what you had wished for. Once you had let the wish slip out, it could never come true.

'Could you teach me the Viennese waltz, Amy? Please,' asked Eliza as they perched on a pair of milking stools in the barn beside the Manse.

'Your parents are not paying tuition fees for me to teach you dancing.'

'If you teach me to waltz, you can come to our Queen's Birthday dance.'

'You have already invited me, Eliza Miller. You cannot take it back. Now let us begin our French lesson.'

'But French is *so* dull, Amy.'

'Not necessarily.' She produced the volume of Monsieur Galland's *Les mille et une nuits* that she had hidden under some straw. The book hadn't been an easy choice, not with Aunt Molly's disclaimer still strong in her mind. But Eliza wasn't a child any more. And the story was so long that Amy could select appropriate passages for translation and avoid anything indelicate.

As soon as Eliza saw the cover with its exotic illustration she began to smile. 'This doesn't look like the primers I used with my governess.'

'Were they little orange books by someone called Lady Bell?'

'Yes, how did you know?'

'That is what we used at Miss Howe's. I still have my copy of *French without Tears*. But this book is much more interesting.'

Amy opened the heavy book at page two hundred and seven – 'Histoire d'Aladdin, ou la lampe merveilleuse'.

'I know this story,' said Eliza. 'I remember my mother telling me about the genie in the lamp. But the princess spoiled everything by exchanging the magic lamp for a new one.'

'She didn't know about its magic powers. Aladdin should have locked it away when he wasn't using it.'

'Like my father's guns.'

Amy was in awe of Eliza's many talents. Over the past couple of weeks she had discovered Eliza could shoot a rifle, ride a horse bareback and shear a sheep. She had even delivered a calf. Still, it wouldn't do to discuss guns or horse-riding, not when there was work to be done.

Soon they were engrossed in the story of the impoverished Aladdin who wanted to be a merchant. And it wasn't long before they found themselves standing alongside him, viewing a royal procession passing through the city streets. Inside the carriage was the princess herself. After pursuing the procession, Aladdin managed to catch a glimpse of the young woman without her veil, pronouncing her face perfectly proportioned and her gaze agreeable and modest.

'It's quite thrilling, isn't it?' said Eliza. 'I fear he has already lost his heart to her. But what a peculiar name she has.'

'Badroulboudour. Yes, it's a tongue-twister.'

'She should have been called something sensible like Amy or Eliza. Still, Aladdin would have thought her lovely whatever her name.'

They examined the engraving of Aladdin in his merchant's finery.

'He is beautiful, isn't he, Amy?'

'Yes, Eliza,' she replied. 'He is indeed . . .'

'Which would you prefer,' Eliza asked, 'a prince with golden hair or someone dark and exotic like Aladdin?'

Amy was about to supply an answer when she realised the French lesson had turned into something else altogether. Putting the book aside, she said: 'I think we have read enough for today. I haven't yet seen your writing skills, Eliza. Perhaps the rest of our afternoon might be spent undertaking a composition.'

Eliza was frowning. 'I'm not talented at inventing stories, Amy. My governess said I had no imagination.'

'I don't expect you to invent a tale. I want you to write something real. About the person you most admire.'

'I suppose I could write about my grandfather, Captain

Alexander Miller. He served under Admiral Nelson at Trafalgar.'

'How wonderful.'

'Yes, he was only a junior officer then, but later he became a master of his own ship. After years of service with the Royal Navy, he was granted two thousand acres of land here in New South Wales. So he emigrated with his family and built a grand villa which he called Millerbrooke House. "Miller" for himself and "Brooke" with an "e" for my grandmother's family. And that is how the town got its name.'

'But it's *Millbrooke*, not Millerbrooke.'

'When people began to settle here, the name was shortened. Nowadays everyone assumes the town was called after the flour mill on the creek, but it is really in honour of the Millers and the Brookes.'

'That is an admirable story, Eliza. It will make an excellent composition.'

A smile began to curl at the corners of Eliza's mouth. 'I've just thought of someone else whose story is equally worthy. Could I write about two people instead of one?'

'No, that would be far too confusing. Surely you can choose between them.'

Eliza seemed to sulk for a moment, before asking, 'How long do I have to write this?'

'Let us say half an hour. If it's not finished, you can complete it at home.' Amy knew how much Eliza detested home lessons. Even if her hand was sore and heavy at the end, the story would be completed on time. They retired to the dining room of the Manse where Eliza sat at a table with a writing paper and pen and ink.

'If I am rushed, there will be smudges,' she warned.

'Your time has already begun,' replied Amy.

Eliza dipped her pen in the ink well and began writing furiously, barely stopping to replenish her pen or blot the page. Amy imagined that 'someone else' referred to Eliza's father, Mr Miller, who was much loved and respected by everyone in Millbrooke. In the meantime Amy began planning her next geography lesson for the boys. They were such restless creatures that she had decided to use their energy in a game, finding capital cities on the linen map of the world her father had purchased for them from Mr Moffitt's stationery store in George Street, Sydney. There would be a prize of a penny for the boy who found the most capitals from the list Amy had composed for them.

At the end of the half hour Eliza was still writing. Amy brought her a cup of tea and gave her another fifteen minutes to finish.

After Eliza and her horse Neddy left for home, Amy read the story, pencil poised to correct any errors. But she found herself so engrossed in Eliza's narrative that the pencil soon slipped from her hand.

Someone I Admire
by Eliza Miller

I was only a baby when the person I most admire came into our lives. He arrived by ship from Canton with his father who was seeking to make his fortune in the goldfields and then return to his wife who had remained behind with their younger son.

The boy and his father had only been at the Millbrooke gold diggings a week or two when everything changed. It was night-time.

The little boy heard a scream and went to investigate. He discovered his father had fallen into one of the deep holes which littered the diggings. It was half full of icy water and his father's head was barely visible above the surface. The boy ran for help. Soon people were lowering bamboo poles into the hole. Finally they were able to drag the father out, but he was barely alive. Someone rode into town and returned with the doctor. However the man could not be revived.

That night the doctor took the boy back to town. The next day my parents, John and Charlotte Miller, who had recently lost a son and a daughter to illness, decided to make the fatherless boy part of their family. He was so small they thought he was only eight, when he was actually eleven, the same age as Joseph, two years older than Daniel and eight years older than I.

Nobody could pronounce his Chinese name so my parents called him something which sounded similar – Charles. He was educated with my two brothers in our family schoolroom next to the kitchen. My grandfather, Captain Alexander Miller, took a special interest in him, and they spent hours together, poring over old maps and planning imaginary journeys.

Charles was a cheerful, obedient boy, but he hated to set foot on the goldfields. It reminded him of the night his father died. He didn't want to be a miner or have anything to do with gold. He said it was a curse. Instead, he set his heart on opening a great store in the main street of Millbrooke, selling ornamental wares from his homeland.

When Charles was fifteen, my grandfather died. In his will he left a bequest to Charles to be claimed on his majority. Five years ago, he used the inheritance to buy a store in Miller Street which became his emporium. Then he sent for his younger brother, whom everyone calls Jimmy, because they cannot pronounce his Chinese name either, and the two of them ran the business and lived in the back room.

The store was so successful, Charles was able to buy an acre of land in Paterson Street where he and Jimmy built a house in the hope their mother might join them. Charles even returned to China to fetch her, but she said she was too old to move to a strange land with different customs.

The little Chinese boy, who looked younger than his years, is now as tall as Joseph and Daniel. They make a handsome trio. Sometimes, on a Sunday morning in St John's Church, I have heard a collective sigh from the ladies of the congregation as the boys walk down the aisle to take their places in our family pew. I love all three, but the one I admire most is Charles. Although there are some townsfolk who mistrust and dislike him because of his race, there are others who hold him in high esteem on account of his hard work and gracious manners.

He is the finest person I know.

The End

When Amy finished reading Eliza's composition, she couldn't help smiling. She would never have guessed that her Chinese merchant was also a well-loved member of Millbrooke's oldest family.

Now

After a long day washing down her bedroom walls with sugar soap, Angie gave herself a reward – dinner at the pub. The Millbrooke Arms was a landmark, standing at the top of the rise at the eastern end of town. Its green iron roof and tall chimneys were the first glimpse of Millbrooke for any visitor arriving from the east. In the old days it would have been a feat for tired horses or bullocks to pull their load up that hill, only a block or two from the last changing station on the mail run, and yet so far.

There was a sign in the bar claiming it was the longest continuously operating hotel in Australia. When Angie commented on the fact, Lisa, the publican confessed: 'I'm not sure that it's true. There are dozens of pubs around Australia making the same claim. Many of them aren't original – just rebuilt on the original site. At least our Georgian inn is still there underneath all the additions. It dates back to the 1830s.'

In 1860 it had been given a Victorian makeover – an extra floor, a wrap-around iron lace verandah and a coat of stucco over the original stone blocks. What vandals those Victorians must have been, thought Angie. It appeared they had messed with most of Millbrooke's original buildings, constructing parapets and adding iron lace in an attempt to show off their assets. Still, it gave the town a certain mystique. When you caught sight of a side wall crafted in granite or sandstone, you knew there were layers beneath the florid exterior. The layers were what made the town interesting.

Lisa's pub was painted orange. She said a heritage expert had taken paint scrapings and discovered the startlingly bright hue was the earliest colour to be used on the Victorian façade. Angie had always felt uncomfortable entering the public bar of a country hotel on her own, but not here. It was the kind of place where nobody would turn to look, let alone leer. Did it have something to do with the preponderance of unattached women in Millbrooke? When she made the observation to Lisa, the publican whispered in reply, 'Millbrooke is a haven for women of all persuasions.'

Was that some form of code? Did Lisa think Angie was gay, or was it just a general statement? That session with the painting ladies had left her unnaturally attuned to codes and connotations.

Angie ordered her meal from the bar, bought a glass of white wine and found herself a table in the corner. Three people were sitting at the cedar bar. The old mirrored shelves behind it, reaching as high as the ceiling, held bottles of spirits. It could have been a saloon in any Western movie. Except the place was almost empty. How did Lisa survive with so few drinkers and one lone diner?

'How are you managing at the Manse?' It was a male voice, soft and mellow, not unlike an announcer on a classical music station.

When Angie looked up, she saw her landlord in a woollen pixie hat and shabby shirt. The voice didn't match the scruffy exterior.

'Pretty well, thanks.' She prayed he wasn't going to join her.

'I hear you're teaching art classes,' he said, taking a seat at the next table.

He must have seen the ad in the paper. 'I hope you don't mind me using your house for my classes. Perhaps I should have asked you first. But it's just one day a week. And only five ladies.'

'That's fine, Mrs Wallace. I'm not from the council.'

'Do they check on people?'

'If they know you're running a business from home. OH&S. Fire regulations. But not for a group of ladies having a pleasant day of painting and conversation. Even the Millbrooke Council wouldn't be that petty.'

Something about his manner made her feel anxious, like a child whose classmate has been reprimanded and feels guilty by association. 'I'm using the dining room as a studio, but I've covered the floor with a groundsheet.'

'I'm not worried about the floor. I've had a family renting that house whose kids used to ride bikes inside.'

Angie winced. Those beautiful floors. 'Eventually I'd like to use the barn for my classes, but it's . . .'

'Full of junk?'

'It certainly needs tidying. Though I suspect there are some treasures among the trash.'

'I'll come over one day and clear it out for you. There's still room in my shed at Millerbrooke.'

'No hurry.'

Angie's dinner had arrived, and so had her landlord's.

'The lamb shanks are good,' he said from the adjoining table, noting they had ordered the same thing. 'It's Millerbrooke lamb.'

Angie sipped her wine. He seemed to be drinking orange juice. It was hard to make out his facial features for stubble, but after Narelle's comment, Angie looked carefully for the telltale signs. She couldn't see whether his cheeks were flushed or not, but he didn't seem to have a drinker's nose.

'Have you painted anything since you arrived?' he asked between mouthfuls.

'I'm about to paint my bedroom. The one with the window seat.'

'I thought you would have chosen the large bedroom.'

'No, I like the small one.'

'It may have belonged to the girl with the golden hair.'

'Which girl?'

'I don't know who she was, except that she must have been a daughter of one of the early Presbyterian ministers. When I bought the house, I found a lot of old things – furniture, odds and ends. Right at the bottom of the upstairs linen cupboard, there was a battered trunk. The lid was stuck and I had to pry it open. It contained a pile of old books and some little keepsakes. And there was an old sepia photo of a girl. I took the trunk back to Millerbrooke and stored it in my shed, along with a chest of drawers.'

'Is it still there?'

'Yes, somewhere at the back. I've accumulated a lot more things since then.'

He reminded Angie of Steptoe, or was it his son? She could imagine furniture and boxes crammed into the rooms. Piles of old newspapers. Cobwebs forming fretwork brackets in the corners, home to daddy-long-legs spiders and dead flies.

'Do you know anything about the history of the Old Manse?' she asked.

'Only that it was built in 1870, not long after the church. It's strange really. The church is typical Calvinist style. Sombre, dour, unadorned. And then they built the Manse which is a complete romantic fantasy.'

'Perhaps the builder got carried away,' suggested Angie. 'Like a hairdresser who takes it into her head to colour your hair some exotic shade, but you only discover it after the shampoo and blow-dry.'

'I wouldn't know about that.'

Had she offended him? She had wondered about that stupid cap. Perhaps he was bald.

'Anyway, I'd love to have a look at the contents of the trunk,' she said.

'I'll drop it off to you. And I have some cans of paint if you need them.'

'What colour?'

'White.'

Angie frowned. 'What kind of white? Warm? Cool? Titanium?'

'We blokes aren't good at colours, Mrs Wallace. It's just an all-purpose white. But you could have it tinted. What colour did you have in mind?'

'Naples yellow hue. The colour of hollandaise sauce.'

'You mean the stuff the café puts on my eggs Benedict?'

'Exactly.'

'I suppose that wouldn't be too bad.'

What a peculiar person he was. Not unintelligent. In fact, quite the opposite. A sixty-something bachelor who owned a lot of property. So why hadn't he been snapped up by one of Millbrooke's single women? Was it the drinking problem or the clothes or both? Maybe he was one of those men so far outside the social norms that a woman would need to be desperate to contemplate a relationship with him. And even the painting ladies with their racy chitchat weren't that desperate.

True to his word, Richard Scott dropped off the trunk the next day. It was brown, with rusty hinges and patches of scuffed leather. No initials or labels. Anonymous. She had to ease the lid open. Finally it swung back on its hinges. As she expected, there was a musty smell. A bunch of lavender tied with a ribbon sat on top. When she picked it up, it crumbled to dust on the kitchen table.

There were a couple of white cotton blouses, slightly marked, with leg-of-mutton sleeves. Below them was a pincushion made of embroidered silk, with rust marks where the pins must have been. Wrapped in yellowing tissue paper was a blue velvet band with a tiny cameo brooch attached. A little tin with a domed lid caught Angie's eye. Its sides were decorated with Oriental motifs. When she opened it, there was black dust inside that might once have been tea leaves. Wedged against the side was a tiny glass bottle which would have held perfume. Angie removed the lid and sniffed. It could have been her imagination, but it seemed to smell of violets. Beside the bottle was a silk fan with an ivory handle.

As she lay the items out on the kitchen table, she realised with growing delight that this wasn't just a dirty old trunk; it was a treasure chest.

In the next layer were some books with linen covers, all a little faded. At the top was *The Poems of Sir Walter Scott*, dated 1861. Then a French volume of *The Arabian Nights* and a copy of *Jane Eyre*, published in 1869 – far too late to be a first edition. There were other familiar titles – *Pride and Prejudice*, *The Mill on the Floss*, *The Woman in White* – and one she didn't know, which sounded quite graphic for Victorian times – *Sylvia's Lovers*. The author was Mrs Gaskell. Hadn't she written the very sedate *Cranford*? Might there have been another side to her? Angie made a mental note to add the book to the pile on her bedside table.

At the bottom of the trunk she found the picture Richard had mentioned, an oval portrait in a heavy frame of a girl in her late teens, her hair piled on her head. She wore a floral dress and a velvet choker around her neck – the one in the trunk.

The photograph had been hand-tinted to give the girl's cheeks a soft blush and her hair a yellow glow. She possessed the kind of eyes a nineteenth-century writer would call 'intelligent'. Although that was usually code for a plain face, the girl in the picture was quite the opposite. Angie looked on the back. There was a label: *Anton Weiss. Millbrooke Photography* and a handwritten name: *Amy*.

Angie returned to the books. Perhaps they contained something else about the girl. She found it inside *Sylvia's Lovers*. A dedication.

For Amy,
As you leave for your new life in Millbrooke.
Loving wishes,
Aunt Molly
2nd March, 1872

There was a barely visible name at the top of the first page, written in pencil. Even with her glasses, Angie found it hard to read. She took the book over to the window. *A. Duncan*.

Amy Duncan. The owner of the trunk.

Afterwards Angie poured herself a glass of wine to celebrate her find. Admittedly, it was only early afternoon and still several hours before the sun was officially over the yardarm, but what the hell! As she sat on the grass overlooking the creek, she saw something that appeared to be a floating piece of wood. Then it slid under the surface with a delicate splash, leaving only ripples behind it. A platypus! She had never seen one before, and here it was blithely duck-diving in full sunshine with the noise of cars and tractors humming in the background. Perhaps it was giving the finger to all those scientists who claimed it was a bashful creature, only appearing at dawn and dusk.

From mysterious treasure chests to strange animals with a lineage harking back to the age of reptiles, Millbrooke was proving to be a town full of surprises.

4
THE BLUE DANUBE

Then

Amy finally gave in to Eliza's entreaties. After their formal lesson, they remained in the barn beside the Manse while she taught Eliza to waltz. Amy had learned singing and dancing at Miss Howe's, something she had never told her father. He only approved of singing when it served to glorify God. But having caught him humming the tune of 'Comin' Thro' the Rye' on several occasions, the family knew he tolerated Scottish airs. Dancing, however, was different. He insisted it was among the worst of venial sins with no purpose save to do the devil's work. Amy often wondered exactly what her father meant by that. Was it because men and women touched hands as they danced? If that were the case, he would be appalled by the intimacy of the newest dancing craze, the Viennese waltz, where partners swept around the room, locked in each other's arms.

On account of her height, Amy had taken the man's part in her dance classes at school. Therefore, she was well able to tutor Eliza in the intricacies of the ballroom. Nevertheless, she was only half concentrating on her task because she was also keeping an anxious eye on the doorway in case her father should appear.

'Just four days until the dance,' said Eliza as they twirled around the hay-strewn floor. 'The boys have been clearing our barn in preparation. We will have tables of cakes and refreshments, and Mother has organised for the Millbrooke band to play. Have you asked your father's permission yet, Amy?'

'No, if I say it is a dance, he will forbid me to go.'

'You shall come to stay from Friday afternoon until Sunday. Then you need not tell him about the dance because it will be one minor aspect of your sojourn at Millerbrooke House.'

Amy considered Eliza's argument. It wasn't a falsehood to omit something, was it? But what if her father asked directly if there would be dancing? And what if the Millers invited her to play cards or offered her a glass of wine or other form of alcohol?

'Amy, you must tell him about the bonfire and the fireworks in celebration of the Queen's Birthday. We do it every year. Your father will like that.'

It was true. Her father admired the Queen as the epitome of virtue and steadfastness.

'The boys have already started building the bonfire, and Charles will be in charge of the fireworks on Friday night. He calls it "waking the dragon". You must come, Amy. You can meet Joseph and Daniel. They're very handsome. And, of course, Charles. He is the most charming of them all.'

Little did Eliza know that Amy was already quite well acquainted with Charles. She resolved to ask her father's permission that very evening. She would tell him about the fireworks display, and that the Miller family desired her to stay on at Millerbrooke House until Sunday. She would even promise to be back in time for morning service. How could her father refuse so innocent a proposal?

On Friday afternoon Eliza sent her brother, Joseph, to the Manse to collect Amy. Joseph, who had been warned not to mention the dance, began telling Amy's father about the huge pile of wood he and Daniel had accumulated from all over the property for the bonfire.

'Reverend Duncan, you will be able to see its light from down here at the Manse. And the fireworks too. Such a fitting celebration for our Queen, don't you think?'

Amy was impressed. Joseph had won over her father. With his fair hair and freckled skin, he might have been Matthew Duncan's son.

'Did you pack your woollen shawl, Amy?' asked her mother.

'Yes, Mama, and I have my cape too,' she replied, pointing to the purple garment draped over her arm.

Her mother kissed her and whispered in her ear, 'Enjoy the dancing, dear girl.'

How did she know? A smile passed between them, before Amy climbed onto the Millers' sulky. Joseph took the reins and they were off.

'What should I wear for the bonfire, Eliza?' asked Amy as she surveyed the clothes from her travelling bag spread out on Eliza's bed.

'You are already perfectly dressed for the occasion. Now hurry up. Supper is almost ready and I want you to meet Daniel and Charles. I can hear them downstairs.'

But Amy continued to play for time, rearranging her hair and smoothing her magenta dress. She longed to keep the magic of Mr Chen and his emporium intact, even if it were only for a few more minutes. Separated from his treasures, she feared he would be an ordinary man, dependent on the exotic backdrop for his allure.

'*Fai dee lah*, Amy,' said Eliza impatiently. Seeing the curious look on her friend's face, she added, 'It means hurry up. I learned it from Charles. Now stop dilly-dallying. It isn't like you at all.'

Amy gave her cheeks a final pinch and checked her dress yet again. Then she followed Eliza down the curved staircase and into the drawing room where three tall young gentlemen stood waiting. From their build they might have been brothers, except that two of them had golden curls, the colour of a wheatfield, like Eliza's, while the third had a head of glossy black hair – black as jet.

Eliza took care of the formal introduction which had been missing from Amy's first meeting with Mr Chen.

'Miss Amy Duncan, may I present Mr Charles Chen?'

'My pleasure, Miss Duncan.' He inclined towards her in a bow.

Was there a knowing smile on his face? Was he enjoying the game of pretending they had never met?

Eliza's parents joined them and made a great fuss of Amy, telling her how much Eliza's handwriting had improved since she had been tutoring her.

'And we are delighted that you have taught Eliza to waltz. It is such an important accomplishment for a young lady,' said Mr Miller.

Amy was mystified that dancing could be such an accomplishment in one house, while it was nothing less than the devil's work in another, and was glad Mr Miller was a parishioner of St John's and not St Aidan's, or he might have let something slip in a Sunday morning conversation with her father at the church door.

Careful to avoid the eye of Mr Chen, she looked around her. Aunt Molly's house was well appointed, but Amy had never seen anything like Millerbrooke, with its marble columns and cedar panels, its vast rooms and stencilled friezes. Gleaming polished floors that must have kept an army of maids busy were carpeted with rugs straight out of *A Thousand and One Nights*. Yet it was also a family home, well worn and not at all stiff or formal.

Mr Miller showed her Captain Miller's study, which, he told her, remained exactly as his father had left it. Amy marvelled at the mahogany desk with its chest of drawers cunningly incorporated into the base and its low bookshelf on top. Mr Miller explained to her that desks such as this had been popular among naval officers, being so compact and portable. Then he pointed out a glass-topped display cabinet in which lay Captain Miller's uniform and hat.

'Did he wear this at the Battle of Trafalgar?' asked Amy.

'No, it is his captain's uniform from the later Napoleonic Wars.'

'Then did he ever meet Lord Nelson?'

'Once, at a reception just before the final fatal battle. But it was at a distance because my father was only a junior officer then.'

How wonderful to have seen Horatio Nelson, if only from afar.

'I hear from Eliza that she is studying the story of Aladdin in her French lessons,' said Mr Miller.

'Yes, it is very long. Like a novel. So we are skipping over some of it.'

'I think it is clever of you to choose the French text of a story with which she is already familiar.'

Amy beamed. She was not used to praise from father figures and immediately began to imagine that she too was a daughter of the Miller house, of a father who encouraged reading and dancing, and who seemed blessed with a happy disposition.

Eliza came in, breaking Amy's reverie, to announce that supper was served in the dining room. Mrs Miller had placed Amy between Eliza's brothers, with Charles Chen seated opposite her. It was the longest dining table Amy had ever seen, lit by two silver candelabras. A bowl of perfect pink roses sat in the centre. The table was laid with a bewildering array of silverware. She thanked her stars that she was acquainted with which pieces of cutlery to use, having learned table etiquette at Miss Howe's, and that she knew to break the bread into pieces and not tip her soup bowl towards her in order to empty the dregs – though she noticed Joseph and Daniel Miller doing those very things. Perhaps the formal rules were not so important after all. In fact, Amy liked the friendliness of a table where people conversed pleasantly during a meal, rather than being seen and not heard as her father insisted.

'Well, Amy, how do you like living in Millbrooke?' Daniel Miller asked her as she was breaking up her bread in a manner that would have met with Miss Howe's approval.

'Very well, thank you, Mr Miller,' she began, resolved that she would not tell how tedious she found her Millbrooke life apart from Mr Chen and this wonderful connection to the Miller family.

'Call me Daniel; we do not stand on ceremony here.'

Across the table, Charles was talking to Mrs Miller about the imminent fireworks. Amy couldn't help noticing his waistcoat, made from the same turquoise silk she had admired in his emporium. She allowed herself a cautious glance at his face, and was unnerved to find that he was suddenly gazing at her. She quickly looked away and went back to sipping her soup with great concentration. When she dared to peek up again, he was talking to Mr Miller.

'I intend to speak at the meeting, sir,' he was saying to Eliza's father. 'It is my hope that you will also say a few words.'

'Of course, Charles, I will join you in every effort,' said Mr Miller.

'What meeting is this?' asked Daniel. 'Have I missed something?'

'Next week there is to be a town meeting called by a group of white miners.'

'So you are going to speak?'

'I must; we simply cannot allow such an injustice to occur,' said Charles quietly.

All other conversation at the table had ceased, and in the momentary silence, Amy found herself saying,

'What injustice do you refer to, Mr Chen? I mean Charles,' she corrected herself, blushing at the nervous quake in her voice. Addressing an entire table was something unfamiliar to her.

'There is a sizeable group of miners who want the Chinese diggers expelled from the Millbrooke goldfields,' he replied.

'They are jealous of how hard the Chinese work,' said Eliza with passion.

'It is true; the Chinese labour diligently,' said Charles, addressing himself directly to Amy. 'They do not interfere with the Europeans, they work the areas that others have left behind, yet they are reviled.'

'There is resentment when a Chinaman finds gold which has been missed by a white miner,' said Mr Miller.

'The white miners mistrust the Chinese for working in groups rather than as individuals,' said Eliza.

'And they are suspicious of Oriental customs,' added Joseph.

'They think we are inferior,' said Charles.

It seemed the whole family reckoned as one. Amy felt a wave of admiration for these ardent Millers and the tall Chinaman they embraced as their own. She wanted very much to be one of them.

'But no person is inferior to another,' she said softly. 'The Bible tells us that the Lord "giveth to all life, and breath, and all things; and hath made of one blood all nations of men to dwell on all faces of the earth".'

'You are right,' responded Charles. 'And they are sacred words. All the same, there are many who have not read the Bible, and others who have done so and even call themselves Christians, yet do not heed the message. The truth is that prejudices live deep within a man's heart and cannot easily be dislodged.'

'But surely the Chinese have as much right to be here as anyone else?' said Amy, who thought Charles spoke like a true orator and hoped to hear more. But it was Mr Miller who answered.

'Many people believe the opposite, including our leaders in Macquarie Street. Back in the sixties they passed an Act of Parliament to restrict Chinese immigration. It was repealed a few years later, but mark my words, they will try it again.'

'I heard a Miners' Protection League is to be formed in Millbrooke,' said Joseph.

'Isn't that a good idea?' said Amy. 'Then every miner will be protected.'

'You would think so, wouldn't you? But in fact, the title is misleading,' said Charles, his eyes glowing amber in the light of the candelabra. 'It is for the protection of white miners only. It might as well be called the Anti-Chinese League.'

Amy was thrilled by his fervour. What a valiant cause. How could she possibly have thought Charles would be disappointing in his role as Eliza's foster brother? As they ate their dessert, she glanced across at him, only to discover he was staring back at her, but she couldn't fathom his expression.

Everyone slept late after the fireworks. The girls were propped up in Eliza's bed, eating the bread and jam which Matilda, the maid, had delivered to them.

'I have never had breakfast in bed before,' remarked Amy, 'but I've read of it in novels. It occurs when the heroine is feeling poorly. Is this a luxury you enjoy every day, Eliza?'

'No. Only on special occasions. Most mornings I'm already up grooming my horse.'

'Will you teach me to ride? Just as I taught you to waltz.'

'Yes, of course I will. But not today. Because if you have a fall, you will be unable to dance this evening.'

The dance had acquired weighty importance in Amy's mind, and most of her thoughts centred on Charles Chen. He had become the object of her daydreams, the most fascinating man she had ever met. Far more attractive than fictional heroes like Mr Darcy or Mr Rochester or even the glamorous Aladdin, to whom Charles bore a striking resemblance. But she didn't dare tell Eliza in case she laughed at Amy's silly infatuation.

Worse still, she might even tell Charles.

The girls spent the morning making lemonade and picking hawthorn branches to arrange in jugs around the barn. Joseph and Daniel were decorating the rafters with streamers and garlands of bright paper dragons which Charles had supplied. Meanwhile *he* was being Mr Chen, running his emporium.

After lunch Amy and Eliza took their baths and began to dress. Amy had brought her corset. How she hated that whalebone contraption, but it produced an hourglass figure, which made her inclined to bear its attendant discomforts with stoicism. Eliza helped her to lace it up.

Then Amy donned her muslin party dress, freshly ironed by Matilda. It had been a gift from Aunt Molly, purchased after the Duncan family's departure for Millbrooke. In Sydney Amy had worn it to concerts and tea dances; in Millbrooke it remained hidden alongside the other forbidden possessions. Her father would have been appalled by the low neckline, immodestly revealing her collarbones, not to mention the lace trim and the floral pattern, clear signs of vanity.

'You look perfect,' pronounced Eliza.

'There's just one more thing,' said Amy, removing a velvet band from her travelling bag. Pinned to the velvet was her grandmother's cameo brooch. Eliza secured it around Amy's neck.

Then it was Eliza's turn. Her gown was a sophisticated creation of green silk with tiers of frills at the back. For a girl who rode horses and delivered calves, she seemed quite at home in evening attire. As a finishing touch she produced a little bottle of perfume from the jumble of jars and phials on her dressing-table.

'It is called attar of violets. Pat it behind your ears,' she told Amy.

'It reminds me of Aunt Molly,' said Amy. 'She always smells of violets.'

'Then keep it,' said Eliza, pressing the bottle into Amy's hand. 'I have plenty of others. My father buys them for Mother and me whenever he visits Sydney. Though mostly I forget to use them.'

Mr and Mrs Miller had arranged for Mr Weiss, the town's

photographer, to take formal family pictures during the afternoon. He was an expert in the process of wet-plate collodions which gave remarkably detailed and lifelike results. Promptly at four o'clock he arrived with a portable dark-tent, bottles of strange-looking chemicals and various glassware, informing a perplexed Matilda that he would need copious amounts of water to rinse his plates. It was decided to take the photographs on the pillared verandah in front of the grand front door with its lunette and sidelights. Amy was to be included in the family photograph, from which only Charles was missing because he was busy at his store. After that, Mr Weiss took individual portraits, allowing his subjects to smile if they wished. How unlike the photographer who had come to Miss Howe's and insisted on poker faces.

By the time Mr Weiss had finished, it was getting dark. Amy could hear the band tuning its instruments in the barn.

Eliza decided she and Amy should make a grand entrance to the dance, once the other guests had arrived. As they reached the door, an exuberant polka was underway. Eliza had barely entered the room when a young man asked her to dance. Where were their dance cards, Amy wondered, before noticing that none of the ladies seemed to have one. Following the polka, there was an old-fashioned quadrille.

Her eyes scanned the barn for Charles. At the opposite side she caught a glimpse of a vivid turquoise waistcoat. Nearby was Daniel Miller. Just as she was wondering why Joseph was missing from the trio, he was suddenly beside her, requesting the next dance, his blond curls bobbing as he spoke. The lively music foreshadowed another polka. Joseph was soon galloping across the room with such verve Amy could barely keep up with him. At the end they were breathless and thirsty and he fetched her a glass of lemonade.

'Are you enjoying your stay here at Millerbrooke House, Amy?'

'I am indeed.'

'And you have taught my sister to dance the waltz.'

'Yes, but it is not a fact I wish to broadcast.'

'So Eliza told me,' he smiled.

They danced a schottische and then a mazurka. Miss Howe had always said it was bad manners to allow a man to monopolise your dance program. But did it really matter here in the Millers' barn?

After the mazurka the band announced an interval. Joseph was still at her side when she noted Charles speaking to a young lady with shiny brown ringlets, who was wearing a diaphanous lilac gown which made Amy's muslin party dress look childish by comparison. Suddenly it wasn't the barn at Millerbrooke any more. It was a scene from *Jane Eyre* – the grand ball at Thornfield. The dark-haired girl in lilac was Blanche and the man in the waistcoat was Mr Rochester. And Amy in her floral-patterned muslin was Jane, and she was wretched. Even so, she made small talk with Joseph and Eliza and tried not to look in Charles's direction.

When a Viennese waltz was announced, Charles was nowhere to be seen. Eliza tugged Joseph's hand.

'Come on, Joseph, I want to show you how well I can waltz.'

'A lady should never ask a gentleman to dance,' he replied.

'We are sister and brother, not lady and gentleman.'

Joseph shrugged his shoulders amiably. 'Will you excuse me, Amy?' he asked.

'Of course,' she replied, taking a seat next to Mrs Miller.

As the band started up, Amy saw a tall figure in a turquoise waistcoat crossing the room. Was the crowd parting to let him through, or was it just her imagination? It seemed to take an age for him to reach her, as if the world had suddenly slowed down. Then she heard his voice close to her asking: 'Would you care to waltz with me, Amy?'

'With pleasure, Charles,' she whispered in reply.

As he took her hand and led her into the centre of the floor, she thought she would swoon. The band was playing the fashionable new melody from Vienna, 'The Blue Danube', and all at once they were spinning around the barn in each other's arms. If there were other dancers on the floor, Amy didn't see them. Shyly she looked up at the brown eyes only to discover his gaze fixed upon her face. What had happened between them?

When the music finished, he kept hold of her hand. The band struck up another barn dance, but he ushered her to the side of the room. Amy's heart was pounding so fast inside her corset that she was tempted to place her other hand against her chest to steady it. For some moments they just stared at each other, neither speaking. Had all her daydreams come true? Did he really feel about her as she did about him? She began to speak, 'Charles, I . . .'

But he spoke over her, 'Please excuse me, Miss Amy. I must take my leave. I have urgent matters to attend to. Good evening.'

And just like Aladdin's genie, he was gone.

That night, as Amy lay sleepless in Eliza's bedroom, she went over the events of the evening, but could not solve the mystery of

Charles's sudden departure. Had he been playing a game, flirting with her and then running off at the end of their waltz?

Had she misread that speechless moment when they had looked into each other's eyes? She had taken it to mean he didn't want to break the magic. Yet there was a simpler explanation for his silence. What if he had nothing to say to her? Did he think of her as an inexperienced child? Was the young lady with the brown ringlets more his type? Was there any hope for Amy at all? She let out such a loud sigh she was certain it would wake Eliza. But the figure lying next to her continued to sleep, a little snore accompanying her every breath.

Amy longed to be versed in the ways of the world, but who could teach her? Perhaps she could write to Aunt Molly for advice. Then again, if she put everything down on paper, it would seem like the silly fantasies of a lovesick girl. For now, at least, she must be satisfied with her novels as a guide to courtship and romance.

Now

Blake and Tim had come down from Sydney for the weekend to help paint the guest room. They had finished Angie's bedroom as well, carefully avoiding the remnants of original wallpaper which she had marked off with a border of masking tape. The Naples yellow hue worked perfectly with her blue and white toile wing chair and the collection of Chinese porcelain, now featuring in the half-finished still-life canvases of Angie's painting ladies.

On Saturday night they went to the pub for Lisa's braised lamb shanks and mash. Richard was there – his home away from home. He invited the three of them to Millerbrooke House on the Sunday, but Angie declined because they needed to finish the painting. She could have made the time, had she really wanted to, but she found Richard disconcerting, though she wasn't sure why.

The Manse had proven to be a much bigger project than Angie had expected. She'd done up a house before, when she and Phil were first married. Although it had been a challenging project, the difficulties were always tempered by a series of little achievements, foreshadowing the glorious home to come. She had imagined the Manse would be the same. A thorough clean, a scattering of rugs, the addition of her lovely furniture and a vase or two of fresh flowers. She'd thought she had the instant recipe to transform a rundown house into an elegant home, in the way a cooking show contestant takes a boring bolognaise sauce and adds five ingredients to make it dazzle the judges. But the house remained shabby. It was telling her to forget the instant makeover. It needed every job to be finished. Only then would it shine.

Vicky was coming on the Queen's Birthday weekend. Angie was excited about her visit but dreading it at the same time. No matter what Angie did with the guest room, Vicky would notice every single fault, the cracks in the plaster, the uneven floorboards, the chips in the skirting boards. She would bemoan the lack of power points and the funny old hot water heater. She would mutter about people who decided in haste and repented at leisure. Then she would question the wisdom of a widow being isolated from her family and friends at a time when they were most important. She would leave Angie feeling drained and unsettled.

Angie often pondered her decision. But lately she was beginning to think it wasn't as rash and stupid as everyone believed. Because Millbrooke had brought her a special gift. Not something she could hold in her hand or see in the daytime, something more elusive, yet precious all the same. For the first time since his death, Phil had returned to her in the night. She had dreamed she was in a vast room. In the centre was a man in a dressing gown, seated in a wheelchair. It was Phil, and she ran to him, saying: 'You're not dead, after all. You were sick, but you recovered.' She was so happy to see him she couldn't stop crying. His face was thin and pale, his skin looked grey, yet he was alive. Then she woke up.

The dream had recurred several times. Sometimes he would be leaning against the doorway and she would rush over to touch him in disbelief. Every time she would experience the same burst of happiness, then the emptiness of waking.

When she told Blake, he said, 'It's likely to be your subconscious mind trying to keep Dad alive.'

'Well, at least I can catch a glimpse of him when I go to sleep. Isn't that a good thing?'

'Yes and no. The problem is that you're blocking out the reality of Dad's death. And when you deny your feelings, they'll always find a way of resurfacing. Like a cold sore that pops up when you least expect it.'

'You don't actually mean that I'll get cold sores, do you?'

'No, it's a metaphor, Mum. But you might be more prone to illness. Or you might do something completely out of character. Something really weird.'

'Like what?'

'Well, you've already run away to a town in the middle of nowhere.'

'It wasn't running away, Blake. It was readjusting.'

Angie didn't like it when her twenty-something son acted

like a parent and treated her as a child. From now on, she would keep her dreams to herself.

Before the boys left for Sydney, she showed them Amy's trunk. For some reason she had hoped they would share her enthusiasm for the Manse's former resident.

'Why are you keeping that battered old thing?' asked Tim. 'Don't they have council clean-ups here in Millbrooke? I'll take it to the tip for you, if you like.'

Ignoring his comment, Angie unwrapped her treasures from the acid-free tissue paper in which she now kept them.

'I'm trying to build up a picture of Amy Duncan, the owner of the trunk.'

'So when did she live here?' asked Blake.

'In the nineteenth century.'

'Spooky! Next thing you'll be seeing dead people,' quipped Tim.

Blake gave him a jab in the arm.

'Tim didn't put it very tactfully, Mum. But I think what he's trying to say is that you should be looking towards the future. Not delving into the past.'

WINTER

*'The crowd acclaimed Aladdin
for his achievements and generosity of spirit
and marvelled at how he had risen
from humble beginnings.'*

'Histoire d'Aladdin, ou la lampe merveilleuse'
Nuit CCCXXXIV [Antoine Galland c.1710]

5

ROLL UP, ROLL UP

Then

When Amy told the Reverend Duncan she wanted to go to the town meeting, he said exactly what she had expected him to say: 'It is not a place for a wee lass and I forbid ye to attend.'

Then she turned to her mother for support.

'Heed your father, Amy. There will undoubtedly be a drunken throng and it could easily become a riot.'

After supper Amy washed and dried the dishes. Her father was in his study, completing the weekly parish accounts, while her mother was reading stories to the boys. She fetched her purple cape and slipped out the back door. Eliza, Joseph and Daniel had tied up their horse and carriage at the end of Church Lane, and they all walked to the School of Arts together. Already a crowd had assembled on the main street. The four of them jostled their way inside and could find seats only towards the back.

Mr Miller and Charles were seated on the stage among several other prospective speakers. Amy hadn't visited Mr Chen's

Emporium since the dance at Millerbrooke two weeks earlier. Seeing him now made her blush and wince at the same time. Fortunately he had not spotted her.

When the local magistrate called the meeting to order, nobody was listening. Finally he brought his gavel down heavily on the table in front of him. As someone began to play 'God Save the Queen' on the pianoforte, everyone stood and sang heartily. The room was so crowded that latecomers had to stand along the side walls. Eliza gave Amy a nudge.

'How many ladies are present, Amy?'

Amy began to count the bonnets. Probably less than twenty. At the back of the room a group of a dozen Chinese stood at the door. She thought they were brave to come.

Daniel pointed to a large banner, painted in red, white and blue, held aloft by two men near the stage. It made Amy cringe. The words read: 'Roll up, roll up. Rout the Chinamen.' Nearby stood a line of policemen in dark serge uniforms – would the presence of the local constabulary be enough to rein in the rabble?

The first speaker was one of the proponents of the Miners' Protection League. As he rose from his seat, he was met with tumultuous applause.

'Gentlemen,' he began. 'And there are some ladies present too, I see.'

Amy noted an English accent. She couldn't pick the dialect, except that it was probably northern.

'We are all familiar with the problems the Celestials bring to the goldfields. The worst of their sins is to waste water. We've all seen their water channels and the way they sluice and wash tailings. They do not seem to appreciate that water is precious. When the creek runs dry owing to their profligacy, we are forced to pay sixpence a bucket for something which should be free.'

Amy heard 'Hear, hear' from the crowd.

'Furthermore, the Celestials bring disease and pestilence wherever they go. Black canker, camp fever, swamp sickness, infantile paralysis, even French pox. When they move on, the diseases disappear. They are a threat to the prosperity of all right-thinking, God-fearing men. They smoke opium and sell it to the weaker among us, so that Westerners have also become addicted to this sorry black substance. They gamble and worship pagan idols. They work on the Sabbath. It cannot continue. They are putting the livelihoods of all white miners at risk.'

A chant began, echoing the words on the banner, and the magistrate called the meeting to order. Several other speakers followed, presenting much the same arguments.

'Why doesn't someone speak against them?' whispered Amy to Joseph.

'My father will. And Charles. Be patient.'

'But I'm afraid these bigots will hold sway with their falsehoods,' she protested.

'Let them vent their bile,' said Eliza. 'It will not go unchallenged.'

At that moment a scuffle broke out at the front of the room. Those who were seated stood up to gain a better look. Being so far towards the back, Amy could see nothing.

'Father and Charles!' cried Eliza. 'Are they all right?'

Joseph tried to push his way into the aisle, but the crowd blocked him. Then they heard police whistles, followed by the magistrate's gavel pounding on the table.

'Order, order! Resume your seats,' he shouted. 'Order! If there is a repeat of this behaviour, I shall have the offenders taken to the lock-up.'

Deborah O'Brien

Somebody laughed.

'If you find that amusing, sir, just consider a June night spent without a fire or a blanket.'

That prospect seemed to settle the audience. Joseph craned forward to check on his father and Charles.

'They are unharmed,' he said to the girls.

When the meeting resumed, it was Mr Miller's turn to speak. There was polite applause from the townsfolk among the crowd.

'Ladies and gentlemen, my name is John Miller of Millerbrooke House. It was my father, Captain Alexander Miller, who founded this town. I have lived here most of my life, so the welfare of this colony and its people is very important to me.'

There were cheers from around the room.

'We have heard a lot of talk tonight. Idle talk and ugly words. I can see a banner at the side of the room.' When he pointed to it, every head turned in that direction. The chant of 'Rout the Chinamen' began again. Mr Miller waited until it subsided. He had a sense of authority about him. Amy decided he had inherited it from his father, the heroic sea captain.

'The banner is nothing to be proud of. In fact, it is the very opposite.'

There were some protests from the crowd. One heckler shouted: 'Chink lover.'

Mr Miller ignored the comment and continued.

'Some eleven years ago a shameful series of events took place at a town called Lambing Flat in this very colony of New South Wales. A mob of one thousand miners descended on the Chinese camp, bearing a banner much like the one we see tonight. They set fire to tents, destroyed belongings, burnt clothing, terrified women and children. They assaulted the men and cut off their pigtails.'

There were a few shouts of 'Hear, hear.'

'For those who think this was a noble act, I want you to imagine something. Picture a horde of angry men coming to your tent or your hut here at the Millbrooke diggings and burning it down. Imagine that they destroyed everything you had and threatened your loved ones. What if they cut off your beard and took your clothing and threw it on a fire?

'What had you done to deserve this persecution? First of all, you looked different. People called you "brown beard" or "round eyes" or even "white devil". You wore a cabbage-tree hat and breeches. You spoke another language. You followed a different faith. People ridiculed your clothes and the way you spoke. And they reviled your faith and your methods of worship. Yet every day you worked industriously and peacefully.

'Did you deserve to be maligned and persecuted in this way? Is that fair play? In the future, men will think back to the Gold Rush days and they will remember Lambing Flat with shame and sadness. But let us give them something they can remember with pride. That the people of Millbrooke, townsfolk and miners alike, refused to allow the Chinese to be run off their diggings.'

He resumed his seat to both applause and booing. Someone called out: 'Rout the barbarians,' and a few more tried to make a chant of it.

Then Charles rose. Other than a shuffling of chairs and a few coughs, the room became silent. Amy caught her breath. He was wearing the turquoise waistcoat. It would be sure to provoke the anti-Chinese brigade. Why hadn't he worn a commonplace black or brown instead?

'Ladies and gentlemen of Millbrooke and district. I am Charles Chen. Some of you know me as the proprietor of the emporium in this very street. I came to the colonies when I was eleven years old. After my father died in an accident, I was taken in by the Miller family who treated me like their own son. I have two brothers and a sister seated at the back of the room, whom I love as dearly as my family in China.'

The audience turned to look at the golden-haired siblings at the back of the hall.

'I am not going to speak about the Chinese situation on the goldfields because Mr Miller has described it so eloquently. I will, however, mention the problem of opium. It is a fact of history that opium was introduced into China by the British East India Company.'

'How dare you blame the British!' called a voice from the direction of the banner.

'This is not to excuse the Chinese use of this pitiful substance,' continued Charles without acknowledging the heckler. 'It is just an explanation. Together with others in the town, I am forming an anti-opium society to rid the Millbrooke goldfields of this curse. But we need to remember opium is both legal and readily available. It will be a long and difficult battle.

'On the matter of gambling, you will be aware that this afflicts both the Chinese and the European communities. And I don't need to remind anyone that alcohol remains a major problem among white miners. If you are in any doubt, you need only visit the main street of Millbrooke later tonight.'

There was a shout of: 'Who are you to judge others? A Celestial in a waistcoat?'

Amy felt sick, but Charles's face remained calm.

'My mode of dress is my business. I would not dream of

dictating what you should wear, sir. I think I deserve the same respect.'

There was a round of applause, smothering the comment of a man in front of Amy who yelled: 'Moon-faced devil.'

'Regarding the subject of disease, I beg to differ with the gentleman who claimed that the Chinese are the cause. Many of the afflictions he mentioned are of Western origin and pre-existed the arrival of Chinese immigrants to this country. I am disinclined to speak about French pox, owing to the number of ladies present. However, it is well known that this is a curse of those who involve themselves in licentious and libertine behaviour, whatever their nationality. The disease is neither French nor Chinese. It is international.'

A cry of 'A pox on you!' came from the floor.

'If I may continue, I have a few final remarks. Not long ago, a wise person told me something I shall not forget. She said you cannot place people in boxes and label them as you might do with tea. As a seller of tea, I found the statement most telling.'

Amy blushed a bright red and sank down in her seat. She hoped the boys and Eliza hadn't noticed that Charles was looking directly at her as he spoke.

'Just because the Chinese look and sound different does not mean they are devils. Let us cast aside the untruths and exaggerations, the fears and false assumptions, and in their place, let us embrace the fact that we are all God's children.'

Then he recited the verse from the New Testament which Amy had quoted only a fortnight earlier at the Millers' dining table.

As Charles returned to his seat, there was scattered applause, but the heckling continued. And it seemed to Amy that the meeting could still go either way. Then Eliza rose from her seat.

'Sit down, Eliza,' Joseph hissed. 'We agreed that I should do it.'

Although Eliza was standing at her full height of five-foot-three, the magistrate couldn't see her. A man in the row behind called out: 'The young lady here wants to say something.' There was snickering. Joseph took Eliza's hand and tried to pull her down into her seat, but she shook herself free and moved into the aisle. As her father had done, she waited until there was silence. Although it was a torturous delay, it was necessary. She required their complete attention.

'Your Honour,' she began and then paused as Joseph whispered something to her. After an awkward few seconds she continued: 'Your Worship, am I correct in thinking this is a public meeting?'

'Yes, young lady, you are indeed correct,' he replied with a puzzled smile.

Every eye was on Eliza with her green cloak and straw bonnet. Amy noted the determined set of her friend's chin.

'Well, in that case, sir,' said Eliza, 'I would like to move a motion for the consideration of those assembled here this evening.'

'You have every right to do so, but perhaps you should introduce yourself first.'

'My name is Eliza Miller and I was born in this colony. Like America, it is a place to make a fresh start, free from the prejudices of the old order. We have the power to create a society where every individual, whether they be Chinese, Caledonian or even Calathumpian, is equal to his ... or *her* neighbour.'

Amy thought she saw a tiny smile form on Eliza's lips at the word 'her'.

'Your Worship, I wish to move the following motion. That

the people of Millbrooke reject any attempt to expel or restrict Chinese miners from our goldfields. Furthermore, we pledge to protect them from persecution and abuse.'

'Do we have a second for Miss Miller's proposition?' asked the magistrate.

Joseph raised his hand. 'Yes, you do, your Worship. Joseph Miller.'

'Do you wish to speak to the motion, sir?'

'No, your Worship. My sister has expressed it most persuasively.'

'Do we have any speakers against?'

Amy held her breath. She felt sure the Miners' Protection League supporters would object. On the other hand, Eliza might have caught them off guard. They weren't expecting a young girl with curls and a green cloak to stand up and address the crowd.

'In that case, I shall put the motion. Please correct me if I misspeak, Miss Miller.' The magistrate read out her proposal from the notes he had taken. 'Those in favour, say aye.' There was a resounding 'Aye'. 'Against, nay.' An equally strong 'Nay' followed.

'We will need to count the hands. Doctor Allen, might you do the honours?'

The doctor performed his task in a deft and businesslike manner. The motion was passed ninety-seven to fifty-one.

'It is a victory,' cheered Joseph, taking Amy's hand and kissing it. When he realised what he had done, he said: 'Please forgive me, Amy. In the excitement I forgot myself.'

'You are forgiven, Joseph,' she replied. 'It has indeed been a stirring evening.'

Amy knew she could never have summoned the courage to do what Eliza had just done. 'I am proud of you,' she said, reaching for her friend's hand. Was brave Eliza shaking?

'I fear there will be fifty-one disgruntled men in Millbrooke tonight,' said Eliza.

'Better that than a resolution routing the Chinese,' said Joseph.

'Let us join Father and Charles,' suggested Daniel.

They stood to make their way to the front, but Amy excused herself. 'I must go home, before my father discovers my absence.' She couldn't face Charles, not since the night he had run out on her without an explanation.

'You should not walk home on your own, Amy,' said Joseph. 'There are drunkards about. Let me escort you.'

As Joseph and Amy made their way outside, she heard: 'Good evening, Amy.' It was a parishioner from St Aidan's.

And it dawned on her that sooner or later her father would learn she had defied him, and then she would be punished for breaking the fifth Commandment. And who knew what else?

When Amy tiptoed into the house, her father was in his study with the door ajar. She climbed the stairs slowly, avoiding the fourth step which always creaked. Just as she was about to disrobe, a cry came from the master bedroom. She rushed to the door to find her mother clutching the bedpost.

'My waters have broken, Amy, and the pains have started. Tell your father to fetch the doctor.'

Amy wasn't sure what her mother meant by 'waters', but the fact that they were broken sounded serious. Much worse, though, was the thought of her mother being in pain. She ran down the stairs, calling: 'Papa, I think the baby is coming. Fetch Doctor Allen and the midwife.'

Her father's face went as pale as chalk. Thankful that she had arrived home in time, Amy fetched his coat and helped him into it. Even so, he appeared to be in no hurry to leave. Suddenly a muffled scream from upstairs seemed to shock him out of his daze. In a second he was down the hallway and opening the front door.

'Take care, Papa. There will be hooligans about after the meeting,' she called out to him. When she returned to the bedroom, her mother was sitting on the edge of the bed with her arms taut and her hands pressed into the mattress. After a minute or two, she relaxed a little, and Amy helped her to lie down. As another surge took hold, Amy held her mother's hand until it passed.

'Shall I fetch you a damp cloth, Mama? For your brow. And some water to drink?'

'Yes, Amy. But don't be long.'

Before she went downstairs, Amy checked the boys. Both were curled up like sleeping angels. She barely had time to fill a jug of water from the bucket in the kitchen when a piercing scream caused her to run back upstairs.

'Has your father gone for the doctor?' her mother asked through gritted teeth.

'They won't be long, Mama.'

Not knowing what else to do, Amy propped pillows behind her mother's back, held her hand and whispered soothing words about everything being all right when she feared just the opposite. With each successive attack, the pain was getting worse, rather than better. And even though there were respites between each bout, they were scarcely long enough for her mother to catch her breath and steel herself for the next onslaught.

As she watched the gentle face contorted into a grotesque mask, it struck Amy that Margaret Duncan was no longer a young woman. Indeed, she was close to forty, old enough to be a grandmother. Was that why the baby was so early and the pain so great? If only Amy knew what to do to ease her mother's suffering. Just when she thought she could stand it no longer, she heard voices downstairs. Thank the Lord, Doctor Allen and the midwife had arrived at last.

'Fetch some clean rags, Amy,' said the midwife. 'And some hot water.'

Amy removed a pile of cloths from the linen press where her mother had left them neatly ironed in preparation for this day. Then she went downstairs to boil water on the stove.

'How is your ma?' her father asked as he sat huddled at the kitchen table.

'She is not well, Papa.' To herself, she thought: Dear God, don't let her die.

Carefully Amy carried the pot of steaming water upstairs. Pausing at the bedroom door, she was shocked at the sight of her mother's face. It was so ashen she might have been a wax doll. Leaning over her, Doctor Allen was shaking his head.

'A breech presentation,' he said to the midwife. 'At any age it's a problem.'

The midwife cleared her throat to indicate Amy's presence.

'We'll call you when there is news,' she said, taking the pot from Amy and placing it on the bureau. 'Look after the good reverend. He'll need some company.'

Before Amy could say a word, they were shooing her out the door.

Amy took a seat opposite her father at the kitchen table, feeling so restless it was impossible to sit still. She boiled more water, made her father a pot of tea and kept the saucepan bubbling – just in case. For the tea she used the smoky leaves from the emporium – the smell of it alone was comforting – and as her father sipped distractedly from his cup, he didn't seem to notice it wasn't his usual brew. Afterwards she went upstairs and waited outside the bedroom door. Every couple of minutes a shriek would break the silence, but Robbie and Billy remained asleep, oblivious to their mother's battle in the other room.

When Amy could stand the screams no longer, she went downstairs to her father's study. On the shelf among his theology books sat a heavy copy of Doctor Johnson's dictionary. She lifted it down, placed the tome under an oil lamp and leafed to the 'B' pages searching for 'breech'. She read the definition, couched in strange words that might have been a foreign language, but she was no closer to finding the meaning. Then she heard the midwife calling from the top of the stairs.

Amy was out of the room so fast she almost collided with her father in the hallway.

'Reverend Duncan, it is a little girl.'

Now

On Tuesday nights Angie had established a routine – roast dinner at the pub, followed by an hour listening to the local jazz quartet which played in the public bar. Richard was always there with his cronies. The two of them had moved from calling each other Mr Scott and Mrs Wallace to the familiarity of first names. The problem was he'd shortened hers to 'Ange'. Maybe he thought it sounded friendly, but it made her cringe. Only one person in the world had ever been allowed to call her Ange, and *he* was gone.

'Have you seen the posters about the information night?' Richard asked her one Tuesday.

'What information night?'

'The one they're holding this Friday. It's about a new tourist initiative. Top secret. Everyone is speculating as to what it might be.'

'Well, I'm not really interested.'

'Where's your civic spirit, Ange? This could be the biggest thing in Millbrooke since fluoridation.'

'Fluoridation?'

'That issue split the town in two. People weren't speaking to each other for months. Eventually the council organised a vote. A kind of plebiscite.'

Angie's interest was piqued. 'Who won?'

'The pro-fluoriders.'

'I had no idea there was fluoride in the water. I came to the country to escape nasty things like chemicals in the water supply.'

'Well, you shouldn't have come to Millbrooke. It's full of them.'

'I'm buying a filter tomorrow.' Angie shuddered.

'You really should go to the information night, Ange. Everyone in town will be there.'

She had a feeling he would nag her until she agreed.

'I'll pick you up from the Manse. Seven-thirty Friday,' he said, returning to his friends at the bar before she could think of an excuse.

On the stage of the School of Arts auditorium men in suits were filling a row of seats.

'Who are they?' Angie asked Richard.

'The bloke on the end is the shire president, but everyone refers to him as the mayor. If we called him "the president", he'd behave even more self-importantly than he does now.'

'I gather you don't like him.'

'He promised he wouldn't put the rates up, and then delivered the casting vote that raised them by twelve percent.'

'That seems like a lot.'

'Bloody hell it is. Do you know how much I pay every year? Enough to fly to London and back. First class.'

'I guess that's the price of being a real estate tycoon,' she replied. Sometimes she wondered whether he had inherited his properties, as Tanya had once suggested. If not, how could a person like Richard have earned the money to buy them? Even in humble Millbrooke, they wouldn't have come cheap.

The chairs on the stage had now been filled.

'The three on the right are from the mining company,' said Richard. 'Songbird Minerals. They're *Americans*.'

'Yes, you told me that before,' said Angie. 'But why are they here tonight?'

'They're funding the tourism initiative. The whole thing is their idea.'

'That's impressive.'

'It's pork-barrelling.'

'Don't politicians do that every election? Winning over the locals with a grant to a school or a new wing for a hospital. It's the way the world operates, Richard.'

'Well, these Americans are the consummate pork-barrellers.'

'But isn't it a win-win situation for Millbrooke?'

'I believe it was Tacitus who said: "Gold will be slave or master."'

'Actually it was Horace,' she replied, pleased she was able to trump Richard Scott. His schoolmaster demeanour was beginning to grate on her. 'Anyway,' she continued, '*if* a mine does go ahead, there'll be extra jobs for Millbrookers.'

'Sure, but not in the numbers people anticipate. Mining is a specialised business. How many locals will be employed? They'll just fly people in and out. And we'll find ourselves with a bunch of outsiders who don't pay council rates.'

'Like me.'

'No, I didn't mean *you*.' Looking embarrassed, he promptly changed the subject. 'See that bloke in the grey suit.'

Angie turned her gaze towards the stage. Was Richard referring to the good-looking man dressed in beige linen? Trust an Aussie bloke not to know the difference between grey and beige.

'He's the Songbird equipment expert – diamond head drills and so on – and doubles as their PR guy. He's likely to do all the talking tonight. The fellow on the left is the money man and the other one is the project manager. The three of them answer directly to the big bosses back in the States.'

'How do you know this stuff?'

'I have a mate at the pub who works as a security guard for Songbird.'

'Oh.'

The mayor was tapping the microphone.

'Good evening, Millbrookers. Thank you for coming out on this chilly evening. We have some exciting news for you.' He pointed to a table covered by a white bedsheet. 'Believe me when I say it's something which will be the making of our town. This initiative will increase jobs and tourist numbers and produce much-needed income to supplement the council's budget. As you know, the problem for Millbrooke, like so many country towns, is our dwindling population.'

Richard leaned over and whispered in Angie's ear, 'If the rates weren't so high, maybe we'd attract more tree-changers.'

'We simply don't have enough people to sustain the services we need,' continued the mayor. 'If this project goes ahead, we should be able to maintain our rates at the existing level for several years to come.' The mayor paused, waiting for applause. A few people clapped.

'Pull the other one,' whispered Richard.

'And now I would like to introduce our guest speaker for the evening. Many of you know him already. He first came to Millbrooke two years ago and he's visited us so often since then that he's almost become one of us. Please welcome Jack Parker.'

'Listen to the mayor currying favour with him,' growled Richard as the broad-shouldered man in the beige suit moved to the microphone amid a round of polite applause.

'Hi, everyone. Thanks for giving up your evening by the fire to come to our information night.'

Angie was surprised at the mild American accent – she'd been expecting a Texan drawl.

'It's great to see such a big turnout. I trust you'll find it worth the effort.'

'He's a real charmer,' whispered Richard. 'As flash as a rat with a gold tooth.'

Angie laughed despite herself. She hadn't heard that expression in years.

'Shhh,' someone hissed behind them.

'Songbird has a proposal to make to the citizens of Millbrooke,' Jack Parker continued. 'It's exciting and innovative and will deliver a boost to the town which will assure its prosperity for years to come. You might even say it's the best thing to happen to Millbrooke since the Gold Rush. The federal and state tourism departments, as well as your own council, have examined the project and given it a positive assessment. In addition, it's been costed by an independent accounting company.'

There was a buzz of conversation among the audience. Jack Parker waited until the chatter subsided and then the lights were dimmed.

'Unlike some other historic towns across the country, Millbrooke has never tapped into the tourism potential of its Gold Rush past, not on a large scale anyway. Now we're rectifying that situation.' He paused dramatically. 'Let me welcome you to Millbrooke's Golden Days.' Behind him the words appeared on a screen as if they were glittering yellow metal. 'It's a multimedia journey through boom-time Millbrooke. Not just a fun park ride, but a virtual trip into the past, during which visitors will see miners at work on the diggings, hear voices from many lands, and experience the sounds and scenes of the main street, bustling with merchants and customers. All by way of projected images and robotic figures.'

'I saw something like this in Oxford years ago,' whispered Angie to Richard. 'The Oxford Story. It was good.'

'Quiet!' came a reprimand from the row behind.

'Millbrooke's Golden Days will become a top tourist destination, attracting an estimated one hundred thousand visitors a year. While they're in town, it's likely they'll buy a meal at a local restaurant or café, browse in your specialty shops and stay in your places of accommodation. In fact, every business in town will benefit. We anticipate the Golden Days initiative will require six full-time and ten part-time staff. All locals, of course. And fifty percent of the profits will go directly to your council to improve the hospital, repair roads, replenish the library and keep your rates at an acceptable level.

'You're probably wondering where the Golden Days will be located. Songbird has purchased two acres of land at the eastern end of town, right behind the Millbrooke museum and opposite the supermarket. We're about to submit a DA to council for a building to house the audiovisual ride and an adjoining parking area. Will it interfere with Millbrooke's historic streetscape? Not at all. It won't even be visible from the main street. Let me show you.'

A computer drawing appeared on the screen, rotating in space.

Then Jack Parker and the mayor took opposite ends of the bedsheet and, on a count of three, removed it as if they were magicians. Underneath was a model of Millbrooke's Golden Days.

'I invite you all to enjoy some refreshments and then come up on stage to take a closer look. Together with the rest of the Songbird staff, I'll be delighted to assist you with any queries you may have concerning the project.'

'Do you want to take a look at the model?' Angie asked Richard as the stage filled with enthusiastic Millbrookers.

'No, but you go ahead.'

'Don't you like it, Richard?'

'It's okay.'

'Well, I *love* the design,' said Angie. 'It's so restrained and compact. It could easily have been a mini theme park, but whoever designed it didn't go overboard with the gold and glitter. And it's a great way to introduce people to the past.'

He squinted at her from below his cap. 'Yeah, I suppose it's not bad for a tourist attraction.'

The next morning Angie was at the pottery café, drinking tea and about to open the *Millbrooke Gazette* when she felt the presence of a tall figure on the other side of the table. She looked up, expecting to see Richard. Instead, there was a man in a beige corduroy jacket, a white open-necked shirt, jeans and cowboy boots.

'Do you mind if I share your table? There don't seem to be any other seats.' He spoke in a soft American accent. It was Jack Parker, Mr Songbird.

'No problem,' said Angie.

He sat down and ordered breakfast and a cappuccino from the passing waitress.

'I saw you last night at the meeting, didn't I?' he said. 'With your husband.'

Angie almost choked on her tea. 'My landlord, I think you mean.'

Jack Parker's eyes darted to her ring finger and back to her face with the deftness of a conjurer performing a sleight of hand.

'I'm Angie Wallace, by the way.'

'Jack Parker.' He extended his hand. 'But you already know that.'

Up close, Angie decided Mr Songbird was very attractive. Not perfect though. There was an asymmetry to his face which was a tad disconcerting. Being a Libran, Angie hankered after symmetry and balance.

'So you've been in Millbrooke for two years,' she said.

'On and off. I go home every few months to see my family.'

He produced a wallet with a collection of photos. Two boys with round, cheeky faces and pudding-basin haircuts and a wife with a blonde bob.

Angie felt she should reciprocate. In her wallet were baby photos of the boys. What kind of mother didn't update her wallet photos?

'They're in their twenties now,' she explained. 'I have some recent pictures on my phone. Blake is doing his Master's in Psychology and Tim's studying medicine and working part-time as a musician.'

'Wow. It must be nice to know they're on the right path.'

'Yes, it is. And I'm glad their father was able to see them succeed at their studies.' As soon as she mentioned Phil, she knew she had to explain. Twisting the ring on her finger, she said, 'My husband passed away last year.'

'I'm sorry to hear that.'

'Thank you.' She blinked away the tears before they could take hold. 'I moved to Millbrooke last autumn.'

'So we have something in common; we're both blow-ins.'

'Yes, I guess that's true. But you seem to have won favour with the mayor.'

'That's because he can see the benefits a mining project would bring to Millbrooke.'

'You mean River Cove? How's it going?'

'We're awaiting the results from the latest assay tests. It's always one step at a time in the mining game. What do you do for a living, Angie?'

He was good. He remembered names. What was the word the Americans used? A schmoozer.

'I'm an artist,' she replied. 'And I'm considering opening a B&B.'

'Where?'

'Church Lane. The Old Manse across the road from St Aidan's Church. It's the two-storey house with the tall gable and the picket fence.'

'Oh, I love that house. It reminds me of home.'

'Where's that?'

'San Francisco.'

'You must really miss your wife and kids.'

'All the time. But we talk on the internet and the boys email me every day.'

'I do the same with my boys. They worry about me being here on my own.'

'Yeah, my wife worries about me too. She thinks I'm working too hard and not eating right.'

'Would you ever consider bringing your family out to Australia?'

'Not really. My job's an itinerant one. A few years in one place, then on to the next. It wouldn't be fair to uproot my wife and kids.'

'So where do you live when you're in Millbrooke?'

'At the motel with the other guys from Songbird.'

'No wonder you come here for breakfast. You must be sick of greasy eggs, fatty bacon, cold toast and tinned baked beans.'

'How did you know that? Have you stayed there too?'

'No,' she laughed. 'That's just a typical motel breakfast. Although sometimes they add grilled tomatoes for variety.'

At that moment Jack's order arrived – poached eggs on potato rosti with wilted spinach and a generous smear of hollandaise sauce.

'Now this is more like it,' he said, sinking his knife into a perfectly cooked egg and watching the yolk ooze out. For a few minutes there was silence as he devoured his breakfast. Then he said, 'Angie, did you say you're running a B&B?'

'Not yet. I've only done up the bedrooms so far.'

'I just had an idea, but you'll probably think it's crazy.' He flashed a toothpaste commercial smile. 'I really hate going back to that bland motel room every night, but there's nowhere else to stay. I've contacted the Schoolhouse B&B, but the proprietor doesn't take long-term lodgers. And the pub's too noisy.'

Was he asking to stay at Angie's place? Mr Songbird certainly had a hide.

'I don't suppose you'd like a guest? I'm paying nine hundred dollars a week at the motel. I'd be glad to match it for a real home.'

Angie had been preparing to say no, but the words 'nine hundred dollars a week' were echoing in her head. She could afford to have the exterior of the house painted by a professional. She might even be able to buy that stunning sideboard she'd seen in the antiques shop. It would be perfect in the dining room.

'It's very basic,' she said. 'The bathroom has a gas hot water heater, circa 1920. And there's only one power point in the guest bedroom.'

'I don't mind. You have a garden, don't you? And a view of the creek. That's all I need.'

Angie started to laugh. 'What about a trial period? For both of us. One month.'

'It's a deal,' he said and reached over to shake her hand.

'I have a friend coming to stay this weekend, so you couldn't move in until after that.'

'Fine,' he said, placing his knife and fork on the plate to indicate he'd finished.

Angie noticed that he'd pushed the pile of wilted spinach to the side of the plate like a naughty toddler refusing to eat his greens.

'Here's my card. I had better get your number too, Angie.'

She wrote it on the back of another of his business cards. Next thing he was standing, ready to leave.

'Must go. I'll give you a call to confirm everything.' He shook her hand again. 'Have a good day. Bye.'

While Mr Songbird was at the counter paying for his breakfast, the implications of what she'd just agreed to do started to hit home. She considered going over to him before he left the café to say it was all a mistake. But Jack Parker was already heading out the door, giving her a wave and a dazzling smile.

'Shit, shit, shit,' she said to herself. 'What have I done?' She must have spoken out loud because two greying tourists at the next table turned to look at her. She gave them a weak smile. Perhaps they would think she was one of those eccentric country people who always seemed to feature in tree-change TV shows.

She had agreed to sub-let a room in Richard Scott's property without even asking his permission. And even worse, she would be accepting a weekly rent which was ten times the amount she was paying Richard.

Jack Parker had won her over, not with mere beads and trinkets, but with the lure of three and a half thousand dollars a month.

6
DISCOVERIES AND LOSSES

Then

Margaret Duncan called the baby Peggy, after the nickname her own parents had bestowed upon her as a child. Margaret had barely left her bed since the birth. Every time she stood up, she would begin to haemorrhage. In the mornings Amy washed her mother's rags in cold water and hung them on the line to dry. Every night she pressed them with a hot iron.

The baby wouldn't suckle. Sometimes she uttered a tiny cry like a kitten, but mostly she was silent. While her mother slept, Amy nursed little Peggy in her arms and sang softly to her. When her father came to the door and heard the songs, he didn't tell her to stop. Perhaps he knew Amy had made a pact with God. As long as she continued to sing, the bairn would remain alive.

On the third day her father baptised the baby, his voice so choked with tears that Amy could barely understand the words. But it lightened her heart just a little to know the stain of original sin had been removed from Peggy's soul and whatever happened now, she would be joined in covenant to God.

On the fourth day, Amy was sitting in the rocker beside her mother's bed, cradling the baby. She must have fallen asleep, because she dreamed Peggy had grown into a bonnie lassie with rosy cheeks and golden braids. The little girl was playing with a wooden doll in the shade of the elm tree while Amy sat nearby, engrossed in a book. After a while she glanced up and realised her sister was gone. Although she called Peggy's name, there was no answer. Frantically she searched the garden, the barn and every corner of the house. She even crossed the lane and scoured the church. Then the panic that had been rising up inside her began to spill out. Her beautiful sister had disappeared. When Amy woke, tears were running down her cheeks and onto the tiny baby in her arms. She touched the baby's face; it was cold.

Amy had never seen her father cry before. Yet for the past two days he had barely stopped. He sat at his desk with his head buried in his hands, sobbing softly. The boys were out in the garden, chasing chooks. Her mother was upstairs in bed, heavy with the draught of laudanum that Doctor Allen had administered.

Peggy was lying in a tiny, satin-lined coffin in the parlour, wrapped in the christening shawl Margaret Duncan had knitted eighteen years earlier for her first child. The garden was bare of flowers so Amy placed a linen handkerchief dabbed with Eliza's attar of violets inside the coffin. At least little Peggy would have something pretty to smell as she lay waiting for her funeral.

The Reverend Arthur Brownlow from St John's was presiding. Amy had gone to see him when she realised her father couldn't manage it himself. The only words he had said to Amy concerning the funeral were: 'Sing a lullaby for the bairn.'

Amy was moved that her father would want a secular song over a hymn. It revealed another side to the otherwise dour man. When she asked Reverend Brownlow about the choice, he replied, 'If your father wants a lullaby, you must sing one.' So she decided on a sweet old Scottish song she had learned long ago from her mother.

Afterwards Amy went to the church and placed two vases of hawthorn branches, still bearing tiny red berries, on the altar. In spite of her position as a minister's daughter, she had never been to a funeral. Before the boys were born, she had been deemed too young, and afterwards, she was required to mind her little brothers so that her mother could play the organ. Death had never touched Amy's life, save for the descriptions in Mr Dickens's novels. And although she often took a shortcut through the town cemetery, she had never thought about the dead people lying beneath the ground. Not as real beings who once lived and breathed. It was inconceivable to think her own sister, the baby she had held in her arms, would soon be one of them.

When Matthew Duncan, his daughter and two sons entered St Aidan's Church, the pews were full. The tiny coffin, transferred from the Manse by Mr Martin, the undertaker, was now sitting in front of the altar beside Amy's hawthorn branches. As they walked down the aisle, they barely looked at the congregation, only the coffin which stood like an obstacle at the end of their path.

Reverend Brownlow spoke beautiful words, yet Amy hardly heard them. The boys were behaving themselves, not because they were particularly distraught, but because they had never seen their father so quiet nor their sister so solemn and pale. Then Amy noticed the minister beckoning to her and knew it was time to sing. She hoped she could remember the words. Would she be able to finish the song without weeping? She took a deep breath and began singing 'O Can Ye Sew Cushions?' Only once did she falter. It was when she came to the line about 'my wee sweet lamb'. A sob escaped before she could stop it, but clenching her hands so tightly that her nails cut into her palms, she continued for her father's sake, and for her mother who lay in the big bedroom of the Manse and might still never leave that room alive.

After Reverend Brownlow delivered the benediction, they rose and followed the coffin out of the church. Mr Martin and another man carried the box, though it was so small Amy could have carried it herself.

The Miller family were seated in the back row of the church. Closest to the aisle, Eliza reached out and touched Amy's arm. As she turned sideways to acknowledge Eliza's gesture of sympathy, Amy glimpsed the girl with the dark ringlets towards the end of the pew, and next to her a flash of turquoise. Then she was outside the church.

Peggy's grave was a small hole in the corner of the Millbrooke graveyard nearest the creek. At the sight of the pile of freshly dug red clay beside the grave, Amy cried some more. Then she saw something sunny where a marble gravestone would soon be erected – a bouquet of yellow orchids. She had seen orchids once before, in a fancy flower shop in Sydney. But where would anyone find orchids in Millbrooke?

Amy had heard the expression 'bone-tired'. Now she knew what it meant. Every day she rose early to buy bread. Then she washed the clothes and hung them out to dry, made breakfast for her father and the boys and prepared a tray for her mother. Although

Margaret Duncan still spent much of the day in bed, she was growing stronger. Even so, she carried purple shadows under her eyes as if someone had hit her, the way Charles Chen had looked following the incident with the drunkard.

After she washed the breakfast things and cleaned the house, Amy would spend an hour or two reading to her mother. Not from the Bible as her father expected, but from the popular novels of Misses Brontë and Austen that she kept hidden in her bureau. There was a particularly pompous clergyman in *Pride and Prejudice*, and whenever Amy read his speeches, she would adopt a Glaswegian accent which always made her mother smile.

Amy treasured those hours, knowing how close the family had come to losing the person who held everything together. The woman who balanced Matthew Duncan's brusqueness with her tenderness.

'Dearest Amy, I know you would rather be in Sydney,' her mother said one morning.

'Not at all, Mama.'

'It's a natural desire for a young girl to wish to live somewhere exciting. And I imagine your Aunt Molly would have made a great fuss of you.'

'That's true, but this is where I am meant to be. And there is no reason why Millbrooke couldn't be exciting too.' In asserting her wish so confidently, Amy hoped it might come true.

When the family had finished the pot of soup which was ever-present on the stove, she would make more. In the afternoon she would bring in the washing and bake biscuits or a cake. Sometimes she stewed and bottled the apples and pears that Mrs Miller sent down from Millerbrooke, usually in a sulky driven by Joseph. His visits were so frequent, Amy wondered whether he was pursuing her romantically, or if he was simply being a good friend. Even her mother, confined to the bedroom, seemed to know about Joseph. In her dealings with him, Amy was careful not to indicate anything more than friendship. She treated him as if he were her elder brother, following Eliza's example.

Amy had postponed her classes with her friend, at least until her mother was stronger. She missed their amiable chatter in the barn. It wasn't gossip – that was the devil's work. They had always been careful not to malign anyone.

Whenever she had a spare moment, Amy would go to the church and practise her organ music – she had replaced her mother, who sometimes acted as organist. And occasionally she might find time to write to Aunt Molly – news about her mother, descriptions of the boys' escapades, and stories about Eliza and her family. The only person who didn't appear in her letters was Charles.

If only she could visit his emporium and lose herself in the aroma of the teas or the magic of the jade figurines, she might ease her sadness, at least temporarily. But the irony was that an excursion to the one place which beckoned as a source of comfort and healing would necessitate an encounter with the man she most wished to avoid.

Now

'He snowed you, didn't he?' said Richard, shaking his head as he sipped his tea.

'Kind of. It just happened before I knew it. He was saying how he loved the Manse and that it reminded him of home. And next thing I had a lodger. We've agreed to a trial period of four weeks.'

'You might be glad of that, Ange.'

The waiter delivered his breakfast – corn fritters with tomato relish and sourdough toast – and Angie's muesli with poached peaches.

'I don't feel comfortable about keeping all of his rent money, Richard. You must be entitled to some of it.'

'No, it's *your* windfall. Enjoy it. But you'll have to pay the extra electricity and water charges.'

'Of course.'

'And you'll have to deal with the flak of having Jack Parker in your house. It's not something you can keep secret, particularly in a small town like this. Some people hate Songbird. They'll say you're consorting with the enemy.'

When he used the words 'consorting with', Angie wondered if he was implying 'sleeping with'.

'You make me sound like a Nazi collaborator.'

Richard was rubbing the stubble on his chin. 'You might find you've made a pact with the devil.'

On the Thursday before the June long weekend, Angie received a phone call from Vicky.

'I've come down with the flu, Angie. I'm not going to be able to make it.'

'That's okay, Vic. We can do it another time. Just concentrate on getting well. I bet Paul's waiting on you hand and foot.'

There was a pause. 'Something like that.'

'Did I tell you that I have a prospective lodger?'

'No. I didn't think you were going to take in guests. Not with the house so dilapidated.'

'He doesn't mind.'

'*He?*'

'Yes, he's an engineer with the mining company.'

'I suppose he might be good company for you, Angie. After all, you've never been on your own before. What's he like?'

'Charming.'

'Do I detect a hint of romance?'

'Hardly. Anyway, we're both married.' Then Angie remembered she wasn't married any more. Perhaps Blake was right about her being in denial. Maybe she was stuck in the past, frozen in a psychological time warp.

'Besides, I'm too old for romance.'

'You're an attractive woman, Angie. One day you'll meet someone.'

'I'm not interested. The sexual feelings are gone.'

'That's what happens to menopausal women, along with the hot flushes,' joked Vicky.

'I'm serious, Vicky. That part of my life is over.'

The next morning Angie ran into Moira in Miller Street.

'The town's chock-a-block with tourists today,' said Moira disparagingly.

'I used to be one myself, not so long ago, Moira.'

'But not the kind who stops to use the toilets, buys a coffee and then heads on to more exciting places.'

'No, I'm a stayer.'

They both laughed.

'Do you want to come back to my place for a coffee?' asked Moira.

'Actually, I was on my way to the museum. I've decided to do some research into the past residents of the Manse.'

'I haven't been there in years. Do you want some company?'

The museum had its home in Millbrooke's first bank, a stately building made from local sandstone. It was a funny old place with dusty display cabinets and handwritten cards.

'You'd never see things like this in a sophisticated city museum,' said Angie, pointing to a stuffed platypus from 1890 and a wombat with missing patches of fur, resembling a well-loved teddy bear.

'Nor this,' said Moira, examining the naval uniform of a captain who had served under Horatio Nelson. 'I'm surprised some big museum hasn't snapped it up.'

Angie followed a sign saying 'Gold Rush Rooms'.

A showcase held a plaster of Paris landscape with a blue-painted river running through it. On either side were dozens of tiny tents bearing flags on matchstick poles. The plaster surface was dotted with square-cut holes to suggest mine shafts. Although the whole thing reminded Angie of a school project, somehow it captured the spirit of Millbrooke. A do-it-yourself kind of place, honest and unpretentious.

Then she spotted a painted canvas banner bearing the words: 'Roll up, roll up. Rout the Chinamen.' On the wall beside the banner was a description created decades earlier on a typewriter:

Racism on the Goldfields

In 1872 a group of European miners called a town meeting, hoping to have the Chinese removed from the Millbrooke diggings. This is the banner they carried to support their cause. Instead of being successful as they had expected, the anti-Chinese miners were out-voted two to one and the Chinese remained.

On the opposite wall hung a series of portraits, all painted in the same slightly naïve style. None of them was signed. Angie wondered if the artist might have been a talented local, or even an itinerant portraitist who had travelled from town to town offering his artistic services. What a pity he hadn't signed his work for the benefit of posterity. The first painting was of a bearded doctor called Allen, the next a clergyman by the name of Brownlow, followed by a succession of unsmiling male faces in carved wooden frames – the graziers, businessmen and eminent citizens of Gold-Rush-era Millbrooke.

'Not a single woman,' said Angie. 'It's as if they didn't exist.'

They were about to head towards the door when she paused to examine a glass-fronted cabinet in the corner, its shelves lined with tiny objects, none of which looked important in its own right: snuff boxes, broken pieces of china, a pair of spectacles, pieces of lace, old buttons. Almost lost among the miscellanea was a hand-painted miniature, so small it could have fitted into the palm of Angie's hand. She put on her glasses to see the details. Inside an oval frame was a painting of a strikingly handsome Chinese man, dressed in a smart black suit and turquoise waistcoat, with a yellow orchid on his lapel.

'Isn't he gorgeous?' she said to Moira.

'Yes. I bet he broke a few hearts.'

The label was typed on a piece of cardboard:

Charles Chen, circa 1870

'I wonder whether he was a miner,' pondered Angie.

'I wouldn't think so. Look at that spiffy waistcoat. Can't imagine a prospector in one of those.'

'Well, whatever he did, I'm glad somebody immortalised him, if only in miniature.'

Despite the museum's fustiness, Angie preferred it to contemporary institutions with their flashy audiovisual presentations and interactive displays which seemed so removed from the past. Behind a counter in the foyer stood a white-haired volunteer whom Moira introduced as Bert, the president of the Millbrooke Historical Society.

Before Angie could explain why she was there, Bert said, 'You're the lady who's renting the Manse, aren't you? Richard told me about you. He said you might turn up, inquiring about the girl who used to live there.'

'There are no secrets in Millbrooke,' Moira whispered in Angie's ear.

'We might find something in this book,' he said, producing a thin red-covered volume from an array on the counter: *A History of the Churches of Millbrooke*.

In the section about St Aidan's Church they learned that the second minister was Reverend Matthew Duncan who held the post from 1871 until his death in 1894.

'Perhaps Amy was his daughter,' suggested Angie. 'Is there some way we can find out?'

'We could have a look in the archives room.'

He led them down a hallway to a small room, its walls lined with shelves, sagging under the weight of books and folders. A long desk held state-of-the-art computers, a large printer and other electronic gadgets that Angie couldn't identify. For some reason she hadn't expected to find twenty-first century technology in Millbrooke's old-fashioned museum.

'We've been digitising our collection of old photographs,' said Bert. 'There's the entire series of plates belonging to Anton

Weiss who ran a photography business in town in the latter decades of the nineteenth century. And we're also transferring our microfilm copies of the *Millbrooke Gazette* into digital format. But we're only volunteers, you understand, so it's taking us some time.'

He sat at a computer and offered Angie and Moira seats on either side. Then he keyed in the name 'Millbrooke photos 1870s', and a series of folders appeared on the screen. He must have opened scores of pictures before they found a studio photograph with the caption: 'New Minister of St Aidan's Church and his Family, October, 1871.' Right there on the screen was the Reverend Duncan with his wife and two young sons. The minister and his wife were standing straight as flagpoles, their faces unsmiling. He had sandy hair, a beard and a thick moustache, while she wore her hair in a bun, drawing attention to her large eyes and high cheekbones. The two boys were dressed in boater hats, white shirts with a bow at the neck, short jackets and trousers. Standing on either side of their parents like attending angels, each boy had angled his body towards the edge of the picture as if he were trying to run away.

But where was Amy?

'I'm sorry,' said Bert. 'There doesn't seem to be a daughter.'

Angie was disappointed until she recalled the dedication inside *Sylvia's Lovers*.

'I know the reason why Amy isn't in the picture. She didn't come to Millbrooke with the rest of the family. She didn't even leave Sydney until March of 1872.'

'How old was she? Do you know?'

'I have a photograph of her by your Anton Weiss, probably taken during her first year in Millbrooke. She looks about seventeen or eighteen.'

'Perhaps we can find Amy later in her life in the parish records. If she was married here, there'll be a listing.'

From a shelf holding a row of black folders he took one with 'St Aidan's Parish Records 1865–1885' written on a label glued to the spine.

'The clergy kept very thorough registers,' he said. 'These are photocopies of the original pages. Now, if she was seventeen in 1872, you probably need to examine every year from 1872 until 1885 by which time she would have been close to thirty. I'll leave you to it.'

Angie removed the relevant pages from the folder and divided them into two piles. She took one and Moira the other. Between them, they found two references to the Duncan family.

The death of a baby daughter in 1872. *Cause of death: Premature birth. Failure to thrive.*

A decade later there was a marriage, though not Amy's. Robert Duncan in 1882. Was Robert one of the sons?

'We can't find any record of Amy,' Angie told Bert when they had finished with the folder.

'Perhaps she remained single,' he said. 'That was the case for many women in the nineteenth century. Being the daughter of a clergyman, she would have had a reasonable education, probably at home. So she may have become a governess or a schoolmistress. They were common professions for single women of limited means.'

Angie bought a copy of the red-covered book about Millbrooke's churches, not so much for the text but for two particular photographs – the newly completed Manse with its lych-gate and picket fence, and St Aidan's Church circa 1865 with a caption explaining the trustees had chosen the quiet laneway because it was well away from the public-houses of Millbrooke's main street. Brothels too, Angie imagined, although they wouldn't have put that in print.

As they were about to leave, Angie asked Bert: 'What do you think of the Golden Days project?'

'Some of my fellow historians are calling it the "Ghost Ride". They say it will be the end of our museum. They think it's a superficial way of presenting history. But it's my belief that you should engage people by whatever means, and then they will want to learn more. After the tourists have had their excitement at the Songbird ride, I hope they'll come over here to the museum to learn the real history.'

'I agree,' said Angie. 'Anyway, there's a long road between a proposal and a reality. It may not even happen.'

Back at the Manse, Angie produced the collodion portrait of Amy.

'So this is the girl who used to sleep in your room,' said Moira. 'Have you seen her ghost yet?'

'I wish I believed in ghosts, Moira. I'd really like to meet Amy.'

'Maybe she'll be waiting for you tonight. Sitting on the window seat,' said Moira, giving her a wink.

But Angie was lost in the portrait. There was something in the expression of the blue eyes, hand-tinted by Anton Weiss, which reminded her of the young girl who first saw Phil Wallace in a Newtown pub back in the late seventies. In those days she was Angela Simmons, not quite eighteen and in her first year at uni. She'd never been to a pub before, but her girlfriends convinced her to go. Nobody will know you're underage, they said. Just wear plenty of eyeliner.

On the makeshift stage a rock band was playing. Although they weren't very good, she couldn't help noticing the bass guitarist. So did her girlfriends. Except for Vicky who said, 'Watch out for bass guitarists, girls. They'll only break your heart.'

'Come on, Vicky,' one of them giggled, 'tell us about this mysterious musician from your past.'

'It was Paul McCartney,' she replied, provoking further laughter. 'As a kid I had a poster of him on my bedroom wall. I'll never forget how devastated I was when he married Linda. I wanted him for myself.'

After the band finished its set, the guitarist came over to their table and introduced himself as Phil. The girls were flirting with him, except for Angie, who was so shy she could barely look him in the eye. Phil went off to do another set, and she was sure she'd seen the last of him. But right at closing time, when only she and Vicky remained, he appeared at her side, so close she found herself blushing. He asked for her phone number and walked them to the bus stop.

The next day, he rang to invite her to the movies. After she hung up the phone, she was so excited she rushed into the lounge room to tell her parents.

Her dad asked, 'What does this fellow do for a living?'

'He plays in a band,' she responded without thinking.

'No daughter of mine is going out with a musician.'

It turned out that Phil Wallace was really a fourth-year medical student, doing pub gigs on Friday and Saturday nights for the hell of it – and to make some money. Five years later, when he was a resident at a major Sydney hospital, they got married and lived happily ever after.

Until the heart attack, which was like a full stop in the middle of a sentence.

7

THE VANISHING PLATYPUS

Then

One afternoon, when she had finished making a stew for dinner and it sat simmering on the stove, Amy decided she would visit the main street. On her morning trips, she always avoided Mr Chen's Emporium, even crossing the road so as not to walk past the door. Nevertheless, its magic lived on in her imagination, and its owner figured often in her thoughts. He had called her wise – not just once, but twice. She had held that word close to her, like a talisman, even though she didn't feel wise at all, certainly not in matters of the heart.

She had searched her novels for a scene similar to the events at the Millers' dance, but she could only find one such instance. It occurred when Mr Rochester left Jane after she saved him from the fire in his bed. That night they exchanged intimate looks and next morning he rode off without a word. Of course, there was a reason for his hasty departure, though Jane wasn't aware of it at the time. Only after her doomed wedding ceremony did she learn Mr Rochester was married to the mad woman in the attic. Charles wasn't married though. Amy knew that for a fact.

But he might well have a secret sweetheart, a Blanche Ingram with dark hair and a sophisticated demeanour. If Charles loved someone else, that would account for him running off. As for his asking Amy to dance, he had done that out of duty, having seen her sitting by the wall without a partner. An act of politeness towards someone he considered a wallflower, albeit a wise one.

Determinedly she brushed her hair, pulling it into a tight knot at the nape of her neck and capturing it in a crocheted hairnet. As she caught a glimpse of herself in the mirror above her bureau, she realised the smart coiffure had done nothing to improve her wan complexion. Even when she pinched her cheeks to make them rosy, she resembled one of those clowns in a travelling circus. Two red spots set in a ghostly white complexion. Still, it would have to do.

Sometimes a winter's day in Millbrooke could produce a blue sky brighter than anything Sydney could offer. Today was such a day. There was a chill in the air that the townsfolk liked to describe as 'brisk'. Shivering in spite of her shawl, Amy dallied outside the drapery, examining every piece of fabric in the window, trying to postpone her visit to the emporium. Yet it had to be done. Even if she and Charles were only to be acquaintances, she couldn't keep avoiding him. And though her feelings for him seemed unrequited, she could love someone who didn't love her, as long as the words remained unspoken. While they were secret, they could exist. Hadn't Little Dorrit pined in silence for Mr Clennam and Jane Eyre for Mr Rochester? They might have won those gentlemen in the end through steadfastness and loyalty, but they had never taken a happy ending for granted.

She stood at the doorway of the emporium. Inside, a man was bent over, unpacking boxes. It reminded her of the March day she had first discovered Aladdin and his treasures. Anxiously she waited for him to turn and face her, but he continued to work, oblivious to her presence, so she raised her hand and rang the brass bells near the door to catch his attention. For some reason, their tinkling sounded hollow. When the man turned, she saw it wasn't Charles but his brother.

'Good afternoon, sir. I am seeking Mr Charles Chen.'

He replied in broken English. 'He go Canton.'

Amy's heart was racing. Canton? That was China. Had she misheard? 'Mr Chen has left for China?'

His brother nodded.

Suddenly the silks were no longer bright and the teas had lost their fragrance.

'You want buy silk?'

'No, thank you.' Panic was sucking the air from her lungs. 'I must speak to Mr Chen. When will he be returning to Millbrooke?'

Charles's brother didn't seem to understand. 'He in Canton.'

She began to cough – a wheezing, rasping death rattle.

'You need doctor?' he asked.

She couldn't breathe. Bent in two, she whispered, 'No. Just some water, please.'

He rushed out the back and returned with a cup.

'You drink this. Make you better.'

She took little sips, gasping for air between each one. It was jasmine tea.

He pulled a stool towards her, one of the little wicker seats from her birthday party with Charles. As she sat there, focusing only on her next breath, finally she began to feel better.

'You go doctor, miss. You sick.'

His gentle manner reminded her of Charles. Tears began to fill her eyes and she wiped them away with her hand.

'Thank you, sir. You have been most kind,' she said, her voice still raspy. 'I shall visit again when Mr Chen returns from Canton. Good afternoon.' Her words were running together. She stumbled out of the store and crossed the road without looking. Although a man driving a horse and cart almost ran into her, she continued down the street, seeing nothing but a blur through her tears.

Charles had gone to Canton. He had run away like Mr Rochester.

In the days after she learned about Charles's departure for China, Amy threw herself into her household chores and duties at the church. She tried to fill her mind with anything other than thoughts of him, but a deep malaise had overtaken her. Her chest ached and she was beset by coughing fits. At night as she lay in bed, trying not to cough because it would waken her mother, she imagined she was the heroine of one of her novels – Elizabeth Bennet, Amy Dorrit or even George Eliot's Maggie Tulliver. What a silly girl that Maggie was, not knowing whom she loved, when Amy had no doubts whatsoever. Finally, as the day was breaking, she would fall asleep, but she didn't dream about Charles. He was gone from her life. He didn't even appear in her dreams.

One afternoon, while the boys were studying the classics with their father, and her mother was napping on the chaise longue in the parlour, Amy wrapped herself in a warm shawl and walked down to the stream at the bottom of the garden.

She found a low boulder, sheltered from the wind, and sat there, looking into the water. A pattern of circular ripples caught her eye. As they dissipated, new ripples appeared a few yards further down the stream. Floating low in the water, there was something brown, resembling a log. Then the brown object disappeared under the water in a duck dive. But it wasn't a duck. Could it be a water rat? More ripples appeared. Concentric circles. In the very centre, the brown log was back. Amy crept to the edge of the bank and peered around a stand of reeds. The creature had a bill, a furry coat and a tail shaped like a paddle. It was little more than eighteen inches long. Like a magician vanishing amid a flash of smoke, the animal disappeared with a splash. She knew the creature's name and what awful things it could do with its hind claws. Yet it seemed so sweet. The boys must have tormented it to make it react in such a hostile manner.

The animal was back again, floating on the surface for several seconds. Amy thought its white-rimmed eye was looking at her. Then it was gone again, leaving only a trio of bubbles on the surface as a souvenir of its presence. Although she didn't take her eyes off the surface, the duck-mole did not return.

Suddenly she was weeping. She didn't even hear the swishing sound of someone coming through the long grass. It was not until a figure sat beside her on the boulder that she looked up and saw it was Eliza.

'Amy, has something happened to your mother?'

'No, she is much better, thank you.'

'What is it then? Are you thinking of little Peggy?'

Amy felt ashamed. She wasn't crying for Peggy but for herself. Wiping her eyes with her hand, she turned towards Eliza. 'It's kind of you to be concerned about me, Eliza, but I can assure you I am fine. However, there is something I need to ask you.'

'Yes?'

'Why has Charles returned to China?'

'Some weeks ago – it must have been shortly after little Peggy's passing – he received a letter from his mother, saying she was very ill. So he left immediately for Sydney and boarded a ship for home.'

'Why didn't you tell me?'

'It didn't cross my mind. Anyway, you must have worked it out when you went to the emporium and saw Jimmy minding the store.'

'I haven't been there. Not since before the Queen's Birthday. Not until today.'

'Well, I don't see why you're making such a fuss. But speaking of Charles, I do hope things go smoothly for him with the Chinese authorities.'

'What do you mean?'

'The Manchus have a rule that all Chinese men should wear a pigtail, even those returning from overseas. But Charles says he is not prepared to comply with such edicts, that it is just another way for the Manchus to impose their will on ordinary Chinese people.'

Amy had no idea what Eliza meant by Manchus, but they sounded exceedingly unpleasant.

'Father says there is no need to worry,' said Eliza. 'Charles is travelling on his British passport and they cannot touch him.'

'I am pleased to hear that,' said Amy, failing to stifle a sob. 'And I trust his mother will make a speedy recovery.'

Suddenly Eliza seemed to grasp the reason for Amy's tears. 'Amy Duncan, is it possible you have feelings for Charles?'

When Amy didn't answer, Eliza continued, 'Now I remember I saw you waltzing with him that night in the barn. Don't you realise that Charles can never marry a European girl or even a Chinese girl living in the colonies? Sooner or later he is required to return to China to find a suitable bride. It is his mother's dearest wish and I don't think he could ever disappoint her.' Eliza lowered her voice. 'I suspect she might even be feigning illness to expedite matters. Speaking of which, Amy, you're doing the exact opposite. Pretending to be well when you're so poorly. Now let's get you inside beside the fire. You'll catch your death out here.'

Amy dried her eyes on her sleeve. If she had been silly enough to imagine a future with Charles, it would never happen now. But she could hold on to the feelings and no-one need ever know. And as soon as her mother was well enough, she would leave Millbrooke and return to Sydney. Her aunt would help her find a position as a governess with a good family. She might only be eighteen, but she had made a grown-up decision. She would never marry, not if she couldn't have Charles Chen.

The following Sunday, Amy was in the ante-room next to the church vestibule, putting away hymn books after the Sunday service, when she overheard Doctor Allen speaking with her father.

'I am concerned about your daughter's health, Reverend Duncan.'

'She is well enough, Doctor. She cooks and cleans and tutors the wee lads.'

'But have you looked at her face? She has a deathly pallor. And surely you must have heard her coughing during the service today.'

'It is just the winter grippe. She will pick up once the weather grows warmer.'

'I'm not so certain about that. I fear the cough could easily turn consumptive. She needs to rest and regain her strength.'

'I could send her to her aunt in Sydney, I suppose.'

'I do believe that would be for the best. Otherwise, you might be burying a second daughter before the year is out.'

Amy remained in the semi-darkness of the ante-room, stifling a cough and reflecting on what the doctor had just said. Consumption. Surely not. That was the dreadful disease which had claimed sweet, young Helen in *Jane Eyre*. Suddenly she felt icy cold. Pulling her shawl around her shoulders, she checked that the vestibule was empty. Then she slipped out of the church and crossed the road to the Manse.

As she entered the house, her father called to her from his study.

'Lass, I have decided ye need a holiday to clear yer lungs and bring the roses back to yer cheeks. Dinna worry about yer ma. The parish ladies will help out in yer absence.'

The very next morning he bid Amy accompany him to the Post and Telegraph Office in the main street. He had never sent a telegram before and so he spent a long time composing his message in order to keep the words to a minimum. Then they both watched the postmaster tapping out the letters. All being well, it would be delivered to Molly Mackenzie by the Newtown Post Office later in the day, informing her of her niece's arrival at Redfern terminal on Friday afternoon.

Amy woke on Saturday morning in the pretty guest room of Aunt Molly's terrace house. The maid had just delivered a breakfast tray with a boiled egg, fresh bread, jam and a pot of steaming hot tea. It reminded Amy of the time Jane Bennet was recuperating at Mr Bingley's house after she fell ill with a fever. Like Miss Bennet, Amy was unwell, though not so poorly she couldn't appreciate the well-appointed room or the thoughtfully prepared tray. The only thing missing was the dashing gentleman. He, of course, was far away, having taken a sea voyage to his native land. How long was a journey to Canton, she wondered. Much shorter than her own trip from Glasgow to Sydney Town. That meant Charles might have already disembarked. Perhaps he was even now being summoned to meet the father of his bride-to-be.

The arrangement between Mr Chen the Elder and the young lady's father would have been made years ago, when Charles was a small child, in the very same way that the Sultan had organised the betrothal of the young princess to the Chief Minister's son in Monsieur Galland's story. Now, all that remained was for the father to inspect the grown-up Charles and bestow his approval. And how could he fail to be impressed with Charles Chen? The perfect son-in-law: clever, congenial and industrious. As for the young Chinese maiden, she would be delighted at her fortune in having been delivered such a handsome husband.

As Amy prodded at the shell of her boiled egg, she allowed her mind to wander to the inevitable day when Charles would return to Millbrooke a married man, with his lovely bride beside him. It might not be for some months, not until spring or even summer. By then, Amy would be fully recovered and back at the Manse helping her mother. Even though she might hide herself away, doing chores and tutoring the boys, one day she would have to venture out. And eventually she would run into the happy couple, promenading along the main street, or more likely at the Miller house where Eliza's father would be holding a reception for the newlyweds. Unaware of Amy's feelings for Charles, Mr Miller would insist that she come. After all, she was almost a member of the family now. Joseph might even drive down to the Manse to collect her.

Everyone would be assembled in the grand drawing room, sipping golden liquid from crystal glasses. When she first glimpsed Charles and his bride, standing close together, their hands touching, Amy might utter a tiny gasp, but she would conceal it by placing her lace fan in front of her face. Then she would lower the fan, her expression composed and inscrutable. No-one would see her shock or pain.

Charles would introduce his bride, a woman as beautiful as the Oriental princess decorating the engravings in Monsieur Galland's book. Golden eyes, bronzed skin and glossy black hair caught in a bun, adorned with an ivory ornament, a gift from her new husband. Her gown would be crafted of pastel silk patterned with butterflies and blossoms. She would nod politely, because she knew no English, and then gaze adoringly at Charles.

At this point, Amy could go no further. She put the egg aside and took a sip of tea to settle her stomach.

'Good, you're awake,' said Aunt Molly as she entered the room to check on her patient. 'I want you to eat all your breakfast. We need to fill those hollows in your cheeks before I can send you back to your dear mother.'

In Amy's first week in Sydney Aunt Molly summoned her medical practitioner, Doctor Fullerton, to examine her niece.

'She has a serious chest infection, but it's unlikely to be consumptive,' he said. 'I suggest regular hot lemon and honey drinks to relieve the congestion. And I recommend daily sessions of back massage to open the airways. I shall return at the end of the week to check her progress.'

Although it should have been blissful to recuperate in Aunt Molly's elegant house, Amy couldn't really enjoy the pampering because she felt guilty. Instead of helping her mother, she was in Sydney, being waited on as if she were Queen Victoria visiting the colonies.

New thoughts about Charles were puzzling her too. He had seemed such an honourable man. After all, he was Eliza's most admired person, and *she* had grown up with him – yet he had flirted with Amy to make Blanche Ingram jealous and then sailed off for home to meet his familial obligations by marrying a Chinese bride. Had he been dallying with both Blanche and Amy? Surely not. Yet the other alternative caused her just as much pain. Could it be true that Charles had never been dallying with her in the first place, that he wasn't even interested?

In Amy's second week of convalescence, she spent the daylight hours in Aunt Molly's sunny north-facing back garden. Amy had forgotten how warm Sydney could be. There were even a few late-flowering blooms remaining on the rose bushes. Aunt Molly's coachman, who also served as her factotum, had set up a divan and a table in the semi-shade of a eucalypt tree, while Aunt Molly had provided an assortment of books for her niece to read. It wasn't long before she was immersed in Mr Dickens's last novel, *Our Mutual Friend*, the story of a young man required to marry a girl he had never met. Amy wondered if it might contain some clues to help her unravel the mysteries of such marriages.

At the end of the week Doctor Fullerton made a house call. He found Amy much improved and advised short walks around the garden and an excursion to the seaside if the weather remained mild.

'Breathing the salty air might prove the restorative she needs,' he said.

So Aunt Molly, who loved an adventure, arranged for her coachman to take them to Circular Quay from whence they availed themselves of the services of the Port Jackson and Manly Steamship Company to travel to Manly. Although Aunt Molly wouldn't permit Amy to walk on the sand, they sat on a bench overlooking the ocean beach and took afternoon tea in a little inn beside the protected harbour cove. Then they returned via the steamer to Circular Quay where the coachman was waiting, and they were home before nightfall because the doctor had warned against the night air.

One afternoon they went to a matinée performance of a minstrel show visiting from America.

'Don't ever tell your father,' said Aunt Molly.

'Of course not,' replied Amy.

As she sat beside her aunt in the packed theatre, Amy couldn't understand why the minstrels were wearing black make-up and woolly wigs. With their blue eyes, they were obviously as white as she was. However, Aunt Molly didn't seem to find it odd. Neither did the audience who greeted each item with growing enthusiasm. Admittedly, the music was enchanting, particularly a song called 'Beautiful Dreamer'. Amy checked the composer's name in the programme. Stephen Foster. It was the last piece he wrote before he died.

Towards the end, a skit took place involving Chinese characters. The actors were white men disguised in grotesque make-up and imitating the dancing gait of the Chinese workers whom Amy had seen in Millbrooke. That might not have been so bad if the Chinese had been represented as decent citizens, but it was quite the opposite. On the stage a den of opium dealers was trying to ruin the white hero. The audience hissed and booed. Amy squirmed in her seat. She didn't want to embarrass Aunt Molly, so she whispered: 'I am feeling poorly, Auntie. I shall go and sit in the foyer for a while.'

In her fourth week Amy received a letter from Eliza containing an exceedingly strange request. Did Aunt Molly live close to the university and would it be possible for Amy to visit the premises and send Eliza a detailed description? After Amy showed her aunt the letter, Molly said they would do the trip that very afternoon. It was only a couple of miles away on the Parramatta Road.

When Amy saw the buildings set high above an embankment, they reminded her of a Scottish castle, except that the stone was a pale gold, the colour of Manly sand. As their carriage reached the gatehouse, Aunt Molly spoke to the gatekeeper and soon the horses were leading them up a rise towards the castle. Amy peered out the window at the students, young gentlemen dressed in black flowing gowns with bundles of books pressed under their arms. She tried hard to remember every detail so she could describe it to Eliza. It was an intriguing and glorious place.

That same week Aunt Molly took Amy to David Jones' store in Barrack Lane.

'You have lost so much weight, Amy, you require a new outfit.'

Instead of the sensible clothes Amy needed, Aunt Molly bought her a ready-made dress of palest pink voile, patterned with textured hail spots.

'How pretty you look, my dear,' said Aunt Molly. 'I shall ask the attendant to pack up your navy dress so that you may wear this one back to Newtown.'

As she pirouetted in front of the mirror in the dressing room, Amy fancied she was Elizabeth Bennet attending a ball at Netherfield.

'You must have a new hat to match,' said Aunt Molly who soon found one, trimmed with a lavish plume of pink feathers and a generous trail of ribbons at the back. Amy could never wear a hat like that in her father's presence, but she could wear it to Millerbrooke. It would give her the courage to face Charles and his new wife.

At the start of Amy's fifth week in Sydney, Aunt Molly's doctor proclaimed her fully cured — not the slightest sign of congestion.

'Amy, you are well in body,' said her aunt, 'but I fear there is a malaise inside you which has persisted in spite of the best care I could provide.'

Amy looked down, unable to answer.

'Is it the loss of your darling wee sister?'

'Partly.'

'And what is the other part, Amy? Is it a young man?'

She nodded.

'Has he broken your heart?'

Amy felt tears filling her eyes.

'What is his name?'

'Charles.'

'Is there any hope of a reconciliation?'

Amy blurted out the answer before she could stop herself: 'No, he has gone to China to marry his betrothed.'

Aunt Molly was silent for quite some time. Then she asked: 'Is he a Chinaman?'

'Yes.' Amy looked into her aunt's eyes, seeking the glint of prejudice she had observed in so many faces that night at the School of Arts, but there was only a look of curiosity and concern on Aunt Molly's face.

'An arranged marriage. I have some experience in that field.'

What did Aunt Molly mean? Amy wanted to know everything.

'When I was about your age, I met a beautiful young man and fell in love. He was the son of the village schoolmaster and was planning to become a teacher himself. Although teaching is a noble profession, it is among the most poorly paid. And my parents didn't approve. I was the elder of two daughters and my family's future depended on me marrying well.'

'Like the Bennet daughters in *Pride and Prejudice*,' said Amy.

'Quite. We considered eloping, but I wasn't brave enough. So I acceded to my parents' wishes and gave him up. Not long afterwards, they introduced me to my second cousin from Edinburgh, an older gentleman whom they had always wanted me to marry. And that was how I became the wife of your Uncle Edward.'

'But you loved Uncle Edward, didn't you?'

'Not when I married him. In fact, I hardly knew him. But I grew to love him. What was the other course? To sulk and seethe? To resent my husband because he wasn't the beautiful young man I had desired? Yet who is to say how *that* might have turned out? We are too easily bewitched by the grand romances that we read about in novels. Yet rarely does an author tell us what happens to the couple when the rapture fades and the real world takes over. Imagine having to tolerate Mr Darcy's prissiness for a lifetime. Or being married to that selfish, manipulating Mr Rochester.'

Amy gasped. How could Aunt Molly say such hideous things about Messrs Darcy and Rochester? 'But, Aunt Molly,' she protested, 'Jane and Mr Rochester were blissfully happy. She said so herself.'

'An unreliable account. I have always believed that Jane would have been better off marrying St John. What a fine man he was. Just like your dear departed Uncle Edward. The truth is that romantic expectations can breed disappointment. On the other hand, when you don't expect happiness, it can creep up on you.'

'Are you saying that Charles and his bride will be happy?'

'If he is a good man, he will do everything in his power to make it work. It is his duty.'

'Was the marriage between my parents an arranged one too?'

Molly laughed. 'No, Amy. Theirs was a love match. Being the younger daughter whose sister had already married a wealthy man, Margaret found our parents much more lenient.'

'A love match?' Amy was puzzled. She couldn't imagine her dour father being romantic.

'Yes, it was. And they still love each other. Your father's love for Margaret is his redeeming feature. His one area of softness.'

Amy tried to reconcile the intractable Matthew Duncan with the notion of softness. And then she remembered the night Peggy was born and her father's concern for his wife and his grief when the baby died. Perhaps Aunt Molly was right.

On her very last day in Sydney, Amy paid a visit to Miss Howe's – the successful ex-student returning to her alma mater. When Miss Howe assembled the students for afternoon tea, they besieged Amy with questions about the goldfields and life in a boom town. She was embarrassed to say her father had never permitted her to visit the diggings. Briefly she considered telling them about the young woman she had encountered the first day and the dozens of similar ladies she had seen since then, venturing furtively into the daylight as if they were nocturnal creatures unused to the glare. But she decided that although ladies of the night might well be fascinating beings, they were not suitable topics of conversation for a group of young female scholars. Instead, she described the wonders of Mr Chen's Emporium, carefully omitting the man himself. Then she spoke about the Chinese shopkeepers and miners, not as the Celestials and Chinks who regularly appeared in newspaper caricatures, but as real people. And when they begged for another Millbrooke story, she told them about the platypus. They found it hard to believe such a creature could exist.

As Amy was preparing to leave, Miss Howe presented her with a gift.

'For outstanding achievement in French.'

It was a French dictionary.

What a perfect present. Now she would be able to devour every single word of Monsieur Galland's '*Histoire d'Aladdin*'.

Amy had barely been back a day when Eliza appeared at the Manse, brimming with excitement.

'Can you keep a confidence, Amy?'

'Of course.' After all, she was an expert at keeping secrets.

'Cross your heart and hope to die?'

Amy repeated the words solemnly, crossing her heart as she spoke.

'I know you have been sad on account of Charles, but I have news which may cheer you. There is someone right here in Millbrooke who has lost his heart to you.'

'To *me*? How do you know? Has the person in question confided in you?' Then a name flashed across her mind. 'It's not Joseph, is it?' she asked warily.

It was a moment before Eliza replied, 'I can tell by the tone in your voice that you do not reciprocate.'

'He is a good man, but I cannot ever feel romantically disposed towards him. Are you cross with me, Eliza?'

'Perhaps a little. But I have to admit you have always been most circumspect in your dealings with him. I shall let him down gently by saying your affections lie elsewhere.'

'Please don't tell Joseph about my feelings for Charles!'

'Of course not. Joseph will assume it is someone at your church. Anyway, once Charles is married, you might be more inclined to consider Joseph in a romantic light. Though, by then, *he* could well have transferred his affections to someone else. After all, there are many young ladies in our congregation who have been known to swoon over him . . .'

Amy let Eliza prattle on, but the comment about Charles's marriage was a reminder that, by holding on to her feelings for him, she would be committing a terrible sin – coveting another woman's husband. Yet, even if it meant condemning her eternal soul to damnation, she could never stop loving Charles Chen.

Now

Everywhere else in the Southern Hemisphere, it was almost spring, but in Millbrooke it was still the depths of winter. A circle of ice lay on the top of the metal birdbath, while the lawn wore its morning coat of frost. To a newcomer who had grown up on the coast, it resembled a light dusting of snow. But Angie had soon come to realise it was something much more sinister, creeping up from the creek while she was asleep to kill her newly planted garden. An invisible fog, like Bram Stoker's vampire, tainting anything in its path.

The French lavender that she thought would fare so well in a climate akin to Provence had been the first to keel over. When she visited the local nursery, they told her she'd planted the wrong variety. Only English lavender had any chance of surviving winter nights, which dipped below zero. So she pulled out the dead bushes and started again. It was the same with the geraniums she'd brought from her Sydney garden – they had wilted in a single night, and now their leaves were crisp and brown. Although she'd been tempted to clip them back – for the sake of neatness – the nurseryman advised her to leave the frost-affected tips in place as protection, like scar tissue, at least until the threat of further damage had passed. They might even produce some new growth in the summer, he said.

Mr Songbird had been her lodger for some weeks now. She would have to stop referring to him by that nickname. Richard had started to do it as well. Soon it would spread to his cronies at the pub and then, like an exotic virus, it would sweep through the town and she would be responsible for an epidemic.

Jack Parker wasn't so bad after all. He never complained about the frugality of his surroundings; he just seemed to be happy living in a home rather than a motel. During the first week Angie had organised for the electrician, Brad Horley of Horley and Sons, to add extra power points in the guest room. At the same time, he checked the wiring and pronounced it sound. Apparently, his dad had rewired the house in the seventies. Whenever Angie cleaned Jack's room, she wrestled with a snake-like tangle of black cords leading to the various power points. She could only guess how many appliances he attached in the evenings.

Angie cooked breakfast for him every day. It was the least she could do for a man who was paying her nine hundred dollars a week in rent. Sometimes they had dinner together as well, in the kitchen, because the table in the dining room was littered with painting paraphernalia. It was her roast lamb he liked best. He said American lamb didn't taste as good. The reason might have been the mustard crust infused with fresh rosemary, but Angie suspected it was more likely to be the fact that Australian lamb wasn't grain-fed.

Wednesday was painting day. The first hour was always spent in banter about men, taking place over tea, coffee and homemade slice. In fact, most of the day was peppered with innuendo and double-entendre. The women made Angie laugh, which was a good thing for someone who still cried a lot.

They all knew about Jack Parker living at the Manse.

'How's the cowboy?' asked Jennie. 'You don't want to swap for one night, do you, Angie? I could stay here at the Manse and you could go to my place.'

'He reminds me of Clint Eastwood in *Play Misty for Me*,' said Moira.

'Never heard of it,' said Tanya.

In fact, nobody except Angie could recall the movie.

'I remember when Clint was young and beautiful.' Moira paused to sigh. 'You should have seen him in *Rawhide*.'

'It's not fair, Angie,' complained Jennie. 'I would have done anything to have him stay at my place.'

'He might come to visit if I told him about my spa bath and the heated towel rail,' said Narelle. 'After all, you only have that crappy old cast-iron bath and an antiquated water heater.'

'Well, I'm glad you have someone to keep you warm at night, Angie,' said Ros.

'He's a paying guest, Ros. I'm not *sleeping* with him,' protested Angie. 'Anyway, he's married.'

'Only kidding. But you never know your luck. And it's early days yet,' said Ros with a wink.

The class hadn't progressed far with their still-life, but at least they'd finished the yellow roses. That was good timing because the rose bush was now bare. The blue and white porcelain, however, was proving to be a problem. Despite Angie's advice about capturing an impression of the swirls and scrolls, the women were trying to paint them in intricate detail.

At lunchtime she brought out a portrait she had started several weeks earlier. A work in progress. Her first painting since Phil's death, apart from walls and ceilings and undercoating her students' canvases. It was a picture of Amy. Almost full-size. Initially Angie had considered putting her under the lych-gate, surrounded by briar roses and dressed in a picture hat and gauzy frills, with a parasol in her hand. A typical nineteenth-century Romantic painting. She'd even done a detailed sketch. Although it was a pleasing composition, it looked Pre-Raphaelite, and Amy didn't seem to be an ethereal kind of girl. Not if her reading material was anything to go by. A young woman who chose to read Jane Austen and George Eliot had to have a practical side to her. So Angie had painted her curled up in the window seat, reading a novel, and if you looked closely you would be able to see the title. She hadn't decided which book yet. That would come at the end.

The women enthused so much over Amy's portrait that Angie showed them the Anton Weiss photograph and the contents of the trunk.

'Imagine having the actual choker from the photo,' said Tanya, gently fingering the velvet band.

'Do you think the picture was taken on her wedding day?' asked Ros.

'We couldn't find anything about a marriage in the church registers,' said Angie.

'Bert told us it was quite likely she didn't marry at all,' added Moira.

'She could have faced the same problems we're experiencing now. Lack of eligible men,' suggested Jennie.

'What about all those miners?' asked Ros.

'They probably went back to the wife and kids in the home country,' suggested Tanya. 'They might have had a fling with a Millbrooke woman, but not a permanent relationship.'

'What's changed?' asked Narelle.

Angie blushed, but nobody seemed to notice. Anyway, there was *nothing* going on between her and Mr Songbird.

'Well, *I'd* like to imagine she married a wealthy man,' said Jennie, 'who took her to his grand house in Sydney where they had lots of servants. And they lived happily ever after.'

Narelle scoffed, 'That's only because *you're* looking for someone rich who will whisk you away from boring old Millbrooke. But you won't find him on the net. Blokes like that don't need to advertise.'

SPRING

*'When Aladdin lifted his head
and saw her after such a long separation,
he greeted her with an abundance of joy.'*

'Histoire d'Aladdin, ou la lampe merveilleuse'
Nuit CCCXLI [Antoine Galland c.1710]

8

A SECRET INFATUATION

Then

Millbrooke in the spring was as enchanting a place as anywhere in Scotland. Daffodils danced in the garden beds. Lilac bushes of white and purple scented the air. New lambs huddled together in the fields. And down in the stream the duck-mole was a daily visitor. Amy could see the ripples in the dawn light as she fetched water from the well. Around noon the creature would reappear, only for a few minutes, and then it would move on. At twilight it returned for a lingering visit, fossicking for food in the pools formed by fallen willow trees and ignoring the ducks cavorting around it. The boys knew the duck-mole's routines better than anyone. After Robbie's encounter with the poison spur, they had acquired a new respect for the strangely engaging creature and no longer tried to disturb its burrow or throw sticks at it. Indeed, Robbie and Billy could crouch for an hour on the edge of the stream, observing the ripples.

One day, when Amy finished her morning chores, she set off to the main street to visit the haberdashery. She needed some lace to brighten up her navy day-dress, which was looking quite shabby. Hanging in the wardrobe was the pink voile ensemble, still pristine. Though it was the kind of gown she could wear with nonchalance in the streets of Sydney Town, it might draw attention in Millbrooke. Nevertheless, she planned to don it this morning. Afterwards she intended to change into something serviceable, before her father returned from his weekly visits to the elderly parishioners of the town. Meanwhile her mother was making a cake for the church bazaar, and the boys were in the dining room, completing the sums Amy had written on their slates. Long division for Robbie and measurement for Billy. He was struggling with rods, poles, perches and chains. Nobody would notice if she slipped out for half an hour.

Aunt Molly had said that Amy would turn heads in the pink dress, but she had not expected the reaction to be so dramatic. Was it the effect of the matching parasol she held over her head and the hat with its frivolous plume of pink feathers? Millbrooke was a prosperous town with many a wealthy family, yet very few had seen a dress like this, direct from Paris via David Jones'. At the haberdashery she spent considerable time perusing the laces, before deciding on a yard and a half of silk bobbin lace from Chantilly. It was an extravagant purchase. Being silk rather than cotton, it wouldn't wash well, yet it was the prettiest trim in the shop.

Amy was already at the butchery when she decided she would buy some jasmine tea – it might cheer her up. Although she hadn't brought her tin with her, she was sure Charles's brother could fill a paper bag for her instead.

She stood at the threshold, listening to the tinkling of the brass bells. Today they sounded cheerful, like the trill of a bird. The aroma of the spices seemed different too, warmer, more inviting.

Dressed in shirtsleeves and a dark waistcoat, the brother had his back to her, loading shelves with porcelain bowls. When the figure turned, it was Charles himself.

'You're back,' she said, forgetting her manners altogether.

'Good morning, Amy.'

If he was surprised to see her, he hid it well.

'I heard you have been unwell. Are you fully recovered now?' he asked.

'Yes, thank you, Charles. I had a good rest in Sydney with my aunt. When did you return from your travels?' She tried to sound matter-of-fact, as if she was indulging in a polite conversation with one of her father's parishioners, but her heart was racing at a ridiculous rate, each beat toppling over the next.

'Only yesterday. I am sorry to be so poorly dressed when you are wearing something so becoming.'

Was Charles Chen flirting with her? How ill-mannered of him. After all, he was a married man now. No doubt his glossy-haired bride would emerge from the back room at any moment.

'How is your mother, Charles? Eliza told me she was poorly. I do hope she has recovered.'

'Yes, she is much stronger, Amy, but it broke her heart to see me leave. How is your own mother?'

'She is better now, thank you.' She looked at his face from under the brim of her hat. He was as beautiful as ever. Marriage agreed with him. 'I trust your bride is finding Millbrooke to be a pleasant locale, although I fear she must be tired after her lengthy journey. Is she resting at home?' Amy pictured the elegant Mrs Chen reclining on a chaise longue, awaiting her husband's return.

'No, she is not.'

'Perhaps she is visiting with the Millers?'

'No, Amy.'

'But your bride returned with you from China, didn't she?'

'I'm afraid not.'

'Is she coming on another ship?'

'No.'

Amy was perplexed. Where was the bride? Had she remained in China, as his mother had done? What kind of marriage would that be?

'But you were married while you were in China, were you not?'

'No, I could not marry because I already love another.'

Another? For a brief moment Amy's heart soared. Just as quickly it plummeted at the thought of Blanche Ingram of the brown ringlets.

'And have you asked for her hand in marriage?' Although it was a bold question, Amy needed to know the answer.

'Not yet.'

'Well, perhaps you should do it expeditiously. She may have found another suitor in your absence.' As soon as the words escaped her mouth, she regretted them. How stupid to encourage him to propose to Blanche.

'I fear that may indeed have happened.'

'But did you not write to her while you were away and remind her of your love?'

'I should have done so; however, the situation was complicated.'

'Why, may I ask?'

'I left for China so suddenly and without explanation, I am afraid she thinks badly of me. But my mother was ill and I had to return home. And I was caught between two worlds. I did not know whether to comply with the customs of my land or abandon the age-old traditions to court the woman I love. It was my mother's most ardent wish that I marry a bride of her choice. And I wanted to please her because she is my mother and although she is no longer ill, she is not young any more. She would like to see me suitably married before she departs this life. But despite the fact that my mother brought many pleasant and suitable young ladies before me, I could not do it.'

'Does the woman you love know that the precipitous nature of your departure was due to your mother's illness?'

'Yes, indeed.'

'And does she have any knowledge of the customs requiring you to marry a lady from your native soil?'

'She does.'

'Then I imagine she would consider your decision to defy tradition as an indication of the depth of your love for her.' What was she saying? She was simply advancing Blanche's cause.

'But suppose that she loves another?' he asked.

'Then there is no hope. If the person you love does not love you in return, it is a matter of lasting despair.'

'So what course of action should I follow, Amy?'

She hesitated. It crossed her mind that this might easily have been a conversation between Jane Eyre and Mr Rochester. She tried to recall what Jane had replied when he asked her a similar question. Finally she said, 'You must decide that for yourself, Charles.'

'Would you be happy for me if I married?'

'It is not my place to be happy or otherwise.' A safe reply, guarding her heart from further damage. But where had those words come from? Jane Eyre again? Amy could feel her throat tightening. Tears were threatening. Although she tried to blink them away, a drop had already dribbled down her cheek.

'Why are you sad, Amy?'

She looked into the golden-brown eyes. If she told him, she would seem like a fool. Worse, she might cry and never stop.

'I'm not sad. It is merely a spring cold.' She was sniffling. When she looked in her purse, there was no handkerchief.

Charles produced one from his pocket. Instead of handing it to her, he began to dry her face, dabbing softly at her skin. She could barely breathe. His face was as close to hers as when they were waltzing. Then he pocketed his silk handkerchief and stood back.

'I hope your cold will soon be better, Amy.'

'Thank you, Charles. I'm sure it will improve with the advent of warmer weather. I must take my leave. I have arithmetic to mark. Good morning.'

Amy was saddened by her unexpected meeting with Charles and the strange conversation which had ensued. No matter how hard she tried to concentrate on preparing for Eliza's lesson, her thoughts kept straying to him and the dark-haired girl he wanted to make his bride. He might even be asking her at this very moment. And Amy had no doubt what the answer would be. Yes, yes, yes.

When Eliza arrived, they decided to sit on the boulders down by the creek while her horse Neddy grazed nearby on the thick spring grass. Although Amy was certain Eliza would know the identity of Charles's young woman, she was equally determined not to raise the subject. She wanted her friend to think she was over her infatuation with Mr Chen and indifferent to his choice of a bride. As it happened, Eliza seemed to have other things on her mind.

'I have brought a French book for us to translate,' said Eliza, producing a volume with a black cover.

'What about 'Aladdin' or even *French without Tears*?'

'This is more important. My father took out a subscription for me. It is a periodical from France.'

Amy expected it to be full of the latest gowns from Paris, but instead it was a journal about medicine and science.

'Why would you wish to read about medical matters, Eliza?'

'Because I intend to be a doctor.'

Amy laughed so loudly that Neddy turned towards her with a curious look. 'Girls can't be doctors.'

'Of course they can. There are women doctors in America.'

'I have never heard of a lady doctor. Only nurses like Miss Nightingale.'

'Well, perhaps I will be the first in the colony.'

'And how, pray, did this interest in doctoring develop? It is a most unladylike hobby.'

'I do not perceive it to be either unladylike or a hobby. Quite the contrary. Medicine is a serious occupation, befitting the woman I wish to become.'

It was the first time Amy had ever heard Eliza sound cross. She was such a placid girl, never ruffled by anything, yet now she was all fiery eyes and flushed cheeks. Suddenly Amy felt ashamed. Eliza had harboured a special dream, and her best friend had just belittled it. Dreams were such fragile things that even the slightest bump could damage them. And Amy had just trampled over Eliza's. Was she her father's daughter after all? Just as she bore his fair complexion, did his holier-than-thou voice live inside her, impossible to silence?

'I am sorry if I have offended you, Eliza, but it is just that I find this notion difficult to understand.'

'Long ago I lost a brother and a sister to illness. I was only a baby and I don't remember either of them, but I do know that my mother continues to grieve – even now. It is my desire to learn as much as I can about the afflictions which curse our lives. Already there is hope that we may be able to guard ourselves against at least some of these scourges. Imagine a world without smallpox.'

'That is not an earthly prospect, Eliza. It is the paradise which God offers to those who believe in Him and His Son, a place free of sickness and pain.'

'One day God will grant us this paradise on earth.' Eliza spoke with such determination that Amy felt like smiling, but adopted a solemn expression instead. She didn't want to upset Eliza yet again.

'Eliza, where will you learn to be a doctor? What school or university would allow a young lady to study medicine?'

'I am intending to write to the University of Sydney, asking to be considered for enrolment as soon as they establish a medical school.'

'I didn't see any ladies when I was there. Only gentlemen.'

'That is true. But times are changing and it will not always be that way.'

'And in the meantime you're planning to read medical journals.'

'Yes.'

'And deliver calves.'

'And last year I set Daniel's leg when he broke it. Doctor Allen was out at Cockatoo Ridge and he couldn't get back until the next day. When he returned, he said I had done such a good job it didn't require re-setting.'

'You are determined to do this.'

'Yes, indeed. And my father supports me in my quest. He is purchasing a microscope for my birthday. Furthermore, he has asked Doctor Allen to order another subscription for me – to the *Boston Medical and Surgical Journal*.'

'Does Doctor Allen approve of you reading medical journals?'

'At first he thought it unseemly that a young lady would want to know about the workings of the human body, but my father convinced him otherwise. And I promised him an English précis of the important articles in my French journal.'

As Eliza shot her a cheeky grin, Amy wasn't sure whether to be galled by her friend's affront or to marvel at the dedication with which she pursued her dream. 'Show me this French periodical, Eliza Miller. Where do you wish to start?'

Eliza chose an article about a Professor Pasteur whose work on fermentation had led him to discover strange creatures called germs that were so tiny you could only see them through a special magnifying device – the microscope of which Eliza had spoken. The translation was an arduous process, much more difficult than 'Aladdin'. Although they used a dictionary, many of the long words were not French but Latin or Greek. It was most confusing, like solving a jigsaw. Nevertheless, Eliza remained enthusiastic, spurring Amy on to the next paragraph and then the one after that.

'How amazing,' Eliza declared, when they had finished translating the first two pages. 'Germs can live on your body and you wouldn't even know. And all the while, they could be spreading disease, like an invisible army.'

'I always thought sickness was spread through poisonous vapours infecting the air,' said Amy.

'You mean miasma. That is what most people believe.'

'Are you saying there is no such thing?'

'I wonder if it might be a myth, like a fire-breathing dragon.'

Amy was shocked. It was as if the basis of everything she knew was crumbling before her. If these germs caused you to become ill and they were unseen and omnipresent, how could you escape them? At least with the bad smell, you would know it was there. You could hold your breath or cover your face or even run away.

'I don't think I want to translate any more of this text, Eliza. It is too frightening. Far more disquieting than *The Woman in White*.'

'It is a time of hope, Amy, not fear. Scientists are making new discoveries all the time. That is why I need to read the journals.'

The sun was low in the sky when Eliza finally set off for home. Amy put the dictionary aside and lay down in the soft grass next to the boulders. Hidden in the reeds, two frogs were having a mumbled conversation. A magpie hopped among the blades of grass, burying its beak in the ground as it looked for worms. The duck-mole was probably playing among the fallen willow branches, but Amy was too tired to look. She must have nodded off to sleep because she dreamed that Charles Chen was standing above her, smiling. When she opened her eyes, he was there.

'Did I disturb you, Amy?'

Realising she was lying on the ground with her skirt in disarray, Amy tried to stand up. A hand reached for hers and lifted her to her feet.

'Shall we sit here?' he asked, indicating one of the lower boulders.

They sat close together.

'Amy, following our talk earlier, there is a matter which requires clarification.'

'Does it pertain to the lady of whom you spoke?'

'It does indeed.'

'Then, I think it is best that you speak to her.'
'I thought so too.'
'I saw her at the Millers' dance. She is very pretty.'
'I think there has been some confusion, Amy.'
'I am not sure what you mean, Charles? You were in animated conversation with a young lady who has dark ringlets. It was before you asked me to waltz.'
'I do not recall that.'
'Are you mocking me?'
'Not at all. But there is something I must ask you, Amy. I trust you will not be offended.'
'How do I know if I will be offended until you ask me?'
'It concerns Joseph. I saw you with him at the dance and then he took you home after the meeting in the School of Arts.'
'Yes, that is correct.'
'Are you and Joseph courting?'
Amy laughed before she could stop herself. 'Why don't you ask him?'
'I was intending to. But as you know, I am only newly returned to Millbrooke, and Joseph is out at Cockatoo Ridge, helping with the shearing.'
'In that case, perhaps I can save you the trouble. Joseph is my friend. It can only ever be a friendship. Nothing more. I have never indicated otherwise. Besides, my heart lies elsewhere.'
'Are you certain?'
'As certain as I have ever been. If you are entitled to ask a question, then may I do likewise?'
'Of course.'
'Why did you leave the dance so abruptly? Was it to meet your secret fiancée?'
'There is no fiancée.'

'Then why did you run away?'

'It was because I was faced with a crushing dilemma. As you are aware, my mother has always expected me to marry a Chinese bride. But I found myself irresistibly drawn to the young lady with whom I was dancing. And I knew I shouldn't feel that way. For my mother's sake and for yours.'

A blush was rising up Amy's face, but while they were speaking frankly, she wanted answers. 'Have you ever been faced with that dilemma before?'

'To be honest, no. I have met many affable young ladies, but none who combined that quality with a sense of justice and compassion.'

He had turned to face her, but she didn't dare look at him.

'Was it you who left the orchids on little Peggy's grave?' she asked with lowered eyes.

'Yes.'

'Thank you.'

'My heart broke for you that day, Amy.'

'Not long afterwards,' she began, 'I went to the emporium to speak with you. To make things right between us. But your brother said you had left for China. And then Eliza told me about the arranged marriage and I decided I would never marry. Not if I couldn't have you.'

She was weeping. He took her hand and put it to his lips.

'When I was in Canton, all I could think about was you, Amy Duncan. I remembered how it felt to be close to you when we waltzed. I told my mother I could not take a Chinese bride, not when there was a young woman whom I loved back in Millbrooke. And I dared to hope you might feel the same. I couldn't wait to come home. I couldn't wait until you came to my store. Then you walked in wearing that pink dress and . . .'

He leaned across and kissed her on the mouth. At last Amy knew how Aladdin's princess felt when Aladdin embraced her. As if she were floating weightless above the ground.

'Will you marry me, Amy Duncan?' he asked.

'Yes, I will, Charles Chen.'

They kissed again. This time she couldn't stop herself from pressing against him and the strangest shiver passed through her body. Gently he pushed her away from him.

'Did I do something wrong?' she asked.

'No, Amy. But you might make it difficult for me to be a gentleman.'

'But you are always a gentleman, Charles.'

'You might be surprised how tempted I am to abandon the decorum and give vent to my unbridled passion. Right at this very moment.'

'Really,' she gasped, until she saw a smile forming on his lips and realised he had been speaking at least partly in jest. All the same, 'unbridled passion' was a thrilling notion. But what exactly did it mean? There were so many mysterious things between men and women that she didn't yet understand.

After a moment Charles spoke again, and this time his tone was serious and urgent.

'Amy, I must ask your father for your hand in marriage. I shall come to see him this evening. After supper.'

Until that point, it could have been a dream. Now Amy woke up. And she felt ill.

'My father won't be happy, Charles.' But she didn't elaborate. She couldn't bear to tell him the names her father had called him.

When she remained silent, Charles said: 'It is because of my race, isn't it? There will be many people who feel that way, Amy.

They will look down on you because of me. They may even call you horrible names. Can you live that way?'

'I don't care what people think.'

'You should. It is your reputation which is at stake.'

'Reputation is simply the way I am viewed in the eyes of others. But I know who I am.'

Charles took her in his arms. 'I love you, Amy. I can hardly believe you feel the same. And that is all that matters. Do not worry about your father. I shall win him over.'

'He's a stubborn man, Charles.'

'I can be stubborn too, when I have a cause that is dear to me.'

From the house she heard the boys' voices. Their Latin lesson must have finished. They were coming out to play. Oh dear. At any moment her father might appear at the back door. And then he would look towards the creek and see his daughter in the arms of the man he had called an infidel and an opium user.

'You must go.'

'I'll return tonight at half past seven.' He kissed her chastely on the cheek, and then seemed to remember something, removing a parcel from inside his jacket.

'I brought this back for you from Canton.'

It was a fan made of silk. As she unfurled it, a charming scene appeared. Outside an Oriental palace, a young man, who might have been Aladdin, and a young woman, who could easily have been the princess, were locked in a tender embrace.

'It's beautiful, Charles. I shall treasure it.'

After she watched him make his way along the creek towards Schoolhouse Road, Amy went inside the Manse and upstairs to her room. From beneath the underclothing in her bureau she took Monsieur Galland's *Arabian Nights*. The book fell open at page three hundred and fifty-four as if it had been waiting for her – Amy's favourite part of the story, Aladdin's reunion with the princess.

It wasn't possible to express the joy they both felt at seeing each other again after being separated for what seemed like forever.

It might have been written for Charles and me, she thought to herself. Then she returned the book to its hiding place.

Amy couldn't wait to tell her mother of Charles's imminent visit. Margaret Duncan might be an ally in what could well prove to be a battle of wills between father and daughter. While they were seated at the kitchen table, peeling potatoes, she asked: 'Mama, have ever you been to Mr Chen's Emporium?'

'Yes, but don't tell your father.' Her mother lowered her voice. 'It was when we first came to Millbrooke. I bought some silk to make a blouse.'

'So you met Mr Chen?'

'Yes, he's a most personable young man.'

Amy continued to peel the potatoes, placing each one in a bowl of water.

'You and Papa fell in love, didn't you?'

'Indeed we did, even though he wasn't the well-to-do husband my parents wanted for me.'

'You put love ahead of everything else.'

'I suppose I did.'

'Mama, how old were you when you married Papa?'

'I was eighteen.'

'So am I.'

Her mother put the knife down and turned to face Amy. 'Amy Duncan, what are you trying to say?'

'A young man has asked me to marry him and I've said "yes". He is coming tonight to ask Papa's permission.'

Margaret held her gaze for what seemed like an eternity. 'It's Mr Chen, isn't it?'

'Yes. I love him, Mama. He is the most extraordinary man I have ever met.'

'Oh, Amy. There are so many suitable young men in Millbrooke and you have to choose the one your father detests. What about Joseph Miller? He's a fine boy and your father likes him.'

'I don't love Joseph.'

'Did your Aunt Molly put this idea in your head?'

'No, but she knows about Charles.'

'Charles? You address him by his first name? Amy, has anything of a forbidden nature happened between the two of you?'

'Only a kiss. This afternoon.'

'Don't tell your father that.'

'Please, Mama, speak to him. Remind him of how you felt when you were young. Tell him Charles and I feel the same way.'

Her mother was shaking her head. 'So he's coming tonight?'

'At half past seven.'

'Amy, don't you realise this cannot possibly end well?'

Now

The painting ladies had been so taken with Angie's picture of Amy that they wanted to have a go at doing portraits themselves.

Although Angie explained the difficulties, particularly in the hands of inexperienced artists, they kept nagging.

'When I was at art school,' she told them, 'we weren't allowed to paint people until third year. The first two years were spent doing bottles and vases. And sometimes we did cubes, prisms and spheres, mostly in monochrome.'

'How boring,' said Narelle.

'I suppose so, but it was also a good grounding.'

'Couldn't you distil the essence of portraiture for us?' asked Moira.

Angie knew she wasn't going to win this one. She might as well give in now. 'All right, but it has to be a painting of a child. Adults are too tricky. With children, you can be a bit chocolate-boxy and get away with it.'

She did a sketch of Jennie's face, showing them the proportions. Then she demonstrated how to mix flesh colours and how to paint hair with a rake brush so that it looked as if you could see every strand.

'Next week bring a large photo with you. It might be your child, your grandchild, niece or nephew. It could even be you when you were little.'

The room was abuzz with enthusiasm. Over the top of the din she shouted, 'Don't expect to win the Archibald Prize with your first attempt.'

It had been a long winter, starting on ANZAC Day and reaching far into September. Since the official arrival of spring, the nights weren't quite as cold – a matter of one hot water bottle rather than two. But although the temperatures had risen, frosts remained a problem, striking when you least expected them. This morning, however, it was easy to forget about winter and its icy aftershocks. The cherry trees were in pink blossom, the lavender aflutter with orange butterflies, and the dead-looking grass had suddenly sprouted into knee-length luxuriance like a teenager having a growth spurt. Richard arrived with a trailer holding his new ride-on mower. It took him two hours to mow the three acres – his old mower had taken two and a half to do the same job.

Now they were sitting in the kitchen, drinking tea and eating leftover lamingtons from Angie's painting class.

'Can't I at least pay you for mowing the grass, Richard?'

He frowned at her as though he was offended that she'd even offered, but then he said, 'You might want to consider getting some goats or alpacas to keep it down. Maybe not goats, because their hooves tend to compact the ground. And they'd probably get loose and eat your garden. Alpacas would be better. They're well-behaved and have soft paws like dogs.'

'Really? I don't know much about alpacas other than they're adorable. There are three or four in the paddock near the school. I love the white ones.'

'Well, think about it. They're not as expensive as they used to be. And they're easier to look after than sheep.'

'You seem to know a lot about them.'

'I have a small herd at Millerbrooke. If you want to buy three or four, let me know. You'll need a wether to guard the flock. Sometimes wethers can be a bit stroppy – like all old bachelors – but generally alpacas are docile. And they're quite aloof, so don't expect to cuddle and pat them as you would with a dog. When you come to my place, I'll introduce you.'

Angie felt guilty. Although there had been numerous invitations to Richard's house, she'd always found an excuse. He unsettled her in a way nobody else could. But she would have to go up there one day. Maybe the next time the boys came for the weekend.

'I like what you've done with the Manse, Ange.' He hadn't been inside the place since autumn when he'd dropped off Amy's trunk.

'After you finish your tea, I'll take you on a tour,' she said.

'How's Mr Songbird?' he asked.

'He's in San Francisco. A flying visit to see his family. And please don't call him that, Richard.'

'You started it.'

'I hope you haven't told anyone that.'

'What do you think I am? The village idiot?'

Whenever she thought about Richard — which wasn't often, despite the fact that she seemed to run into him so much — she didn't perceive him to be stupid, just eccentric and slightly Dickensian, with his funny cap and down-at-heel clothes.

'Is he enjoying his holiday?'

'How would I know?' she replied crossly. 'We don't exchange emails.'

'I hear they've applied to the government for approval to build a mine.'

'I wouldn't know anything about that. He's my lodger. We don't discuss his work.'

'It was in the paper.'

'Well, if it's in the paper, it must be true,' she said, fed up with the conversation. 'But you needn't worry. It's not going to happen overnight. In the mining game, it's always one step at a time.' She smiled at her clever use of the quote from Jack.

'No doubt Mr Songbird is consulting with his superiors at

this very moment as to how best to lobby the government,' said Richard.

Angie didn't bother to reply. There was no point in engaging in a debate. Particularly when it concerned something she didn't care about.

As for Jack, he had paid his rent in advance to cover the period he was away. Eighteen hundred dollars had bought Angie a brass daybed she had been longing for ever since she first saw it in the antiques shop. And thanks to her Songbird windfall, the exterior of the Manse was finished at last, looking as smart as when the house was first built. This week the painters were beginning work on the picket fence. It had been a recurring nightmare for Angie and she had often experienced restless, sweaty dreams about sanding and priming hundreds of pickets. Now she could pay somebody else to do it.

After they had finished their tea, she showed Richard the newly finished sitting room with its cosy sofas and checked wing chair. Above the fireplace hung Angie's portrait of Amy, now framed in sturdy, dark wood. Amy was sitting in the window seat with her legs curled up under her. Her hair was piled on top of her head, but the odd ringlet had escaped, falling onto her shoulders. She wore a white dress patterned with flower sprigs. At her neck was the choker with the black jet cameo. The silk pincushion lay on the seat, together with an abandoned piece of embroidery. Beside her was a stack of books, there to suggest Amy was a person of substance. You could see the names on the spines. Amy's own books – *Jane Eyre*, *The Mill on the Floss* and *Sylvia's Lovers*. Angie decided the latter was a nice touch, implying there might be more to Amy than just a straitlaced Victorian girl. Another novel lay open in her lap, but you could only see impressionistic scribble for text. Even when the painting was finished, Angie hadn't been able to decide which book Amy was reading. When she told her painting ladies, they said it didn't matter. But it mattered to Angie.

Finally it had come to her. On the back of the painting she'd written: 'Amy Duncan and *Pride and Prejudice*'.

Angie ushered Richard across the hall to the dining room, where the antique dresser, purchased with her first fortnight's rent money, had been joined by a matching table with ten balloon-back chairs. Her painting equipment, easel, folding table and vinyl chairs no longer cluttered the room. Instead, they had been moved to the barn where Richard had recently cleared out a section big enough for a class of twenty. He'd turned up so quietly that she hadn't realised he'd been until a few days later when she looked inside the empty barn. Empty except for the cartons of old magazines. How had he known to leave them behind?

In the upstairs bathroom, Angie gave him a demonstration of the new hot water tap. She had retained the gas heater for historical value.

'You realise it's not original to the house, don't you, Ange? It's unlikely they would have had an internal bathroom in the 1870s. Just a bathtub in the washhouse and an outside dunny. You can have it removed, if you like.'

'No, in a strange kind of way, I like it.'

'*If* I decide to buy the house, I want to make some changes,' Angie said when they were back in the kitchen, having another cup of tea and eating the last of the lamingtons. 'I'd like to install ensuite bathrooms. Do you think that's possible?'

She produced her sketchbook with the rough drawings she'd done on the return car trip from the girls' weekend in March.

As Richard examined Angie's sketches, he began to smile.

'I know I'm not a draughtsman, Richard, but is it *that* bad?'

'No, I was just smiling at your knot garden. It's so typical of you, Ange.'

Did he mean she was all tied up in knots? Or was he referring to the puzzling Gordian kind, where you couldn't find the end?

When she frowned he said: 'I meant whimsical. In a nice kind of way, of course.'

He continued to pore over her drawings. 'The plan looks fine, but then again, what would I know? May I borrow a pencil for a moment?' He turned to a new page of the sketchbook. Before Angie had finished her next lamington, he had produced two floor plans – upstairs and down.

'You could convert that funny little ante-room next to your bedroom into a bathroom and make a doorway between the two. And there's room for an ensuite along the east wall of the third bedroom. That's where most of the pipes are anyway, so it wouldn't involve a lot of plumbing work.'

She had always wondered what Richard Scott did before he became a property owner and a semi-permanent resident of the Millbrooke pub. He must have been a builder. That might be useful.

'I like your conservatory,' he continued. 'It makes the most of the north-facing aspect. You could create a solar-passive space there. But I don't like the half hexagon effect – it doesn't work with the structure of the house. Look at this.' He pointed to the outlines of the building. 'The Manse is all straight lines –

a sideways T. You need to make your conservatory rectangular to maintain the integrity of the footprint.'

Wow. She would persuade Richard to come out of retirement to do her job. But there was no point in asking him yet. Not until she was absolutely sure about buying the place.

Angie wondered whether her interest in Amy Duncan was becoming obsessive. At first it had been about the physical resemblance she had seen to her own younger self. But lately she had found her thoughts drifting to the character of the girl in the photograph, her interests and passions. There was something intriguingly modern about Amy. Sure, she read Victorian novels, but not the cheap romances or gothic thrillers you might have expected from a girl of that era. Amy's books were the classics that Angie had loved when she was young, and continued to read even now.

And what was it about Amy's little treasures that drew Angie back to them, time and again? Taken individually, they meant little; yet as a group, they formed a collection which bridged two worlds – the exotic silk pincushion, the fan and the tin, all representing the Orient, and the cameo, the perfume and the portrait, reflecting an Anglo-Celtic girl of the era. What did that fusion say about Amy?

Angie had become a regular at the museum, not just searching for Amy, but exploring the archives and building a mental picture of boom-time Millbrooke. Today, something sent her back to the photos of the 1870s. She worked systematically through every decade until the turn of the century. After three hours she hadn't found a single caption referring to Amy Duncan. Maybe Amy really had left Millbrooke and never returned.

Before she went home, Angie paid a visit to Charles Chen in his glass-fronted cabinet. It was something she did every time she came to the museum. She wasn't sure why. A little ritual, a secret infatuation. As usual, he was waiting for her. There was a confidence about him, a sense of entitlement that she found compelling, yet he didn't appear arrogant. And he didn't seem the type of person who would have been subjected to the appalling racism exemplified by the ugly anti-Chinese banner which hung not far from his miniature portrait. Then again, someone who wore Western clothes and appeared to be self-assured might have been even more of a target than a stereotypical 'Chinaman'.

Angie sighed. If she had been a young woman in 1870s Millbrooke, she would have fallen hard for Charles Chen. He was the most attractive man she'd ever seen. There must have been plenty of young ladies smitten with him. Did he ever get married, or had he remained a footloose bachelor, like Richard Scott? No, she laughed to herself. Not like Richard. Charles was immaculately dressed and drop-dead gorgeous.

Jack had slipped back into town like one of those glamorous outlaws from an old Western movie. You knew he shouldn't be in your house, but you wanted him there anyway.

A week or two after his return, they were sharing a bottle of white Zinfandel to accompany Tasmanian salmon topped with lemon thyme from the herb garden. There were even kipfler potatoes Angie had grown herself.

'I missed you, Angie,' he said.

'I missed your talk about gravity circuits and froth flotation,' she replied.

'You remember.' He was smiling, showing off those perfect teeth, a credit to American dentistry.

They sipped their wine in comfortable silence. He was an uncomplicated person to have around. No hidden agendas. No layers. He didn't nag like Vicky or sermonise like Blake. And he didn't patronise her like Richard. In fact, Jack was so amiable and laidback, he had slotted into her life without a single drama. Which was why she had to be careful. She could easily become dependent on him. There were signs the process had already started. Simple things like accepting his help in opening a jar or checking the oil in her car. Not to mention the comfort of sharing a meal and a glass of wine, and the reassurance of knowing another person was sleeping in the room across the hall. But what concerned her most about Mr Songbird was the music he made, whistling a tune in the shower, or singing as he worked at his laptop. She could easily get used to that.

'Any decisions on River Cove?' she asked, making conversation.

'Not yet. We're still waiting on a couple of assessments. And the pollies want to be damned sure the electorate is onside. They don't want to lose the seat.'

'What if the mine's rejected?'

'We'll cut our losses and leave.'

'No Golden Days for Millbrooke then?'

'Of course not. It's a total package, Angie. Millbrooke can't have the tourist attraction without the mine. Songbird can't keep dispensing favours without receiving something in return.'

Angie considered his words as she finished her second glass of Zinfandel.

'Have you won enough hearts and minds, Jack?'

'Not quite yet. But I'm working on it.'

After dinner, they had coffee in the sitting room. As they sat together on the sofa, he leaned over and kissed her on the mouth. Mr Songbird had soft, cool lips which aroused sensations in her body she'd thought were gone forever. But she reminded herself that Jack Parker had just returned from a fortnight with his family. And Angie Wallace had been a widow for barely a year.

As she pulled away, she placed her fingers on his lips, though not in an encouraging way.

'Not a wise idea, Jack. I can't afford to get hurt. And you're a married man.'

'Okay,' he said. 'But you know that most of Millbrooke thinks we're sleeping together anyway.'

One morning Angie decided to try the new Gold Rush Café which had opened in the old hotel on the corner of St John's Road. As she drank her tea, she read through the menu, which contained a page about Millbrooke's glory days in the mid-nineteenth century, when a small farming community was suddenly transformed into a bustling town, thanks to the discovery of gold nuggets nearby.

What was the attraction of gold anyway? What made it more desirable than silver? Angie herself had always preferred the latter, even for her wedding ring. But it was the yellow metal, not the silver, which had drawn men across oceans to dig holes with shovels and sift through tailings by hand. Backbreaking work, yet they barely scratched the surface of the treasure-trove, and very few of them became wealthy men. These days, mining companies, with their hi-tech drills, could bore hundreds of metres into the earth, and the men they employed were among the most highly paid workers in the country. What would an old-time prospector make of that?

Angie had finished her tea and was considering whether to order another, when she saw Richard waving at her through the window. He had tracked her down. He shambled in and took a seat opposite her.

'Where's your loyalty, Ange? As soon as a glitzy new café opens, you abandon the old place.'

'I just thought I'd try it, Richard. And they make a nice Lapsang Souchong.'

'Have you read the front page of the *Gazette*?' he asked, unfurling his copy.

'Not yet. I was reading the historical stuff inside the menu and thinking about the Gold Rush.'

He pointed to the headline: 'Millbrookers to Protest Proposed Mine'. 'Look at this. They're planning a big parade down Miller Street and a rally afterwards in the park, right next to the platypus statue. And there's a TV crew coming from Sydney to film everything for a current affairs program about foreign mining companies.' He put the paper on the table in front of her. 'Mr Songbird won't be happy about this.'

'Shhhh,' whispered Angie. 'You do that on purpose, don't you?'

'So what do you think about the mine proposal, Ange?' he challenged.

'I don't know, Richard. To tell you the truth, I haven't given it much thought.' Didn't he realise she had to focus all her emotional energy on getting through the day? Couldn't he see she had nothing left for issues other than her own?

'There's a Latin proverb which might interest you, Ange. "Even the just may sin with an open chest of gold before them." That's the problem for Millbrooke. *Aureo hamo piscari.* Songbird is fishing with a golden hook.'

She didn't bother responding. He reminded her of a headmaster denouncing the evils of smoking in the toilets – his comments could make you squirm, even though you hadn't been party to the misdemeanour in the first place.

Then, as he bid her good morning, accompanied by yet another of his piercing looks, Angie wondered if the conversation hadn't been more about her dealings with Mr Songbird than about the mine itself.

9
OUR MUTUAL FRIEND

Then

As the long-case clock in the hallway was tolling the half hour, there was a knock at the front door. Amy, who hadn't been able to eat her dinner, ran to open it. Charles was standing at the threshold in his black suit and a conservative grey silk waistcoat. In his hands were two bunches of flowers.

'Is your father expecting me?' he asked.

What should have been one of the happiest evenings of her life was going to be a nightmare.

'My mother is telling him now. We thought it best to leave it until the last moment.'

Charles gave her a curious look but said nothing.

'Please come into the parlour, Charles. They won't be long.'

As he placed the flowers on the credenza, two little boys peered into the room from the doorway. Then she heard her father's study door open and the sound of his footsteps as he crossed the hall. Amy had never seen his face look so livid. He ignored Charles, who was standing in the centre of the room, and addressed his words to Amy instead.

'What is this ungodly proposal yer mama is telling me about? I canna possibly countenance the idea of ma wee daughter consorting with a Celestial. It is unnatural. An abomination.' He turned on Charles. 'How dare ye consider asking fer Amy's hand in marriage? It makes me ill to contemplate ye even touching her. Dinnae ye realise that any bairns ye might have would be outcasts? Half-breeds. I want ye to leave ma house now and I forbid ye to see her again. And *ye*, Amy Duncan, will not leave the Manse without yer mama or me accompanying ye. Ye are not to be trusted.'

Amy was too shocked to cry. She had expected something awful, but not as vicious as this. She looked at the floor, ashamed of placing Charles in such an invidious position. Finally she heard him speak, slowly and calmly.

'I am sorry if you find it distasteful that I love your daughter and she loves me in return. It is the most wondrous thing that has ever happened to me. A blessing from God. *Your* God. *My* God. I thank Him every day for bringing Amy into my life. You have raised a fine daughter, Reverend Duncan, and I will not let her go so easily.' He nodded to Amy's mother. 'It has been a pleasure to see you again, Mrs Duncan. Goodnight, Amy.'

Amy followed Charles to the door.

He turned as he stepped over the threshold. 'I love you, Amy,' he declared.

Then Matthew Duncan slammed the door in his face.

Amy had never defied her father. Not openly. But she had never been so outraged. She looked straight into his eyes, pale against the flushed skin. 'It seems you have forgotten what the Bible says: "There is neither Jew nor Greek, there is neither bond nor free, there is neither male nor female: for you are all one in Christ Jesus."'

'Don't ye dare quote Galatians at me. Perhaps ye have forgotten Ecclesiasticus: "If thy daughter be shameless, keep her in straitly, lest she abuse herself through overmuch liberty."'

Amy took a deep breath. Angry words were forming inside her head. She wanted to say: 'You may be a reverend, but you are not a Christian. You are rude, ignorant and intolerant. You have humiliated a good man, and you should seek forgiveness.' But instead she ran down the hall, up the stairs and into her bedroom where she slammed the door so hard the walls shook as if there had been an earth tremor.

Amy lay in her bed, hitting the pillow because she couldn't hit her father. He had vilified Charles who, in his goodness and nobility, had turned the other cheek. What generosity of spirit to forgive the vicious words even as they burst forth from her father's mouth. Or did Charles consider it best not to burn bridges this early in the battle? Did he really think he could win over Matthew Duncan through patient negotiation?

Clearly Charles was an optimist. He looked forward to better times. He believed in the power of conciliation and arbitration. He would make an excellent diplomat. Amy, on the other hand, didn't feel diplomatic at all.

She rose from the bed, wiped her face on a handkerchief, turned up the kerosene lamp and fetched her pen and ink.

Dearest Charles,
How can I possibly apologise for the vile behaviour of my father? Please do not heed his words. They are but a reflection of his prejudices. I hate them, but I cannot hate my father. It is a sin to do so.

Please know you are the finest, most wonderful person I have ever met. This evening you behaved with such dignity and grace that it only made me love you more, if that is possible. Somehow we will be together.

I cannot sleep tonight and if I could escape this house and be with you, I would. But you would likely send me home because you know what is right and you always adhere to it. I wish I could be like you.

Yours always,
Amy

She blotted the ink, folded the note, placed it in an envelope and slipped it inside her French dictionary, ready to give Eliza tomorrow afternoon. Although Eliza didn't know it yet, Amy had already designated her as their go-between.

The next day, when Eliza arrived for her lesson, the first thing Amy did was to hand over the envelope.

'I shall deliver it on my way home,' she promised. 'Shall I wait for "Our Mutual Friend" to write a reply? Then I can bring it tomorrow.'

'Yes, please.'

It was no burden to Eliza who was excited by the intrigue.

The correspondence ended after the first exchange of letters. Though Eliza found it a great adventure, Charles felt unhappy about involving his sister in the subterfuge. So they devised something better, a way of meeting face to face which precluded the use of messages or the involvement of a third party. It was simple and foolproof. Charles would be at the creek at five every afternoon, hidden behind the largest outcrop of boulders. If Amy couldn't come, she would place a bucket outside the back door. But most days there was no problem. It was almost suppertime. Everyone was busy. She only had to concoct a reasonable excuse to allow her to be absent for a few minutes – picking vegetables, collecting eggs, fetching lemons from the tree by the creek.

Today Amy slipped out under the pretence of picking parsley to accompany the fish her mother was cooking for supper.

'There is a solution, Charles, if you want us to be together,' she said, once they were seated on a low boulder out of view of the house.

'Of course I do. But while your father refuses to give us his blessing, there is no solution.'

'But there is. Do you remember "Lochinvar"?' She recited the lines from Sir Walter Scott.

One touch to her hand, and one word in her ear,
When they reach'd the hall-door, and the charger stood near;
So light to the croupe the fair lady he swung,
So light to the saddle before her he sprung!

'Amy, that is only a poem. If we eloped, he would never forgive you. There are still diplomatic channels we should pursue.'

'All the channels have been exhausted, Charles.'

'Surely not. And to take such a rash course of action would only reinforce your father's notion that I am an evil seducer trying to abduct his daughter. Then there would never be a reconciliation.'

'Charles, I have learned something during eighteen years of being Matthew Duncan's daughter. There is no negotiating with him. He has become more obstinate by the day, more hardened in his prejudice. I feel as though I'm suffocating in that house.'

'But, Amy, I don't want you to be estranged from your father.'

'If it has to be that way, I can accept it. If it is the only way to be together, we must do it.'

'I am not convinced of that.'

'You haven't changed your mind about me, have you?' As soon as she said the words, she felt guilty for having asked such a wheedling question of Charles, more so when she heard his answer.

'Never. How could you ask me that, Amy? I love you more than I could ever have imagined.'

And then he proved it by kissing her with such passion that she understood what Monsieur Galland had meant when he wrote Aladdin burned with desire for his princess.

Now

The old Millbrooke cemetery filled a couple of acres at the western side of town. According to the information sheet Angie had found on the shelves of the tourist office, the oldest graves dated back more than a hundred and fifty years. There were miners and merchants, pastoralists and pioneers, tradesmen and artisans. English, Scottish, Irish and those born in the colony. Angie wandered through the cemetery, noting the different sections, delineated by low picket fences – Anglicans, Presbyterians, Methodists, Congregationalists and Catholics.

A few old rose bushes survived among the weeds which had taken over the pathways between the graves. Finally she made her way to the section marked 'Presbyterian'. It didn't take her long to find the Duncans. The grave lay within a fence composed of cast-iron spears. A large grey headstone sat in the centre of a block of marble. Around it the grass was interspersed with clumps of yellow jonquils. Three names appeared one below the other:

> In Loving Memory of
> **Peggy Ann Duncan**
> Dearly loved daughter of
> Matthew and Margaret Duncan
> Died 13th June, 1872
> Aged four days
> Safe in the arms of Jesus
>
> **Revd Matthew Duncan**
> Incumbent of
> St Aidan's Millbrooke
> Native of Scotland
> Emigrated 1864
> Died 15th June, 1894
> Aged 63 years
> Asleep in Christ
>
> **Margaret Jean Duncan**
> nee Macdonald
> Beloved mother of Amy, Robert and William,
> And Peggy (deceased)
> Much loved wife of Matthew (deceased)
> And dear sister of Molly (deceased)
> Died of pneumonic influenza

Deborah O'Brien

21st August, 1919
Age 84 years
R.I.P.

May angels guard thee in thy rest

Although they had all three been dead for such a long time, Angie felt strangely sad to find them here. Then she realised the good news. Margaret Duncan's inscription indicated that, as late as 1919, Amy was still alive, aged in her mid-sixties.

There was another important piece of information Angie could glean from the headstone. Amy's parents didn't emigrate to the colonies until 1864. That meant Amy was born in Scotland, not New South Wales. Angie took a photograph of the grave. She would add it to her growing folder of material about Amy Duncan.

The following morning Richard turned up at the Manse with a horse float which he drove across the grass and down to the back paddock. Then he removed three alpacas – white, black and tan. The tan alpaca had a cheeky black nose and a circle of black around his eyes like thick kohl pencil.

'I've checked your wire fences and they're sound,' he said. 'You can have these three on trial. If it works out, you can pay me later.'

'I want to hug them,' said Angie. 'Particularly the little white one.'

'That's the female. The vet says she may be infertile, but we'll see. The big tan boy is a wether. He'll guard the other two. And the black one is a stud male, but he's almost past his prime.

They only have a few good breeding years in them and then they're replaced by a newer model.'

'Like modern appliances,' said Angie. She reached out to stroke the white female who turned her head away.

'Don't rush them. They like their personal space. Let them get to know you.'

They were uttering little bleats, like tiny lambs.

'Do they have names?'

He rolled his eyes.

'Well, they do now,' she said. 'The brown wether with the Egyptian eyes is Tutankhamun, the white girl is Snow White and the black male is Jet.'

'*Anyway*,' Richard said, shaking his head, 'they're easy to care for, Ange, as long as you remember two important things. Rake up the dung and remove it. It's a breeding ground for worms. And clean out the feeder and water trough regularly.'

'I can do that,' said Angie. 'It's just good housekeeping.'

'When I have a chance, I'll build a sandpit for them.'

'A sandpit?'

'You've seen wombats having a sand bath down by the river. Well, alpacas like to roll in the dust too. And you can imagine how your lovely white girl would look after that. And coming from the Andes, they don't like the heat. So you should wet down the sand in the summer to keep them cool.'

'What else?' she asked.

'They need shelter, but there's that old elm tree down by the creek. In a bad storm you might want to move them into the barn until it's over. I'll come and visit every day for the first couple of weeks and if you have a problem, we can sort it out then.'

'Thank you, Richard. My own personal vet.'

She stood on her toes and kissed him on his stubbly cheek.

'This isn't a gift, Ange. I'm not the gift-giving type.'

'I know that, Richard.' Her heels hit the ground with a bump. 'I don't need a trial period. I can pay for them now, if you like.'

'No, let's see how you feel in a month or two. Think about all those well-intentioned people who buy cute little puppies at Christmas and want to return them in January.'

'I'm not one of those people, Richard. Once I make a commitment, I stick to it.'

'Where did the llamas come from?' asked Jack as he carried a bottle of wine and crystal glasses to the back of the house, the potential location of Angie's longed-for conservatory. She would need a year's worth of Songbird rent to pay for that. For the time being, she had set up a table and chairs on a paved area overlooking the creek.

'Richard dropped them off. And they're alpacas, not llamas.'

'Don't they spit?'

'Only when they're upset.'

He poured two glasses of chablis.

'That documentary about foreign mining companies is on TV tonight,' he said. 'They filmed the entire protest march. I bet we'll see those little schoolkids dressed in platypus costumes. What kind of parent lets their kids get mixed up in something like that? It's child exploitation. They should have been in school where they belong, not being politicised by their greenie parents and leftie teachers.'

Angie sipped her wine and let Jack vent his frustration, as if he were a caller to a talkback radio show.

'You know, Angie, every single business in Millbrooke

supports the mine, but they didn't interview anyone from the business community.'

'They interviewed you though. You should let your kids know about it, so they can watch the show online.'

'That's not a bad idea.'

'Any news on the environmental assessment?'

'The planning people have had it for months. The problem is those frigging platypuses. Everyone loves them. They're like your llamas. So damned cute.'

She could see the alpacas grazing in the paddock. She was already in love with them. How could she return to the city now that she had these adorable woolly creatures?

They said their usual goodnights in the hallway. She closed the door and settled into her wing chair. On the side table sat Amy's copy of *Sylvia's Lovers*. Despite the scandalous title, it had proven to be a very moral and formulaic melodrama. Although Angie kept waiting for something sensational to happen, it didn't. Finally she placed a marker in the book, removed her dressing gown and hopped into bed. She left her table lamp on. She had done it ever since Phil died. The woman who had always embraced the night-time was now frightened of the dark.

As she hovered on the edge of sleep, she heard a tap on the door.

'Angie, are you awake?'

She could have pretended to be asleep, and Jack would have returned to his room. Instead she said, 'Yes.'

'May I come in and talk?'

'Okay,' she replied tentatively. Angie knew the meaning of 'talk' from the dating dictionary of the painting ladies. Just as 'companionship' wasn't platonic, 'talk' didn't mean 'conversation'. She watched the door open. There, in the soft light of her table lamp stood Jack Parker in his silk boxer shorts. The painting ladies' fantasy – Moira's Clint Eastwood circa 1970. Although it was exciting, part of her was viewing the scene in a clinical way, like a painter framing up a composition.

He sat on the edge of the bed. 'I was thinking about you, Angie,' he whispered, although there was no need to do so – the nearest house was fifty metres away. 'I haven't been able to get you out of my head.'

She knew he was waiting for her to give him a cue. After a long pause she said, 'You'll catch a cold if you sit there like that.' She wasn't sure where those words had come from. Was it an old movie script? Maybe it was just those two glasses of chablis. She'd never been a good drinker.

When he slipped under the covers, it was as if his body had its own central heating.

'You don't know how long I've wanted you,' he whispered, his lips on her bare shoulders. 'It's been driving me crazy.'

'Jack, I haven't done this in a long time.'

'I know.' His hand was already between her thighs.

She caught her breath. She hadn't felt as aroused as this in . . . probably years.

Angie lay in the half world between sleeping and waking, trying to hold on to the dream that had filled her night, but it stayed out of reach. Then the garbage truck came rumbling down the street, its air brakes whooshing, and she was wide awake. Beside her the sleeping cowboy was oblivious to the crash of a bin being dropped on the road.

Her first impulse was to jump out of bed, have a long, hot shower and pretend it never happened. But she didn't move. Had she just cheated on Phil? Not in a technical sense perhaps, but it felt like a betrayal. An ill-advised attempt to seek comfort from her grief.

There had been no words of love, of course, because love didn't come into it. It was simply about emptying her head of everything except the sensation of Jack's body coupled with hers. And had that been bland and disappointing, she might have dismissed the episode as an aberration, but it had been quite the opposite.

What had happened to the circumspect widow, the respectable middle-aged woman who had buried the sexual side of her life with her dead husband, the only lover she'd ever had? Until now. Had she become a different person in Millbrooke? Good old Angie, a slave to convention, had done something completely out of character, and she felt guilty and exhilarated, both at the same time.

As Jack began to stir beside her, she wondered what he would think of Angie Wallace without make-up. Apparently he didn't notice.

'Why haven't we been doing this for the past few months, Angie?'

It probably wasn't the right moment to remind him about the woman with the blonde bob and the two chubby-faced boys. He would have to deal with that in his own way and in his own time. And so would Angie.

'You're so beautiful,' Jack mumbled as he kissed her breasts.

She knew he was lying, but words could be a self-fulfilling prophecy. Then she felt him hard against her thigh. This time she couldn't rationalise her response by blaming the wine. It was no longer a tipsy one-night stand. This time she was making a choice.

Richard was in the supermarket, dressed in camouflage pants and a pixie cap pulled low over his forehead, looking more like a derelict than a property owner as he pushed his trolley along the aisle.

'You weren't at the café this morning.' His tone was accusatory.

'I slept in.'

'Is it okay if I pop in to see the alpacas this afternoon?'

Something in his tone made her wonder whether he had guessed about Jack. Was there a look on her face which announced she had just had sex with Mr Songbird – not simply once, but twice?

'Of course. You don't need to ask.'

'I won't be disturbing you, will I?'

'Not at all.'

She was about to walk away when he blurted out: 'Don't forget it's jazz night at the pub, Ange. You might want to drop in.'

'Thanks. But I have some preparation to do for my painting class tomorrow. We're starting a new project. Aspects of Millbrooke.'

In fact, she was planning a romantic dinner with Jack. But if Richard knew that, he would fulminate about Faustian pacts and selling one's soul.

'Jack, tell me honestly,' asked Angie as she opened a bottle of sauvignon blanc, 'can we have the mine and protect the local platypus population too?'

It was late afternoon and Jack was sitting at the kitchen table as Angie began preparing dinner.

'The EIS says we can. After all, they've been around for a hundred million years.'

'That's the point, isn't it? They're the earliest form of mammal. An ancient species, swimming in the creeks of Gondwanaland when dinosaurs still roamed the earth.'

'Exactly. And when an asteroid annihilated the dinosaurs, who survived? Steropodon – the ancestor of the little critter living in your creek. What does that tell you, Angie? They're tough and resilient.'

Angie couldn't help smiling. Jack Parker could convince you of anything. Even that you should take him into your bed when commonsense warned you otherwise. Before she knew it, they were kissing, up against the kitchen counter. Just as he was struggling with the zip of her jeans, there was a knock at the door.

'Shit, who can that be?' Jack asked.

'It must be Richard. I forgot about him coming round. He wants to check the alpacas.'

'Can't you get rid of him?'

Angie was already on her way to the door, straightening her T-shirt and zipping up her jeans. As she passed the mirror of the hallstand, she took a quick look. Her face was flushed and her hair was awry where Jack had run his hands through it. Quickly she smoothed it down. There was nothing she could do about the flush.

Yes, it was Richard. He was wearing a new cap for the occasion – one of those knitted hats from Peru with side flaps like a beagle's ears.

'Hi, Ange.' He was looking at her oddly, and instantly she

imagined there were little antennae on the top of his head hidden by his trademark cap. He *knew*. 'I've brought a book about alpacas,' he said by way of greeting.

'Thanks.'

He continued to stand there, playing with a long woollen tassel which hung from the bottom of one of the beagle ears.

'Would you like to come in for a drink?'

'Well, maybe just a quick juice.'

Why did he bother maintaining the façade of being a teetotaller? It was ridiculous. Angie led the way down the hall to the kitchen where Jack was sitting with his feet up on the table, like the county sheriff. She almost expected him to say, 'Howdy', but instead he smiled: 'Hi. It's Richard, isn't it? We met at the information evening. Nice to see you. Would you like a glass of wine?'

'No, thanks.'

'I'll get you an orange juice,' said Angie. 'Have a seat.'

Mr Songbird and the owner of Millerbrooke faced each other off across the table.

'How are things at the drill site?' asked Richard, his tone making 'drill site' sound like something dire and evil.

'Everything's proceeding according to plan. We're publishing updated information about the feasibility studies on our website this week.'

'I'll look forward to it.'

'It's about openness and accountability, Richard.'

'I'm all for that.'

Angie offered olives and cheese. 'I noticed Snow White spitting at Jet today,' she said to change the subject. 'What does that mean, Richard? Is she pissed off with him?'

'Maybe. It could also mean she's pregnant. We'll get the vet to check her over. How's Tutankhamun?'

'A bit stroppy, poor darling. Perhaps he fancies Snow White and there's nothing he can do about it.'

'Except gaze at her from afar,' interjected Jack.

Angie had finished her wine.

'Another?' Jack asked, stroking her hand. Although she withdrew it quickly, she knew Jack's casual caress hadn't escaped Richard's attention.

'Will you stay for dinner, Richard?' Angie asked, praying he would decline.

'It smells good, but there's a rabbit casserole on the stove at Millerbrooke.'

Angie shuddered. 'I know they're pests, but how can you eat them? They're so sweet.'

'So are lambs, Ange, and you eat *them*. Thanks for the juice. I'd better get back. Enjoy your dinner.'

She saw him to the door. As he turned to go, he said: 'I almost forgot to give you the book.' He produced a pocket-sized volume from his coat, *Alpacas and You*, with a baby alpaca on the cover looking like a floppy soft toy.

'Thanks. And I hope Snow White really is pregnant.'

'Don't count on it. More likely she was just telling him to back off. She's an independent girl. Doesn't want to get involved with a glamorous womaniser like Jet. He'll just break her heart. And she's too nice to have that happen to her.'

10
YOUNG LOCHINVAR

Then

The next day Amy and Charles met at the rocks.

'Amy, I have been considering young Lochinvar's actions. If we *were* to choose that path, we would need to plan it carefully.'

She threw her arms around him. 'Do you mean we are going to be married?'

'You told me you couldn't breathe in that house. And I cannot have you suffocating, can I?'

She hugged him even tighter.

'But, Amy, there is a problem,' he said, disengaging himself from the hug and bidding her to sit down. 'I have checked with Mr Thomas, the solicitor. You are only eighteen. The law requires you to be twenty-one before you can marry, unless you have permission from your parents or there is a special reason.'

'Is it not special reason enough that we love each other and want to be together?'

'Unfortunately, being in love is not a reason to dispense with the law. Neither is suffocating.'

'Don't make fun of me, Charles.'

'I'm sorry. I was trying to make you smile.' He took her hand. 'By special reason, I imagine the law is referring to a young woman who is with child, in which case a marriage would be expedient.'

Amy's mouth fell open. You could have a baby and not be married?

'Forgive me, Amy. I should not speak of such things.'

'If you do not, I shall never learn what happens in the world.'

He had a smile on his face. 'I have thought of another way though. It involves your aunt. Is she on friendly terms with your father?'

'Aunt Molly says the only redeeming feature my father possesses is his love for my mother.'

'So she would be our ally rather than his?'

'Yes, of course.'

'She was your guardian when you remained in Sydney?'

'I suppose she was. After my parents left for Millbrooke, Aunt Molly would write letters to Miss Howe giving me permission to attend a theatrical performance or a concert. And she always wrote "Guardian" in brackets after her signature.'

'Do you think we could persuade her to give her consent?'

Amy sat up straighter. 'I'm sure we could – once she meets you. Otherwise, I could just pretend I'm twenty-one. Then I wouldn't need anyone's consent.'

Charles gave her a stern look. 'If we go to your aunt,' he said, 'we would need to decide whether to travel together or apart.'

'Together, of course. That is what we shall be doing for the rest of our lives.'

∞

The following afternoon, Amy's mother asked her to fetch some lemons to make lemon butter. Once she had picked them, she ran to the creek and found Charles pacing behind the rocks.

'Amy, I have devised a plan. I shall commission Mr Thomas, in strictest confidence, via one of his colleagues in Sydney, to seek out a city minister who will marry us. But it is not a matter of arriving one day and marrying the next. There will be a waiting period of three weeks for the reading of the banns. In the meantime, your father will probably come looking for us.'

'We shall hide at Aunt Molly's. She has a lovely house.'

'That is the first place your father would look.'

'Then we shall stay in a hotel. Under assumed names.'

When Charles gave her a questioning look, she continued: 'We can't very well use our real names, Charles. You could be Mr Wickham and I Lydia Bennet.' She giggled.

'What is so funny?'

'They eloped together in *Pride and Prejudice*.' Then, as she recalled that Mr Wickham was a scoundrel, Amy flushed with embarrassment, but Charles didn't appear to have read Miss Austen.

'Amy, we should stay in separate rooms. For the sake of propriety.'

'If we travel together, we should lodge together.'

'But people might think I had sullied your honour.'

'You wouldn't do that,' replied Amy, not exactly sure what he meant by 'honour'.

'No, of course not.'

'Well, that is settled.'

When he laughed in exasperation, Amy knew she had won. He was still smiling when he said, 'There is also the manner of our departure to consider. It may well be sudden and rushed.

You might have little more than a few hours' notice. You must bring only your travelling bag and nothing else.'

'Neither my pink dress nor my parasol?'

'No, Amy Duncan, nor your collection of bonnets. We shall travel light.'

Years of living under her father's iron rule, nodding obediently when she was inwardly rebelling, reading behind a closed door, and sneaking out to forbidden places, had made Amy skilled at pretence. Even though she could barely contain her excitement, day after day she played the perfect daughter, silent and compliant. No doubt her father thought her resigned to his judgment.

Although she wanted to have her bag packed and ready, she couldn't do it without giving the plan away. However, there was something she could do in advance – hide the prohibited books. After the elopement Amy didn't want her father checking to see what was missing and finding *Sylvia's Lovers* and other volumes tucked away in a drawer. But where could she put all her secret things? Not in the wardrobe. That was far too obvious. Then she recalled her trunk. It was sitting at the bottom of the linen press – empty, except for some old blouses which were too small.

She gathered the books and all the other forbidden treasures – the perfume bottle, now empty, the pincushion, the picture from the weekend at Millerbrooke, the fan and the tin. She couldn't decide whether to include the cameo or to take it with her. Probably best to leave her grandmother's brooch behind. She arranged everything in the trunk and laid the blouses on top. Then she slipped out to the garden, picked a bunch of lavender, tied it with a piece of ribbon and placed it inside.

The lavender would keep everything fresh until her return. And nobody would ever imagine that the trunk contained anything but old clothes.

As she was closing the lid, Amy felt a shiver pass up the back of her neck. It didn't last more than a second or two, and it wasn't frightening like the icy fingers which brushed her skin when she read Mr Collins's *The Woman in White* by candlelight. In fact, it had been so warm and comforting, she wondered if it was really a shiver at all. But whatever it was, it seemed to have something to do with the treasures in the trunk. As if someone was surveying the contents and smiling at them. She wasn't sure who that might be – certainly not anyone in this household.

Then she remembered the note from Charles, his reply to the letter she had written the night her father sent him away. After some thought, she hid it beneath the wallpaper lining in the bottom drawer of her bureau. It would be safe there until her homecoming as a married woman.

On the final day of November, as Amy arrived for their secret afternoon rendezvous, Charles was leaning against the largest boulder, watching the duck-mole.

'He is such an amusing creature, Amy.'

'Charles, what makes you think the duck-mole is a he?'

'I don't really know. Possibly the fact that he is always on his own.'

'Perhaps *she* is an independent type.'

'Like my Amy.' He stole a quick kiss.

'Do you believe in ladies being independent, Charles?'

'How could I say otherwise? After all, my betrothed is a person with a mind of her own.'

As the duck-mole floated on the surface, they sat close and silent for a moment.

'Amy dearest, I almost forgot the news I have come to deliver. We are leaving tonight.'

She threw her arms around him so tightly that he laughed and gently pushed her away.

'Will your parents be asleep by eleven?'

'Yes, they are always abed well before then.'

'Then we shall meet at half past eleven by the elm tree at the end of Church Lane. You won't have long to pack. Can you manage?'

'I am travelling light, remember.'

There was a voice at the back door. It was her mother calling her.

'I must go, Charles. I love you.'

'And I love you. Until tonight then.' He kissed her tenderly. When they drew apart, she saw an ardent look in his eyes that made her tremble. With a smile, he strode off, following the line of the creek towards the main street. Soon he was out of sight.

Amy skirted around the rocks and up the hill to the herb garden where she quickly filled her basket with sprigs of parsley and spikes of rosemary. Then, like a little girl, she skipped towards the back door.

Now

Most afternoons, just before sunset, Angie would check the next day's weather forecast on the internet – a routine which had developed since her lavender hedge was burnt by the frost.

Having pulled out the dead plants and replaced them with *Lavandula angustifolia* – on the recommendation of the local nursery – she was now tending the new plants as if they were babies, naked and vulnerable. If the frost indicator suggested a problem, she would collect hessian from the shed and cover each plant. It was a tedious process because every piece needed to be tied gently in place and then removed in the morning, once the threat had passed.

According to the Bureau of Meteorology, tomorrow morning promised to bring a severe frost, so she gathered the squares of hessian and was about to start work when Moira turned up with a sketchbook under her arm.

'Do you need a hand?' she asked.

'Thanks, Moira; it's a real chore doing this.'

In ten minutes the two of them had finished the hedge and covered the crab-apple with an old sheet, just as a precaution.

'Two years ago we had a frost that burnt all the fruit trees,' said Moira. 'It was the last week of November when everyone thought the frosts were over.'

'Did the trees recover?'

'The leaves fell off and there was no fruit that year, but most of them survived. Not many apples last season though. We'll see what happens with the summer fruit.'

In the dying light they drank tea on the terrace at the back of the Manse.

'Jack not home yet?' asked Moira.

'No, not for an hour or two.'

Moira opened her sketchbook and showed Angie a drawing she'd done in coloured pencil.

'I based it on a photo I took a few years ago when we had a heavy snowfall.'

'It's beautiful. I like the way you've covered St John's tower in snow. And there's even a snowman.'

'I thought I might use it for the exhibition. What do you think, Angie?'

'I love it. You could even do a series. The four seasons in Millbrooke.'

'That's not a bad idea.'

The sky had turned orange and purple. In the creek the platypus was diving for worms and insects. If it was lucky, it might even snare a yabby for dinner.

'Don't you worry about the fate of the platypuses, Angie?'

'I don't want to talk about it, Moira. I get enough of that from Richard.'

'But if you care about the platypuses, you should make a stand. After all, you're in a position to exert some influence on Jack.'

Angie gave Moira a dark look. 'We've spoken about it and he says they'll be okay.'

'Of course he'd say that.'

'Look, Moira, I don't want to upset things between Jack and me. I need him right now. Sometimes I think if I didn't have him in my life, I'd fall apart.'

'That's not healthy, Angie.'

'It's not forever. Just to tide me over until I can manage on my own.'

'That's what drug addicts say,' Moira mumbled.

When Jack arrived home, it was half past seven so Angie dispensed with pre-dinner drinks and served their meal right away. She enjoyed their evenings at the table – perhaps it was the flirtatious anticipation of the night to come.

'How was your day?' she asked.

'We had a meeting with the anti-mine people. They're calling themselves MAM. Millbrooke against Mines. I wonder sometimes whether they'd rather see this town dwindle away to nothing than have a mine built here. And of course I'm the focus of all their hostility – the dastardly villain who's out to ruin Millbrooke.'

'But that's not the general view. The business sector thinks you're God's gift to the town. My painting ladies like you too.'

'Really? I would have thought they hated me for having my evil way with their art teacher.'

She was about to tell him that Jennie and Narelle would have given anything to be in Angie's place, but decided his ego was already healthy enough.

'So if there are so many different takes on Jack Parker, who are you really?' she asked as they ate their meal.

'I'm just an ordinary Californian boy who's worked hard and made good.'

'Seriously though, Jack, what do you want from life, what do you hope for?'

'Well, I'm not sure that I hope for anything. I like my life. I know what I'm good at, and the fact I can make a decent living out of it. I like being married; I'm a good husband and father.'

'Oh really,' Angie said.

'Okay, I'm away a lot, but that's good for my marriage too. And if I didn't have this going with you, I'd be less than what I could be. My wife doesn't need to know. Maybe she guesses, but she keeps quiet if she does, and I do too. It works. And I like that I'm a good lover. Well, I don't have to tell you that . . . do I?'

'Are you telling me or asking me?'

'Do we have time for a demonstration?'

SUMMER

*'Never fear, my adorable princess,
your honour is safe with me.
No matter how strong my passion
or how powerful your charms,
I pledge to treat you with the deepest respect.'*

'Histoire d'Aladdin, ou la lampe merveilleuse'
Nuit CCCXXX [Antoine Galland c.1710]

11
ALADDIN AND THE INVISIBLE SWORD

Then

On the most important night of Amy's life, her mother and father had stayed up late, selecting the texts for the Festival of Lessons and Carols which Reverend Duncan was delivering the next morning to celebrate the first day of Advent. It was almost half past eleven when Amy heard the door to her parents' bedroom click shut. Lying fully dressed under the bedclothes, she waited a few minutes to be certain they had settled for the night. Then she hopped out of bed and opened the curtains of the bay window so that silvery moonlight filled the room. From her bureau she snatched clothes and piled them into her bag. She had considered doing it earlier in the evening, but had been afraid her mother might pop her head around the door and catch her in the act. When the hall clock chimed the three-quarter hour, she began to panic. Her purple cape wouldn't fit in the bag so she decided to wear it instead, together with her favourite bonnet, the one with the magenta ribbons. Charles had said not to bring the entire collection, but surely he wouldn't mind if she was wearing one of them.

It was such a warm night she was already damp with perspiration. The cape didn't help. She considered leaving it behind, but Miss Howe had always said a cape was essential when one went out at night, no matter what the season.

As Amy bent over to pick up the leather bag, something fell onto the floor. She felt around with her hand and retrieved the bunch of velvet violets which had come loose from her bonnet. After trying unsuccessfully to re-attach them, she gave up and threw them in the bottom drawer of her bureau, where Charles's letter lay hidden. She had barely finished lacing her boots when the long-case clock began to chime the hour. Oh dear. Gingerly she opened the bedroom door. The third chime was sounding. She held her breath and crept down the stairs, taking care to avoid the noisiest, the fourth step from the bottom. As she passed the hallstand, she dropped an envelope addressed to her mother on the shelf. Just the briefest of notes, saying she would be in touch and not to worry. Another letter sat in her pocket, waiting to be mailed later. By the tenth chime she was at the front door and on the twelfth she was closing it behind her.

'I'm sorry I'm late, Charles.' She was out of breath from running up the lane with the heavy bag.

'I thought you had changed your mind.' Charles was smiling.

'Not likely.' She gazed up at the moon. 'What a perfect night. Look at that marvellous sky.'

'While I was waiting for you, I saw a shooting star.'

'Did you make a wish?'

'Of course.'

'Will you tell me what you wished for?'

'I shall. Once we are married. Now *fai dee lah*. They're waiting for us.'

Charles took her bag in one hand and grabbed Amy's wrist with the other. She was walking so fast she didn't have the breath to ask who 'they' were. At the eastern end of the main street, she had her answer. Standing outside the School of Arts were all three Miller siblings and Charles's brother Jimmy, who was carrying a large box. Beside them was the Millerbrooke dray and two black horses.

'Joseph will take you to Granthurst,' said Eliza. 'You cannot wait for the morning coach because it doesn't leave until eight. Your father might notice you missing and the first thing he would do is come down to the coach stop. So we have provided you with your own coachman. It is not exactly Cinderella's carriage, but it will have to do.'

Eliza was only trying to lighten the mood, but her remarks alarmed Amy. She and Charles had considered the possibility of Matthew Duncan pursuing them, but what if her father alerted the constabulary?

'You will have a good head start,' said Daniel, as if reading her mind. 'And you will be safe in Granthurst by the morning. In time to catch the Sydney train.'

Amy looked around her at the drunkards who were meandering along the pavement and the ladies of ill-repute leaning over the iron lace verandahs of the public-houses. Late at night, Millbrooke was a different town altogether – an eerie, grey world containing grotesque characters worthy of Mr Dickens. For a moment the hellish scene around her seemed to be a portent of things to come and she was paralysed by anxiety. Then Eliza was beside her, squeezing her hand.

'I wish I could have been your bridesmaid,' she whispered.

'I wish so too, Eliza.' Then Amy lowered her voice: 'Never mind, you will be the godmother of our first child instead.'

As dawn rose over the violet-tinted ranges, the town of Granthurst became visible in the valley below, its church steeples and iron-roofed houses emerging from the shadows of the night. Amy had slept through most of the journey, her head resting on Charles's shoulder. They had made good time, even allowing for the regular breaks that Joseph took to rest and water the horses. When they arrived at the railway station, the town was still asleep.

'We are here, my darling,' Charles said, rousing her.

She had been lost in a dream about Charles. Then she opened her eyes and knew it was real. Before her was the deep yellow of the station building with its central clock tower and iron columns. They had an hour before the Sydney train left.

'Let us find an inn and partake of some breakfast,' suggested Charles.

'I shall leave you now,' said Joseph.

'No, Joseph, please come and eat with us,' said Amy. 'You have been such a dear friend to me and a loyal brother to Charles. Do not leave us yet.' She wondered whether he still had feelings for her. It was impossible to tell from the expression on his face.

Soon they were seated inside an inn directly opposite the railway station. The proprietor couldn't keep his eyes off the blond-haired boy and the girl who might have been his sister, travelling with a well-dressed Chinaman. Charles caught the man staring.

'Are you sure about this, Amy? We will never be anonymous. We cannot simply disappear into a crowd like everybody else.'

'I know. But I don't care what other people might think about us,' she said defiantly.

Just before nine Joseph bade them farewell. He was going to buy supplies for Millerbrooke in Granthurst's famed general store and then begin the long journey home.

'I almost forgot,' he said, producing from his pocket a small box tied with a ribbon. 'This is from Eliza, Daniel and me. Open it on your wedding day.'

In the distance the church bells of Granthurst were tolling the nine o'clock service. While Charles was buying the train tickets, Amy slipped away to the red pillar-box outside the station and dropped in a letter addressed to her parents.

Dearest Mama and Papa,
I am sorry I have worried you by my sudden departure and I pray you will forgive me for disobeying you. Sadly you have left me no choice but to elope with the man I love.

There is no point in contacting Aunt Molly. She is far away in Sydney and I have not informed her of where I am lodging.

When Charles and I return to Millbrooke as a married couple, I pray that we will all be reunited as a family.

Please give the boys a kiss for me.
Ever your loving daughter,
Amy

It wasn't full of falsehoods, just the evasions at which she was so skilled. More than anything she was hoping the letter with its Granthurst postmark would divert her father's attention from Sydney and have him scouring closer to home for a Chinaman with a white fiancée.

'Why don't you try to sleep?' Amy whispered to Charles as they sat in a compartment opposite an elderly lady who was reading.

'I shall try,' said Charles, but she noticed him waking every few minutes as if he were on guard duty.

The woman was holding her book so high in front of her face that Amy could read the title printed in gold on the cover. It was *The Pilgrim's Progress*. Even her father would approve of John Bunyan.

Whenever Charles dozed, Amy observed his face. Two vertical frown lines, which she hadn't noticed before, had appeared between his brows. She raised her hand to smooth them away and then realised the elderly lady opposite her was no longer reading but staring at her and Charles instead. Although she knew it was rude to do so, Amy stared back. The woman lowered her eyes and continued reading.

Where had the worried expression on Charles's face come from? Amy knew he hated deception and lies. Dishonesty was against his nature. How could an honourable man like Charles justify an elopement? It would eat away at him.

She felt ill. It was her fault. She knew how much he loved her and she had pressured him until he gave in. She had tainted him with her impatience and her capacity for deceit.

While Charles napped, she stroked his hand and didn't care whether the woman saw or not. All the same, a tiny nugget of fear lodged deep inside her.

From Redfern terminal, they took a carriage to the inn that Charles's solicitor had organised for them in George Street. Then, using the services of a messenger employed by the innkeeper, they sent notes to the minister of religion and to Aunt Molly, seeking meetings for the next day.

Dearest Aunt Molly,

By now you may have received a telegram from my father and if you have, you will be acquainted with the events which have occurred these past days. I am sorry to involve you in this situation.

You know, of course, of my feelings for Charles Chen. What you do not know is that he returned from China without a bride. He could not bring himself to follow the traditions of his homeland or to satisfy the long-held expectations of his dear mother. The reason, as you might have guessed by now, is that he was already in love with someone else. A Scottish girl living in Millbrooke! He asked me to marry him and naturally I accepted. However, when he sought consent from my father, he was met by insults and abuse. It broke my heart to see him treated in that way. Nevertheless, Charles was determined to persuade my father of his cause, but you and I are familiar with the intransigence of Matthew Duncan. Aunt Molly, there was <u>no</u> hope of my father changing his mind.

So I convinced Charles we should elope. We are here in Sydney, lodging in George Street. We need your assistance in presenting our case to a minister of religion with whom Charles has been in touch via his solicitor. Would it be convenient for us to come to see you tomorrow morning to discuss these matters?

When you meet Charles, you will understand.

Your loving niece,

Amy

P.S. The messenger will wait for your reply.

On Sunday night as they were preparing for bed, the innkeeper knocked at the door.

'Mr and Mrs Miller, I thought you might care for some tea and biscuits.' He was holding a tray.

'Thank you, sir. Please set it on the table,' said Charles.

The man's probing stare made Amy wonder if the refreshments weren't simply a pretext to spy on them. Apparently Charles was thinking the same thing because his next words were uncharacteristically terse.

'That will be all, thank you,' he said, walking the innkeeper to the bedroom door and shutting it firmly behind him.

When they finished their tea, Charles offered to sleep in an armchair. Then Amy told him how Aladdin was so distraught about the prospect of his beloved princess spending her wedding night with the Chief Minister's son that he had his faithful genie imprison the bridegroom for the night. And afterwards Aladdin took the groom's place in the princess's bed, placing a sword between them.

'We shall have an imaginary sword,' she said.

'It is a fairytale, Amy. I'm not sure that I can sleep so close to you.'

Like Aladdin and his princess, they lay down on the bed with an invisible sword separating them. Although Amy was tired, she couldn't sleep. Not when Charles was beside her, taking every breath in unison with hers. She wanted to reach across the barrier and place her hand in his, but something told her that if she embarked upon such a step, there would be no going back. When his breathing became softer, she knew he was finally asleep. Then she too succumbed to the tiredness that had been dogging her all day.

On Monday afternoon at two o'clock, Charles Chen, Amy Duncan and Molly Mackenzie were seated on a sofa opposite the Reverend Jacob Foster in the parlour of his rectory.

'Mrs Mackenzie, I understand you acted as Miss Duncan's guardian while she was residing in Sydney.'

'That is correct. I can supply a letter from a Miss Howe of Miss Howe's School for Ladies verifying that I have been Amy's guardian.'

Amy squirmed. Poor Aunt Molly. It wasn't technically a falsehood. Although no such letter actually existed, theoretically they could obtain one, should they choose to contact Miss Howe, but the truth was that Amy had been reluctant to do so. Not yet. The fewer people who knew, the better.

Reverend Foster considered the statement and then replied: 'In that case, I can see no problem regarding consent. There are, however, other matters we need to clarify.' He directed his next words to Amy and Charles. 'Is either of you already married?'

They both shook their heads.

'There is also the matter of kinship. This refers to the prohibition on a brother and sister marrying. But it is obvious in this case that there is no such relationship between the two parties.'

Amy and Charles exchanged smiles. Something which had caused her father to reject the marriage was now a point in their favour.

'Before we proceed, I need to counsel you both that you have chosen a difficult path. You will be shunned by many in our society.'

'We have taken that into account, Reverend Foster,' said Charles.

'And our love for each other is strong enough to withstand the censure,' said Amy.

'I am pleased to hear that and I pray it is so. You realise, of course, that the banns must be read for three successive Sundays. I understand that the respective parish churches of the two parties are distant from here. Nevertheless, we could organise the notification by letter.'

'But, Reverend Foster,' said Aunt Molly, 'we have already established there is no impediment to the marriage of Amy and Charles. So there is no need for notification elsewhere. Surely, it would be sufficient to post the banns here at St Paul's. After all, Sydney Town is the very heart of the colony.'

Amy held her breath.

'Yes, I concur, Mrs Mackenzie. And I would be delighted to solemnise the union of this charming couple. Shall we make a date for the ceremony?'

It was agreed that the wedding would take place on the Monday following the third reading of the banns: 23rd December, 1872.

Aladdin and Badroulboudour slept chaste and unmarried in the same bed for less than a week, yet it seemed like a lifetime to the young man who wanted only to be with her. Afterwards her father dissolved the marriage with the Chief Minister's son on the grounds of non-consummation. Only when Aladdin was able to convince the Sultan of the worthiness of his suit, did he wed the princess. But for Amy and Charles, there was no convincing her father, and it wasn't just a few nights, but three weeks before they could be married. Three weeks of the invisible sword. In Amy's case, those nights together had ignited new feelings within her. She had always assumed that the heart was the site of all things pertaining to love, but now she suspected there was somewhere else, a secret place whose power would be unlocked when she and Charles were finally married.

At the end of their first week in Sydney, a letter arrived at Charles's Sydney solicitor's office, addressed to Miss Amy Duncan.

My dearest Amy,
I trust that you are both well. There has been a big kerfuffle in your absence, involving your father and mine. The night after you left, the Reverend stormed up to Millerbrooke and accused Joseph of aiding in your elopement. Poor Joseph, who had only just returned from Granthurst, was so tired he could barely speak.

Then your father called me a wicked girl for encouraging you to disobey your parents. My father stood his ground and declared that if the Reverend had behaved in a Godly manner, none of this would have happened. He even called your father a narrow-minded bigot. It was a rousing sight.

Never fear, Amy, we did not disclose your whereabouts. Then again, I might have let the word 'Granthurst' slip during the conversation...
Yours ever,
Eliza

Charles kept himself busy by visiting the warehouses which lined the wharves of Pyrmont, and sometimes Amy accompanied him. She was fascinated by the rows of tea chests stamped with exotic writing.

'You must teach me Cantonese, Charles.'

That very evening, he taught her to say the numbers from one to ten. When he wrote them down, she marvelled at his calligraphy.

'I don't think I will ever be able to write it,' she said.

'As long as you can understand and read, you will manage. But once we get back to Millbrooke, I fear I will be too busy to teach you.'

'Perhaps I can teach your brother English and he can teach me Chinese in return.'

'He would like that, Amy.'

Sometimes they took tea in one of the eating-houses near the harbour, and reminded each other of the day they drank cinnamon tisane when he was Mr Chen, the merchant, and she his customer.

'When did you fall in love with me, Charles?' she would ask him as they sipped their tea.

'I have already told you, Amy,' he would reply.

'Tell me again.'

'It was when I saw you silhouetted against the doorway that very first morning. With your halo of golden hair I thought you were an angel.'

Every Sunday for three weeks they attended St Paul's Church where their banns were read in front of the congregation. The first Sunday, there had been some shocked looks and a chorus of whispers as they entered the church. The next week they were greeted with fewer inquisitive looks and even some smiles. By the third week they were taking morning tea with the rest of the congregation following the service. Although there were some who refused to converse with them, there were many others who were charmed by Charles's exquisite manners and gentle ways.

A few days before the wedding Amy was buying white hair ribbon in a haberdashery near their lodgings when she heard an excited voice saying: 'Amy Duncan! Is that really you?'

Amy looked around to see a young woman in a smart striped dress and jaunty black bonnet trimmed with matching feathers. It was Dora Barnes who had been at Miss Howe's, two years ahead of Amy. Although they had never been confidantes or even close friends, Amy had been suitably impressed when Dora left to complete her education at a finishing school on the Continent.

'Dora Barnes. How lovely to see you.'

'It's Dora Digby-Watts now,' she said, indicating a thick gold wedding band. 'So much has happened since I last saw you, Amy. Do you have time for a cup of tea and I shall tell you everything?'

Dora swept Amy out of the shop and around the corner to a tearoom filled with well-dressed ladies partaking of high tea and speaking in low voices.

'I met my husband when I was in London for the season,' said Dora, once they were seated at a table in the bay window overlooking the street. 'For some years he had been considering the idea of emigrating to New South Wales, but he had always procrastinated. After he met me, he knew his future lay here rather than in England.'

'How romantic,' sighed Amy.

'Yes, indeed. He followed me home on the next ship and sought my father's permission for us to marry.'

'Was your father in agreement?'

'Why, of course he was. Rupert is a wealthy man from a good English family.'

'He sounds very nice.'

'You must come and meet him. Perhaps next week.'

'That may be difficult. I am afraid I shan't be in Sydney very long. I'm just visiting.'

The waiter delivered a tiered stand holding tiny sandwiches and scones, and then returned with a teapot decorated with roses.

'Where do you live now?' asked Dora, helping herself to a scone.

'Millbrooke. My father was posted there last year.'

'I have never heard of it.'

'It's a gold town.'

'I expect Rupert would know it. Gold is his livelihood.'

'Is he a prospector?'

'Heavens, no,' laughed Dora. 'He is an assayer. Precious metals. He has a big office down by the Quay with a view of the harbour. He can watch the ships coming in.'

'That must be very pleasant.'

'Not when a boat is loaded with Celestials. He says they march off in their funny hats and pigtails and head straight for the latest boom town. They actually *walk* there! What a primitive lot they are!'

Dora didn't pause long enough for Amy to respond.

'Too many of them are here already, Rupert says. They should be shipped back to where they came from. That would deter the others.' She lowered her voice to a whisper. 'They are sent here by secret societies in China who plan to overrun the colony.'

'Did Rupert tell you this?'

'Everyone knows it, Amy. The Celestials are a strange people. We do not need types like that in our country.'

Amy almost choked on the morsel of scone she had just placed in her mouth. It struck her that there would be many similar conversations in her future, and she would have to decide how to deal with them, whether to listen meekly to the ignorant hearsay or to take a stand. She cleared her throat.

'There is something you should know, Dora. I am about to

marry a Chinaman. He is the best person I have ever met. As for judging others by the colour of their skin, their place of birth or any such generality, it is an unreliable measure. Someone might walk into this tearoom right now and think you and I were alike. A *type*, as you call it. We both have yellow hair and pale complexions. But in our hearts, we are as different as ...' She hesitated, trying to think of the perfect simile. Nothing came to mind, and her voice trailed off.

She removed some coins from her purse and placed them on the table. 'I must take my leave. I have wedding matters awaiting my attention. Good afternoon.' Then she rose and walked towards the door. Not once did she look back.

That afternoon, Charles persuaded Amy to send a note to Miss Howe's School, asking Amy's two closest friends to be her attendants and inviting the headmistress and her students to St Paul's Church for the wedding.

'It is a futile gesture, Charles. I very much doubt that any of them will attend. Not even Miss Howe.'

'Do it regardless, Amy. Let us not assume everyone is like Dora.'

Reverend Foster had warned them it was bad luck to see the bride before the service, offering Charles an invitation to spend the morning hours at his rectory instead. By the time Amy woke in their room at the inn, Charles was already gone. There was a note written in his elegant script beside the bed.

Dearest One,
Soon we will belong to each other, not just for the rest of our lives but forever.

Tonight we can banish the sword from our bed.
Yours always,
Charles

Outside the window, Sydney Town was bustling with merchants touting their wares and Christmas shoppers rushing about in the heat. Meanwhile Amy and her two friends were unpacking a large box delivered that morning by messenger. The girls had turned up at half past ten in the white dresses they reserved for Sunday best.

'Just imagine,' said one of them, 'in a few hours you will be Mrs Chen. It is such an exotic name.'

'Is he handsome, Amy?' asked the other.

'You'll have to wait and see,' Amy teased, relieved that these two, at least, seemed pleased about her imminent nuptials.

When they finally removed the string and opened the box, they squealed with excitement. Inside was the most exquisite gown any of them had ever seen – Aunt Molly's wedding dress. Carefully, Amy stepped into it, taking pains not to stand on the long lace train. Her friends secured the column of tiny buttons running down the back. It fitted perfectly.

As Amy's carriage arrived at the church, Aunt Molly was there to greet her. So was Doctor Fullerton, who had been kind to her when she was ill.

'Would you allow me to walk you down the aisle, Miss Amy?' he asked.

'I would be delighted,' she replied.

Molly fussed with Amy's train and plumped the folds of her skirt.

'After I wed your Uncle Edward, I dreamed of having a

daughter to wear this dress, but we were never blessed with children. Instead, I have been blessed with a special niece. You are a courageous girl, Amy. I don't know if I could have done it.'

Then Molly followed the others into the church. Amy looked around, fearing her father might be lurking outside, ready to rush up and declare an impediment. The Granthurst ruse had worked for a while, but then he must have suspected his sister-in-law's involvement because there had been a stream of telegrams and letters seeking the whereabouts of his daughter, and since Amy and Charles had never informed her of the address of their lodging house, Molly could truthfully say she had no idea. Even the delivery of the wedding gown had taken place via the solicitor's office.

As she walked down the aisle on Doctor Fullerton's arm, the sense of unease Amy had experienced outside the church hung over her like a dark cloud. Only by keeping her gaze fixed on Charles standing at the altar was she able to calm herself. When she reached his side, he mouthed the words, 'I love you.' Focusing on his liquid eyes, she told herself to think of nothing else.

Reverend Foster's sermon was gentle and encouraging. He didn't mention their differences; only that they were a fine young couple with a promising life ahead of them. She prayed it would be so. Finally it was time for their vows. Charles repeated his in a strong, determined voice. Amy spoke softly but didn't falter. After the minister declared them man and wife, the congregation applauded.

Suddenly they were outside in the sunshine and the feeling of foreboding was gone. Nobody could separate them now, not even Matthew Duncan.

After the service, they retired to Aunt Molly's house for a reception. She had hung a white chiffon bow on the front door and arranged large urns of yellow roses in the drawing room. There were canapés on silver trays and champagne served in crystal flutes. Miss Howe was there and a few of her pupils. Amy wondered about the others. Were they absent simply because it was a school day, or did they find the idea of their friend marrying a Chinaman repugnant? She couldn't bring herself to ask Miss Howe.

When Amy went upstairs to change into her magenta dress, she found a large box on the bed. She recalled seeing it once before – in Jimmy's arms on the night of the elopement. Inside was yet another gown. But whereas the wedding dress was white and virginal, this one was turquoise silk, fit for an Oriental empress. She ran her hand over the fabric, which was lavishly embroidered with sprigs of flowers like a *mille-fleurs* tapestry.

'My husband had this dress made for me,' she told her attendants proudly.

Late in the afternoon, Amy in her new gown and Charles in his smart black suit caught the steamer to Manly. Charles had booked a room in a little hostelry overlooking the ocean beach. After supper they opened the box from the Miller siblings. Inside was a scroll containing a text in Eliza's writing.

Dearest Charles and Darling Amy,
We wanted to give you the best crystal or the most delicate porcelain, but it would not have survived the journey to Granthurst. Not in the Millerbrooke dray, at any rate. Instead, we are offering you our love, friendship and loyalty. If you need any one of us, or all three for that matter, we will be at your service. Do not fear to ask. We love you both dearly.
Your devoted friends,
Eliza, Joseph and Daniel

That night Amy learned what had happened to Aladdin and the princess after the nuptial festivities were over, when the invisible sword was banished from their marital bed. No wonder there was a gap in the story, followed by the words 'next morning'. It was the most wonderful secret of all.

Now

There were times when Angie regretted even dreaming up the 'Aspects of Millbrooke' project. It had become bigger than *Ben-Hur*, or in Millbrooke terms, bigger than the Millbrooke Agricultural Show, the premier social event of the district.

The painting class, however, had embraced the project with enthusiasm.

'Where shall we hold the exhibition, Angie?' asked Ros.

'I thought we might try to book a room in the library.'

'Surely we could do better than that,' said Narelle. 'What about the School of Arts?'

'We could have an opening night with champagne and nibbles,' suggested Jennie.

'And Devonshire teas for sale during the day,' added Moira.

'You could invite entries from the whole community, even the school,' said Ros.

'And the TAFE students in Granthurst,' said Tanya.

'We could ask Sam Porter to open it,' said Moira.

'Who's he?' asked Narelle.

'Crikey, Narelle, wake up!' said Jennie. 'He's your local MP.'

'We don't want bloody politicians involved,' protested Narelle, neatly ducking Jennie's allusion to her indifference to politics.

'What about Jack?' asked Jennie. 'Angie, you could ask him.'

'Hmm,' said Angie, wondering how she could calm them down.

'We could give the profits to a local charity,' said Moira.

'Which one?' asked Jennie.

A debate ensued about the possibilities.

'We don't even have our artworks finished yet,' said Angie, trying to focus them on the task at hand.

'Jennie and I have made a lot of progress on ours,' said Narelle. Behind them was a large canvas wrapped in old sheets. 'Do you want to see it?'

The two women triumphantly unveiled their painting; it was divided into four columns and five rows, each of the twenty rectangles framed by a black border.

'We used rolls of masking tape to mark the borders,' explained Narelle. 'But when we stripped it off, the black paint had seeped underneath.'

'We fixed it though,' said Jennie.

Inside each rectangle they had pencilled in the name of a Millbrooke personality. In a few of the rectangles a finished portrait appeared, recognisable, if slightly caricatured. There was Lisa from the pub and Nola from the B&B. Near the centre was an image which made Angie smile broadly. It was herself, with the Manse in the background.

'So that was why you took all those pictures of me last week.'

'Do you like it?' Jennie asked.

'I think it's wonderful.'

'We have a confession to make,' whispered Narelle. 'We used photos and traced the outlines.'

'It doesn't matter,' said Angie. 'They're *your* photos. And I credit, Richard, who had known about the contents for years, had kept the collection intact in their original trunk.

As she reached the story of Aladdin, Angie found something folded inside. Four sheets of what appeared to be a story, written in copperplate script with pen and ink. Nobody wrote like that any more. She put on her glasses and began to read. The text was by an Eliza Miller who had lived at Millerbrooke House, Richard Scott's place.

It was an homage to Charles Chen.

Why would a piece of writing by Eliza Miller be sitting inside Amy Duncan's book? Were they friends? Even so, why give Amy your story? Angie couldn't wait to tell the painting ladies about her discovery. No doubt they would have their own theories as to its significance, but surely Charles Chen had to be the link. Could there have been a romance between Charles and Amy? It seemed unlikely – a Chinese man and a Scottish girl. Not in the 1870s. Unless Amy had harboured a secret crush on him. Just like Angie's. Yet another connection between the two of them – Amy infatuated with the flesh-and-blood man and Angie with his miniature portrait.

12

HIC SUNT DRACONES: HERE BE DRAGONS

1872–1873

On the third day of Christmas Amy and Charles returned to Millbrooke as Mr and Mrs Chen. Charles was of a mind to go directly to the Manse to speak with Amy's father.

'Now we are married, he will have to relent. He will realise my intentions have always been honourable. He will see we are happy. And he will welcome you back into his life.'

Amy didn't believe that, and she wasn't ready for a confrontation with her father, not while she was still basking in the glow of her honeymoon. Instead, she suggested they go to Charles's house in Paterson Street. After all, she had never been inside.

From the street it resembled most of the residences in Millbrooke: single storey, timber construction, tin roof with a verandah stretching around three sides. However, one aspect differed very colourfully from its neighbours – a glossy red front door. As Charles carried Amy over the threshold, she entered a world which could have been created by Aladdin's genie.

The parlour contained an overstuffed sofa and stiff velvet armchairs of the kind you might expect in the house of any well-to-do merchant, except that they were strewn with red brocade cushions, trimmed with gold tassels. Rosewood side tables held brassware and cloisonné bowls. The walls were hung with traditional English landscapes, but also hand-painted Chinese scrolls. At the far end of the room stood a cabinet whose glass doors bore a criss-cross pattern of mock bamboo. Amy ran her fingers over the intricate fretwork.

'It is called Chinese Chippendale,' said Charles.

Behind the glass a collection of Staffordshire figurines was arranged among pieces of blue and white Oriental porcelain. She discovered a statue of Lord Nelson and a pair of English spaniels. There was even a china figure of George Washington.

'Lord Nelson and General Washington,' said Amy. 'They are my heroes.'

'Mine too,' Charles said.

Over the fireplace was a large scroll decorated with a dragon looking towards the sky. Below it she spotted a miniature painting among the porcelain boxes arranged on the mantel.

'Charles, it's you,' she exclaimed with delight, 'in your turquoise waistcoat.' Carefully she picked up the tiny picture and placed it in her hand. 'It's exquisite. Look at the details. Imagine being able to paint something so small.'

'It was a gift from my family – my Millerbrooke family. I shall commission the same artist to paint one of you so that we can be together on the mantel.'

Amy beamed. She had never dreamed of having her portrait painted, even in miniature. That was for rich people.

Then Charles took her by the hand. 'Now come and see our bedroom.'

Behind a gold-leaf screen decorated with birds on the wing and twining flowers hid a four-poster bed covered with a jade-green silk coverlet and piles of embroidered pillows.

'Oh, it's beautiful,' said Amy. 'I'm afraid I should never want to leave this room.' She sat down on the bed and patted the coverlet. 'Come here, husband.'

They sat together, hand in hand, and Amy felt abundantly blessed to be the mistress of this house, wife of this man.

'I suppose you should show me the rest of the house,' she said after a while.

'Jimmy's room is across the hall,' said Charles, 'but he will be staying at the emporium now we are back.'

'No, he must remain here, Charles,' said Amy. 'It is his home too.'

'Well, he is not here now, Amy,' said Charles with a wicked smile, 'so let us celebrate our first day back in Millbrooke.'

And they spent the afternoon in their silken bed.

On the first Sunday after their homecoming – the last in December – Amy and Charles set off to attend the morning service at St Aidan's. As they made their way down the aisle, hand in hand, heads turned like marionettes on strings, and whispers hummed like bees swarming through the congregation. They took a seat in the second row, behind Margaret Duncan and her sons. When the boys turned around to check the source of the ruckus, they could not contain themselves.

'Mama, it's Amy. She's back!'

Robbie and Billy stood in unison, as if to embrace their sister. Amy's mother turned and gave her a quick smile, before telling the boys to sit still because the service was about to begin.

At that moment Reverend Duncan entered the chancel from the vestry and climbed the steps to the lectern. The organist began to play the first few bars of 'And Can It Be That I Should Gain?'. As the congregation rose from the pews, Matthew Duncan saw Amy and Charles. His face turned a molten red and his mouth dropped open, though not in song. Amy flinched at the thought that he might stride down from the lectern and give vent to the violence she could read in his face. But he did not move. The congregation was already in full throat.

> *No condemnation now I dread;*
> *Jesus, and all in Him, is mine;*
> *Alive in Him, my living Head,*
> *And clothed in righteousness divine,*
> *Bold I approach th' eternal throne,*
> *And claim the crown, through Christ my own.*

'No condemnation now I dread,' whispered Charles to Amy.

She held his hand and breathed deeply. 'There is nothing he can do to us,' she whispered to herself.

'Today I am abandoning the sermon about the Three Wise Men that I had planned to deliver on this fifth day of Christmas,' announced Matthew Duncan to the congregation. 'I intend to tell ye a story instead. Children, listen well. It is a warning about the dangers of dealing with the devil.'

Amy swallowed hard. She had not expected this, that her father would make his feelings public.

'Once upon a time there was a wee white duckling. Her parents raised her to be virtuous and god-fearing. Instead, she grew up to be headstrong and deceitful. One day, they sent her to do the messages and warned her not to go near the slant-eyed mole. But the silly duck was tempted by the fancy wares the mole was selling. He persuaded her to come inside his burrow where he gave her a magic potion disguised as tea. No sooner had she taken a wee sip, than she found herself in his thrall. When the father duck learned about her visit, he made her promise ne'er to see the mole again. But she began meeting him in secret. Soon he convinced her to run away with him. Aided by a flock of wild ducks who should have known better, the mismatched pair travelled to a distant city known for its licentiousness. There they broke the laws of God by consorting with each other. A duck and a mole – it was a perversion. A few weeks later, they returned, thinking all would be forgiven. But how could her parents forgive the wee white duck when she had openly defied them?'

Amy felt Charles's hand gripping hers. She didn't dare look at his face. Silently she prayed: Please, God, let this be over soon.

'The duck and the mole paraded around the town as if they were the Prince and Princess of Wales. But their sins wouldna go unpunished. One day the duck laid an egg. When it finally cracked open, she screamed in horror at what lay inside. Instead of a fluffy white duckling, there was an ungodly creature no-one had e'er seen before. Instead of feathers, it was covered in fur. Where there should have been a delicate beak, a leathery snout protruded like a deformity. And the eyes were so tiny, it could scarcely see. The creature was a travesty. A mongrel. The child of the devil. Can anyone tell me the name of the offspring of the white duck and the slant-eyed mole?'

In the front row Robbie put his hand up. 'A duck-mole, Papa.'

'That is correct, Robert. And there is an important lesson to be learned from the story of the duck and the mole. When ye consort with the devil, ye *will* be punished.

'"But the fearful, and unbelieving, and the abominable, and murderers, and whoremongers, and sorcerers, and idolaters, and all liars, shall have their part in the lake which burneth with fire and brimstone: which is the second death." Revelations 21:8.

'We shall now sing hymn number two hundred and thirty-nine, "Praise My Soul the King of Heaven".'

Amy's throat was dry. She couldn't sing. She looked across at her husband. His cheeks were flushed, but he was standing tall and singing with conviction.

As soon as the benediction was over, Reverend Duncan left the chancel, proceeding down the aisle with his gaze fixed straight ahead. Margaret Duncan turned around with tears in her eyes.

'I am so sorry, Amy.'

As they left their pew, Charles made to leave by the front door, but this time it was Amy who chose to avoid a confrontation.

'Charles, I am as upset as you are. But there is no point in making a scene in front of the entire St Aidan's congregation. Let us make a dignified exit. And next Sunday we shall attend St John's instead.'

On Monday night the Miller family held a reception for the newlyweds at Millerbrooke House. Although Mr Miller had specifically invited Jimmy, he declined to attend. Amy tried to persuade him to change his mind, but in vain.

'He is embarrassed about his English,' explained Charles when he and Amy were alone.

'The Millers would understand.'

'You and I know that, but he would be uncomfortable trying to keep up with the conversation.'

So Amy and Charles went on their own, he in his turquoise waistcoat and she in her matching dress. While she had been convalescing in Sydney, she had tormented herself with the picture of an evening like this, imagining somebody else as the object of Charles's adoration. How life had turned topsy-turvy. The rival from Amy's daydreams was seated on the sofa. The young lady with the dark ringlets. But she wasn't called Blanche Ingram. Her name was Flora and she was the sweetheart of Daniel Miller, which explained why she had been seated in the Millers' pew at Peggy's funeral. Next to Flora sat another young woman, who wore her hair in golden curls like Amy's. Judging by the attention Joseph was lavishing on her, it appeared he had found his true love. Amy couldn't help smiling at the swiftness with which he had transferred his affections.

'Our maid, Matilda, attends your father's church,' Eliza whispered to Amy. 'She told me what happened yesterday.'

'It was as hideous as the night Charles came to the Manse to ask for my hand in marriage.'

'Matilda thought the sermon was cruel. She said you and Charles have several supporters in the congregation, but they are too afraid of your father to speak up.'

'I suspect my mother is one of them.'

'Can you blame her, Amy? She has been forced to choose between you and your father.'

'No, I cannot. It is her duty, I suppose. Still, I miss my family.'

'Of course you do, but you have all of us.'

'I do indeed. And I cannot imagine anything more wonderful than being Mrs Chen. Charles is such a gentle and considerate husband.'

'I told you he is the finest person I know,' said Eliza with a grin. 'By-the-bye, Amy, I have some news for you.'

'Have you met a special young man?'

'Of course not. It is far more serious than that! My father has obtained a subscription to *The Lancet*.'

'The what?'

'It is a medical journal from England.'

'How will you ever find time to read all these journals, Eliza?'

'I won't waste my time reading silly novels,' she replied with a smile. 'Speaking of journals, another one has arrived in the post from France. I shall need help in translating it. Can we resume our classes, Amy?'

Amy laughed. 'Why don't you come tomorrow afternoon? Then you can stay for Jimmy's lesson. I am teaching him English and he is teaching me Chinese.'

'Chinese might be useful for a doctor. What do you think?'

'I think a doctor fluent in English, French and Chinese would be unique, especially if she were a woman.'

'Are you making fun of me?'

'No, I admire your determination, Eliza. I just wonder what will happen when a handsome young man comes along and steals your heart.'

'If I were forced to choose between love and vocation, I would choose the latter.'

'Do you think it might ever be possible for women to have both?'

'No, Amy, I do not. Not in a world where men are rulers and women subordinates. Not when women cannot control their own lives or even their ability to procreate.'

Amy caught her breath. Sometimes Eliza could say the most shocking things.

Not long after their return, Charles and Jimmy planned to spend a day at the diggings as part of the anti-opium campaign, distributing pamphlets and speaking to the miners. Meanwhile Amy had volunteered to watch over the emporium. Although it wasn't generally considered proper for a lady to serve behind the counter, she had convinced Charles there was nothing wrong with her helping out now and again.

'Are you sure you can manage on your own, Amy?'

'Of course, Charles. After all, I am well informed on the subject of tea, having been taught by an expert,' she teased, skimming her hand along the lids of the boxes. 'And I can hold a discourse on the silks if required. You may find they have all been sold by the time you return, and that your shelves of porcelain have been rearranged.' She picked up a red bowl, placed it on the shelf containing blue and white items, and waited for Charles's reaction.

But he just laughed and hugged her. 'We shall be back before nightfall.'

'Good,' she said. 'You shouldn't be there after dark.'

She knew from Eliza's composition why Charles hated the goldfields.

'Next time you go, I would like to come with you,' she said. In all the months she had been living in Millbrooke, she had never once been to the diggings. Although her father ran a service every Sunday afternoon for the miners, he hadn't allowed her to accompany him.

It was a particularly busy day at the emporium and Amy barely had time to make herself a cup of tea. She was looking forward to Charles's return so she could tell him about selling a china platter, a brocade tablecloth and a lacquered chest which had only arrived that very week. Just before closing time, a customer who was purchasing a tin of tea remarked affably, 'That Mr Chen is a real gent.'

Amy smiled warmly in response.

Then he added, 'He's as honest as a white man.'

The last sentence echoed in her head. Was it a compliment or something altogether different? Amy knew for a fact that honesty had nothing to do with race or skin colour.

The following week, Amy and Charles went to the goldfields while Jimmy ran the store. Although it was early in the day, the January sun was already hot, and in spite of her bonnet, Amy could feel her face burning. She wished she possessed golden skin like her husband's, instead of a pale Scottish complexion which reddened in the heat and freckled in the sunlight. When they reached the hill leading down to the river, she was amazed at the city of tents and bark huts spread out before her.

'Look at the flags, Charles. It is an international assemblage.' She picked out the blue St Andrew's cross, the red cross of St George and even the *tricolore*. 'What is the flag with the white star?'

'That's the lone star of Texas.'

'And the star and the bear?'

'California. They had a Gold Rush there too.'

'Where are the Chinese?'

'They have their own camp, on the other side of the river at a place called Chinaman's Cove,' he said, pointing across the broad expanse of water.

'Do they choose to live separately for their safety?'

'I suspect so. In spite of Eliza's courageous resolution, they are still wary. They travel back and forth each day by barge.'

Charles pulled up the cart not far from a group of Chinese miners who were working a pile of tailings left by the other prospectors. He got down and began calling out in Chinese. The miners stopped work and gathered around him. Dressed in his smart brown suit and hat, he looked as if he had come directly from the city. Then he began to address the crowd. Although Amy couldn't understand a word of what Charles was saying, she could sense that his address was compelling. Why else would his audience be so silent and still?

'What did you say to them?' she asked when the group had dispersed.

'I am warning that opium is the path to dissipation and ruin, and they will find themselves spending all their money on the fearful substance and having nothing to send home to their families. And I am reminding them that by frequenting opium dens, they are only fuelling the stories some Westerners spread about the Chinese.'

During the morning, Charles moved from group to group, repeating his message, while Amy walked among the crowd, handing out pamphlets written in their language, bearing an illustration of an opium pipe with a cross drawn through it.

At noon she produced a basket with bread and cold meat, after which Charles returned to his speeches. As the light began to wane, she tugged on his arm.

'We must leave before dark, Charles.'

'Just one more group,' he said.

By the time he had finished speaking, the sky was almost black, save for a streak of orange over the horizon. Barges had begun to ferry the Chinese miners across the river to their camp. As the couple made their way back to the horse and cart, he stopped abruptly, as if a ghost had crossed his path.

'Don't move, Amy,' he said, holding her by the arm.

'What is it?'

In the fading light he pointed to a hole in the ground. It wasn't square and reinforced with timber like a European mine shaft, but circular. Peering into the hole, Amy saw that it was half filled with water.

'It is all right, Charles. You realised the danger in time. Nothing will happen to us. We are safe.'

When they were seated in the cart, Charles whispered: 'Do you know why the Chinese dig circular shafts? So that evil spirits cannot hide in the corners. But whether a hole has corners or not, it always has the power to kill.'

Amy clasped his hand reassuringly. Even though it had been fifteen years since the accident, the little boy who tried in vain to save his drowning father still lived deep inside Charles Chen.

Now

Jack Parker was one of those old-fashioned cowboys who tipped their hat to the ladies with a 'Howdy, ma'am.' Every night he would knock at Angie's door. And mostly she would reply, 'Come in. The door's not locked,' and he would appear in his boxer shorts.

Although he didn't actually call her 'ma'am', he didn't take her favours for granted. It was partly his innate good manners, and partly that Angie had made a rule for herself. Despite the fact that she might want the comfort of sex and the warmth of his body, there were nights when she would say no. Then he would wish her a goodnight through the closed door and pad across the hall to his room. She would hear him turn off the light and climb into his own bed. It was important that he didn't become indispensable to her, that she could spend a night without Mr Songbird.

Lately, he had been confiding in her, as they lay in each other's arms after making love. Not about personal things, but about River Cove and the endless negotiations with the government and its departments. He had heard rumours of a new tax to be imposed on foreign mining companies. Already other multi-nationals were heading for more profitable locations. And Jack couldn't escape the presence of the platypuses. They were looming as the biggest obstacle to the mine, the symbol of everything that might be endangered if the project was approved. All around town, opponents of the project had taken to wearing black T-shirts featuring a fluoro-pink platypus.

Even when Jack was relaxing on the paved area at the back of the Manse, having a twilight drink, the platypus would be nearby, its circlets of ripples taunting him, so that he would retreat inside and finish his drink in the kitchen.

'You need to learn how to clip their nails,' said Richard as they stood in the centre of the alpaca paddock.

'Can't *you* just clip their nails for me?' The thought of it made Angie nervous. What if she cut their soft little feet? 'I couldn't even bring myself to cut the boys' nails when they were babies. Phil always did it for me.' There, she had said his name and her eyes remained dry.

'Well, I suppose I could do it for you,' said Richard, proceeding to give them a manicure in a very professional fashion, almost as if he were a vet.

'Thanks, Richard. I don't mind raking up dung or cleaning the feeder, but cutting nails sets my teeth on edge.'

Richard had brought a photo of his latest alpaca baby. 'Other people have grandchildren. I have crias.'

Even though he said it in a joking way, Angie wondered if there wasn't an undertone.

'I've never seen anything so adorable, Richard. Much cuter than a human baby. I hope Snow White gets pregnant. I think she fancies Jet.'

'You're probably right. He's a ladies' man. Handsome, confident, charming. Poor old Tutankhamun doesn't stand a chance.'

'Is this a conversation about alpacas or what?' Angie asked with a strained laugh.

He seemed to catch the edge in her voice and changed the subject. 'Anyway, theoretically, the female can get pregnant at any time. There's always an egg waiting to be fertilised.'

'That doesn't sound particularly erotic.'

'They're animals, Ange, not people. It's not about eroticism – it's about reproducing.'

'Well, I hope it happens soon. Snow White wants a baby and I want to be a grandmother.'

'You'd be the best-looking grandma in Millbrooke.'

Could Richard Scott be flirting with her? Glowing red as cadmium scarlet paint, he quickly changed the subject.

'I have some books on alpaca breeding, Ange. You can borrow them, if you like. I'll bring them down next time I come.'

'I've booked the School of Arts for the Easter weekend,' Angie told the painting ladies as they drank their tea and coffee in the kitchen before their lesson in the barn. 'And I've been in touch with the school. The principal likes the idea. She wants every class involved.'

'My children will be exhibiting in the same exhibition as their mum,' said Tanya.

'That's a good thing,' said Angie.

'Not if their paintings are better than mine.'

Everyone laughed.

'I was thinking the little ones might like to work on a theme – animals and birds of Millbrooke.'

'You know which animal they'll choose, don't you?' said Narelle.

'How's *your* project going, Angie?' asked Moira.

'I'll show you.' After all her equivocating about what to do, she'd finally decided on the subject – Amy's Millbrooke. Carefully she removed a sheet of drawing paper from between two pieces of cardboard. It was a pen and ink sketch of the Manse, so detailed that every intricate curl of the cast-iron lace was visible. There was a sigh of admiration from the painting class.

'This is just the first,' she said. 'I'm going to do a series.'

'What other buildings do you have in mind?' asked Moira.

'That's the problem,' replied Angie. 'There's St Aidan's, of course, but apart from that, I don't know. I'll have to do some more research. I know Amy was still alive in 1919, because her name appears without "deceased" after it on her mother's headstone. But whether she was living in Millbrooke or not is another question.'

The day after the painting class, Angie began work on her sketch of St Aidan's, a plain, no-nonsense kind of church you might expect to see on the American prairies. Although she didn't dislike the 'old maid' quality, its austerity was difficult to transfer to the page. After an hour she gave up, went inside and made herself a cup of tea. Tea was always conducive to clear thinking. Before the cup was even empty, she decided to visit the museum. Perhaps there was something in the archives she'd missed.

It was lunchtime when she arrived and the information desk was unattended. She didn't want to go directly to the archives room without permission so she decided to visit the beautiful Charles Chen instead. A shiver ran down her spine whenever she set eyes on the little portrait. A *coup de foudre*, repeated every time she entered the room and found him waiting for her.

You couldn't fall in love with a painting, could you? Only in one of those sad old Hollywood movies with Jennifer Jones and Joseph Cotton.

When she returned to the entrance, Bert was smiling at her from behind his desk.

'Angie, you'll be pleased to know our microfilm copies of the *Millbrooke Gazette* are now digitised.'

He showed her where the folders were located on the computer desktop and left her to it. In spite of her intention to work through the pages briskly, she soon became immersed in the stories, personal notices and classified advertisements. When she looked at her watch, it was three o'clock and she was still in 1872.

At quarter to five Bert appeared at the door to tell her the museum was closing in fifteen minutes. She didn't fancy the idea of being left alone among the dusty showcases and cobwebby corners. Not even the thought of Charles Chen, ensconced in his cabinet, smoothing his moustache, rearranging his tie and giving his orchid a tweak, could tempt her to stay in the museum after hours.

She was just about to call it a day when she caught sight of his name in an article concerning the crusade against opium. It was dated January, 1873. At the end was a sentence which caused Angie to catch her breath:

Mr Chen is accompanied on his regular excursions by his brother, Mr Jimmy Chen, and on occasions, by his wife, the former Miss Amy Duncan.

'Strike me lucky!' said Angie aloud. She had never used that expression before. Wasn't it something her grandfather used to say?

'Strike me lucky,' she repeated, this time more of a whisper, and looked up to see Bert standing beside her.

'I gather you've found something,' he said.

Bert placed the 'Closed' sign on the front door and made them both a cup of tea.

'If you go back to the pictures folders, you might find a photograph of them together. Charles Chen was important enough to have his portrait painted, albeit in miniature, so you never know.'

'But Moira and I looked at every photo right up until the mid-1880s. And I checked a second time.'

'You were looking for Amy Duncan, not Mrs Charles Chen. You could easily have missed her if the image was fuzzy or in a context you weren't expecting.'

By the time they finished their tea, they'd found it. A photograph from 1873 of two Chinese men, one in an English suit, the other in a loose shirt and trousers, and a European woman holding a frilly parasol. They were standing bolt upright – in the Victorian photographic tradition – outside a wooden building with large windows and double doors. A verandah awning across the front was supported by columns decorated with iron lace brackets. The caption read:

Mr Chen's Emporium

*Mr and Mrs Charles Chen and Mr Jimmy Chen
outside their Emporium*

Angie enlarged the image to two hundred percent. Yes, there they were – her old friends, Amy and Charles, *together*, standing beside Charles's brother. Everything made sense now – Eliza's story in Amy's book, the Oriental treasures in the trunk; all the clues were leading her to this moment. Then she zoomed closer to read the lettering on the window.

MR CHEN'S EMPORIUM
IMPORTER OF FINE GOODS AND DEALER IN ORNAMENTAL WARES

'Do you know whether the building still exists?' she asked Bert.

'Probably not. A lot of those Gold Rush stores were demolished in the bad old days before the government introduced heritage listings. Or they were so extensively renovated that they're unrecognisable. Don't get your hopes up,' he said, printing out the image and handing it to her.

Afterwards they went to Lisa's pub for a celebratory drink.

'It's bizarre, isn't it, Bert? Celebrating a marriage that took place in the nineteenth century. People would think we were crazy if we told them.'

They raised their glasses and toasted Amy and Charles. Yet despite her joy at the union, Angie felt a twinge of jealousy. It was irrational, of course, but in her imagination she had wanted him for herself.

First thing next morning, the printout tucked safely in her handbag, Angie headed for Miller Street. She had no idea where to start, so she decided to be systematic and walk its length, east to west, and then the reverse. But in the back of her mind Bert's warning was flashing like a hazard light.

The task proved much harder than she'd expected, mainly because so many of Millbrooke's buildings seemed to have double doors with windows on either side. The only clue was the dragon design on the verandah brackets, *if*, in fact, they still existed. She couldn't remember whether she'd seen that particular motif before. Perhaps Charles had commissioned a foundry to make them just for him. To be honest, she'd never paid much attention to the intricacies of the iron lace decoration which seemed to festoon every second building in Millbrooke. Like a flower, you might appreciate its overall beauty, but it was only when you came to draw it that you noticed the number of petals or the veining on the leaves. In fact, until she began sketching the Manse she hadn't even bothered to scrutinise the complex pattern of swirls, scallops and fleurs-de-lis trimming her very own verandah.

Angie was almost at the end of her second lap when she found herself outside the pottery café. Definitely time for a Lapsang Souchong. As she approached the doorway, she glanced at the posts holding up the old awning that protected shoppers from the weather. At the top were rusting iron brackets, one on each end-post and two on the others.

'Dragons!' she screamed and began laughing in a way she hadn't done in over a year. A pair of grey nomads, who had just alighted from their motorhome, gave her a curious look and wisely kept walking.

As she stepped over the threshold, it was as if she were entering the building for the first time. Everything had taken on a new meaning. She half-closed her eyes, a habit acquired from sizing up the tonal values within a painting, and instantly the ceramic bowls, displayed on wooden shelves reaching to the cornices, were transformed into Oriental porcelain. She ran her hand over the cedar shelving and leaned down to smell it. Was there a hint of cinnamon and cloves? Maybe a whiff of ginger too.

The counter was all steel and Perspex – nothing original there – but the floor was hardwood; wide boards of the type you could only find nowadays at restoration specialists. Through a doorway was the kitchen. Like the counter, it was ultra-modern. What had it been in Charles's day? A storeroom? An office? She imagined him sitting at his roll-top desk, doing the accounts, dipping his pen into the ink well and wiping off the excess, before writing rows of numbers in copperplate script.

The waiter looked up from behind the counter where he was making coffee and asked: 'Your usual, Angie?'

'No, thanks, Ben. Not today.' For some reason, the thought of a fragrant, floral tea was suddenly appealing. 'I think I'll have jasmine tea and one of those currant buns, please,' she said, pointing to a cake stand topped by a glass cloche.

'Actually, Angie, they're choc-chip scones.'

'Oh,' she said, looking closely at the items lying under the glass. How could she have possibly thought they were currant buns?

When she finished her tea and scones, Angie crossed Miller Street and appraised the café from the other side. Above the awning a parapet stretched right across the front of the building. In the very centre there were three embossed initials. Just like the dragon brackets, they'd been there all along – in plain sight yet unseen. A code waiting to be deciphered:

M C E

Deborah O'Brien

Wouldn't Amy be pleased that the twenty-first century woman who had delighted in her treasures was also the one to rediscover the emporium?

Afterwards, Angie dropped into Moira's to share the news about Amy and Charles.

'I know about the marriage,' said Moira. 'Bert told me this morning when I ran into him at the pharmacy.'

Angie couldn't help laughing. Who needed text-messaging when the Millbrooke grapevine worked so efficiently?

'But I bet he didn't tell you what happened to the emporium.'

'He said you were trying to find it.'

'Well, I did – just now. Guess which building it is.'

'Not the supermarket?'

'No,' laughed Angie. 'That would be a travesty.'

'Well, I give up.'

'It's the pottery café!'

'The place where you have breakfast. That's a nice connection, Angie. And I'm delighted about Amy and Charles.'

'So am I. I can't wait to tell the painting class. I thought we might have a little party with cupcakes and champagne.'

'There won't be much painting done after that!' said Moira with a laugh. Then her expression changed as something seemed to dawn on her. 'You know, I'm surprised Amy's parents allowed her to marry a Chinese man. Wouldn't a mixed marriage have been taboo in those days?'

'I don't think they *did* give their permission. There's a clue I found in one of Amy's books. The poem about Lochinvar.'

'I remember "Lochinvar". We had to learn it by heart when I was in primary school. Those were the days.'

Hiding a smile, Angie said, 'Well, as you know, it's a ballad about a knight who runs away with the woman he loves. There's one particular line that Amy has underlined so heavily she's practically cut through the page: "I long woo'd your daughter, my suit you denied..."'

'So you think her dad said no, and then Amy and Charles eloped? I suppose that would explain why we couldn't find any record of her marriage in the parish registers.'

'It was such a daring thing to do, Moira, particularly for the daughter of a clergyman. Can you imagine her parents' reaction when they found out?'

'A real shit storm,' said Moira with a smile.

Angie gave her an oblique glance. She had never heard genteel Moira swear before, not even to say 'bloody'.

'Do you think *you* would have run off with George if your parents hadn't approved of him?' asked Angie.

'It's academic really. They both adored George. What about you and Phil?'

'Same thing, apart from a hiccup at the start.' She smiled, recalling her father's belief that any male who played in a rock band was a sex-crazed hippie. 'But seriously, I wonder if I would have found the courage to defy my parents if they'd forbidden me to see him. I'd like to think I'd have been brave like Amy. After all, Phil was the love of my life.'

'Your life isn't over yet, Angie,' Moira replied cryptically.

It was Phil's birthday. Last year's, coming only a couple of months after his death, had hit Angie like one disastrous frost after another. Blake had suggested they plant a tree. It was among his better ideas. The three of them had gone to a nursery and chosen a Huon pine, a species whose propensity to live for centuries, even millennia, seemed to provide a glimpse of eternity which Angie had found comforting. This year, she hoped the day would be easier. She had been rallying her inner resources, keeping busy with the sketches of St Aidan's, the emporium and Millerbrooke House. For her drawing of Millerbrooke, she was using the original architectural elevations in the museum as a guide and guessing the rest because she hadn't actually visited the house itself. She couldn't bring herself to do it. She'd evaded so many invitations, how would it look if she went now, when she suspected Richard fancied her? Of course, she might have imagined he was flirting with her. It was so clumsy, it could have meant anything. All the same, she had a feeling there was more to her landlord than the dishevelled eccentric he appeared to be.

Today though, all the psychological preparation, not to mention the busyness of the last weeks, didn't mean a thing. She could feel a major crying jag threatening, one of those gut-wrenching sessions that left her wrung out for days.

Mr Songbird had set off early for the drill site, creeping out so quietly Angie hadn't heard him. He'd even made his own breakfast and put the cereal bowl in her newly purchased dishwasher afterwards. The perfect lodger.

On a day like this, she thought to herself, it might be better to be surrounded by people. Then she wouldn't surrender to the crying. So she picked up her handbag and sunglasses and headed for the emporium café – that's what she called it now. Maybe in the future it would become common usage among Millbrookers, just as Jack Parker was now familiarly known as Mr Songbird.

On the way she bought a Sydney paper and the *Millbrooke Gazette*. The café was busy with the last of its regular breakfast diners. Angie noticed one of the anti-mine campaigners, her T-shirt emblazoned with a shocking-pink platypus, sitting in the corner facing towards the wall. At a table for four, the plants lady was drinking coffee and writing frantically in one of those old-fashioned legal pads. Was it her next film script? Would it be a whimsical story about the eccentric habitués of the emporium café? Angie liked to think so.

She was about to open the paper when she heard a soft cowboy voice asking: 'Is this chair taken, ma'am?'

'I thought you were at River Cove.'

'Yeah, I put in a few hours out there, but I have a meeting with the regional planning guy from Granthurst at eleven. We were intending to come here, though that might not be such a good idea.' He inclined his head towards the platypus woman who was bent over a folder with her back to them. 'I'll just text him with a new meeting place. What's that café up the hill called?'

'The Gold Rush Café. Corner of St John's.'

'Are you going to eat those sausages, Angie?'

She pushed her plate towards him. 'I'm not hungry. I only ordered them out of habit.'

'Is anything wrong?' He had adopted his concerned look, the asymmetry of his face accentuated by the raised eyebrows and lopsided half smile.

'It's Phil's birthday.' She hadn't intended to tell him.

There was a pause during which he seemed to be searching his brain for the significance of a man called Phil.

'Oh, your husband. I'm sorry.' He reached over and patted her hand. 'I'll take you out for dinner tonight. That will cheer you up. We'll go to the Italian place.'

Angie smiled despite herself. How inappropriate to ask her out to dinner on her dead husband's birthday. But Mr Songbird didn't seem to notice. He thought he was being kind, trying to take her mind off Phil.

'I've thawed a leg of lamb,' said Angie, 'so we probably should eat at home tonight.'

'Well, in that case, let's go out tomorrow night.' He had finished her plate. 'Must fly. Keep your chin up, Angie.'

It was fortunate that songbirds were renowned for their melodies rather than their empathy. Otherwise, you might let them into your heart when you were at your most vulnerable.

As Jack stood to go, he bent over and kissed her on the mouth. Just a brief kiss, but significant to an outsider observing the widow and the miner. When he walked to the counter to pay, Angie scanned the room to see if anyone had noticed. Then she spotted her landlord coming into the café. He and Jack crossed paths at the door. There was an exchange of greetings, like two cowboys tipping their hats, and Mr Songbird was gone.

'Anyone sitting here, Ange?' The question was loaded with innuendo.

'It's all yours.'

'Another Lapsang Souchong?' he asked as he placed his order.

'No, thanks. I really should go. I have a sketch to finish.'

'Of what?'

She couldn't very well tell him it was a drawing of his own house. 'My contribution to the exhibition.'

'I saw the poster. You girls are getting serious about this, aren't you?'

'It's a serious thing, Richard.'

'I didn't mean to imply otherwise.'

'Some people might think we're just a bunch of dilettantes with pretensions.' After she said it, she realised it was probably an accurate description.

Suddenly her phone rang. When she answered it, she heard Phil. For a moment she thought he'd come back to her. Then she realised it was her son.

'I was going to call you later, darling. And Tim as well.' She lowered her voice. 'I wish we could be together today.'

It was difficult to hold a personal phone conversation when there was a man sitting opposite her, wearing a pixie hat which covered antennae that could pick up every nuance. Whether the aerials were the metal kind or similar to those horny growths protruding from a giraffe's head, she hadn't yet determined.

'We thought we might come and visit you,' said Blake. 'Not this weekend, the one after. Is that okay with you, Mum?'

Thank goodness Mr Songbird had scheduled a trip to Canberra for Wednesday week. He would be away until the following Monday. The boys knew about Jack's existence, of course, but she had implied he was a nerdy old engineer. She wasn't sure how they would cope with a handsome cowboy living in their mother's house.

'That would be lovely, Blake. I miss you both so much, especially today.'

'Have you been all right?'

'Kind of.' She didn't want to say anything in front of Richard, even though he appeared to be engrossed in her copy of the *Gazette*.

'It's natural to be upset on a day like this, Mum. It's called anniversary syndrome.'

Trust Blake to have a diagnosis.

'Are you still having those denial dreams? The ones about Dad recovering.'

'Actually, they haven't happened in quite a while.' What did that mean? No doubt Blake would tell her.

'That indicates you're making progress.'

'So it's a good thing?'

'Yeah, it looks like you're coming out of denial. But grieving isn't a straightforward process, you know.'

'I didn't think it was. So where am I now?' she asked warily, not expecting to hear: 'You seem to be angry.'

'No, I'm not. I'm perfectly calm,' she said, moderating her voice accordingly.

'It's repressed anger, Mum. You're resentful at Dad for leaving you. That's probably the reason you're not seeing him in your dreams.'

'But it doesn't make sense. It's not as though he ran off with another woman.' She had dropped her voice to a whisper, aware of the man opposite her. 'He had no choice in the matter.'

'You understand that on a rational level, but your subconscious has a mind of its own.'

She heard him chuckle at his little pun.

'You really need to look after yourself, Mum,' he said, sounding serious again.

'But I do.'

'I'm speaking in an emotional sense. You're fragile right now. You could easily do something you'd regret down the track. You might even find yourself falling apart.'

'I'm not the type.'

'It happens. People do all kinds of things to ease the pain. Drinking too much, taking drugs, having an affair.'

'No likelihood of any of those.' Angie laughed, perhaps a little too heartily. 'Anyway, I'd better let you go, sweetheart.' She didn't want to discuss her feelings any longer. 'Thank you for calling me today. I love you, darling.'

'Ditto, Mum.'

As she looked across at Richard, his hat bent over the newspaper, she could almost hear the antennae humming beneath their woollen covering.

On a Wednesday in early February Angie found herself with only one student – Moira. The others were at an open day at the school, except for Jennie who was in Granthurst, visiting her latest internet man. They intended to meet in a café overlooking the park – a neutral setting, as advised by the dating website – and if all went well, they would have lunch together.

'And then what?' Angie had asked tentatively.

'I'll come home. I never sleep with them on the first date. They'd think I'm an easy lay.'

'So you wait a month or two?'

'Not necessarily. The second date is negotiable.'

Angie didn't know whether to be shocked or to laugh out loud. Fortunately the conversation had taken place over the phone and Jennie couldn't see her twitching face.

Angie and Moira observed the usual tradition of coffee and cake before the lesson, but because there were only two of them, the introductory banter extended to lunchtime, and they still hadn't started to paint. Moira had lived in Millbrooke all her life and knew everybody's secrets. She didn't gossip though. Moira was discreet. You could trust her as a repository of your confidences. Unlike the others, she never disclosed the details of her own internet adventures, even though it seemed to Angie that there had been several, if not in person, then of the online variety. Moira was a seventy-year-old woman still interested in men and presumably in sex. It was intriguing and, Angie had to admit, inspirational.

'Do you agree with Tanya about the man drought?' asked Angie.

'There aren't many available men in my age group, Angie. And when a man does lose his wife, there's a string of women waiting to become the replacement. You can see them lining up at the funeral. The next day, they turn up with a casserole or a spag bol, offering solace. Before too long, the silly old bloke will find himself snared. And after a respectable interval, there'll be a quiet wedding.'

'It sounds as though you've had some experience of this.'

'It happened to my best friend's husband after she died of cancer.'

'Funny how it doesn't work the other way around, the men lining up.'

'Yes, funny, isn't it?'

'I think women always cope better when they lose their partner. We're stronger than men.'

'You're right, Angie. Just look at you. You've come a long way this year. I've watched you start to laugh again.'

'Really?'

'Like a flower unfurling in slow motion in one of those nature documentaries.'

'Perhaps Millbrooke is good for me. Even the winter weather.'

'Do you think you'll buy the Manse?'

'Richard's given me a year to decide. But I think I might.'

'What do you know about Richard?' asked Moira.

'Nothing really, except that he's a bit of a dero who needs to ditch the beanie and get some decent clothes.'

'And that's it?'

'No, there's another thing.' Angie lowered her voice, even though it was only the two of them. 'I'm convinced he's an alcoholic.'

'What makes you think that?'

'Narelle said as much. And he spends a lot of time at the pub.'

'Have you ever seen Richard drunk or even hung over?'

'No, but he might be one of those types who can drink and not let it show.'

'Is there anything else you know about him?'

'I'm pretty sure he used to be a builder. Or maybe a carpenter. He sketched some rough floor plans for me, and they weren't half bad. He would have made a good architect if he'd put his mind to it.'

Angie wondered why Moira was grinning at her.

'Angie, you're such a card.'

'What's so funny?'

'You and Richard meet up almost every morning, and yet you don't know a single thing about him.'

'Firstly, Moira, we don't meet as such. Richard just turns up at the café when I'm having my breakfast. And secondly, what makes you think I'm wrong about him?'

'Because Richard Scott really *is* an architect, a well-respected one.'

'Okay, I suppose that makes sense. He was talking about passive solar and the integrity of the design. That's the way architects speak, isn't it? But you can't tell me he doesn't have issues with alcohol.'

'He hasn't had a drink in years.'

'How do you know all this stuff about him anyway?' Then Angie hesitated. 'Oh my God. I wondered how you could be so sure about Richard not being gay. And now it makes sense. The two of you are having an affair, aren't you?'

Moira's whole body began to shake, causing the brown liquid in her mug to spill onto the table.

'He's not interested in me, Angie!' she replied, breathless with laughter. Then she mopped up the puddles of tea with a paper napkin. 'Never has been.'

'So you've known him a long time?'

'Ever since he first came to Millbrooke with his wife.'

Angie's mouth dropped open. 'His wife? Richard had a wife?'

'Yes, indeed. It would have been the late eighties, I suppose. He was a first-rate architect from Sydney, specialising in heritage restorations. He'd made his money buying old houses in the inner city, doing them up and selling them at a profit. Then he and his wife came here to inspect Millerbrooke House which was up for sale, after the last of the Millers had died. The place was in a bad way with a damaged roof and broken windows, but Richard was smitten with the Georgian façade. So they bought it and he spent all his time working on the renovations. I guess that's when the marriage started to go wrong. She missed Sydney and didn't like being stuck up there in a draughty old house with mould on the walls.'

'So did she leave him and go back to Sydney?'

'Not exactly. I'm telling you this in confidence, Angie. Because I trust you. I'd never say it in front of the others.'

'I wouldn't breathe a word to anyone, Moira.'

'Well, it wasn't long after they moved here that George and I got to know them. We wanted to restore our cottage. So Richard did an assessment and drew up the plans. He and George became good friends. That's how we found out Diana, Richard's wife, was having an affair with the local solicitor.'

'Jim Holbrook?'

'No, the one before him. George went up there one night to discuss the renovations and found Richard distraught. She'd left him to go and live with the solicitor. And she'd told him she was pregnant, but it wasn't his. Apparently they'd been trying for years to have a baby and then the lawyer got her pregnant in the first few weeks.'

'That's sad.'

'Yes, it was. Richard used to bump into her in town and she had a bulging belly. It was a big scandal, but people have forgotten it now. New scandals, new controversies.'

'What happened to him after that?'

'He started drinking. He let his consulting practice slide. George tried to help him, but he wouldn't listen. There were a couple of bad years. Then George had his first heart attack and a second.' She paused to take a breath. 'After George died, Richard seemed to wake up to himself. He stopped drinking and resumed his design work. He still operates the consulting business from home. But I don't think he's ever gotten over Diana. She and the solicitor moved down to the coast years ago. I heard they had a daughter. And poor Richard continued to live in that big old house and spend his evenings drinking with his cronies at the pub – though these days it's only orange juice.'

'I wonder why he still spends so much time in the pub,' said Angie. 'You'd think that would be torture for him.'

'Lisa welcomes him there. She has a collection of oddballs from all over the district. Nobody else notices them in their beanies and worn-out clothes. In fact, everybody's so used to them, they might as well be invisible.'

After a moment Angie said, 'In the mornings when I see Richard in the café, I'm always caught up in my own life. And he's just a foil, someone I bounce my problems off. I've never given much thought to what his story might be. I guess that's pretty selfish.'

'It's been a time in your life when you've needed to be selfish, to take care of yourself. Now you can start to reach out to people again.' Moira smiled at her and took her hand. 'Do you remember our first painting class? Everyone was chatting and nobody was in a hurry to get started. I could see you becoming stressed, looking at your watch, wondering if you should hurry us along. You didn't realise we'd come as much for the social side as for the painting. It was the same with the lace-making and the quilting before that. You might think it's an art class, but it's really our weekly therapy session.'

That evening Angie and Jack were having their usual drinks on the terrace.

'Angie, in all these weeks we've been together, you've never asked anything of me.'

'Why would I? You're always helping around the house – making your bed and loading the dishwasher.'

'I didn't mean housework. I was talking about you wanting something deeper – emotionally.'

'I thought the boundaries were clear from the start. After all, you're married. And I'm not looking for a grand romance.'

'Women always want more.'

'Not *this* one. I like things exactly as they are.'

'But, Angie, don't you love me just a little?'

He sounded like a little boy craving his mother's attention. Had Jack been expecting Angie to fall in love with him? She really couldn't blame him – grown women became simpering adolescents in Jack's presence, even the happily married Ros. He could be endearing and tender, but Angie could never love him, not even a little. Not while she was still in love with her husband.

And she couldn't just extinguish a love story that had lasted more than three decades, as she might snuff out a candle.

Angie was silent for so long, Jack began tickling her ribs, trying to tease the information out of her. Just as she was begging for him to stop, she came up with a response she thought would please him.

'You're lovable, Jack. *Very* lovable.'

'But you don't *love* me, do you?'

It might have been her imagination, but Jack Parker seemed miffed.

13
SECRETS AND SONGBIRDS

Then

Amy and Eliza had resumed their daily lessons and were grappling with the French scientific journal. Their work was assisted by a medical dictionary Charles had acquired for them in Sydney. Sometimes Eliza would stay for supper and afterwards Jimmy would join them for their language lesson. Amy tutored Jimmy in English, using Bible stories Eliza and her brothers had read as children. For his part, Jimmy taught Amy and Eliza to speak Chinese by way of drawings, mime and simply pointing to objects.

Amy was fond of Jimmy. He reminded her of Charles. Not just in looks, but in his gracious manner. Jimmy respected their privacy, keeping to himself in the evenings and knocking loudly on the back door before he entered the house, even though the door was never locked.

Charles confided to Amy that their mother had sent a letter in which she expressed her desire for Jimmy to return home and find a bride. She feared her younger son might also fall in love with a white girl. To Amy, that implied Charles's mother didn't approve of him marrying her, but she said nothing. After all, her own father had done far more than disapprove. He had castigated them in the most public way imaginable.

One afternoon in February, Eliza arrived to find Amy cat-napping on the sofa.

'I thought we had a lesson this afternoon, Amy Chen, and here you are in dreamland.'

Amy yawned and stretched her arms. 'I'm sorry. I have been so tired of late.'

Eliza frowned and lowered her voice. 'When were you last on the rag?'

'Eliza!' How could she be so vulgar? Female matters weren't things to be mentioned in polite society, even by a girl who wanted to be a doctor. Aunt Molly, who was the most progressive of people, had never brought up so intimate a topic, and after Amy's mother showed her how to sew rags together, the subject hadn't been broached again.

'Do you understand what I'm talking about, Amy?'

'Of course.' Then she whispered her answer: 'In December.'

'When exactly?'

'Oh dear, Eliza, I don't remember. Why do you need to know such information?'

'It is important, Amy, to confirm my suspicions or otherwise.'

Amy knew there was no point in arguing with Eliza. She would persist, no matter how hard she protested. 'The second week in Sydney.'

'And you haven't considered the absence of your monthlies to be odd?'

'No. Isn't it because I'm a married woman?'

Eliza laughed. 'Who told you such a ridiculous thing, Amy?

Or did you invent it in your imagination? The reason they have stopped is that you are with child.'

Amy's eyes widened. 'A bairn?'

'Yes, and it may have begun on your honeymoon.' Eliza counted on her fingers. 'Which means you and Charles will have a baby in September!'

It was such a shock Amy couldn't speak.

'You're happy about the baby, aren't you, Amy?'

'Yes, of course. But I am also fearful. I saw Mama screaming in agony. I wish the story about the stork was true.'

'Don't be anxious, Amy. There are anaesthetic measures which can relieve the pain – chloroform and ether. I have read about them in my journals.'

'Why weren't these measures used to alleviate my mother's distress?'

'Some doctors believe it's a woman's duty to bear the pain.'

'Will Doctor Allen allow me to have this chlor . . .'

'Chloroform. I shall insist on it.'

'What if the baby is born feet first?'

'It is too soon to worry yourself about that, Amy. And it is unlikely you will have a breech birth.'

'That is a relief.'

'There is something else. It would be best not to tell Charles that you are with child. Not for a month or two.'

'But why? Surely he will be pleased?'

'I have no doubt. But you should be aware that things can go wrong during the early months.'

'Now I am even more frightened.'

'You must be careful not to overexert yourself. And some doctors say you should avoid loud noises as the shock can dislodge the baby.'

'You are so well versed in the subject of babies, Eliza, are you sure you don't want to become a midwife rather than a doctor?'

'I'm certain. I shall continue to read my journals and deliver calves and foals. And one day a letter will come from the university offering me a place as a student in the faculty of medicine. Professor Pasteur once said that scientists should prepare their minds for the time when chance favours them. And that is what I intend to do.'

Now

While Angie's boys were in town for the weekend, she finally accepted a lunch invitation to Millerbrooke. Richard had been quite insistent about it, which she found peculiar. In the past, his invitations had always been easy to decline.

Because it was her first visit, she considered taking a gift – a plant or a box of chocolates. But Richard didn't do presents, and a bottle of wine was out of the question. So she made a *tarte tatin*, using the abundant harvest of Royal Galas from her apple tree. The trick was to add just a few drops of lemon juice to balance the sweetness of the brown sugar. They had lunch in Millerbrooke's vast dining room at a table which was longer than Angie's ten-seater. Richard was full of surprises. The house was elegant and uncluttered. And he could actually cook. Yabbies from the dam, followed by his free-range chicken. As she looked around the dining room, Angie wondered if he didn't have his own aesthetic, based on creating beauty in his surroundings, rather than worrying about his personal appearance.

Deborah O'Brien

After lunch he took them on a tour. If the Old Manse was quaint and romantic, Millerbrooke was a grand colonial mansion.

'What do you call this style?' asked Blake.

'Georgian. It's all about symmetry and classical proportions.'

At the back of the house a series of outbuildings formed a courtyard. Richard showed them the old kitchen where the cook used to prepare the meals and the adjoining schoolroom in which the Miller children were educated by a governess.

'There's one more thing you should see,' he said, sounding as excited as a child at Christmastime.

They followed him towards a stand of elm trees.

'It's a graveyard!' exclaimed Angie. 'No wonder I couldn't find any Millers in the town cemetery.'

'Yes, they're all here.'

The graveyard was delineated by a low box hedge. Angie found Captain Miller immediately. His was an impressive obelisk with an urn on top. There was a joint headstone for John and Charlotte. Behind them was their daughter, Eliza. Angie couldn't help thinking she had only recently met Eliza, courtesy of the story hidden inside Amy's book. And here she was in her grave.

> **In loving memory of**
> **Eliza May Miller**
> **A pioneering woman**
> **Who departed this life**
> **6th June, 1927**
> **Aged 72 years**

'Dans les champs de l'observation
le hasard ne favorise que les
esprits préparés.'

Blessed are the dead which die in
the Lord

What was the significance of the French quote, Angie wondered. She took a photo of the inscription and resolved to search on the internet.

Next to Eliza were Joseph and his wife. The younger brother, Daniel, was missing. Perhaps he had moved away. Towards the back was a large headstone with an arched top, shaded by a rose bush heavy with yellow flowers. Parts of the inscription were covered in mould; other sections had worn away. In places the stone looked bleached, as if someone had tried to scrub it clean.

Amy Chen
Native of Scotland
Loving wife of Charles
and   he to is   n,
r es   ander (ea)
Departed this life 28th May 1933
Aged 79 years
Reunited with her darling loved ones
Blessed are the pure in heart for they
shall see Jesus

Sacred to the Memory of
Charles Chen
Native of Canton

Deborah O'Brien

Late of Paterson Street, Millbrooke
Much loved husband of Amy
Called to rest
24th February, 1873
Aged 26 years

My darling one has gone before
I'll meet you on the other shore

It was such a surprise that for a few seconds Angie couldn't breathe. She had found Amy but lost Charles.

Richard made her a cup of tea.

'I'm sorry, Ange. I thought you'd be pleased about finding Amy. But now I see it was silly of me not to break it to you gently.'

'How long have you known?' asked Angie, blotting her eyes.

'I only twigged to it recently when I started cleaning up the gravestones. The ones at the back were in the worst condition. That was when I found Amy and Charles. But I didn't get far with the clean-up because the stone kept disintegrating and I realised I was doing more harm than good.'

Angie hadn't touched her tea. 'I can't believe Charles is dead. Sometimes I visit him in the museum.' The boys were giving her puzzled looks. 'His portrait, I mean. Bert and I had a celebration when we discovered Charles had married Amy. I liked to think of them having a long life together as Mr and Mrs Chen; I even imagined him breaking through the cultural barrier and becoming president of the chamber of commerce or mayor of Millbrooke.' She stared into her tea cup. 'What a waste. He was so young.'

'Life was hard back then,' said Richard. 'It might have been an accident. Or an illness.'

'Whatever happened, it isn't bloody fair. Can you imagine what it must have been like for poor Amy, losing the love of her life after less than a year?'

'Mum, get a grip; it's not as if you know these people,' said Tim. 'You're acting as if they're your long-lost relatives when they're just people from the nineteenth century. They have *no* relevance to *your* life.'

'Your mum has become very close to Amy,' said Richard quietly. 'Through researching her life and painting her portrait.'

'It's just so sad,' Angie said. Tears were filling her eyes once more. 'Sorry.' She went into the hallway so they wouldn't see her crying. This time she couldn't stop. The sobs were so loud she put her hand over her mouth to stifle them. Then she felt a hand on her shoulder.

'It's okay to cry, Ange.'

The painting ladies had become stakeholders in Angie's quest for Amy. When there was finally a pause in the Wednesday morning chatter, she broke the news.

'To die so young,' said Ros. 'It's a tragedy. And they were only newlyweds. Do you know what happened?'

'No. There isn't any cause of death on the inscription or in the *Gazette* – I looked in the archives yesterday. But I did wonder if it might have been a racist attack or a robbery or a combination of the two.'

'Surely there would have been a hint of something so untoward on the headstone,' said Ros.

'Or in the papers,' said Jennie.

'You'd think so. Maybe it was a riding accident. Or snakebite or even a cut that turned septic,' suggested Narelle.

'Poor Amy,' sighed Moira. 'A teenage widow.'

'Would she have inherited the house and emporium?' asked Ros.

'It depends on Charles's will, I suppose,' said Angie. 'If he even had one. Who expects to die when they're twenty-six?'

'I wonder if her parents were there for her, with him being a vicar and all,' said Tanya.

'I doubt it. The fact that the trunk remained at the Manse is the clue. She never returned for her treasures because she couldn't or wouldn't enter that house.'

'Is there any mention of a second marriage on Amy's headstone?'

'None that I could see, but parts of it were worn away.'

'It's hard to believe she didn't marry again,' mused Ros. 'Half a century is a long time to be a widow.'

'Perhaps she was like Queen Victoria,' said Angie. 'And Charles was her Prince Albert.'

'Yes, but Victoria was middle-aged when Albert died, and Amy was a teenager with her life ahead of her. Surely she could have found someone else.'

'Maybe she didn't want to,' said Moira. 'She might have carried a torch for Charles for the rest of her life.'

'What would you have done, Angie?' asked Narelle. 'If you'd been Amy?'

'I can't imagine marrying again. After all, how could you ever find anyone to compare with Charles Chen?' Or Phil Wallace, she could have added.

It was difficult to settle down to work after that. A strange sense of loss lingered into the afternoon.

'I feel as though I've just been to a funeral,' said Jennie.

'Maybe we should have a wake,' suggested Narelle.

Jennie and Narelle were working on their portraits for the 'Faces of Millbrooke'. The layout reminded Angie of the old *Hollywood Squares* TV show where the celebrities were seated in rows to form a grid. There was Jonathan, the woodworker cum newspaper editor; Doug, the real estate agent; Jim, the solicitor; Ben, the ceramicist; Don, the baker; Brad, the electrician; Bert, the historian; Senior Sergeant Peters; even the mayor himself. Twenty Millbrookers in total.

Meanwhile Angie was busy on her own project, inking the sketch of the emporium, the last in her quartet of significant buildings in Amy's life. She was keen to do it justice and her pen hovered nervously over the page. A technically accurate rendering might be satisfactory for the others, but Mr Chen's Emporium required something extra. A touch of magic.

After her students had left and Angie was tidying the barn, a thought crossed her mind. Someone was missing from the 'Faces of Millbrooke' – the owner of the district's oldest property. Narelle and Jennie had forgotten all about him. And nobody had noticed. It was just as Moira said – Richard had made himself invisible.

Since Moira's revelations, Angie had pondered whether to tell Richard that she knew about him being an architect. She didn't want to implicate Moira, and she certainly didn't want him working out that she knew about his marriage break-up and bout with the bottle.

One afternoon, when he came to check on the alpacas, Angie said: 'I was thinking about those drawings you did for me, Richard. The floor plans. They were brilliant. And all your talk about symmetry and classical proportions. Are you an architect?' She posed the question with a serious face and an unwavering gaze, hoping this would get past his antennae.

He smiled. 'Guilty as charged.'

'It's not something to be ashamed of.'

'Nobody cares what I do. They just assume I'm an ageing eccentric who owns a lot of Millbrooke real estate.'

Angie started to laugh. 'But you are.'

Dismissing her with a frown, he continued: 'I like to stay under the radar.'

'But why?'

'It's a safer place to be.'

Vicky was coming from Sydney for the Millbrooke Village Fair. Her husband Paul couldn't make it, and so it would be just the two of them – and Jack, of course.

When Angie told him about her old friend's visit, he said: 'She can have my room. I'll spend the weekend at the motel.'

'That's generous of you, but there's no need. Anyway, the motel will be booked out because of the fair. I'll put Vicky in the third bedroom.'

'I guess I'd better not call on you then, while your friend is staying.'

'Call on you' – he was such an old-fashioned cowboy. Shucks, ma'am, I don't want to cause you any embarrassment.

'We'll make up for it on Sunday night,' he promised with a grin.

Vicky was dazzled by the transformation to the Manse and adored the alpacas.

'I'm going to be a grandmother,' announced Angie as they patted Snow White on the neck – she hated anyone touching her head. 'I only found out this week.'

Vicky looked shocked.

Angie quivered with laughter. 'It's not Blake or Tim. It's Snow White.'

'Oh,' said Vicky, staring at each animal in turn. 'So who's the father? The brown one?'

'No, he's a wether.'

'A what?'

'He's been neutered. He can't make babies.'

'And when is this baby due?'

'January of next year. It's a very long gestation.'

'Does that mean you're staying?'

'Maybe.'

When Jack arrived home on Friday afternoon, Angie could see he was unsettled. There had been a visit from the planning bureaucrats who were intending to stay overnight at the motel. In an hour or two Jack and the team would attempt what he called 'a last-ditch wooing'. It would take place over dinner at the Millbrooke RSL, where they had booked a private function room because they didn't want any locals eavesdropping. Angie had wondered about the use of 'last-ditch'. What exactly did he mean by that? Surely they weren't going to abandon the project, not when they'd come so far. Perhaps it was just a reflection of Jack's growing impatience with the whole process, although that was odd, considering he'd been the one to say that in the mining game, it was always one step at a time.

Lately it seemed the more stressed he became, the more he

clung to Angie. She cooked him fancy meals, listened to his problems and soothed his frustrations. But he wanted more – he needed her to love him. It was ironic really, because she was certain he didn't love *her* at all. And that's the way it had to be. Wouldn't the painting ladies think it weird if they knew the truth? Angie wanted Jack for his body, and Jack just wanted to be loved.

While Angie, Vicky and Jack had a drink outside in the garden, the platypus was making ripples in the creek.

'They're amazing,' said Vicky. It was her first-ever platypus spotting. She tried to take some photos, but the animal was too quick for her, either lying low in the water like a tiny crocodile or duck-diving so fast she could only manage to get a fuzzy image of its back.

'They're not easy to photograph, are they?'

'They like to retain their mystique,' said Angie. 'The Greta Garbo of the animal kingdom.'

Meanwhile, Jack was preoccupied, excusing himself and wandering out of earshot to make calls. Angie observed him, holding his phone to his ear and gesticulating wildly with his free arm. From a distance he looked like a marionette being manipulated by an invisible puppeteer. What were those bigwigs in the US saying to make him so agitated? And what had happened to her easygoing cowboy? He was acting like a neurotic character from a Woody Allen movie.

'You didn't tell me he was gorgeous,' whispered Vicky.

'The ladies in my painting class are smitten with him,' Angie whispered back.

'He oozes charm, doesn't he? But not of the used car salesman variety.'

'Mr Songbird's charm runs deep.'

'Are you sleeping with him, Angie?'

Angie just smiled.

'You *are*, I know you are!'

Later Jack left for his dinner at the RSL, and Angie and Vicky ate at the Italian restaurant.

'So you're sleeping with a married man,' said Vicky who had never been known for her tact. 'No kids, I hope.'

'Actually he has two boys.'

'You never mentioned he had children.' Her tone was serious.

'Vicky, it's not forever. For either of us.'

'You mean it's just a fling?'

'I don't know what you'd call it. Not really a fling, but not a great love story either.'

'What about the wife and kids?'

'I'm no threat to them. He loves his family and I'm still in love with Phil. I could never see myself growing old with Jack. Once the mine is up and running, he'll fly away home.' As an afterthought, she asked: 'Do I sound callous?'

'Not callous. Just different to the Angie I know. But I guess I only ever saw you with Phil.'

'I was a different person then. I wouldn't have dreamed of sleeping with someone I didn't love. But now I'm in a strange place where the old rules don't apply. It's enough that I like Jack. I don't need to love him.' She lowered her voice, even though the restaurant was full of tourists and there wasn't a local in sight, other than the waiter. 'To tell you the truth, Vicky, Jack and I have very little in common, apart from . . .' She cut the sentence short, suddenly aware that the waiter was approaching with their bottle of wine.

On Sunday, Richard offered to show Vicky over his house, followed by afternoon tea. It meant she would catch all the Sunday afternoon traffic on her way back to Sydney, but she didn't seem to care. She wanted to see the grandest house in town, she said. Angie suspected Vicky was also curious about her mysterious landlord.

The man in question answered the door, wearing a striped woollen cap and camouflage gear. Perhaps it was a misguided attempt at dressing up. All the same, the visit went smoothly. Vicky was suitably impressed by the Georgian architecture, and Richard served them tea and homemade pumpkin scones in the drawing room. As they were saying their goodbyes, Angie remembered the flowers she had brought to lay on Amy's grave.

'Richard, do you mind if we pop down to the graveyard before we leave?'

'I'll come with you,' he said.

She collected her flowers from the bucket in the back of the car. Yellow roses from the Manse and Singapore orchids from the florist in town. She had wanted cymbidiums to match the yellow orchid worn by Charles in the painting at the museum, but they were out of season.

At the base of the headstone shared by Amy and Charles was a little bouquet of wilted flowers. It was hard to determine what species they had once been. Daisies, perhaps. The February heat had fried them to a crisp brown. Nevertheless, it was good to see someone else had paid a visit to the Chens. As she took the dead flowers away and replaced them with her own, she looked up at Richard. His eyes were squinting more than usual, owing to the sun, and also because he was smiling.

'Does he wear that crazy hat all the time, or was it just for my benefit?' asked Vicky when they were in the car driving back down the gravel road to Richard's gate.

'He has a range of headgear – caps, beanies, beagle hats. They hide his antennae.'

'Antennae?'

'The ones he uses to pry into other people's business.'

'And what's *his* business?'

'He's an architect.'

'Well, that explains it.'

Angie glanced across to see if Vicky was smiling, but she wasn't.

They had almost reached the Manse when Vicky said: 'I think he has a crush on you, Angie.'

'Who? Jack?'

'No, *Richard*. Your landlord.'

'Richard? That's ridiculous,' she protested. All the same, she clearly remembered the day when he'd seemed to be flirting.

Once they were back at the Manse, Angie waited for Vicky to pack her things and rush away. Instead, she sat down at the kitchen table and accepted Angie's offer of a cup of tea. Finally she announced: 'I don't really need to be back in Sydney until tomorrow. Do you mind if I stay another night?'

Tonight was to be Angie's reunion with Jack.

'Of course you can stay, Vicky. Do you want to go somewhere for dinner? I can make a booking.'

'No, thanks. Just a toasted sandwich would be fine.'

The next morning, Angie took Vicky for breakfast at the emporium café. Richard passed the window, waved, but didn't come inside. Perhaps he knew this was girl-talk.

'Angie, there's something I've been trying to tell you all weekend.' Vicky was staring into the powdered chocolate on her cappuccino as if it could predict the future.

'You're not ill, are you?'

'No, it's nothing like that.'

Was it going to be a guessing game, Angie wondered.

'It's Paul,' Vicky said, not looking up from the coffee. 'He's having an affair.'

At first Angie thought it was a joke. Not Paul. He and Vicky were a given. 'Are you sure?'

'I saw them together. In a café in Darling Harbour, holding hands. Alfie was with them.'

Angie had to think for a second. Of course. Alfie was the dog.

'How dare he involve Alfie in his sleazy affair?' Vicky stirred her coffee but didn't drink it. 'When he came home, I confronted him and he started to cry. It was pathetic.'

'I can't believe he'd do something so stupid.'

'Neither could I.'

'How did he meet her in the first place?'

'He takes Alfie for a walk every morning. Around Blackwattle Bay. And she was walking her bloody dog. They started having coffee together and then . . .'

'How long has it been going on?'

'A few months, or so he says.'

'Oh, Vicky, I'm really sorry. Are they still seeing each other?'

'He claims it's over, but I don't believe him. He's texting all the time and making furtive phone calls out on the balcony. And last week I had a call from my skin therapist to confirm an appointment for a top-up.' Vicky was a devotee of wrinkle injections. 'I told her I'm not due for a couple of months. Then she replied, "Sorry, Mrs Lamb, I've just realised that it's Mr Lamb's appointment, not yours. Can you remind him?" I was shaking so much I could barely hold the phone. He's always made fun of my cosmetic enhancements and now he's doing it himself. And if it's over, why is he having top-ups?'

Angie couldn't supply an answer. Instead she said, 'You and Paul have always been so solid – maybe it will burn itself out.'

'Do you really think so? I'm no expert in this kind of thing. I've never had an adulterous husband before now. Well, not that I know about. And I've never had an affair.'

Angie frowned. 'So you think *I'm* some kind of expert in extramarital relationships? That I'm doing to Jack's wife what the Blackwattle woman is doing to you?'

'No, I didn't mean it that way, Angie. They're completely different situations.'

But Vicky didn't sound convincing. They finished their breakfast in an icy silence which hardened by the minute. Finally, when Angie could stand it no longer, she broke the impasse. 'It's probably a belated mid-life crisis, Vic. Any day now he'll wake up and realise what an idiot he's been.'

Vicky answered as if the awkwardness had never happened. 'I hope so. I should have guessed there was something amiss. After Phil died, Paul started to talk about seizing the day and enjoying life before it was too late. I thought it was just a string of empty catchphrases, but he actually went out and did it. Do you know the worst part, Angie? She's thirty-eight years old. How can I compete with that? Whether I spend a fortune on wrinkle injections or not.'

∽

On Monday night Angie sat in bed, awaiting Jack's knock. She had dimmed the bedside lamps so that the room glowed with an even light which was becoming to ladies of a certain age – bright side lights were the enemy of mature skin; everyone past fifty knew that. She had donned a new nightie she'd found on a recent shopping trip to Granthurst. Turquoise silk with coffee lace and shoestring straps. With her hair piled on top and the scanty outfit, she felt like Miss Kitty from *Gunsmoke*.

'Angie, are you awake?' The question was accompanied by the customary tap at the door.

'Yes. Come in. The door's not locked.' It was a script they performed like actors.

Jack was dressed in a towelling robe. That was strange. He rarely wore a robe – Mr Songbird liked to show off his cowboy physique. Instead of getting into the bed, he sat on the edge.

'I'm sorry, Angie. Just got a text. Problems with the drill site in Venezuela.'

'Is it serious?'

'I don't think so. Just an equipment glitch, but sometimes that kind of thing can take a while to sort out.'

'I was going to do some reading anyway.'

'Well, don't wait up on my account.' He kissed her lightly on the forehead.

After Jack returned to his room, Angie leaned over to her side table where a pile of Amy's books had been collecting. She took the heaviest volume – the French version of *The Arabian Nights* – rearranged the pillows and put on her reading glasses. Jack didn't know about the glasses. She never wore them when he was around. The book fell open at the story of Aladdin. As she flipped through it, she couldn't help thinking it was almost as long as a novel. She hadn't read any French since her schooldays, but it wasn't as difficult as she thought. From time to time a word would stump her, and then she would look it up on her phone. How amazing that the internet could offer instant translations. What would Amy have made of that?

Soon Angie was engrossed in the story of the ne'er-do-well boy who found fame, fortune and love, then almost lost it all. Amy had littered the margins with pencilled exclamation marks. Certain words were underlined two or three times – abstract nouns like *désir*, *passion*, *amour*, *extase*, *tendresse*. A young girl's romantic wish list. A middle-aged woman's too, for that matter. Angie fingered the impressions left on the paper by Amy's ardent annotations, and felt closer to her than ever before.

It was clear that Amy had seen parallels between Charles and Aladdin. On a simplistic level, she was right, of course. Both were Chinese merchants who started with nothing, but the fairytale character seemed shallow and greedy compared to the real man. According to Eliza's account, Charles had been hard-working and noble. Yet, in one respect they were the same. Each had fallen in love and never wavered in his affections. And perhaps that connection, and not the obvious similarities, was the core of Amy's fascination with the story.

When Angie reached the reunion between Aladdin and the princess, she found a surfeit of exclamation marks and underlining. And no wonder. This was definitely a book of fairytales for adults. She put the book on her bedside table and turned off the lamp.

During the night Angie dreamed that she and Jack were making love. A leisurely and hypnotic fantasy. When she woke at dawn, their bodies were entwined. It wasn't a dream after all. As she looked at the sleeping man beside her, she pondered Moira's warning about becoming addicted to Jack. It had troubled her. Was he her drug of choice? Yet he wasn't sinister or dangerous like heroin. More like a tonic you took at bedtime. Hearty and invigorating in small doses, but trouble if you became dependent on it.

One afternoon Angie dropped in to Richard's place to return the alpaca books he had lent her. She hadn't read any of them. She wanted her herd to grow naturally, without human interference. The titles alone were off-putting: *Servicing Your Female*, *Selective Breeding Programs*, *Studs and Maidens* – that one sounded like a porno movie.

While Richard was returning the various volumes to the bookcase in his study, Angie wandered around the room, admiring the architectural details created by clever nineteenth-century artisans. Like all the rooms at Millerbrooke, it was impressive. High ceilings, elegant proportions, glowing timber. In the corner was a large drawing board, piled with tracing paper plans.

Idly she leafed through them. The one on the top looked familiar. Well, well. It was a front elevation of Millbrooke's Golden Days. In the bottom right corner was a box with the words: 'Scott Architectural Design'.

Still sorting through the books, Richard was oblivious to Angie's discovery. She could have easily pretended she hadn't seen the plans, but there were so many questions in her head, she couldn't contain herself. 'Richard Scott, what have you been up to?'

When he turned, his head was tilted to the side, like a dog listening to its owner, the tiny pompom at the top of his hat bobbing in time with the movement.

'*You* designed the bloody Golden Days project, didn't you?'

He was looking at the floor. 'Yes.'

'Have you and Jack been keeping this thing secret?'

'No, Ange. He doesn't know.'

'How could he not know? He's the bloody mining engineer. One of Songbird's local triumvirate.'

'Just calm down. *Aequam servare mentem*.'

'Don't you go quoting Virgil at me.'

'It's Horace, not Virgil, and I'll get you a glass of water.'

'Don't you dare run away. Sit down and tell me the whole story or I'll take all your damned hats and burn them. And those horrible flannelette shirts too.'

Looking sheepish, he leaned against his desk. It was a few seconds before he spoke and even then the words were so soft she could barely hear them. 'About eighteen months ago the US headquarters of Songbird contacted an architectural firm in Sydney about designing a multimedia tourist attraction. The brief was that it had to be integrated within a heritage setting. They commissioned me as their heritage adviser and I ended up designing the whole thing. Back in Sydney they tweaked it a bit and constructed a model. Their name is on the final plans and so is mine – in small print as Scott Architectural Design. Jack doesn't have a clue who the designer is. Neither do his buddies. They don't care about the architectural merit or who designed it, as long as it serves Songbird's purpose. Millbrooke's Golden Days is simply a lever to win support for the mine. That's Jack's job, Ange. Lobbying and sweet-talking.'

'You always turn things around so that Jack is the despicable villain and you're the hero. But what about your role in this saga? All along you've been haranguing me about making a pact with the devil, when you did something far worse. If this mine is approved, it will be at least partly because of the building *you* designed. The town might be divided over the mine, but the Golden Days project has huge community support.'

'You can't compare my situation with yours.'

'What do you mean by that?'

'You've been consorting with him.'

'My relationship – or otherwise – with Jack Parker is none of your business. You and I both took his money. We're as bad as each other. I've been banking his rent every fortnight. And *you* were probably paid a motza for *your* efforts.' She paused to catch her breath. 'When you started working on the project, did you connect Golden Days with the drilling?'

'Not for a couple of months. Then I heard about what was happening out at Chinaman's Cove. Same parent company. And I put two and two together.'

'Had you finished your design by then?'

'No, it took almost six months in all.'

'So you knew and yet you continued to do the job. You're a hypocrite, Richard Scott.'

She waited for him to justify himself, but instead he said with anger in his voice: 'Mr Songbird was coming on to you from that very first night at the School of Arts. And you fell for it like a starstruck teenager. Couldn't you see he just wanted to get into your . . .'

'My what?' she challenged.

'Your house.' His reply was barely audible.

She picked up her car keys and stormed out of the study, down the graceful hallway and through the panelled front door. She was still fuming as she stumbled towards the gravel parking area where she'd left her car.

Richard Scott, self-appointed arbiter of integrity and secret designer of Millbrooke's Golden Days, had been playing games all along. Not just with Angie Wallace, but with the entire town.

14
BEAUTIFUL DREAMER

Then

It was the last week of February. Although the Millbrooke days were still hot and humid, the nights had already turned chilly. Amy wondered whether it was the altitude. Was that why the early hours of the morning felt more like Scotland than New South Wales? Shivering in her silk pyjamas, she pulled up the coverlet. Outside, she could hear the raucous cries of a kookaburra, waking from a nightmare. Then it was silent, and she fell asleep again, until a queasy feeling in her stomach woke her. It happened every morning, but if she lay still for a while, it would always pass. Nestling against Charles, she sighed contentedly as she felt the warmth of his body. After a while she noticed his back was damp and wondered if he wasn't feverish. She propped herself up on her arm and examined his sleeping face. His brow was wet. Then she noticed his breathing. He was making a dry, wheezing sound. Was he coming down with something?

Quietly she slipped out of bed and put on the jade-green robe Charles had bought to match her pyjamas. By the time she had washed her face and brushed her hair, his breathing was quieter.

Nevertheless, she would suggest to him that he stay at home today. Jimmy was perfectly capable of running the emporium on his own.

Adhering to her morning routine, she dressed and lit the wood stove in the kitchen, then went up to the bakery to buy her husband a special treat — some spicy currant buns. She could always smell them at least two shops away. Just as she reached the bakery, her brother emerged from the doorway, basket in hand.

'I'm not allowed to talk to you,' said Billy sheepishly.

'Don't then,' Amy replied.

He continued to stand there, as if he were reluctant to go home.

'How is your arithmetic?' she asked. 'Have you remembered how many poles there are in a perch?'

'That is a trick question because they are all the same.'

'Well then, Billy Duncan, I wonder if you know how many rods are in a pole.'

He started to smile. 'It is the same trick.'

'How many yards in a rod, pole or perch?' she asked.

'Five and a half.'

'You are right. You must have had a good teacher.'

'It was you.'

'I know.'

They both laughed.

'You don't look like an evil woman, Amy.'

'I'm not, Billy.'

'But Papa says you are married to the devil.'

'He's wrong. I am married to the best man in the world. You must come and have afternoon tea with us one day and you can see for yourself.'

'Maybe I shall. But I won't tell Papa.'

He gave her a hug and ran down the hill towards Church Lane. She blinked the tears from her eyes and entered the bakery.

As soon as she got back, Amy checked on Charles, who was awake, propped up against the pillows. She made him a cup of tea and placed it on a tray next to the currant buns. At the last moment she added a yellow rose from the bush outside the back door and carried everything into the bedroom. Sometimes it was pleasant to be served a tray in bed. She often recalled those indulgent mornings of her convalescence at Aunt Molly's.

'You have come down with a fever, Charles. I think you should stay home today.'

'It is nothing, Amy. Just a cold. I shall feel better after breakfast.' His voice was hoarse and his face glossy with sweat. He drank the tea but left the buns.

'I'm not hungry, my darling,' he said. 'I shall eat later.'

She watched him put on his clothes. Except for the sweating and the raspy voice, he didn't *seem* ill. She brushed his hair with a tortoiseshell hairbrush until it was shiny as silk. Then he kissed her and went off to work.

Towards lunchtime Amy filled a basket with bread and slices of chicken she had cooked the day before. She added some boiled fruitcake and covered everything with a clean cloth. As she did most days, she walked to the emporium to have lunch with Charles and Jimmy. Sometimes, if the store was busy, Amy would stay and help behind the counter for an hour or two before returning home for her lesson with Eliza. Today, it was quiet and Charles was in the storeroom, doing the accounts. When he looked up, she saw his face was glistening.

'You *are* ill, Charles. I am taking you home *now* and calling Doctor Allen.'

Before he could protest, she said: 'Don't argue with me, Charles Chen. Because you *will not win*.'

Doctor Allen checked Charles's breathing and looked down his throat.

'I fear it is an attack of quinsy. I have seen several cases of it already this month.'

'What is quinsy?' asked Amy.

'An infection of the tonsils which causes difficulty in swallowing.'

Charles added in a hoarse voice: 'Isn't quinsy the affliction that killed George Washington?'

Amy looked at him in horror. 'You are not going to die. Washington was an old man. You are young and strong.'

'It can be serious, Amy,' said Doctor Allen. 'If the swelling of the tonsils becomes extreme, the patient cannot swallow food or drink.'

'How do we prevent that?' she asked.

'We will commence by putting Charles in a hot bath to induce sweating.'

'But he has a fever already.'

The doctor continued as if he hadn't heard her. 'Then you should dry him thoroughly and wrap him in blankets. I also recommend a poultice wrung in hot water to be applied to the neck area. And a sip of brandy wouldn't hurt.'

Amy followed Doctor Allen's advice, but she was doubtful about its efficacy. When Jimmy returned from the emporium, she sent him up to Millerbrooke with a note for Eliza.

An hour later, Eliza arrived with a pot of vegetable broth. When Amy described Doctor Allen's treatment regime, the young woman looked askance.

'I do not see how the hot baths and sweating will help,' Eliza said, confirming Amy's own judgment. 'But it may be possible to break up the blockage in his throat by using steam.'

Jimmy boiled a kettle and they filled a bowl with hot water so that Charles could inhale it. Meanwhile Amy stood at the door, not wanting to interfere and feeling utterly helpless.

'Be careful not to scald him,' she said in a strained voice that didn't seem to belong to her.

'I will test the steam first,' Eliza reassured her.

Charles's neck had become swollen and that frightened Amy. So did the harsh cough which almost rent him in two. After the inhalation he expelled a plug of greyish mucus which Eliza disposed of in a spittoon.

'The blockage is gone, thank the Lord,' said Amy.

Charles was breathing more easily.

Later that evening, Doctor Allen returned. He sent Amy to the kitchen to make a pot of tea, while he spoke with Eliza in the sitting room.

'I am afraid it might not be quinsy at all, but something more sinister. I am particularly concerned about the swelling in his neck. It is symptomatic of black canker. Some people know it as putrid throat.'

'I had it, Doctor Allen, when I was a baby, long before you came to Millbrooke. My mother has always called it the strangling angel. Children all over the district died, including my older brother and sister. That explains the gap in years between Daniel and myself.'

They heard a cry and turned to see Amy standing in the doorway.

'Why is it called the strangling angel?' she asked in an unsteady voice.

'In some cases, it strangles the sufferer so they cannot breathe,' said Doctor Allen. 'But people survive the black canker, Amy. Look at Eliza. Now try to get some rest. I shall return in the morning.'

Once the doctor left, and on his advice, Eliza collected sage leaves from the herb garden, steeped them in boiling water, and strained the cooled liquid to make a gargle. However, when Charles tried to use it, he gagged and almost choked.

'We shall make a hot lemon and honey drink instead,' said Amy. 'It helped me when I was ill.'

Amy fed it to Charles from a spoon. Afterwards he seemed stronger. The wheezing was gone and soon he was asleep.

'Do you think the crisis has passed?' Amy asked Eliza anxiously.

'I do not know. But while Charles is sleeping, you should too.'

Amy began to climb into bed next to Charles.

'You really should sleep in another room, Amy. Don't you remember Professor Pasteur's theory about germs?'

'Yes, of course I do. It is a most peculiar idea.' She was in no mood to discuss Eliza's invisible creatures.

'Not at all, Amy. I have been reading in *The Lancet* about a Professor Lister and his antiseptic principles in surgical practice. He too believes in the existence of germs, only he calls them "minute organisms".'

What did any of this have to do with Charles? Sometimes Eliza and her medical talk could be exceedingly tedious.

'Germs can spread easily,' continued Eliza, oblivious to Amy's growing impatience. 'Anyone who touches Charles must wash his hands. And it is best if *you* do not go too close to him.'

'Charles is my husband. I need to be close to him, especially when he is poorly.'

'You are with child, Amy, and you cannot afford to fall ill.'

'What about you, Eliza? You have touched Charles today. Why is it that you can do these things and I cannot?'

'Because I am immune.'

'What does that mean?'

'I have endured the black canker. And it is unlikely I will catch it again. Now go and take a nap on the sofa and I shall watch over Charles.'

But Amy was having none of it. 'Eliza, I know you mean well; however, I intend to sleep in my own bed. With my husband. And you cannot tell me otherwise.'

While Amy slept, she dreamed of Charles and the baby. It was a boy, and he was talking to his father. Even in a dream, she thought it strange that a bairn could speak, but then she decided he must be very clever. Charles and his son were conversing in an animated fashion about all manner of things – George Washington, Lord Nelson, the price of a bolt of silk. When she woke, she remembered the dream. She was going to have a little boy who would be happy, healthy and smart. Nothing like the abominable chimera prophesied by her father.

Towards morning the coughing and wheezing returned. Sometimes there would be a brief respite when Charles would close his eyes and rest, but his voice was barely a whisper, and his neck so swollen it was no longer in proportion with his face. They gave him water through a paper straw.

'Charles is going to die, isn't he?' Amy said to Eliza, the tears suddenly flooding her eyes.

'He may still recover. The inhalations are helping.'

'Eliza, when I looked out of the window just now, I saw a dark shadow.' Amy was trembling. 'I fear it was the strangling angel. She is outside waiting.'

'Amy, stop it. There is no angel. It is a name someone invented for a disease. Now listen to me. I know I warned you not to say anything to Charles about the baby, but it is time to tell him.'

'Because you think he is dying.'

'Because it will lift his spirits. It will make him fight this illness in a way that nothing else can.'

'Then I shall tell him right away.'

After Amy told Charles the good news, his breathing settled, but his voice remained a whisper.

'You have brought me great joy, Amy. With our marriage and now the baby.'

'It is my joy too.'

'When is our baby due?'

'September.'

'Just in time for spring.'

Tears were streaming down her face, but she managed to keep her voice calm. 'It is a boy, Charles.'

'How can you know?'

'I dreamed it.'

He took her hand and tried to squeeze it, but didn't have the strength.

'What shall we call him?' he asked.

'Charles, of course.'

'Charles Alexander Chen.'

She kissed him on the lips, even though she knew she shouldn't do so, in case she became infected by the invisible germs.

The entire Miller family had gathered in the parlour at Paterson Street. Amy asked them to visit with Charles one at a time. She didn't want to tire him, or for him to think it was a death-bed gathering and give up hope.

In the afternoon Eliza sent for Reverend Brownlow. Full of nervous energy, Amy paced up and down the hall, awaiting his arrival. At the sound of his knock, she ushered him inside and quickly closed the door behind him. She didn't want the strangling angel following the clergyman into the house. He prayed with the family, spent time with Charles and then spoke to Amy alone.

'How are you, my dear?'

'I feel helpless, sir,' said Amy, trying to conceal the desperation in her voice. 'I do not understand why Charles has been afflicted by this illness. If it is caused by germs, as Eliza has said, why did they attack Charles and not me or Jimmy?'

'We cannot know why this has happened to Charles, but I do know that we should hand the Lord our troubles and He will comfort us.'

'Reverend Brownlow, what if this is a punishment?'

'What are you talking about, Amy? Why would God punish Charles?'

'For marrying me! My father foresaw it. He said Charles and I would be punished. I fear that I have caused this. If Charles hadn't married me, he would be strong and well.'

'Amy, if he hadn't married you, he wouldn't have had the

happiness of the last few months. And the illness would have come anyway.'

She shook her head. 'I wish I could believe you.'

'Charles told me it is his love for you which is sustaining him – that and his faith. Now go and sit with him and do not blame yourself.'

A little later, there was a knock at the front door. Eliza went to see who it was and then returned to the bedroom, indicating that Amy should follow her. Standing at the threshold was Margaret Duncan, carrying a pot of stew.

'Amy, I'm so sorry to hear about Charles,' she said, handing the stew to Eliza.

For a few seconds Amy remained motionless, as if she were in shock. Then she threw herself into her mother's arms.

'I love him so much, Mama. I can't lose him.'

'I know, dear girl. I know.' Margaret held her daughter, stroking her hair. Finally Amy detached herself and wiped her face on her apron.

'Please come in, Mama. Just for a cup of tea. I have some of the tisane that you like.'

'I wish I could, Amy, but your father doesn't know I'm here. I'll try to come again, perhaps tomorrow. And I shall pray for Charles's recovery.'

'Will Papa pray for Charles too?' asked Amy, even though she already knew the answer.

'Be strong, Amy. For Charles.' Margaret kissed Amy on the forehead and was gone so quickly she might have been an apparition.

In spite of Eliza's disapproval, Amy lay on the bed beside Charles, holding his hand.

'Sing to me, Amy,' he whispered.

She sang the song she had heard in Sydney – 'Beautiful Dreamer'.

> *Beautiful dreamer, wake unto me,*
> *Starlight and dewdrops are waiting for thee;*
> *Sounds of the rude world, heard in the day,*
> *Lull'd by the moonlight have all pass'd away!*

She kept singing, though Charles's coughing was breaking her heart. Afterwards he dozed for a while, only to wake and cough again. Every hour, Eliza came in and felt his wrist. Sometimes she put her head against his chest.

When the light faded, Amy heard the dark angel flapping at the windows. She rose and checked that the curtains were closed and the windows locked, before returning to Charles's side and humming the melody softly as he napped. She must have fallen asleep herself because when she woke it was the grey hour before dawn. Charles seemed better. He was sleeping and the wheezing was gone. Perhaps the crisis was over. She climbed off the bed carefully and tiptoed into the parlour where Joseph and Daniel were dozing at either end of the sofa, and Jimmy was curled up in an armchair because he had given up his room for Eliza. She, in turn, had not slept at all. A kerosene lamp was burning in Charles's study where Amy could see her bent over the desk, writing something. She went to the door and spoke quietly, so as not to startle her friend: 'Eliza, Charles is sleeping and his breathing is quiet. Do you think the worst has passed?'

Eliza followed her back to the bedroom where the first light was filtering through the muslin curtains.

'I cannot hear the angel any more, thank heavens,' said Amy as they approached the bed. 'Do you think she has flown away and left Charles in peace?'

Eliza put her fingers on Charles's wrist and lowered her head against his chest. Finally she looked up, her eyes meeting Amy's. For a few seconds neither spoke. Then Amy's body began to crumple. Eliza caught her just before she hit the floor. As she lay in a half faint in Eliza's arms, Amy saw the dark angel smiling at her.

Now

In Millbrooke, locals couldn't just sit in a café, drink a coffee and eat a snack – they had to be doing something. In the corner Jonathan, the woodworker, was bent over his laptop, writing an editorial for the *Millbrooke Gazette*. At another table, the plants woman was making changes to her screenplay – in longhand with a fountain pen. Next to the window, Angie Wallace was putting the final touches to her sketch of Mr Chen's Emporium. She had completed everything, bar the dragon-shaped brackets at the top of each verandah post. Being so intricate, they were the most difficult thing to draw. As she inked in the details, she kept glancing out the window to check she had everything right. Then she noticed a tall figure in a flannelette shirt crossing the street. Quickly she leaned away from the plate glass, but he had already spotted her.

Richard started speaking even before he was seated. 'I'm sorry about the other day, Ange. And I regret not telling you from the start. I suppose I'm so used to holding things close to myself and not sharing them with others that I just do it automatically. But I should have told *you*. Do you forgive me?'

For some silly reason Angie had tears in her eyes. 'Yes, of course. And I shouldn't have said you're a hypocrite. It was mean and unfair.'

'I'm sorry about the other thing too.'

'What other thing?'

'The consorting remark. And the stuff I almost said. About your pants.'

'So you should be!' But she was smiling.

'Have you heard the latest rumours?' he asked.

'I thought you didn't deal in rumours. Aren't they the resort of those with nothing better to do?'

Ignoring her, he continued: 'Scuttlebutt has it that Songbird Minerals is pulling the plug on Millbrooke.'

'Pulling the plug?'

'Bailing out, folding up their tents, scarpering.'

Sometimes Richard Scott could be very irritating. 'You don't have to supply a thesaurus. I understand what you're saying.'

'They've stopped the test-drilling. My mate, the security guard, told me that the big bosses in the States are pissed off with the delays, but what's got them really incensed is the mooted tax on foreign mining companies.'

When Angie remained silent, he continued. 'They're claiming it would be an unreasonable impost on their already tight profit margin, that it's nothing more than a blatant cash grab. And they're scared that once it's introduced, the government will keep upping the rate. So Songbird is cutting its losses. Doing a dummy spit. Flying the coop.'

'Will you stop the mixed metaphors, Richard. I get what you're saying!'

He squinted at her. 'Jack hasn't told you, has he? Well, apparently the company has some other project stewing in South America.'

'Of course I know about Venezuela,' she said, trying to keep her voice calm. 'But they wouldn't ditch Millbrooke. Not after all the money they've put into test-drilling and feasibility studies. Plus the investment in the Golden Days project. Are you forgetting that they've bought two acres of prime land right in the middle of town?'

'That's chickenfeed to Songbird. They'll just put the property back on the market.' He scratched his head through the woollen beanie. 'If the price is right, I might even consider buying it.'

'But what about the emotional investment they've made in the local community?'

'Mining companies don't operate according to an emotional agenda, Ange. It's all about making money for the investors. They drill holes in the earth, but they don't necessarily put down roots.'

'I'm surprised you don't have a Latin proverb to sum up those sentiments,' she said archly. All the same, she suspected Richard was right. Mining was a transient business. It always had been. Extract the ore and then move on to a new El Dorado, or Hell Dorado, as the case might be.

After a moment she said, 'You must be disappointed your design won't be built.'

'Not really. It's an architect's lot to design things that never become a reality. If you knew the number of tenders I've prepared which didn't win. And the competitions I've entered without success. To tell you the truth, I've always suspected Millbrooke's Golden Days would remain an architectural model collecting dust in a storeroom somewhere.'

'It's sad though. I really liked that building. And it would have given the town such a boost.'

'Ange, I learned long ago that life is predicated on unfinished business and unresolved dreams. And some disappointments hurt more than others.'

His expression gave nothing away.

'At least this turn of events lets *you* off the hook,' she said. 'No more inner conflict about hating the mine and loving the Golden Days.'

'Yeah, fate seems to have liberated me from a tricky moral dilemma. And I could say the same for *you*.'

Angie didn't bother to answer. She was thinking about Jack, the lodger, who had become a lover. It wasn't only the money and the sex she would miss, or even his ability to open difficult jars and kill the odd cockroach. Mr Songbird had given her a glimpse of the sun when she'd thought it was forever clouded.

AUTUMN

'The princess was inconsolable
at being separated from Aladdin,
her dear husband, whom she had loved
from the very beginning
and would love forever more.'

'Histoire d'Aladdin, ou la lampe merveilleuse'
Nuit CCCXLII [Antoine Galland c.1710]

15
REVELATIONS

Then

By the end of March Amy's belly had formed a bump, so slight only she could see it. All the same, she moved differently now, constantly aware of the bronze-skinned, brown-eyed son growing inside her. He would resemble his father. She knew it from the dream.

As she carried her basket along Miller Street, Amy couldn't help running her other hand over her stomach. It had become a comforting habit which always made her smile. That was a good thing for a young woman who rarely smiled any more. When she reached the Post and Telegraph Office, she saw a bulky figure in a black suit and dog-collar coming towards her from the eastern end of town. He hadn't seen her yet. He was too far away, but the gap was closing quickly.

Surely he couldn't maintain the hostility. Not when his only living daughter was a widow. Not once she told him she was expecting his first grandchild. In turn, Amy would forgive him his sins. After all, Matthew Duncan was her father, and although she might not like the man and his bigotry, a part of her still loved him, the part which recalled his overwhelming grief at the death of Peggy. If he smiled and wished her a good morning, she would open her heart to him. They might even have a discourse about the bairn. It would be the first step in their reconciliation. And soon Amy would be visiting the Manse, taking tea in the kitchen with her mother and playing with the boys.

Anxious to reunite with her father, Amy began to walk faster. There had always been something reassuring about his strong shoulders and husky Glaswegian accent. When they were within ten yards of each other, she gave a tentative smile, awaiting at least a nod in return. Their eyes met, and she searched his face for a reaction. But it was blank. Blank as a tin soldier staring into space.

Then he stepped off the boardwalk and crossed to the other side of the road, continuing his way up Miller Street as if she were a lady of the night he had been forced to avoid. Amy stopped dead, the smile melting on her face. Slowly her expression turned from expectation to anguish. Tears were stinging her eyes, but she wasn't going to let the citizens of Millbrooke see her crying. Taking a deep breath, she tilted her chin upwards and threw her shoulders back. She continued down Miller Street, using her free hand to cradle the little bump that would soon be her son.

By the time she reached the emporium, Amy had composed herself. As was her practice before entering the store, she glanced up at the sign above the door saying: 'C. Chen, Proprietor'. She and Jimmy might have inherited the property, but they would never be its owners, merely the caretakers of Charles's legacy.

After hanging her cloak on the stand in the back room, she went straight to the counter, where she aligned the tea boxes in a perfect row, skimming her fingers across the labels, so elegantly written in Charles's own hand. Until those boxes were as they should be, she couldn't think of anything else. Then she picked up a feather duster and ran it over the large porcelain urns standing on the floor. After that, she went to the cabinet where the silks were displayed. Someone had put a red bolt among the blues and greens – a careless customer perhaps, who didn't understand the need for everything to be in its place. Once she had returned the errant silk to its shelf and rolled up any loose ends, she set about tidying the stacks of plates, bowls and cups. Plain white on one shelf, patterned on the next, alternating them in the way Charles used to do. Only two months ago she had teased him about rearranging the shelves while he was out at the diggings. Now the thought of changing anything was anathema to her.

When the porcelain was in order, she took a cloth and polished the brass lantern until it shone as bright as the summer sun. There would be no genie, of course, no matter how hard she rubbed the lamp. Genies were the stuff of dreams, like fairy godmothers, invented by optimistic human beings, yearning for the impossible. If Amy had once believed in fairytales, she did so no longer. Her happy-ever-after had ended that grey February dawn when a demonic angel stole her husband and laughed in her face.

Now

The rumours had proven true. Songbird Minerals would soon be decamping, together with its movie-star engineer. After a respite in San Francisco, Mr Songbird would be flying south to new goldfields in South America. There would be another lonely woman, of course. He would meet her in one of those tropical bars with rattan ceiling fans flapping in relentless circles. She would be of a certain age, sitting at a table on her own, sipping tea – the iced variety, since it was steamy Venezuela, rather than chilly Millbrooke. He would chat to her about his family. She might even show him pictures of her own children – baby photos because she hadn't put new ones in her wallet. She would explain in an embarrassed kind of way that the children were grown-up now. She might even share the fact she lived alone. Then he would tell her how he yearned to be in a real home, not a bland motel. Somehow he would end up as her boarder. And, sooner or later, she would welcome him into her bed.

It was the second last painting class before the Easter exhibition, but nobody felt much like painting. Instead, they drew up rosters and discussed catering arrangements for opening night – a twilight preview. Now that their Clint Eastwood lookalike had left for warmer climes, the painting ladies were at a loss to know who to ask to open the show. So Angie decided a Millbrooker should do the honours, Nola from the Schoolhouse B&B. Unlike Mr Songbird, *she* was a real celebrity, at least for the baby boomer generation, particularly the males, who retained fond memories of her days as the rather buxom star of a seventies soap opera.

As the women sat around the kitchen table, sipping their tea and coffee and nibbling on Angie's ginger sponge, Jennie said: 'We have a surprise for you, Angie, to say thank you for teaching us and organising the exhibition.'

'You didn't need to do that,' said Angie, expecting a box of chocolates.

'Who's going to start?' Jennie asked.

'I will,' said Tanya, standing up. 'Angie, you've been so busy lately with the preparations for the show that you've had to neglect Amy. So we've done a bit of investigating for you. We had a little meeting and delegated the research. It was my job to find out what happened to Amy between 1873 and 1933. I've even come up with another building for you to draw, but I guess it's a little late for that, at least if you want to finish it in time for the exhibition.'

'Which building?' asked Angie.

'Well, Amy Chen became quite the real estate entrepreneur. She bought the big block of land next to the emporium where she built a hotel which opened in 1886.'

'Do you mean the Boutique Hotel? I love that building,' said Angie. 'If I ever win the lottery, that's the place I'd like to buy.'

'Back then,' said Tanya, 'it was known as the Emporium Hotel. And according to the ads in the *Millbrooke Gazette*, it was a very fancy place to stay, with exotic interiors and every possible mod con. There were even internal bathrooms at the end of the corridors. Ladies at the south and gents at the north.'

Tanya produced a sheet of printout.

EMPORIUM HOTEL

TWENTY-FIVE COMMODIOUS ROOMS, DECORATED IN ORIENTAL STYLE.

EVERY ATTENTION GIVEN TO TOURISTS AND COMMERCIAL GENTLEMEN.

LETTERS AND TELEGRAMS PROMPTLY DEALT WITH.

EFFICIENT COACH SERVICE DAILY, EXCEPT SUNDAYS, TO AND FROM GRANTHURST RAILWAY STATION.

MRS CHARLES CHEN, PROPRIETRESS.

'I also found a photograph from February 1917,' said Tanya.

In the picture Amy was standing in front of a huge table with a silver candelabra as the centrepiece. In spite of her sixty-two years, she was dressed in a big picture hat and an elegant Edwardian gown. Her waist still looked slim.

The caption read:

> *Mrs Charles Chen, proprietress of the Emporium Hotel, celebrates its thirty-first anniversary by holding a luncheon to raise money for our troops.*

Angie couldn't take her eyes off the photo of Amy as a mature woman. For so long there had been an image burnt onto her brain of a teenage bride, forever young.

'I guess it's my turn next,' said Narelle. 'I looked into the Chens. First of all, I have some good news. There's a baby. I found the birth notice in the *Gazette*.'

Angie's eyes widened. 'A baby. Amy's baby?'

'Yes, she must have been pregnant when Charles died. It was a boy.'

'A boy!' Angie put her hand to her mouth to suppress the squeal of excitement building in her throat. It was a few seconds before she could speak. 'What did she call him?'

'Charles Alexander Chen.'

'Of course,' said Angie, tears pricking her eyes. 'What happened to him?'

'I don't know yet. I haven't checked the newspapers, but I *did* visit the cemetery and he's not there.'

'Well, he's not at Millerbrooke either,' said Angie. 'Or I would have found him. Actually, it's a wonder I didn't see his name on Amy's gravestone.' Then she remembered that parts of the inscription had been worn away. 'Maybe I should go back and take another look.'

'Do you think he might have moved to the city?' asked Moira. 'That's what young people do nowadays.'

'I'll keep searching for him,' promised Narelle.

'I'm next,' said Moira. 'And my assignment is the saddest. We were all curious about the cause of Charles's death. So I checked the parish register. It was black canker.'

'What the hell is that?' asked Narelle.

'It sounds horrible,' said Jennie.

'You can say that again,' said Moira. 'They had several names for it back then – all pretty graphic. In those days it killed more Australians than any other disease.'

'So what is it?' asked Narelle impatiently.

'Diphtheria.'

Nobody spoke for a few seconds. Then Jennie stood up.

'My contribution is a cheerful one, thank goodness. Do you all remember the day Angie read out Eliza's story? I decided I'd like to know more about her. So I made some phone calls. Although it's not as common a name as Smith and Jones, there are a helluva lot of Millers in the district. Anyway, only one claims a connection to the Millerbrooke Millers. Her name's Mary and she lives at Cockatoo Ridge. She was married to a Ted Miller who passed away about five years ago. It turns out Ted was the grandson of James Miller, Joseph's son. So I drove out to her house for a chat. Mary had some old photos of James. What a good-looking man he was. Blond, curly hair and at least six foot tall.'

'I bet if he were alive today,' Narelle interjected, 'Jennie would be trying to crack onto him on a social media site.'

Ignoring her, Jennie continued: 'Mary told me something very interesting about Eliza. She wanted to be a doctor, but there was nowhere in Australia that accepted female students. So she went overseas. By then she would have been in her late twenties, and that was considered too old to be a student, so she lied about her age and said she was eighteen instead. Mary told me it started a family tradition. Ever since then, the Miller women have put their age back by ten years.'

'Don't we all do that anyway?' interrupted Narelle. 'On my internet profile I'm thirty-six.'

'I didn't know you were forty-six!' exclaimed Jennie. 'I thought you were *my* age.'

'And how old is that?'

'Twenty-eight.'

'Yeah, sure!'

'Jennie, what happened to Eliza?' asked Angie, trying to change the subject.

Directing a dark look at Narelle, Jennie returned to her explanation. 'Once Eliza graduated, she returned to Australia, but she wasn't allowed to practise in a hospital. I don't know whether it was because she was a woman or on account of the overseas qualification or a bit of both. Anyway, she came back here and helped run the general practice.'

'So that's why it says "A pioneering woman" on her gravestone,' said Angie. 'And it also explains the quotation from Pasteur about grasping opportunities.'

'But there's more,' said Jennie. 'This is the part *none* of you know about. Not even Narelle.' She gave her friend a superior smile. 'While I was there, Mary told me about her son who's a teacher at the local primary school. He's divorced with two little girls. Anyway, they're staying with Mary until they can find a place of their own. Just as I was leaving, her son turned up. And guess what? His name's Mark. He looks just like James Miller. And he asked for my phone number.'

There was a silence while mouths dropped open. Then everyone was talking at once.

'That's not the end of the story,' said Jennie, interrupting them. 'He rang me the same night and we went out last Sunday.'

'A real man, Jennie,' said Angie, giving her a hug. 'And you met him face to face. In the old-fashioned way.'

'We're going to the pizzeria tonight. He's bringing his kids. And I want you girls to know something important.' Jennie took a deep breath as if she was about to give evidence in court. 'I've decided I'm not going to sleep with him until at least the third date.'

They laughed until their faces were wet with tears. Finally Ros took something silver out of her pocket – a memory stick.

'Angie, we've put everything we found on this flash drive, so you can add it to your Amy Chen file.'

'Thank you, everybody,' said Angie through her tears. She wasn't sure if they were from laughing or crying. 'I wonder what Amy would make of her life being squeezed onto a tiny circuit board the size of her thumb.'

'She would have embraced the technology,' said Moira. 'Look what she did with the Emporium Hotel. All the latest innovations.'

'We're so proud of Amy,' said Ros. 'She kept on going despite the loss of her husband. She rebuilt her life and achieved something positive. She was the kind of woman we'd all like for a friend. In fact, Angie, she reminds us a lot of you.'

After they left, Angie put the USB into her laptop and browsed through the material. She lingered over the photograph of Amy in her grand dining room at the Emporium Hotel, looking so elegant in her dress and hat.

Then she read the caption again.

Mrs Charles Chen, proprietress of the Emporium Hotel, celebrates its thirty-first anniversary by holding a luncheon to raise money for our troops.

A disturbing line of thought was building inside her head. Was Amy raising money for the troops because it was a good cause, or did she have a personal stake in the war effort? Was her only child, Charles Junior, away at the Western Front? Angie did the sums. He would have been forty-three years old. Too old to serve. Thank goodness. Just to be sure, she checked on the net. The age range for enlistment was nineteen to thirty-eight. What a relief. Then she scrolled down the page, only to find an addendum. In 1915 the upper age was extended to forty-five.

Angie rushed downstairs, put on her straw hat and sunglasses and went out the front door, not even bothering to lock it behind her – nobody ever locked their houses in Millbrooke. At Miller Street she turned right and almost ran up the road, past the Emporium Hotel and the café. On the corner of Paterson Street at the highest point in the town, she stopped, out of breath, in front of the War Memorial. It was like hundreds of similar shrines across Australia. A slender stone monument, and atop it, a white marble digger in a slouch hat, looking towards the distant hills.

Angie stepped over the chain encircling the monument. Tentatively she placed her hand against the polished granite. She ran her fingers over the indentations made by the names, but didn't dare to read them.

Please don't be there, she said to herself.

She found Charles Junior on the western side, facing the setting sun. He was second from the top under a heading which read 'Killed in action'.

MAJOR C. A. CHEN (ACD)

She sat on the stone plinth for quite some time, not crying – she felt too numb to do that – but thinking about the son who had given his mother a reason to keep going after she lost her husband. Then she recalled the words Phil had said to her as he lay in the intensive care unit, attached to tubes and monitors. 'We should be grateful it's not Blake or Tim lying in this bed. A child shouldn't die before his parents.'

Phil was right. A mother shouldn't lose her forty-three-year-old son, and certainly not in a war that began in the Balkans and involved empires far distant from Australia. Those beautiful young men buried in foreign soil. Angie counted the names on the Honour Roll. There were fourteen – all different surnames. Fourteen mothers who had lost their sons. Her heart ached for every one of them, and for Amy most of all. How could you recover from something like that? Losing the person who's the centre of your life? Not once, but twice in a lifetime.

She wasn't sure how long she'd been sitting there when she heard a woman's voice. It was Lisa from the pub.

'Angie, are you all right? I saw you from my window and I thought you might be sick.'

'Thanks, Lisa, I'm okay. I just found Amy's son. He died in the First World War.'

For a moment, Lisa looked puzzled. Then she said: 'Is that the Amy who used to live in the Manse? Richard told me you were researching her. I'm sorry to hear about her son.'

Angie gave a little strangled laugh. 'It's silly really. It was almost a century ago and I'm acting as if he's my own child.'

'Come and have a drink. You look like you need one.'

'That's kind of you, Lisa, but I think I'll go home.'

When Angie said the word 'home', she didn't simply mean the place where she lived. It was much more than that now.

Back at the Manse, Angie looked up Major Chen's military record on the internet, only to find forty pages of scanned documents. The attestation papers were signed in an exquisite script with heavy downstrokes and elegant loops. On the enlistment form was a thumbnail description: six feet tall, one hundred and eighty pounds, olive complexion, brown eyes and black hair – just like his dad. He was married to M. Chen. In 1916 he enlisted in the Army Chaplains' Department, known as the ACD for short, and was assigned the rank of captain. At the beginning of 1917 he was promoted to major. Chaplain-Major Chen died at Bullecourt on April 11, 1917 from a bullet wound sustained while praying over a dying soldier on the battlefield. He was buried in the cemetery at Noreuil.

On his enlistment form there was a question asking: 'What is your trade or calling?' In reply, he had written: *Minister of religion*.

Angie sank into the wing chair in Amy's room and let the tears fall, unsure whether she was crying for Charles Junior, or for

Amy and Charles, or even Angie and Phil. Maybe it was for all of them. She cried so hard, it reminded her of the weeks after Phil died. Finally, when she couldn't cry any longer, she closed her eyes. It was four o'clock and sunlight was flooding through the arched window. Outside a kookaburra gave a startled laugh. Further down the street someone was mowing their lawn.

She dozed and dreamed of Amy and Charles. They were celebrating their golden wedding anniversary in the dining room of the Emporium Hotel. Charles Junior was there too. He had a limp from a shrapnel injury, but had survived the war. The room was full of people dressed in evening clothes. Angie was wearing jeans and a T-shirt and felt out of place. At the far table, hard against the side wall, there was someone familiar. A man with grey hair. He had his arm around Blake. Angie exchanged smiles with him.

When she woke to the sound of wattlebirds outside her window, the dream remained vivid. Amy and Charles growing old together. Wish fulfilment, of course, but it made her smile. Then she recalled the man at the far table.

It was Phil.

Afterwards the dream lingered in her head like the smell of a freshly baked sponge cake. Warm and comforting. Although Phil had been part of her dream, it hadn't resembled the ones from those early weeks in Millbrooke. Back then, her husband had been the star, miraculously returned from the dead, causing her to rejoice and then to crumple when she woke. Today he had been nothing more than a supporting player, just off to the side. She hadn't rushed to him. In fact, she hadn't been surprised to see him at all.

What did it mean? Should she consult Blake? No, she was sure she could work it out for herself. As she sat in her chair, looking at the patches of Amy's wallpaper still glued to the bedroom wall, she thought she saw something out of the corner of her eye. A flittering movement. Surely not an apparition – she didn't believe in them anyway. When she turned, she realised it was only the sun flashing through a gap in the curtain. And suddenly Phil's cameo appearance in her dream made sense. At last she'd found a place for her dead husband – not as a ghost, or as an imaginary friend nobody else could see, but as a source of strength, just there on the periphery of her vision.

EPILOGUE

Angie and Richard were seated in the office of Millbrooke's solicitor, Jim Holbrook, who was presiding over the exchange of contracts. Such matters were handled at a distance in the city. Sometimes a purchaser never met a vendor. But this was Millbrooke, a town where documents were handled in the old-fashioned way with the buyer and seller in the same room. Not only was Angie's vendor sitting beside her, but he had been a constant in her life from the very first weekend she came to town.

This morning Richard wasn't wearing one of his signature woollen caps and Angie was relieved to see there weren't any antennae emerging from his scalp, just a mane of silver hair. It was really quite attractive. Why did he hide it under those silly hats? He'd also shaved off his grey stubble and donned a denim shirt – he'd even ironed it. Angie had never really noticed him before. Not as a man. He was just Richard, shabby, irritating, reliable, kind, funny and oddly appealing. All the same, it wasn't one of those miraculous makeovers where ten years had been scrubbed from his age. Nor had he turned into an instant heart-throb.

Why did that make her think of Jack? She hadn't heard from him since he returned to his family in San Francisco. Not an email or even a text message. Then again, she hadn't tried to contact *him* either. There was no unfinished business between them, no need to keep in touch. Did she miss him? Sometimes at twilight when she recalled their evening drinks in the garden. Sometimes at night when she thought about the empty bedroom across the hallway. And in the morning when she woke up alone under the toile-patterned quilt.

Yet there were also moments when she wondered if the relationship hadn't been a figment of her imagination all along.

After the formalities were over, Richard and Angie retired to the emporium café for a Lapsang Souchong.

'By the way, how was your conference?' she asked him. He had only returned the day before from an architecture symposium in Sydney.

'Good, but I was homesick.' When he said 'homesick', he was looking directly at Angie.

'Did you wear a suit?'

'Don't own one, Ange. But it's okay for architects to look eccentric. People expect us to be a bit odd. Like artists.'

She kicked him under the table.

'How are things going with the art show?'

'Oh, I almost forgot. Here's your ticket for Thursday's twilight preview,' she said, fishing in her handbag.

'What do I owe you?' He went to take out his wallet.

'It's complimentary.'

'Thanks. Can I help with anything?'

'We could do with some blokes to put up display panels and

handle the heavy jobs. And Moira's painted wardrobe needs to be moved.'

'I'm available and I'll round up a few of my mates from the pub.'

'Great. Blake and Tim are driving down Wednesday afternoon. And you remember my friend, Vicky? She's staying for the weekend.'

'How is she now?'

'What do you mean by *now*?'

'When she came to my place, she seemed to be going through some kind of emotional crisis.'

For the second time that morning Angie looked at him closely. There were definitely no antennae. So how had he known there was something wrong with Vicky, when Angie, her best friend, hadn't noticed a thing?

'Vicky's dealing with some unpleasant stuff,' said Angie who wasn't prepared to share the details of her friend's situation. Besides, it wasn't a happy ending. No reconciliation, only rancour. Paul wanted a divorce to marry his thirty-eight-year-old girlfriend. There was a dispute looming over his super and a custody battle for the dog.

When they finished their drinks, Richard produced a grey plastic shopping bag.

'I thought you might like this,' he announced. 'It's not a present. Just something I found in that old chest of drawers in the shed, the one that used to be in the Manse.'

Inside the plastic bag was something soft. As Angie removed it from the bag, she began to smile. It was a crumpled posy of velvet violets.

'It may have belonged to Amy,' he said. 'I thought Charles might have given it to her.'

'It's possible. Or it could have come off a hat or dress. But it's definitely Amy's.'

'How can you be so sure?'

'Violets were her flower.'

'This is for you as well.' He handed her a large envelope with 'For Ange' written stylishly across the centre with a fountain pen.

'A card?'

'No, I don't do cards either. Just open it.'

She removed a hand-written letter from the envelope.

Dearest One,
Know that I love you more each day. Over the time we have been apart, I have been recalling that autumn morning when you first walked into the emporium, looking like an angel. We introduced ourselves and drank tea together. By the time you left, I was already falling in love with you. After that, I watched for you every day, and whenever we met, my heart would soar.

I never expected to feel like this. Romantic love is not something I have allowed myself, until now. It is both a joy and a torture. A joy when I am with you and a torture when we are apart.

I will always love you.
Your Devoted Suitor

The script was copperplate. The paper was covered in foxing marks, resembling tea stains. When Angie looked up, Richard was smiling. His eyes were hazel, fringed by dark lashes. Tutankhamun's eyes. She hadn't noticed before.

'It's a lovely letter. Thank you. I'll add it to my Amy Duncan collection.' But she wondered if it mightn't equally apply to

Richard's feelings for her, or was that making far too big an assumption?

'Where did you find it?' she asked, steering the conversation to safer ground.

'In the same chest of drawers that I found the flowers. I decided to clean it up, thinking you might like it for the Manse. So I started to remove the lining paper from the drawers and that's when I found the letter hidden underneath.'

'You didn't throw away the lining, did you?'

'Of course not. I'm not the town idiot, or a vandal, for that matter.'

His response left her feeling foolish. She should have known a heritage specialist wouldn't mess with such a precious piece of furniture. Why was she always underestimating him? After a moment she ventured: 'There's something that's been puzzling me.'

'Yes?' He was looking directly at her with those inquisitive eyes.

'Everyone, including my best friend, calls me Angie, but *you* insist on calling me *Ange*.'

'Don't you like it?'

She was about to say that there was only one person in the world allowed to use that name, before realising she didn't mind it at all. 'No,' she said gently, 'I was just wondering why.'

'You studied French at school, didn't you, Ange?'

'That was a long time ago,' she replied, wondering where this could possibly be heading. 'But I suppose my French has improved lately from reading Amy's Aladdin story.'

'In that case, you might know the meaning of the word *a-n-g-e*.'

As she struggled to remember, he supplied the answer in the manner of an impatient schoolteacher: 'From the Ancient Greek via Latin. It means *angel*.'

For a second Angie could have been a teenage girl hearing a boy she fancied declaring his love for her. Then she decided that this was Richard Scott and *he* was simply being flippant.

Why was it that she was seeing sub-text in everything people said? Even in a letter from Charles Chen to the woman he loved. If you lived in Millbrooke long enough, you could fall victim to the Millbrooke phenomenon. You'd begin to look for the layers in everything and everyone – the layers of history hidden in every old building and the layers inside every inhabitant. If you were only passing through the town, you wouldn't even notice. You might have a coffee in the emporium café and not see the ceramicist doing his day job as a waiter, and you wouldn't look twice at the middle-aged woman who happened to be both an artist and the proprietor of a soon-to-open B&B. Even if you happened to be a Millbrooke resident, it would take you a while to become aware of the architect behind the street person. And it would be a year before you realised he was a man you liked a lot.

Should you visit Millbrooke in the winter, you might wonder how the locals managed to endure the icy winds, the sub-zero nights and the frosty mornings. But if you chose to make Millbrooke your home, you would become accustomed to the weather. You would learn that a harsh winter often brings a sumptuous spring, a glorious summer and a golden autumn. You might still complain about frost burning your lavender and wilting the geraniums, but secretly you would stand at the window and marvel at the morning view, glistening with icy crystals. And despite the frost, your garden would continue to grow.

AUTHOR'S NOTE

The story of Aladdin, or 'L'histoire d'Aladdin, ou la lampe merveilleuse', first appeared in *Les mille et une nuits: contes arabes*, collected and translated by Antoine Galland c.1710. There are twelve volumes of Galland's stories, which became known in English as *The Arabian Nights* or *One Thousand and One Nights*. Each volume contained several tales. Amy owned Volume IV, a hefty 474 pages. Her edition was annotated and published by Edouard Gauttier du Lys d'Arc in 1822.

In spite of its age, Galland's 'L'histoire d'Aladdin' (sometimes spelled *Aladin*) is an engaging and accessible read. The quotes appearing in this novel are my own loose translations of the original text. Although the 1822 edition contains engravings, there are none that seem to relate to Aladdin. Therefore, the illustration discussed by Amy and Eliza is merely a product of my imagination.

I am grateful to the following museums for their online and/or actual resources: the Beechworth Chinese Cultural Centre; the

Braidwood Museum; the Burke Museum, Beechworth; the Chinese Museum, Melbourne; the Lambing Flat Folk Museum (home of the anti-Chinese 'Roll up' banner c. 1860, the 'prototype' for the Millbrooke banner); Melbourne Museum and the National Museum of Australia. I am also indebted to the National Archives in Canberra, the Original Gold Rush Colony, previously known as Old Mogo Town, and the State Library of NSW.

From the many books and websites I have used as research, I would particularly like to mention the following sources:

Margaret Scarlett Tart's wonderful book, *The Life of Quong Tart: How a Foreigner Succeeded in a British Community*, first published in 1911 by W M Maclardy (University of Sydney Press), about her husband, Mei Quong Tart, was an inspiration in creating aspects of a prosperous nineteenth-century Chinese merchant in the colony of New South Wales. I found *Golden Shadows on a White Land* by Kate Bagnall (University of Sydney Department of History, 2006) a very readable and illuminating analysis of relationships between Chinese men and European women in the Australia of the second half of the nineteenth century and the early twentieth century. Michael Williams's *Chinese Settlement in NSW: A Thematic History* (A Report for the NSW Heritage Office, 1999) was most useful in providing an overview of the occupations of Chinese settlers and the European attitudes towards them.

The Practical Home Physician and *Encyclopedia of Medicine* by Henry Munson Lyman et al (World Publishing Company, 1892) provided a nineteenth-century perspective on treating a perceived case of quinsy.

For a wealth of Victorian-era miscellanea, I am indebted to the Australian National Library's amazing online collection of old newspapers at http://trove.nla.gov.au/newspaper.

I discovered the term 'duck-mole' in *Austral English: A Dictionary of Australasian Words, Phrases and Usages* by Edward E Morris (1898).

The Lancet was established in 1823. The *Boston Medical and Surgical Journal*, founded in 1812 as the *New England Journal of Medicine and Surgery*, is now the *New England Journal of Medicine*.

ABOUT THE AUTHOR

Deborah O'Brien is a teacher, visual artist and writer. Although she was born and educated in Sydney, she has family links to rural New South Wales by way of her father and her maternal grandmother.

Together with her husband and son, she divides her time between the city and a country cottage, overlooking a creek frequented by platypuses. It is her dream to own a small herd of alpacas.

She has authored several non-fiction books, contributed articles to a variety of magazines and written short stories. *Mr Chen's Emporium* is her first novel. Its sequel, *The Jade Widow*, will publish in September 2013.

www.deborahobrien.com.au

ACKNOWLEDGEMENTS

Many thanks to the friends who sustained me with their generous and valuable comments during the development of this book, particularly Judy Allen, Judy and Colin Briscoe, Gilly Burke, Carol Fulker, Margaret Grainger, Jo and Mark Hill, Henrietta Kit-lan Holden, Lena Kotevich, Kerrie James, Marilyn McCann, Jan Norris, Angelika Roper, Sue Schipp, Joyce Spencer, Chrissie Whipper and Margaret Wong.

I am indebted to Sean Doyle of Lynk Manuscript Assessment Service for his wise counsel. Special thanks to Carrolline Rhodes, whose astute and supportive advice gave me the impetus to keep writing, to Janet Blagg for her illuminating ideas and psychological insights, and Jan Dawkins, who brought her delightful sense of humour and perceptive feedback to our regular coffee sessions.

I am deeply grateful to my agent, Sheila Drummond, for championing *Mr Chen* so enthusiastically, and to my publisher, Beverley Cousins, who believed in this book from the moment it 'pinged into her inbox', contributed inspirational ideas for enhancing the manuscript, and lovingly nurtured it to publication. A big thank you to my very capable and patient RHA editor Elena Gomez, designer Christa Moffitt, publicist Kirsty Noffke, Tobie Mann in marketing, and everyone who worked on the book.

Heartfelt thanks to my husband who patiently listened for hours – and sometimes fell asleep – as I read aloud from the manuscript. And to my son for his loving encouragement.

Lastly, I am immensely grateful to my mother for her love and support and for her unswerving belief in my ability as a writer.

Q&A
WITH DEBORAH O'BRIEN

Warning: These questions may contain spoilers, so we recommend reading them after you have finished the book.

Your novel celebrates the resilience of the human spirit, but it also shows the darker side of human nature in terms of racism and prejudice. How do these opposing themes play out in the book?
The concept of finding hope and renewal runs through both storylines. It's a universal constant no matter what the era. Family, friends and faith have always been among the primary sources of comfort for those who have suffered a loss. These days, people can also access counselling services, which didn't exist in Amy's time, and modern thinking on the grieving process has been very much informed by the groundbreaking work of Elisabeth Kübler-Ross.

There are a number of characters in the novel, both in the past and the present, who suffer the death of a partner or a child, or the break-up of a marriage. Some, like Angie, reach a degree of acceptance and begin to rebuild their lives; others, like Vicky, are still dealing with unfinished business.

As for prejudice and intolerance, it is arguably the most pernicious curse of mankind. The 1870s thread highlights the appalling racism directed at Chinese immigrants. In his role as a merchant, Charles earned a level of acceptance, even respect from the Millbrooke community (or at least a good number of them); nevertheless he would have been expected to 'know his place'. The widespread view was that business dealings with 'Celestials' were acceptable, but personal relationships, particularly intimate ones, were not. Apart from a few progressives such as the Miller family who embraced Charles as an equal, most of Millbrooke's citizens would have disapproved of a marriage between a 'Chinaman' and a white woman. The prevailing attitude, codified nationally thirty years later in the deplorable *Immigration Restriction Act 1901*, was that Australia should be a country for whites only.

What is the role of historical research in the novel?

I love to undertake research – it satisfies my natural curiosity (I should have been a detective) and it affords me the chance to visit museums, which I consider among the most interesting places on earth.

As an artist, I'm particularly excited by visual discoveries: objects, photographs, paintings, drawings, posters. I fell in love with a rickety Cobb and Co coach belonging to Museum Victoria (one of the few remaining) and an old travelling trunk I saw online, and decided both had to appear in the novel. I was intrigued by an 1870s photo of Sydney University, so different to the vast, leafy place I attended a century later. This prompted Amy's visit there with Aunt Molly. An illustration of a nineteenth-century forceps inspired some rather graphic text in the draft childbirth scene, which you will be pleased to know I later deleted.

I'm also fascinated by old newspapers. They can take you back to the very date in question and reveal so much about what was going on in people's lives and in society as a whole. Now that they're conveniently available online, it's easy to spend hours lost in those archives, just reading the classifieds and personal notices.

I must also offer a disclaimer. Even though I like the factual details to be correct, I don't purport to be a purist. Often there has to be compromise – for the sake of the story or a host of other reasons. After all, this is an imaginary tale, not a work of historical non-fiction.

The structure of the novel with its past and present threads seems complex. Did you plan it?
There was no plan as such, just a starting point (Amy and Angie arriving as blow-ins in different eras) and some possible key incidents along the way. Though I'm fond of making checklists and plans in everyday life, I'm quite the opposite when it comes to writing. Other than a few 'guideposts', I tend to let my characters loose and allow the story to unfold.

I was helped greatly by the seasonal nature of the book which gave it a natural rhythm and structure. Within that framework, the individual chapters and parallel storylines evolved, for the most part, in a spontaneous way. For instance, I didn't plan to have both town meetings occurring in the same chapter. But when I saw what had happened, I was delighted. It seemed like magic, though I suspect my subconscious had also played a part. Angie's discovery of the emporium building in the modern-day was also a surprise which unfolded as my fingers tapped the keys, complete to the incident with the currant buns. That kind of scene, where the writing process takes on a momentum of its own, often turns out better than something which is meticulously orchestrated.

How do you create your characters? Are they based on real people?
Not at all. I usually begin with one or two elements and build the character from there – a mannerism, an accent, a personal trait, a way of dressing. In creating Amy, it was the books which provided my starting point. Early on, we see her escapist fantasy about being held up by a highwayman – it could easily be a scene out of Sir Walter Scott, except, of course, for the Freudian undertones. The fact that she has to read her novels in secret mirrors the experience of my own grandmother who used to hide in the barn reading Dickens.

The first time I saw Charles Chen in my imagination, he was wearing a vividly coloured silk waistcoat. So that became his emblem. As I wrote his scenes, they were informed by the research I had done into nineteenth-century merchant, Quong Tart. There are many echoes of the revered historical figure in Charles Chen's story, but also many differences.

With Richard, the genesis was the woollen beanie and checked flannelette shirt. At first I wanted him to be invisible – to the other characters and even to the reader. But soon he was insinuating his way into the heart of the story. Once I realised what was happening, I let the growing relationship between Angie and Richard evolve, not sure where it was heading. Even at the end there's a degree of ambivalence.

The township of Millbrooke is a potent presence in the book. Is it based on a real town?
No, Millbrooke is an imaginary place rather than a specific one. I see it as an archetypal former Gold Rush town, like so many scattered across NSW and Victoria. However, the strong sense of community and friendship which characterises Millbrooke is something real and tangible that I've encountered in many country towns, including my own. It's what makes rural living so special. As for the setting and climate, I've found most gold towns in south-eastern Australia seem to be located in picturesque areas with four distinct seasons, including a bracingly cold winter and the attendant frosty mornings. In terms of the architecture, I've created a composite town in my mind's eye, made up of my favourite Georgian and Victorian buildings taken from many different places.

Will there be a sequel to Amy's story?
Yes, Amy's sequel, called *The Jade Widow*, picks up her life in early 1885 when she and Eliza are thirty. It's a chance to revisit some of the characters from *Mr Chen's Emporium* and meet a few intriguing newcomers.

READING GROUP QUESTIONS

These questions may contain spoilers, so we recommend reading them after you have finished the book.

1. Which do you prefer – the present-day storyline or the past? Why?
2. What themes and motifs connect the two storylines?
3. Angie and Amy are very different women, yet they have much in common. Discuss the similarities and differences.
4. Amy often sees the world through the lens of her reading material. Is this a help or a hindrance? Does there come a point when she begins to rely on her own judgment rather than seeking answers from her books?
5. How did the people of 1870s Millbrooke feel about the Chinese population? Did opinions vary? How have society's attitudes to interracial relationships changed since Amy's day? Compare the attitude of Matthew Duncan in 1872 with the reaction of Angie and the painting ladies to the relationship between Amy and Charles.

6. The novel's past/present structure highlights many social changes relating to women. Consider one or more of the following issues – courting and dating practices, childbirth, education – and discuss the differences between then and now.
7. The emporium is virtually a character in its own right. What is its role in the Amy/Charles relationship and in the novel as a whole?
8. How did you feel about Angie's affair with Jack Parker? What does it reveal about her?
9. Would you like to live in a town like Millbrooke? Why or why not?
10. Did you find Angie's and Amy's stories empowering?